HIGH FIRES

HIGH FIRES

BY

MARJORIE BARKLEY McCLURE

BOSTON
LITTLE, BROWN, AND COMPANY
1924

THIS BOOK IS LOVINGLY DEDICATED
TO THE MEMORY OF
Mary Conwell Barkley and James Morrison Barkley;
TO ALL WHO, LIKE THEM, ARE ANIMATED BY THE
HIGH FIRES OF THE SPIRIT AND TEMPERED BY THE
KINDLY HUMOR OF UNDERSTANDING; AND TO ALL
WHO LOVE MUCH AND MANY, BUT THEMSELVES
THE LEAST.

CONTENTS

BOOK ONE

BOOK ONE

INTRODUCES THE STANHOPES AND THE STEVENSONS, THEIR
SONS AND DAUGHTERS AND DETROIT IN 1905

HIGH FIRES

BOOK ONE

CHAPTER I

I

On a Monday morning in May, at a little before eight
o'clock, Felix Stanhope and his small daughter Charlotte
sat alone at the breakfast table and observed the tapping
of a twig of budded lilac against the dining-room window. A noisy wind romped through the shrubbery and
shook the bordering daffodils as it leaped toward a paper
caught under the hedge and tossed it, whirling up, up,
toward a mountain of clouds just visible to Felix
through a gap in the trees.

"I don't believe it's as cold as it looks," he murmured
half to himself and, finishing his fruit, reached for the
morning paper.

As his eager eye ran over the largest of the headlines
he asked, dutifully irritable, "What in the world is keeping Richard? I thought he was dressed long ago."

Although the question was but the male parent's dis-
charge of a morning obligation and in no sense a desire
for information, Charlotte, a saucy-faced young person
of eight years, gave the information. Sitting in her
youth's chair, her shoulders were well above the table on
which she rested her elbows comfortably. One hand was
lost among the blond curls at her neck, the other jabbed
at her orange with a gold-bowled spoon.

" He was dressed, but mother took him back to change his blouse. There was choc'lut from last night down the front."

A humming sound from Felix was prolonged unduly. "Hmmm . . . Yes . . ." He was deep in the morning news. He tipped his chair on its two back legs and balanced easily, rocking slowly, absently, as he read. He was lost from Charlotte's view behind the *Free Press.* Only the edges of his blue-striped cuffs and the bronzed hands holding the paper were visible to her above the table. She took advantage of the opportunity to eat the remaining half of her orange the comfortable way. The comfortable way obviated the necessity of the spoon and the possibility of juice in the eye, but was certain to call forth unpleasant comment upon the condition of her face. That, however, she could bear, and she clapped the half orange over her mouth and went to work with sparkling eyes alert for a movement of the paper.

The oranges on green majolica plates, set at the four sides of the table, made bright, repeating spots of color in the room. " This decorative scheme, this room," Rita had said when she was planning it, " is to set you off, Felix; you and Richey, since you are just alike."

Felix had admitted the æsthetic resemblance with a mentally reserved " not particularly subtle." The black carved oak furniture and highly polished black floor and woodwork, the wrought-iron fixtures and the black-bordered rug needed dull golds and blues for relief, he thought. He knew a little something about houses and color, but without consulting him Rita had introduced tremendous contrast by using orange brocades; and the orange wall panels set off by the black woodwork were decorated with dragons that at first had stirred Felix to humor. His chaffing was not appreciated, however, and he dropped it after the Sunday when he heard Rita telling a group of callers that the dragon was the central detail from the old Stanhope coat of arms.

" ' The old Stanhope coat of arms ! ' " Felix repeated to himself. " Good Lord, since when a coat of arms ? " No use combating that idea in her if she had it firmly fixed. That it was firmly fixed he knew, when later he discovered stationery on the library writing table richly embossed with their new address under a shield and dragon done in black.

She explained that his absurd idea of saying nothing about his wonderful English ancestry was too quixotic, and she produced a book on heraldry that gave the Stanhope coat of arms with its Latin *fortiter et recte*, the crossed lances and all. " There now," she said triumphantly, " there it is ! "

" That's all right," Felix had cried, " of course; but how do we know I'm that Stanhope ? I don't know that I am. I don't know that originally I was a Stanhope. All sorts of things are done to names over here in this melting pot." He knew perfectly well that he was " that Stanhope," but to admit it to Rita in so many words would be to have the fact used as an advertising slogan. Even questioning it as he did made not the slightest change in her thought of it. She enjoyed the importance of the coat of arms and the dining-room dragons gave her an excuse for showing it.

Felix let it pass, but he began to dislike the dining room. For one thing, unless the flowers were blue or pale yellow they were utterly killed by the pervading orange. Pink and red were Felix' favorites, Jack roses and American beauties, pink carnations and sweet peas, but for the dining room they must hunt up stringy little bachelor buttons and hyacinths out of season, virginal white things and yellows that wouldn't clash.

" Like a woman with carrot hair and a red face," Felix

grumbled once when a dinner party was in preparation, "we have to either match it or have cool things to counteract the room's complexion."

II

As to the room's function in framing Felix and Richard, — it did succeed perhaps. He didn't know. He was himself black and bronze with not a note of color anywhere. He was keen, clean, close-cropped; a nervous type of less bulk than length. He stooped slightly, rather attractively, his head thrust forward as if to see better through the heavy lenses that made shifting bars of light across his jetty eyes. His thick, crisp, black hair and the dull copper of his skin suggested the idealized Amerindian, high cheek bones, nose slightly flattened, a tense, purposeful chin and jaw.

Richard was like him, like him exactly in pigment and features, but the boy, just turned twelve, lacked the stamp of fineness his father's keen intelligence had set in his face. The son was the raw material, the father the finished product.

From the pantry a maid entered with a platter of bacon and eggs.

From the hall came Richard a bound ahead of his mother, who cast a critical eye over the table. The flowers were missing. She flashed a disciplinary glance at the maid and silently lifted a bowl of hyacinths from the sideboard to the centerpiece.

She was slight and blond and so rigidly erect that despite cleverly draped clothing she never gave off a suggestion either of softness or grace. There was nothing of repose in her nature. Life was, to her, deadly earnest; humor was merely one of the social necessities. One must smile, one must joke, one must laugh. Like cocktail sauce to the oyster, jest was accessory to conversation, but there was nothing of mirth in the controlled modulations of her laugh. Her smile, according to the nature of the need, was invariably correct. In such matters her instinct was flawless and yet — baffling. Felix had tried to analyze it. Life was to her a series of defeats. It was people themselves, human beings, the right ones and the wrong ones, the dividing line between, who eluded her. Bad judgment, a lack of sensitiveness together with a snobbishness that was to Felix a stupid defect, "like shopping only by price; she overlooks the best values — the real bargains." Bargains in the world of human nature were common if you had a discerning eye. But Rita couldn't see it that way. She overlooked much, paid high prices for little, was cheated and bitterly disappointed — socially that is — and the whole thing constituted the defeat that meant exclusion from "the drawing-rooms of the best people." The words were Rita's.

At thirty-six Rita had yet to learn that the best people were not the snobs.

III

She seated herself opposite Felix and opened her napkin, at the same time observing Charlotte.

"Your face! Felix, haven't you been watching Charlotte?" And to Charlotte, frowning, "You've had your nose in your orange!"

Felix laughed, twinkling at Charlotte, and lowered the front legs of his chair. He tossed his paper aside and lifted the serving spoon above the platter of eggs, but turned his black eyes upon his son.

"Late again, Dick. Isn't this the morning you're supposed to be at school early? It's a bad habit. School is your business just as surely as automobiles are mine. You must wake up to it."

Richard, disposing of his orange with an energy that called his shoulders into play, glanced up at his father. "I was dressed. It's mother. She doesn't know school is my business. Only thing she ever thinks of is the scrub team, always making me wash."

Felix smiled and served an egg, forgot the bacon and was reminded by Rita, whose tone was patient. To show, however, that she forgave the oversight, she asked pleasantly, "What's the news this morning?"

The humming sound again from Felix. "Hmmm — that man Stevenson is kicking as usual, the Reverend Angus Stevenson. Sunday baseball this time. The *Free Press* puts him on the front page. Nothing else to report, I suppose."

"I know his little girl, Frances," Charlotte offered with the eagerness children feel when grown-up talk offers them opportunity for a contribution. "She goes to my school and she's in my room. I don't like her."

Felix made a quick gesture of reproof, but Rita said, encouragingly, "Why not?"

"Oh, she has funny clothes. On Friday when we're all dressed up for dancing school, she just wears the same old dress. I guess they're poor. She told teacher her father didn't let her go to dancing school because he doesn't believe in it." Charlotte's tone slid from scorn to inquiry. "Why doesn't he believe in it?"

"Oh, bigotry! Because he's a minister he can't dance and of course he doesn't want anybody else to. It's all so absurd and archaic!"

Bigotry, archaic. Charlotte's brief participation in the breakfast table talk was over. She applied herself to fresh toast passed by the maid.

"And now he's against Sunday baseball? What next!

How can Sunday baseball possibly do him any harm? ”

“ If you read the paper you'll find out. He tells you why. European Sunday a bad thing in this country whose strength is in its God-fearing principles. Foreign invasion of America breaking this down. The German Sunday a menace, et cetera, et cetera. It's pretty much a case of kicking on general principles. If a thing's pleasant it's wicked.”

“ It's hypocrisy and bigotry! That's what it is,” Rita said rather heatedly, and Felix, reaching for the paper again, took an irritating tone.

“ I wouldn't use quite such strong words if I were you.”

Rita flashed back. “ Those are the very words you used about this same man a few weeks ago when he preached all that stuff about the automobile being a menace to the quiet Sunday. You know you did.”

Felix laughed and flushed a little under the bronze. “ He was poking his nose in my business that time. Sunday ball, one way or another, doesn't bother me.”

Richard, looking across at Charlotte, said, “ Every day when I cross Second to call for Tom I see that little Stevenson kid. She's cute, I think, and she wears the funniest shoes. Gee! I wonder where she gets them! ”

IV

The wearer of the funny shoes was sitting on the curbstone in front of her father's house at the moment when Richard crossed over for Tom. One short little foot was crowded back against the curbing, the other rested, sole on instep, against its mate.

Richard grinned down on the shoes and Frances wriggled consciously. That boy always looked at her feet.

The Second Avenue pavement was being mended

again.   All through the spring Frances had seen the
engines and the squad of black men approaching slowly·
from way down the street.   Every day they moved a
little nearer and the smell of asphalt became a little more
persistent.   When the wind came fanning in from the
south, as it often did in Detroit, the smell was very
strong and Frances could hear the men singing sometimes as they worked.   Last Saturday noon they had
finished just exactly at the corner below.   Now on Monday morning the steam roller and the squad of men and
the black wagon of tar with a fire glowing under it were
close enough to be watched from the window, but Frances
elected to observe operations from the curb.

There were ten minutes yet before she had to start for
school.   She could wait till after that Stanhope boy
passed if she hippety-hopped good and fast part of the
way.   Hippety-hop for half a block and walk half a
block, hippety-hop some more and walk some more.
That made the journey seem shorter.

Frances hummed as she watched the black man swing
his pick.   They were going to cut holes in the asphalt all
around everywhere and pour in new asphalt and smooth
it over with hot irons and then roll and roll it with the
steam roller.   It was the steam roller that thrilled
Frances most, great black looming thing with smoke
pouring out, and the rumbly sound of its heavy iron
wheels.   It came toward you fast and just as you scurried for the curb it turned aside so you needn't have run
at all.   That was the exciting thing about steam rollers.
They had no tracks.   Street cars and trains had tracks
and stayed on them, but steam rollers could curve around
and back and turn over all the street, any way they
wished.

It was cold on this morning in May after days of warm
sunshine and soft winds.   All the trees were full of

leaves and the lilacs would soon be out. Over in Tom's yard was the bush mother loved to look at, the big greenish-yellow Forsythia that mother said was like a flame of happy sunlight against the ivied wall.

Frances snuggled her coat closer about her neck.

She was a chubby little person with very round cheeks, round eyes and a little round, knobby nose. Her red felt tam was pulled down close over her forehead against the wind and, from under its band, silky brown ringlets muffed her ears. She looked for all the world like a chilly sparrow perched there on the curb, hugging herself to keep warm, her hands tucked under her arms. During the first hot days she had begged to wear socks and Mary, always indulgent with the children, had been willing that she should do as she pleased and learn by experience the unreliability of summer in May. This morning Frances was learning. Her brief skirts barely covered the turn of her bare knees and lacked several inches of meeting the blue socks that were scarcely more than a band of decoration upon her short little legs.

She had lost her mittens the week before and hadn't bothered to hunt for them, nor had she reported the loss. She hadn't supposed there would be any need for mittens again this summer, but to-day — Frances' humming gave way to articulation. She sang sweetly, absently, a line from a little Sunday-school song, her eyes on the big black man with the pick.

" ' Jesus loves even me. Jesus loves even me. Jesus loves — ' " Frances stopped. Why did Jesus love Eve and Frances especially? They had been singing that song in Sunday school for a long, long time and Frances had always wondered and never asked. Jesus loved all the world and died for it. Everybody knew that, except the heathen, and yet the song spoke 'specially of Eve and Frances. Well maybe — Frances was good at speculation — maybe it was because Eve was the first woman and Frances, being only seven, was almost the last woman. If Jesus loved the first one and the last one, almost the last at least, then of course he loved all the ones that came in between. Jesus loved *everybody in the whole world.* Frances knew that well enough!

The Stanhope boy came out of Tom's house and looked across at her, smiling. He said something to Tom and they both laughed as they walked away, looking back over their shoulders at her feet. Frances tried to draw them closer against the curb. Impossible that. Already, to make room for the workmen, they occupied as little space as possible on the asphalt, one pressed upon the other cozily.

It was Frances' funny shoes that made them laugh, those big boys being so mean to a little girl! It wasn't polite to stare and make fun. When they had gone Frances looked at her shoes. She hated them. Nobody else ever had that kind. Other little girls wore patent leather with cloth tops on dancing-school day and tan shoes laced up high on other days, but Frances had to wear these things with toes wider than the heels all the time and never anything pretty about them after the tassels were lost off.

It was daddy's idea. He always explained to the shoe man that the heel must fit close and grip her snugly, then the toes could be as wide as need be, or wider. "Plenty of room to spread out in when you hop around, Francie," he would say and snuggle her and exclaim, "My! My! What enchanting tassels! What more could a little girl want?"

There was no answer to that. The tassels were enchanting and one didn't want anything more. The trouble was one wanted less, less toe, very much less toe at the very ends.

V

From the front window where she was dusting Mary saw Frances hippety-hop off to school. She looked after her and smiled. "That Frances!" she murmured. "That little funny Frances. Angus, you won't forget to take her down about her tooth this afternoon? I'm sure it will have to come out and it isn't loose." She paused, looking after Frances still hopping, her red cap a bobbing spot of color, her arms balancing like bird wings.

"And, Angus, if it hurts pretty badly and she is brave, I think she ought to have a new doll carriage." Mary laughed and a mist of tears filmed her eyes. "The wheel of the old one keeps coming off and she cried the other day after playing out of doors for hours because she said it 'made her heart ache to see poor Suzanne always sitting up straight in the buggy, when she was tired and needing so terribly to lie down and sleep.' I made the mistake of getting the new Christmas doll too big for the old carriage."

Angus chuckled sympathetically but kept his eye on the paper. "I'll see about it," he promised and immediately his tone changed from tenderness to impatience. "They've reported my sermon wrong again! Why don't I learn that the newspaper men will fasten on the least thing that can be twisted into sensationalism? They come bothering me for news and when I try to help them they misquote me. Anything to get a headline!"

CHAPTER II

I

ANGUS STEVENSON on his way to the study that Monday morning, was supposed to be taking it easy, for it was his rest day, the day after Sunday, when he took part in five services, at two of which he preached. He was supposed to stroll on that morning, if on no other, and observe the beauties of spring, inhale deeply of the sweet, cool, May air and note the clouds that looked like the floating islands of meringue on his favorite dessert. But strolling for Angus on Monday or any other day was an impossibility and incompatible with that strenuous urgency of purpose that kept him keyed to a high pitch of endeavor. He walked rapidly, with a swinging stride and an aggressive movement of his shoulders as if he were making his way through a crowd.

He turned the corner on to Wood Avenue and looked up at the name plate fastened at one side of the entrance to the church he had served for twenty-two years. It was done in old English lettering, gold on black — SECOND PRESBYTERIAN CHURCH — and under the name in block letters were listed the services for the week with the additional statement that

ALL ARE WELCOME.

In very small letters at the bottom Angus' own name looked down on him and in letters the same size and just beneath—Hamilton Heath, Custodian. Telephone Grand 5762J.

"Ham and I," he was wont to muse, when his eye noted the sign at all, " Hammie and I do the stoking."

This morning he saw the two names, but made no whimsical jest to that other fellow who was usually about with him, that fellow whose philosophy and humor and perpetual youth were Angus the beloved. For, like some men and all women, he was two very distinct persons.

There was first, and always dominant, the heroic figure Angus, the servant of God whose feet stood in a path as narrow as the soles of his shoes: a path granite-walled like a canyon whose canopy is sky. That first Angus was of the tribe of Prometheus, the world on his shoulders, the flare of a brimstone hell in his vision. All the tragedy of the reformer was in his soul, all the exaltation of a seer radiated from his heart. It was this Angus that saved souls, that drew followers, whose beaming eye prodded shame to consciousness in men; but it was this Angus too who made enemies. So tensely, earnestly, exaltedly the saver of souls was he — that dominant Angus — that but for the other fellow of philosophical humor and irrepressible youth he might have grown top-heavy.

It was the other fellow who made Angus popular here and there among the many. He was quick to see a joke, quicker to tell one, a mimic whose sermons, though they hurled brickbats, also tossed confetti at times just to leaven things, and his audiences were quite used to sudden transition from squirming resentfulness to snickering mirth. He knew how to turn the trick, yet he did it, sometimes, not because he cherished an ambition for oratorical popularity but because, sensitively, he felt the squirming resentfulness and heard the voice of the other Angus whispering, " Curtain and lights! Hurry."

Usually he obeyed, against his inclination, recognizing the narrow margin of human endurance for the truth,

and wanting above all things to have his sermons win, not
antagonize; and in the matter of curtain and lights he
would pause, shut his lips — not merely in the sense that
he ceased speaking but shut them as he shut the Bible
when he had finished reading the morning lesson — and
fade out of the picture imperceptibly.   His place would
be taken by the other fellow, deep shining eyes alight,
mouth a bit awry from smiling, a twinkle of comrade-
ship illumining the features, and then — a brief sentence, quietly spoken, a rustle all through the congregation and, to Angus up there in the pulpit, the gleam
of teeth.

There were times, when his digestion was upset, that
he went against the voice of the other fellow and shoul-
dered him back out of audience — would not listen —
knew better — and went on with the brickbats despite the
squirming resentfulness.

Those were the Sundays when he leaned on the dinner
table at noon and said soberly to Mary, " I was an ass
to-day.   I didn't keep the people with me."   And Mary,
whose love was the comfortable sort that sensed all the
distinctions between tact and truth, would say, " You
were wonderful!   Wonderful and brave and honest!
You're hungry now, dear, and tired.   After dinner you
must have a nap."

II

Angus mounted the tower stairs toward his study and
passed across one end of the church gallery.   A dull
light coming through the stained glass of a memorial
window made patches of color on the red carpet.   A
breath of tomb-like chill rose from the auditorium, a
deadly cold, vastly different from the sweet, sharp May
wind Angus had left with the closing of the heavy door
downstairs.

He paused a moment and looked about. Wrinkled and torn programs of the Sunday services littered the place, hymn books sprawled on the seats and floor, and in the aisle lay a small crumpled handkerchief, very much soiled.

Ham was nowhere to be seen.

"In my study," Angus thought and went toward the door at the end of the passage. But Ham was not there, though the room gave evidence of his recent visitation. The air was fresh and warm. There was a faint hiss of steam from the radiator, and a window raised a few inches admitted a wedge of wind that ruffled the leaves of a magazine on the broad seat.

Angus hung up his coat and moved toward his desk, planning the day that was before him. He would luxuriate in leisure this morning, do the pleasant things that were waiting to be done, read a little, write a few letters and some pages in his notebook. He had had some thoughts yesterday that must be caught while they were in the front of his mind. Then he must lunch downtown with several of the committee of which he was chairman to talk over the campaign for more city playgrounds. The mayor had asked him to take up the matter and had given him a list of willing property owners who would serve with him.

At two he must be uptown for the Bissinger funeral. Between now and then he would have to think out a brief funeral sermon. What to say! Old Bissinger had been a hard customer with all his respectability. There was not much to be said for him, but to comfort his family and give them something to hold to. The funeral would take until four probably; he would have to go to the cemetery and then hurry down home for Frances, who must be taken to the dentist. Mary had been

bound to some club engagement before the trouble with
the tooth began, a baby tooth of course. He rather
dreaded that — standing by the little duck while she
went through a small experience of surgery, for the tooth
would have to come out, no doubt. She would cry. She
seemed to have none of her mother's cool courage at the
prospect of pain. The sight of blood blanched her
cheeks as it did his, and she had always declined the
honor of viewing other children's wounds. Poor little
soul, with that sort of sensitiveness and a woman's life
before her.

He sighed. " Francie," he said aloud tenderly. " Little Francie! "

He picked up the book that was, after all, the only
item on his program which suggested leisure, and that
hardly, since it was a new life of Saint Paul which he
needed to go over before beginning his next Sunday's
sermon, but it counted as leisure because it was a thing he
wanted to do.

The doctor had told him to get out on to the golf links
Mondays, but somehow there were always so many
things crowding on him that it had seemed simpler to
postpone golfing — at present anyway. It was almost
impossible to keep Mondays for play. This funeral
now was a hard job but one there was no avoiding. The
widow clung to him for comfort, looked to him to see
her through the ordeal of parting. He knew how to do
it and what to say. Mary often teased him about the old
lady in his congregation who had said, " Dr. Stevenson
is always so happy at funerals." Well, it ought not to
weary a man to serve people in trouble That was a
privilege, not work exactly, and yet, compared to the
same number of hours on the golf links — He shut the
book with a slap of the pages and, sighing, tossed it to the
table. The thought of golf — why had he ever let his

mind get around that way? The letters had to be done,
the book didn't. He must get at something necessary.

He turned in his swivel chair and bent forward to the
left of his desk where the rug, for a space of some four
square feet, was covered with magazines, books, papers
and letters. They were in piles — more or less tentative — and were, to the uninformed beholder, a litter of
disorder. To Angus they were as good as a filing cabi-
net. There was, for instance, a stack of *Homiletic
Reviews* to be gone over for clippings, another pile of the
same magazine to be sent to a young home missionary
in Utah. There were *Atlantic Monthlys* with special,
marked articles; books of reference that were ever
needed and always falling off the table when put there;
a two-volume dictionary that should have had a stand
for looks, but not for convenience, and letters — letters
everywhere in apparent confusion.

It was not that Angus had any absurd notions about
not using his desk. The great roll-top affair was jammed
with papers. Every pigeonhole spewed forth letters.
Letters piled the spaces in front. The tools of his profession, great and small, crowded and jostled each other
for space. Angus, usually in a desperate hurry, impatient of confusion, deepened the confusion daily by his
scrambling searchings for elusive documents.

Ham, on cleaning days, was the evil genius who made
the chaos worse confounded. Angus' system inspired no
awe in Ham. A letter on the floor and another letter on
the floor were all letters out of place and belonging in one
pile, and he therefore piled them thus, although he knew
he would hear in that beloved, kindly, irascible voice,
"Ham Heath, why in the nation do you insist on getting
my papers mixed? Haven't I told you every week since
you came here not to muss them up so?"

"Yessir," Ham would say solemnly, "but I can't

never get no broom around them piles and the vac'um jest boun' to suck 'em up."

"You clean too much. A little dust is comfortable. We're all made of dust. I don't mind it. Now after this you clean around my papers and leave them just as you find them."

"Yessir," Ham would promise, "I will." But he never did.

"I'll write those five letters for the five people who want me to vouch for their characters and one to the Northern Motor Company, and see if they have a place for old man Powell, watchman or something like that. Poor old fellow, I must get him a berth if he's to have one at all."

He reached forward but his hand was held suspended among the papers. The five requests for characters were not where he had left them. In their place was a packet of church bills to be looked over. He shuffled about carefully, hoping to come upon the desired five without stirring things up too much. No use. They had disappeared.

"Confound that Ham," he muttered pleasantly, "he's worse than Mary with her everlasting fixing of things. Too much Martha in homes these days, anyway; too little respect for individuality, too much soul-crushing system." He permitted himself to become extravagantly gloomy as he hunted, but that other fellow, that other Angus, reminded him of Mary's name for the small alcove off their bedroom which was his for papers, books, clippings and things. Home Branch of Débris she called it and the boys had taken it up. From their point of view, Angus admitted, the name was descriptive. He laughed, pawed a bit less impatiently and found the five letters together, but under the correspondence *re* the new playground committee.

III

That was the way this particular rest day in May began for Angus.

The writing of the third character was stopped by a caller, a young stranger with pale-blue eyes in a face like a fig, so brown it was, so folded and lined. He introduced himself standing in a slouching attitude before Angus and waiting, seemingly for recognition.

" My name's Mason," he had thrown out as if to begin so was enough; but seeing Angus' puzzled look he continued, " I heard your sermon last night on Sunday ball and I — "

" Oh, of course! " Angus' face broke into smiles. " You're Jack Mason of the Tigers. I should have known you at once in your other clothes. These things make you look so different. Come in! Come in and have a chair."

Angus was genuinely cordial. This was the famous third baseman of his own team, the pride of Detroit and a native son. He knew his record as he knew the names of the books of the Bible. He had seen him from the grand stand a score of times. He had considered him picturesque, a young panther of a fellow with his easy swing and winged heels. But his face above a linen collar seemed an anachronism, like finding the wild beauty of an Arab harnessed into a flunkey's trappings.

They talked baseball, Mason warming to the subject as he met Angus' shining response. But he broke into a discussion of Charlie Bennett's batting average suddenly to exclaim, " Why, if you love ball like this, do you go so hard after the Sunday game? "

Angus' steady blue gaze deepened. " Because that's

my principle, Jack. That's the thing I stand for and fight for, righteousness in American life. Why have you come here?"

Jack tipped his chair back and shoved his hands deep into his pockets.

"Well, I'll tell you. It's like this. I like your kicking and I don't like it, and because my father was a preacher I have a sympathy for your point of view, and because I play ball I understand the other fellows, and I just wanted to talk it over."

"I see. I'm glad you came. I remember now seeing you in the audience with a young girl, about to your shoulder when you stood up for hymns, with purplish things on her hat."

"Carolyn Harrigan. It's violets on her hat. It's like this. We're about the same as engaged. Carolyn's folks are Catholic and mine were pretty straight Baptist. They press on me about my becoming a Catholic and I suppose because I'm cross-grained or something it all makes me kind of want to show the world I'm dyed-in-the-wool Protestant."

Angus laughed and settled himself more comfortably to listen.

"So yesterday I was telling her all about my father, how he worked for a salary of twelve hundred a year out Royal Oak way, preaching and having meetings and doing all kinds of hard things for people and never having a doggone bit of fun! It seems to me as I look back that his life was all doing without, while he worked for rich farmers."

His dark skin fell into lines of resentment, but Angus laughed at him.

"I know, Jack, but he had compensation of a sort you don't experience perhaps. He didn't pity himself, did he? Then you mustn't do it. He had another happiness.

The burden of want came on your mother and you children. There were several?"

"There was a complete baseball team if you include
girls and I was next to the oldest. I had to work, you
can bet, and after father died I worked all the time, quit
school and started at the Detroit Stove Works. They
had a baseball nine and I got on it. That's how I began.
After my first season I knew it would be ball, not stoves
for me. All that privation and work and misery set me
against religion pretty badly. I kept away from every
old thing that looked like the third cousin of a church,
but now that Carolyn and her folks have started this
stuff about me being a Catholic, I just naturally wanted to
show what a good Protestant I am, so last night I
brought her here and you happened to hit on Sunday
ball."

"And you agree and disagree? How — just
exactly?"

"Well, Doctor, I agree and I think you're absolutely
white and kind about your wanting the ball player to have
his rest day like the others. Your point about every
form of mechanism, whether it's steel or human, needing
a day of rest out of every seven is right, and I made up
my mind last night that just because my father was the
sort you are I'd make that my principle, that nobody
should ever have to lift a hand to entertain me on Sunday.
I'll keep away from theaters and shows, and if I can't
put in a good Sunday amusing myself I'll go without.
Anybody can find enough pleasant things to do on
Sunday if they want to, but the place I disagree with
you is that about us ball players: we *want* to play on
Sunday. Unless we're in our home town or got religious
scruples — and some of them have all right — we'd
rather play than sit around hotels. We're in the
game because we love it and playing isn't work to us,

not half the work that sitting in a lobby is, swapping stories. You see you don't get much sympathy from the players and they're half the thing you're fighting for."

Angus' clear eyes winced a little. " They don't want it? The players don't want their Sunday? You fellows play in the big cities where the hotels are luxurious. You don't want a whole afternoon to read, to walk in the country, to see friends — do something *different?* That's it, re-creation is doing things that are different, usually. You know that."

" Yes. Some of the fellows want to do those things. I said that. Some of them go to church. Some like to read. A few have friends in other cities, but not many. Most of them want to play ball and even in their home town they like to have their friends come to the game and see them play. You see, you're making this fight, but you're going to lose it. What's the use? "

Jack rolled in his chair and sat with a long blue serge arm draped over the back. Angus stared past him out the window, across the open lot where he could see his own collie, Sir Walter Scott, running in circles excitedly.

" The use, Jack, is that I fight for a principle — for what I think is right." He brought his palms together with a smack and thrust his face forward, looking keenly into the younger man's eyes. " I don't fight because I expect to win, though I hope to, of course. After you get your Sunday ball and your German beer gardens and your open business houses on Sunday, and peace and quiet and the apartness of the Sabbath are gone, I shall still go on fighting and when I die I hope my torch will be carried on by some American who remembers that America's first great reason for existence was a refuge for religious freedom, not pleasure madness! We are slipping into the very slough of self-indulgence that is rotting the soul out of Europe. Read history, Jack. You'll find it there!"

Angus rose and walked a few steps, pausing by the bookcase, where he took up a volume and shook it at Jack. "Read Carlyle. He'll tell you." He put the book back and stood looking through the window.

Sir Walter had left the field and was trotting across the street toward the church. "Coming to see me," thought Angus and heard Jack say, "Gee, but you have a lot of books, Doctor. Have you read them all?"

Angus looked about at the "lot of books." "Yes," he said, "I've read them all the way President Patton of Princeton taught me to read. It was after I had been graduated. James McCosh was president in my day, but in Patton's study once I asked him that same question, 'Have you read all these books, Doctor Patton?' and he smiled and said, 'Yes, in my own way. I just rip out the guts and go on. There are some books that I read and re-read for texture, but most books are only worth reading for their thought."

Young Mason was grinning. He passed his hand across his chin slowly. "That's going to give me courage, that story, to use my own language the way I want to. If the President of Princeton can talk to you about ripping out the guts, I can say some good old Anglo-Saxon myself on occasion."

"There are occasions when it is a relief and a pleasure. It's one of my luxuries."

"Tell you what —" Jack stood in the study doorway, turning the brass knob absently. "I really came up here to see if you'd come down to the hotel to-morrow and have dinner and give the fellows a talk. We got into an argument at breakfast over your sermon in the paper, and I thought it might be a good idea for the fellows to know you, and you to know the fellows, and you could make a speech and all that."

He glanced up at Angus and met the keen scrutiny of twinkling eyes. The look embarrassed him painfully. He began to back away. Angus followed and put a big hand on his shoulder.

" Jack, you fought my battles for me this morning, that's what you did, and you want to give me a chance to get right with your pals, and there you stand acting as if you were afraid I'd find out that you're my friend; as if you're ashamed of yourself! " The hand on the knotty shoulder squeezed. Jack's fig-brown face widened in a grin. He wagged his head and backed still further, swaying awkwardly. " I understand how you feel, I think, and I'm glad to have the chance you give me. I'll be with you whenever you say."

" You're all right, Doctor. I knew you were. You meet me to-morrow night at six at the Cadillac and we'll put it over."

CHAPTER III

I

ALTHOUGH in 1905 (which is the year Frances was seven and Charlotte eight; Richard twelve and the Stevenson twins fourteen) there were so many automobiles on the streets of Detroit that it was beginning already to be called the automobile city, the luxury of motors did not extend to the funeral vehicles owned by the old and conservative and first-class house of A. Harrington, Sons and Company.

It was thought by A. Harrington, who was a very dapper gentleman of some fifty-odd years, that there was something indelicate about a motor-driven hearse. It suggested speed, modernism, faddishness in a ceremony that above all things should be conservative, quiet and deliberate. To rush the body of a " dear departed " from the home — its last sad exit from that sacred place — to the cemetery — that last sad resting place — would be shockingly indelicate. Black horses in spans, a black hearse for all adults with the touching concession of white, drawn by white ponies, for little children, was Mr. A. Harrington's idea of correct form in the business he understood so well and in which he had succeeded unquestionably.

The Bissinger family had called for the services of A. Harrington upon the death of their husband and father. Likewise, they had sought Doctor Stevenson because they had known him long and favorably and he

was said to have a great talent for being extremely comforting at funerals. He had been extremely comforting
during his first call on the bereaved family. He had
read beautifully and with a deep, quiet voice, things
from the Bible that the Bissinger girls had never known
were in it. They had been moved and lifted out of
their grief to a sincere impulse to join Doctor Stevenson's church — some day. His hand-clasp, his straight,
steady, blue gaze, above all his strong certainty of
immortality and the wisdom of an infinitely understanding Father, had been inspiring and comforting to a family who had given less thought to immortality than to
old age.

"Dr. Stevenson," Mrs. Bissinger had wailed, shedding
the first tears since the moment of her husband's demise,
"what will God do with Phillip? He wasn't good in the
Bible way. He didn't believe, he didn't care. He was —
Oh, I'm afraid he was an infidel — but he was good to
us. He loved us and was generous and brave and kind.
What will God *say* to him?"

Angus laid the open Bible on her knee. "Read this,"
he said. "This about the thief on the cross, what Jesus
said to him —"

"Oh, but that man confessed his sin and repented.
Phillip didn't!"

"You don't know, Mrs. Bissinger. He lay here many
hours alone with his memories and his sins and his
beliefs. He may have faced his Maker and confessed.
Confessions come in all sorts of ways. God sees the
heart, you know."

The widow grasped at the might-have-been and was
comforted. Angus left her quiet, and she watched his
departure through the lace curtains, her handkerchief
against her lips and her consciousness acutely perceptive
of infinite wisdom.

" Infinite — " she told the girls, looking intently into
their red-rimmed eyes. " Infinite! Without limit of any
sort, boundless as the ether, everywhere, seeing, hearing,
understanding even the beat of a heart — that is what
he said. An Infinite Creator understands, of course he
understands, and if he understood Phillip's heart he will
forgive him."

II

Angus conducted the funeral at the house, but, as was
his custom, he refused a seat in the carriage for the
cemetery. Instead he walked rapidly out to the Woodward Avenue car and climbed aboard.

A little book entitled " Great Friendships" came out
of his pocket and he rode, reading, through the May
sunshine, out along the long, broad, heterogeneous
avenue of past glory and deserving fame.

At Hancock Avenue he closed his book and consulted a
memorandum. This was about the address of the man
Stanhope, a member of the playground committee, a new
citizen, and production manager of the Northern Motors
Company. Nice, quiet chap, keen, handsome in that
Indian way and evidently generously inclined. Angus
must call there and offer them — strangers — his church
hospitality. He caught the number of the house in large
brass numerals on the foundation stone of a granite
column. " Pretentious house, old Alderny home. A
queer place for new people who could afford to get out
north among the daisies. Right here on the chief
thoroughfare, dust and racket and automobiles snorting
around. I must remember to look them up."

He opened " Great Friendships." Abélard and
Héloïse, a beautiful friendship that, purely platonic, a
rare relationship. He must tell the boys about them, the

twins, James McCosh and John Calvin, thumping fellows
but with appreciation of fine things.

He read till he reached the cemetery and made a few
notes on a theme for an address to young people on great
friendships. Leaving the car at Woodlawn, he walked a
trifle more slowly than was his wont, crossing the grassy
reaches toward the Bissinger lot.

It was all so very beautiful — the green, gently rolling
park lands, tree-trimmed and flower-starred with winding
drives and footpaths. A new cemetery, comparatively,
since Detroit was a very old city, but one that happily
suggested peace and the sunny quiet of open spaces.
After the roar of Woodward Avenue and the trolley car
the stillness of the place was like muted music.

"The garden of the dead, humming with the most
beautiful of all life, birds," Angus mused. He paused
as the whir of wings reached his ears and was rewarded
for his attentive waiting by the distant call of a meadow
lark.

About him were granite stones of a limited variety
and he had but to turn slowly to see the names of many
of his old friends — his first Detroit friends — some of
whom he had escorted to this fair resting place. So
often he had been here, so many times he had stood with
bared head reading the burial service to bereaved families,
that he had grown to love the spot. Not that he felt any
morbid desire to lie there out of the rush of life; not that,
for him, before need be, but when that time came, to
sleep in Woodlawn among his friends was at least a social
if sentimental prospect. Cremation perhaps was more
sanitary than burial, but not so comfortable. "Dust unto
dust" he accepted — for some far day — in preference
to "ashes to ashes." He shivered, remembering other
quotations not so pleasant, and walked toward an iron
bench that had its back to the sun. He was whispering,

and smiling as he did so, Walt Whitman's pardonable
conceit, " I find no sweeter fat than sticks to my own
bones."

He sat with " Great Friendships " in his hand looking
away across the smooth green to the Herrick mausoleum
where the old colonel had taken up his last abode a year
before.   To the east fluffy white clouds were piled
against the blue, drifted there by the morning wind and
left in graceful confusion.   The gentlest of breezes
stirred the shrubbery, birds darted and sang with piercing
sweetness.   The sun was warm on his back but the
shadows that stretched beneath the trees were greenish
blue, cold and amber-edged.   It was the most beautiful of
all lights, clean, fresh, penetrating, that both revealed and
clothed all objects kindly.

Soon the mourners would arrive and after another
quarter hour of reading and prayer he would be free
again.   Frances was his next engagement.   The tooth.
He mustn't forget the doll carriage.

III

Frances, the little cuddly creature, was a continuously
joyous surprise to him, who had been fifty the year of
her birth.   The twins had come at the end of the third
year of his marriage to Mary and they were seven and
rough and noisy and perennially in need of hot water
and soap when Frances came, a pink rose of a baby to
make mush of his foolish old heart.   Not that fifty was
old!   In Angus' case fifty was peculiarly young, for he
was unjaded.   Ennui of any variety was as foreign to his
nature as dishonesty.   He had a keen and highly developed delight in small things as well as great.   It is a
quality that includes sympathy and understanding.

Angus had married very late.   It was because of the

thing he had mentioned to Jack Mason in the morning. He believed that a man who chooses the ministry because his love of his fellow man is so great as to minimize all other joys finds compensation in a way others cannot understand; poverty is shorn of some of its thorns; worldly pleasures are crowded out of the category of needs by bigger things — for himself; but not for his family. He had promised himself that he would not marry. He might love a woman whose vision, like his own, saw worlds beyond this world, but they in turn, he felt, had small right to force children into a life of renunciation.

His children, Angus knew, had every chance for being as he had been before his conversion — passionate natures of strong desires and aggressiveness. If they were, and if they failed to hear the call as he had heard it, home would be a tragedy, for with all the love he would feel for his own, he knew he never could give an inch in the matter of worldly pleasures. His children should not give their leisure to cards, to dancing, to the support of the theater and general vapidness. He could not endure that they should. He would love them too much to permit such vanities. Better no child life at all in his home than that. Worse than a feud it would be, if his flesh should become enraptured of the flesh of mammon. He would not countenance it. He had in his youth, long lifetimes ago it seemed, been wildly, madly in love with the world. He had seemed to have every bad tendency that a fundamentally nice boy could develop, and he had begun a rapid journey on the down path. He had not gone far for — when he was little more than seventeen — the great revelation had been made to him and from that hour on his dynamic qualities had unceasingly generated power for the upward climb.

He never, not even in his darkest discouragements, had

looked upon his profession as a life of self-sacrifice. It was to him a life of privilege. He loved it and he worked tirelessly either in the cause of humanity or as a student praying to be the voice to call other souls to account. He was actively engaged by day in church, civic, philanthropical and personal work, and his nights — way into the small hours — were devoted to study and writing.

That had been his life, until Mary had come into it eighteen years before — Mary of great gentleness and humor, Mary of the big, sweet voice and whimsical philosophy. He had heard her sing the soprano solo parts of "The Messiah." She had worn a soft frock that later she had told Angus, when he inquired, was ash of rose silk. Ash of rose silk! Ash of rose. Angus thought it the most beautiful and descriptive group of words in the language. He said it to himself, and when he said it he saw, not so much the silk as the woman, flushed and smiling — shy under his admiring eyes, her dark hair framing her face softly, her cheeks lifting when she smiled.

He loved her, and he told her so and all the reasons why, at forty, he was still unmarried, and Mary, who was twenty-five and much sought, listened with grave eyes trying not to twinkle, and then she cleared her throat in a little way she had that was partly habit and partly from need as a singer in the Great Lakes climate, and told Angus all about a magazine article she had read entitled " What Civilization Owes the Parsonage." How of all the professions it stands far and away first in its gifts of brains, of originality, of genius. She talked about Charlotte Brontë and Emerson, Henry Ward Beecher, and Jane Austen, Louise Alcott and Lord Nelson, children of the clergy, while Angus listened and watched the lift of her cheeks and the sweep of her eyelashes and the play of color in her face. When she had finished he sat silent looking at her, so that, to relieve the strain of it, she had begun again and said he was wicked to make such a vow, that he was denying possible human beings the joy of life, for it would be joy to live with the equipment of honor and courage and intelligence he could give his children. " What is money compared to the gifts you have to bequeath? What is the loss of dancing and cards and theaters to the other activities you can provide? "

Mary was logical and she spoke truth from her heart, for she felt that some woman was missing a thrilling lover and she wasn't sure but that she was that unfortunate woman.

When she finished that time, Angus told her it lay with her to decide whether or not he should continue celibate.

Before she answered Mary learned that all she had thought about Angus as a lover was correct. He was indeed thrilling and tremendously convincing; so much so that Mary married him within two months. During the eighteen years that followed they had been happier than any couple since the world was made. Their marriage had to be a success for there was no back door out of it for them. They planned it all during the weeks of their engagement as a partnership of perfect confidence and mutual understanding. There were difficult times, of course, but less as the years went on, and by the time Frances had come ("God's sweet afterthought," a sentimentally unctuous and sanctimonious old woman had called her) they were as nearly perfectly one as two humans can be.

CHAPTER IV

I

On the way to the dentist Frances was very happy. Her experience in matters of surgery was nil. She had sat up bravely to have her hair trimmed since that first time when she had wept in a panic of fear because she had known her hair would bleed when it was cut. Her finger had bled when it was pinched by the scissors and Jimmie's mouth had bled when they clipped his tonsils and, therefore, how logical that hair should bleed too.

The barber had succeeded in applying the scissors, and because her hair had not hurt or bled, her faith was established and she went blithely, unapprehensively to the dentist's chair.

Angus did not feel so gay. His sympathetic heart quickened a beat or two and, because he wished it had not to be, he was very jolly and entertaining.

Going to the street car he pretended to hippety-hop with Frances. She clung to his hand and worked with all her might to send her legs over the slabs of stone. Angus, smiling down at her, rose on his toes a little, springily, which gave Frances a perfect illusion of companionable hippety-hopping.

In the car they read advertisements, Frances spelling and pronouncing phonetically, " O-h-a-r-r-i-g-a-n-. O-hair-a-gain. O-hair-again f-o-r for c-o-a-l coal." She summed it up happily, " Oh Hairagain for coal."

" O'Harrigan," Angus corrected in a whisper, eliding properly.

"Coal for the furnace," said Frances, accepting his pronunciation. She moved to the next card. "C-a-r-t-e-r-s. What's that?"

"Carter's," said Angus.

"Carter's Little L-i-v- liv, e-r er. I know 'little' when I see it without spelling. Carter's Little Liver P-i-double l-s."

The car stopped and Francie's slow young voice rang out with the joy of discovery. She looked up at Angus. "Oo-o, I know. It's Carter's Little Liver Pills. You take them, don't you, daddy, when you're bilious?"

Angus laughed and met the twinkling eyes of a half dozen smiling passengers; he directed Frances' attention to a sign that advertised Heinz Bazaar, the Toy Emporium, and asked her to guess what might be for sale in a toy emporium.

Frances guessed doll buggies first of all and dolls, bicycles and little furniture, dishes and parasols and swings. It was Angus who wearied first of the game. He thought of another. Anything to keep the tooth out of mind.

"I'll sing something," he whispered. "Listen. And using the name of Frances' best friend he sang, composing as he went along:

> "Oh, little Nan McKee,
> She's the girl for me,
> Her face is very round and fair,
> I love her curly golden hair."

Frances smiled, but immediately the smile trembled on her lips and faded from her eyes, and Angus said, "What's the matter?"

Frances made answer, "Oh, nothing," so vaguely, that Angus thought, "It's the tooth. She's remembered."

But Frances hadn't remembered. It was the song.

" Little Nan McKee, she's the girl for me! " For the first time in all her guileless, loved and loving years, Francie was stabbed with jealousy. Nan McKee, who went to dancing school and had white shoes and brown shoes with toes not too wide, and dresses for Friday afternoon that had lace and things with ribbons — and now too, added to the shoes and clothes and dancing school, this song — from daddy — Francie's own special daddy!

No tooth, Angus, could ever send a shaft like that.

For years and years, until she was old enough and understanding enough to tell him, Angus called up that inane little rhyme in moments of Francie's need for comfort. And always it stabbed. He thought, blundering man in his ways with women, that for him to sing of Francie's best friend would please Francie, and she, woman to the very soles of her boots, suffered and wouldn't let it be seen; but she never forgot.

> " Oh, little Nan McKee,
> She's the girl for me,
> Her face is very round and fair,
> I love her curly golden hair."

" Of all things," cried Angus, when he was told long, long after. " That little china doll of a Nan! You Francie! "

When they reached the dentist's waiting room, redolent of lysol and creosote and all the pungent, poignant, clean odors so familiar to the intelligent modern, Angus broke the news of a probable hurt.

He took a lightly casual tone as if he but repeated well-known truths about which nobody, least of all Francie, could have the least doubt, and he tried nodding with an elaborate air of persuasiveness. He was cheerful and so pleasantly negligible in manner that

Frances trustfully nodded too in entire agreement with all he said.

The dentist smelled very soapy and fragrant. He wore a clean white coat and rubbed his pink palms together. He was so pleasant and joky with Angus and laughed so long over one of Angus' very old stories that Francie privately decided there could be no hurt about the tooth. Nobody who was going to hurt anybody could laugh like that *just before.*

The dentist had a bird in his office, he said, a bird who sang beautifully when the sun shone. He wanted to show Frances, whom he supposed like birds. Was he right? Had he been a good guesser? Did she really like birds?

Frances told about the sparrows, so cold and hungry in the snow all winter.

The dentist was much more polite than most grown-up people. He listened exactly as if it had been mother talking and opened his eyes very wide, exclaiming, " Well, well! — " and " You don't say! " Certainly birds interested him immensely. Frances saw his own bird in a cage that hung between a big velvet throne for a king and a side window where the sun was shining. It was shining straight in, almost on the cage, but the bird was not singing. He was hopping and eating seeds from a glass dish at the side. The dentist had said he sang when the sun shone. Frances wondered about that.

The dentist wanted to see in Frances' mouth. He would like to know if her throat was the singing kind of throat like the bird's. Francie opened her mouth and he looked in, murmuring questions to Angus, who murmured back. The dentist touched the bad tooth with a small nutpick, smaller than the ones at home, and pressed.

That was the tooth, Angus said, and the dentist nodded and removed the pick, but forgot to tell Francie if her throat were the singing kind. She reminded him almost immediately and he hastened to assure her that he thought undoubtedly it was a singing throat. It was very pleasantly red, he said, and wide open so that the songs could get out, and he thought if Francie took good deep breaths and held her tummy in tight she would sing to rival the birds.

Francie beamed at Angus and lifted her brows in a confidential aside, whispering, " Like mother."

Angus raised his eyebrows the very same way and nodded. Undoubtedly he was pleased too.

" We are very careful never to deceive the children or shock them," said Angus to the dentist in a low voice, and the dentist replied:

" I wish more people were that way. I have children come here in an agony of fear because I have been held as a whip over them for misdeeds. Now, Frances," he said, " this little tooth will have to come out. If you'll open your mouth again wide, I will have it where you can see it in a minute."

Frances looked at Angus. Angus smiled and nodded and took her hand.

Frances opened her mouth.

" Shut your eyes tight."

She shut her eyes tight. A movement and just at the crucial moment she sat up. " May I have the tooth to take home and show Nan and John and Jimmie and Mother and Maggie and Tom?"

" Yes," a duet, tenor and bass. " Of course you may!"

" Now," tenor solo, " open mouth wide, shut eyes tight; there's that lovely red singing throat." A pause, a muffled cry, " There's the wretched little old tooth."

Frances was crying, blood on her chin, trembling, clinging to Angus.

" All over, Dearlove, all over and here's the tooth.

My, my! What a vicious-looking tusk, every bit as large as a grain of rice!"

There was really no sense in so many tears; they came and came just as if a little tap had been opened somewhere back of Frances' eyes. She caught her breath in sobs, tried to stop and could not.

"Very sensitive, unusually so," said Angus to the dentist.

"It's the shock. No matter how wisely we prepare them, there is a shock about even so slight a violence. Luckily the young forget quickly."

Angus remembered the plight of poor Suzanne, the doll carriage, Heinz toy emporium — and made haste to mention that fairyland of delight.

Before they left Francie saw Angus go down into his pocket and draw out a bill. The dentist raised protesting hands, his pink palms outspread. "Not to the cloth," he said, "not at all."

Angus flushed. "I don't allow that, Doctor. It's a matter of self-respect."

In the end the bill went into the dentist's hand but four more bills were returned to Angus.

Francie wondered but not for long. To give one bill and get back four was a nice arrangement. In Sunday school you gave five cents and got back nothing.

The tooth, snugly wrapped in a piece of cotton, was tucked far down in the safest pocket of her coat. A doll carriage was in immediate prospect. Nothing else was much worth thinking about.

II

The little tap back of Frances' eyes was turned off as effectively as it had been turned on. She radiated joy in the toy emporium. A brief sweeping glance about and she made straight for the doll carriages. There were nine or ten; big ones, little ones, willow ones, black ones, and most beautiful of all, a white willow carriage with a hood, and rubber tires on the wheels, and real springs that made it sway comfortably when Francie pushed it.

"I'll take this one," she decided, beaming at Angus. But Angus was not beaming in return. He was smiling a little worriedly. The carriage Frances had selected was the largest and most luxurious of them all.

To the clerk Angus said, "What is the price of that one?" and with graceful indifference the clerk said, "Eighteen dollars."

"What are the others worth?" Angus asked, looking more worried.

The clerk indicated and gave figures, dividing sheep from goats. Angus stood looking down at a little brown carriage not much longer than the one at home with the recalcitrant wheel.

"Would this one be long enough for Suzanne, Francie?"

Francie looked up in amazement. "Oh, not that one," she said, incredulous of Angus' choice. "I like this big one best. I'll take this. It would be plenty large for Suzanne."

Angus bent over her. "Francie, the one you like best is eighteen dollars, this brown one is seven, and this gray one is seven, and this other here is seven-fifty. You may have either of these three, dear, but not that one."

Frances stared at him. Angus met her eyes with thoughtful scrutiny. It was a long look. Turning to the clerk he said, "We do not talk money at our house. She doesn't understand."

He led Frances aside and, sitting on a bench near the elevator, drew her between his knees.

"Daughter," he said, clearing his throat and groping

through the several languages he knew for the right words, " you know you and mother and John and Jimmie and I all live together in our house, and we love each other and are a family. I work for our church. I go to the study and write and plan. I preach and make calls on sick people and sad people, lead prayer meetings and go to —" Angus had not paused but Frances promptly supplied:

" Old committee meetings."

" Yes, thank you, old committee meetings and mission classes and — "

" Frun'rals."

" Yes, funerals. You understand. For doing all those things the church pays me a salary. That means they give me some money each month (more or less) so that we can buy bread and shoes and strawberries and meat and sheets and clothes and coal from O'Harrigan's and — "

" Carter's little liver pills," Frances offered helpfully.

Angus laughed. " Carter's little liver pills," he repeated, chuckling.

" You see, that salary has to do a very great deal for us five. It has to pay kind old Maggie, too, and give to missions and everything. Now then, mother and I have to sit down with a pencil and say, ' This much is John's share and this much is Jimmie's share and this much is Francie's share,' and so on, and then you and Jimmie and John can have whatever your share will buy."

" I'll take the big buggy with my share," Frances decided. If this was the denouement to which Angus was leading, she could easily anticipate and cut short the explaining.

" Now that's the point, dear. Your share isn't enough to buy that baby carriage for Suzanne. It costs twelve dollars too much. It costs so much that if you should take it I would have to use John's share and Jimmie's share and mother's share too. Then when mother wanted a new pair of gloves or the boys wanted skates. or tennis racquets we'd have to say, ' No, Francie used all your share when she bought the doll carriage that cost so much! "

Frances squirmed about in his arms and looked over at the carriages in silence. Angus rose and took her hand. " Now let's go back and look at those for seven dollars. You may have any of those you like."

Frances deliberated. She wheeled first the brown one, then the gray, but her eyes turned back to the large, luxurious first love. Angus waited, conversing quietly with the clerk.

There were very few customers in the store; it was Monday and May, a poor time in toys. Miss Kroeger had made but one sale that day, a lawn swing of the smallest size. She liked Angus. Any man that would take that much pains with a greedy little child was rather nice. Most fathers would just have said, " Take this or none " and let it go at that.

" How do you keep from talking money at your house? " she asked with mild curiosity. " Seems the only subject important enough to talk about these days."

" I know. It is as important as air, as necessary. Its management is only secondary to that in importance but we settle our budget in private and live within our income without talking it before our children. There are better things to discuss."

" Must be some income," Miss Kroeger murmured, losing interest. " That's what keeps us talking at our house, keeping within the income."

" I am sure that is true. It isn't easy when one's taste prescribes such gowns as you are wearing now.

And theaters? I fancy theaters dispose of a good bit of your income."

As Angus said it, the reference to her gown was both a compliment and a reproof. Miss Kroeger accepted it with heightened color and a lifting of the eyebrows. You couldn't tell an old fellow like this one not to be fresh. She answered the reference to the theater as it deserved, with finality.

" Theaters, I guess yes! You've certainly got to do something to make you forget your troubles for a minute once in a while."

" Yes, you have. I know that, but there are better ways than theaters."

" Great old sports, I'll bet — not," thought Miss Kroeger with a hand to her coiffeur. " Highbrow ! "

Francie was standing beside her first love again, looking at Angus. He went to her.

" I want this one," she said sweetly, a suggestion of tears in her eyes. " Wouldn't the lady let me have it for my share? "

" No. She couldn't do that. Would you rather not have any, Francie? We can fix the wheel on the old one and Suzanne can sleep on your bed while you're at school."

Telling Mary about it later, Angus described that moment as the deadlock. " There was no moving Francie. It was the Big and Gorgeous or tears. The clerk was the channel for the miracle that saved us."

Miss Kroeger, seeing her sale vanishing, bit her thumb nail and applied herself to a solution of this cranky man's problem. She stooped beside Francie and patted the seven-dollar perambulators, let her hands linger caressingly on the imitation leather and tawdry parasols. Francie held aloof. She was not to be beguiled by any such smooth methods. Too often her mother had caressed the wild locks of some pock-marked *papier-mâché* child whom any eye could see was past redemption. This time Francie would stand firm. It was not that she wanted to use more than her share. Angus might have spared himself the effort of repeating how John and Jimmie would have to go without skates and things. The right and natural thing to do was to change the price of the Big and Gorgeous. There were more carriages in the toy emporium than they needed, anyway.

The moment arrived for the miracle. Miss Kroeger said, "Wait a minute," and walking rapidly down the store disappeared. When she emerged from a walled-off corner she was pushing a perambulator a size smaller than the Big and Gorgeous, but otherwise almost exactly like it. Almost —

She explained that this one had been sold and when it was on the delivery wagon there had been some sort of an accident and the corduroy cushions had been split and the handle twisted a little. As she talked she tried to right the handle and she showed them how, with a little new corduroy, it would be very easy indeed to cover the cushions, and then it would be just exactly as good as the Big and Gorgeous.

" And would it cost my share? " asked Frances, warming to the bargain, for in her heart she realized that it was more nearly her size than the Big and Gorgeous; she had no need to reach up to the handle. It came to exactly the right spot on her — that spot — that funny place in the middle of her tummy that she called a button-hole.

The good news — passed from floor manager to Miss Kroeger and from Miss Kroeger to Angus to the effect that the damaged buggy (almost as good as new) could be had for nine dollars — finished the deal. Angus paid the nine in that delightful way of giving one, and receiving one in return, and they beamed upon each other.

"Mother can show the boys exactly how to put new covers on the cushions and they can do it with their kit of tools," said Angus.

"They'll be glad to," said Frances, willing to hope for the best.

"Yes, indeed," said Angus, and —

"Take or send," said the clerk.

"Take. Take, daddy," Frances' eyes implored.

"All right. I'll carry it."

They went away toward the elevator, Frances dancing all around Angus, the carriage partially wrapped in clean smooth paper against his shoulder.

CHAPTER V

I

FELIX turned his car into the graveled drive beside his house and chugging slowly to the right position under the *porte-cochère* brought it to a standstill. There was a loud explosion in the muffler, a spasm of whirring and wheezing and grinding before the thresh of the motor was stilled and Felix free to climb out.

It was dinner time and late. Rita might have some plan for the evening; he would leave the automobile in the drive immediately accessible for use. With his hand on the house-door knob he turned to admire the plump contours of this latest product of the Northern Motors Company.

The light May wind, much softer since morning, Felix noted, caught the tails of his mohair dust coat and waved them around his legs. His driving cap was pulled close down over his forehead, where it met a pair of owl-eyed driving goggles that drew large black circles around the smaller lenses beneath. Through the two thicknesses of glass Felix peered back at the car.

" Beautiful work! " he thought admiringly. " A handsome, luxurious vehicle fit for a prince." If ever the engineers reduced the noise, automobiling would be one of life's supreme delights.

The car in the drive that so enthralled Felix was not called a car at all in those days. It was known as an auto to the brief and thoughtless, but to Felix and his kind, it was an automobile. They were particular about using the longer word and they pronounced it with consciousness of its derivation. *Auto,* meaning self, Felix explained to Richard, *mobile,* moving. Self-moving. *Automobile.* Accent on the first and third syllables. There were those, not quite of Felix kind, but nearly, who mouthed the word as they said it and made it *auto-mobul.* Felix disliked that even more than auto. Auto was an honest and careless pronunciation. Automobul was affected, like program for program.

At that time the word car was still unknown as a name applied to the newest member of the travel world. When it did arrive it was exclusively descriptive of the most luxurious, the heaviest, the most expensive. To hear a Ford driver, who had never before owned a private vehicle more pretentious than a wheelbarrow, say casually, " Get in my car there and I'll motor you down to the office " (or the theater or the church — whichever) was to know him for a bounder.

As a development of and from the first self-propelling vehicles Felix' automobile was really " beautiful work, handsome and luxurious." It was chubby, bulging, large-tired, deep-cushioned. The pneumatic rubber tires were as superior to the first cushion tires as a hair mattress is superior to corn husks. It was painted red, a warm, deep, crimson, called maroon, that earned from its sporting admirers the pleasant sobriquet " red devil."

Felix was no sport, but he liked mightily the feeling that gripped him when he drove at daring speed, twenty miles an hour, say, over the smooth asphalt in his " red devil." At top speed the engine snorted until it was easy to imagine sparks flying from the wheels, streaming behind like Rita's veil, and the admiring glances he caught as he drove thus recklessly were secretly very exhilarating.

The car had the delightful advantage of a tonneau —

if one wished a tonneau. It was complete, a perfect unit, with or without, like the much-advertised beans. Without the tonneau two could ride in a body stripped for speed and graceful as a firefly. When driving became a family jaunt, there was the tonneau, put on in a jiffy, ready to welcome a considerable load through its rear door — in the middle of the back.

But for the talk among the machinists at the factory, Felix would have seen no room for improvement, but the engineers, whose business it was first to tear down and then to improve, scowled over the exhaust, the lines, the short circuiting on rainy days and the possible advantage of more speed.

There was violent disagreement on the question of more speed. Fifteen miles an hour was swift, dangerous, but highly satisfactory at a time when hustle was the catchword of the day. Twenty miles an hour was exhilarating of course, but wicked, unnecessarily risky and a menace, against which every town in the United States would one day have to take action. The mayor of Detroit had made a strong speech advising that warning notices be posted at the city limits on every road proclaiming eight miles an hour the limit of speed, any violation thereof to be punishable by law.

Felix felt this to be wise and just. As a principle it was absolutely right. Nevertheless, he, as an individual, would occasionally permit himself the thrill of a swift fifteen miles. And semi-occasionally he would dare twenty.

Richard's keen love of speed worried Felix a little. At forty he was sobering into the cautiousness of middle age as a very desirable quality in those younger than himself. He had begun to fear the very youth that he had but just outgrown. "Reckless, heady, think they know more than their parents." These were the sins he saw foreshadowed in Richard. Certainly, he, of all others, should have understood Richard, for the son was like the father. They were so like, and Felix understood so well, that he let worry on the boy's account crowd out the sympathy he had needed himself at Richard's age.

"When your time comes for driving, Dick," he had said, answering Richard's thrilled response to the daredevil pace of twenty miles an hour, "you must be prepared to stand strong for moderation in this matter of speed mania. Think now, as you go through your teens, that yours is a call to the privilege of standing always for the conservative. Twenty miles an hour is legitimate when there's a straight-away boulevard, good pavement, no pedestrians ahead and a sober, intelligent man at the wheel. Only then! Remember that."

Of all the advice Felix gave in those days Richard remembered that about speed especially. He remembered it because, secretly, he thought his father pretty much an old fogey on that subject and he was a little ashamed of his grudge against Felix for forgetting how it felt to be a boy.

II

The library, the drawing-room, and the den at the end of the hall of the big, newly done over, old house on Woodward Avenue were deserted and quiet when Felix visited them in search of his family. It was after six, the dining table was set for dinner but the quiet rooms, lit softly by the last clear light of the May afternoon gave no evidence of recent occupation.

He ran upstairs, two steps at a time, and put his head in the door of his wife's room. She was lying on her bed, covered with a satin, down-filled comforter that fell in soft outline about her slender length. Richard stood beside the bed and Charlotte, seated at the head, was passing her short, dimpled hands across her mother's forehead.

"What now?" said Felix, walking in.

"Headache. Too much literary club. Sharley's nurse."

Richard moved aside and made way for his father. He tiptoed from the room and was followed immediately by Charlotte.

Felix seated himself on his own bed and leaned toward Rita. She had given him no sign of greeting. Her face was motionless save for an expression of tense pain.

"Are you awake, dear?"

"Of course. Could I sleep with all the moving about?"

"I suppose not. What's the trouble?" His voice was dutifully concerned. His intent gaze showed suspicion.

"Such a boresome program and a close room. My head aches dreadfully."

Felix put a warm hand on Rita's forehead. It was cool and smooth. With an impulse of affection he bent and kissed her between the eyes, but she turned her face from him in annoyance.

He drew back and was about to leave the room when he heard, from the lower hall, Charlotte's voice suddenly shrieking a command: "Theresa! Mother says to serve the soup; father'll be down in a minit."

III

Rita's chair was empty that night and Felix ate almost in complete silence, his brows drawn together in a worried frown.

When he had finished his soup he asked Richard, looking at him sharply, " Did your mother tell you what happened this afternoon to upset her? "

" No. She just said her head ached and she cried. She was ready to get in bed when I came home from school and she put her face in the pillow and cried to beat the band. I was sorry for her."

" She told me there was a horrid woman at the club made her simply sick," said Charlotte.

Felix was silent. It was as he thought. Rita had blundered again undoubtedly. She had been careful to tell him everything but the truth, with her plea of nerves and an uninteresting program. It was the old story. He knew.

He pushed his plate from him and sat frowning at the children. "Eat more slowly, Charlotte. Don't bolt your food. Where's your pusher? You're not too old to use a pusher until you're old enough to keep your fingers out of your plate."

This, thought Felix, after the interruption in his thought, was the first serious breach since they had come to Detroit. He had hoped, heaven only knew how he had hoped, that Rita had learned and would begin right in the new home city. He had not wanted to leave Bessemer and his berth in the Pennsylvania Steel Company, but to give Rita her chance to begin over from the beginning, to start with the capital of her past mistakes, he had given up his ambition in steel and had accepted the Northern Motor's offer.

Now, it would appear; the same old, bitter round of disappointment had begun again. She longed to be a leader among the socially important, to preside over a salon of intellectual brilliancy, and she strove for it with a desperate gravity the while she invited defeat by indulging her strong dislikes, by tactlessness and a superiority that, in her blind adherence to her own erring instinct, persistently misguided her.

Felix ran over her glittering faults with a distaste that deepened as he remembered her recent underhanded dealings with him in the purchase of this house. She had persuaded her father, old Sensenbrenner of Chicago, to advance her money and she had put the deal through, with his connivance, before Felix had known the real price of the property. There was no injustice in calling her dealings with him underhanded. They were.

Long ago, when Dick was a baby, he had learned the futility of advising Rita. To speak, even in tenderest understanding, of her faults, had brought upon him a season of pouting that he had vowed finally never to call down upon himself again. He had watched and suffered with her in silence. In his heart of hearts he had known he could not endure it always, but he had hoped that, with experience, she might change, and she had changed, but not for the better.

He sat there at the table, his eyes on the children, his thought far, far from the treble of their conversation, but suddenly he saw them and their impressionable youth. With a pang he realized that he was leaving them too much to Rita; he was neglecting them. There was danger. He must do something about it, but what he did not know. With characteristic impulsiveness he turned to Charlotte, who was eating cottage pudding with much enjoyment, a drop of sauce on her chin.

"Wipe your mouth," said Felix, venting something of his unhappiness upon the child. "Charlotte, I want to talk to you. You listen, too, Dick; this won't hurt you. This morning at breakfast we were talking about Doctor Stevenson, who preached against Sunday baseball. We called him a bigot. Remember?"

They nodded, still engaged with cottage pudding. Felix had pushed his dish away but he could smell the nutmeg.

"You said you didn't like his little girl, that she wore her old dress on Friday and didn't go to dancing school. And you, Richard, said her shoes were funny." Felix sent the words out with a snappy sound.

"I don't want to hear that sort of talk again in this house."

"I said she was a cute little kid," Richard shouted. "Don't you remember I said — "

"Don't raise the roof with your loud talking. Yes, you said she was cute. I met her father this noon and I liked him. He may be a bigot. Never mind. I don't agree with him. I don't believe in his God or his ridiculous old superstitions and don't intend that you shall, either, but he has a right to his bigotry as much as I have to my way of thinking. A man who told me about him says he's given himself to the church in Detroit for more than twenty years. That's why he's poor. He doesn't go in for money-making. I won't have you children snobs, and if ever I hear any more such talk from you as that stuff Charlotte got off this morning, I'll punish you!"

Charlotte was pouting. Her moist, red mouth was thrust at Felix. Only her spoon, pressed against her lower lip, saved her from a charge of impudence. The spoon was a babyish touch.

"Mother doesn't care if I say things like that."

Felix flamed. "Don't answer me that way. You do as I say. Now leave the table. Wash your face. You, too, Dick."

"Aw, gee! Dad!" They all rose and Dick slipped his hand into his father's arm. "Don't give me these baby lectures. I'm no snob. That little kid is cute. I said so. I know her brothers, too. They're in high school. They're twins, and John is a peach of a ath-a-lete."

" Not athalete, I have told you. Athlete. Two syllables."

Felix went to the library and Dick, lingering in the hall, heard a squeaky little whistle from the shadows on the upper part of the staircase. It was Charlotte peering down at him. " Big-gut, big-gut, big-gut "— she sang naughtily. " Snobby, snobby, snob."

The words had caught in her memory.

CHAPTER VI

I

VERY soon after her arrival in Detroit Rita had been voted into membership of the exclusive Olla Podrida club. Her name had been suggested by the president herself, Mrs. Henry Grieve, wife of the president of the Northern Motors Company, and she had accepted the compliment without delay.

It was evident to the eye of even a lonely stranger that Olla Podrida numbered among its members the very best of the intellectually fashionable, and Rita reported discussions of the subjects she liked best, life as reflected in the seven arts.

During the next month Felix heard Olla Podrida, Olla Podrida rolled importantly so often that he made a point of asking Mrs. Grieve the meaning of the phrase. She explained, " It means something a little like *pot pourri,* a diversified or varied collection. It is Spanish, of course, and broadly interpreted it means a general program of study. That was what we wanted, especially, and we thought, compared to such club names as The Jolly Twelve and The You and I club, it sounded rather distinctive."

Felix agreed that it did. But he was not satisfied with her translation of the two words. One Sunday — the day of the callers and the dragon as a detail from the Stanhope coat of arms — he looked it up. He had some difficulty running it to earth but he found it at last and, alone in the library, lay back in his chair and enjoyed himself.

" If I should tell Rita! If I should try teasing her to get back for the dragon, how the sparks would fly! If only she could enjoy it. — If it wasn't for a possible offense to Mrs. Grieve through Rita's tactlessness, I'd do it."

He didn't do it, didn't tell, but whenever Rita rolled Olla Podrida importantly, he told himself what the dictionary had told him, Olla Podrida (*po dre da*) n. (Sp., lit., a rotten pot. See olio). Any incongruous mixture or miscellaneous collection; an olio; a hodgepodge; a medley.

Rita had been a faithful member of Olla Podrida from the very first. Even during the months of remodeling the old Alderny home and the move, she had stopped every alternate Monday to attend the club meeting and had brought home glowing reports of her part in the discussions.

But she had missed the first May meeting and she took her silk work bag and the Olla Podrida Year Book on that Monday when Richard had been late to breakfast and Charlotte had put her whole face in her orange, and went forth to meeting.

On the way she met Mrs. Mont and they strolled down Cass Avenue together. As they neared the door of the house where the meeting was to be held Rita remembered her absence from the last session, and asked Mrs. Mont if anything important had happened.

With her foot on the lower step Mrs. Mont had said, half whispering, " We voted to extend the membership limit to twenty-eight and take in three new people. We found that Myra Lamotte, whose family is an old French original here in Detroit, would like to come in. Then there is Mrs. Webb Manchester, whose husband is getting enormous prices for his marines. You've seen his canvases in the art museum, wonderful things, enormous

waves. I always want my furs when I look at them.
She has lived in Europe and knows ever so many of the
great artists. We thought she was an asset."

Other members were arriving, coming up the walk, and
Mrs. Mont finished hurriedly, "And Mrs. Angus Stevenson — you know, the minister's wife."

Rita's expressive eyebrows went up. The new ar-
rivals surrounded them, but she said, incredulity edging
her voice, "Not that bigot's wife? Surely *not!*"

Mrs. Mont said, "Surely *yes*" and laughed. "Is that
the way you feel about orthodox religion, too?"

The "too" was a spur to Rita's indignation. It was
annoying that they could not go on and discuss the thing.
Rita borrowed a word from the Rev. Angus to express
her feeling — menace; a person of that sort, narrow,
bigoted, self-righteous, was a menace to the best life of
the club!

She was carried along with the crowd to the bedrooms
and carried down again to the living-rooms, and to her
surprise she found that she was a little late. The president's gavel played a sharp assembly against the fireplace
tile as she slipped into a chair near the hall door.

The business of the club moved along rapidly. Women
are natural parliamentarians and it was not long until
Rita heard Mrs. Grieve say, "We are ready now to vote
upon the names of the new members."

A voice from the dining room said, "Madame President, I move that we dispense with the formality of the
ballot and vote these friends into membership with an
aye."

The motion was seconded.

Madame President asked the secretary to read the
names of the proposed new members once more, and the
secretary complied, "Miss Myra Lamotte, Mrs. Webb
Manchester and Mrs. Angus Stevenson."

Rita, quivering in every nerve, looked eagerly at Mrs. Grieve. She saw Mrs. Mont beyond her, telegraphing understanding of her silent protest. Mrs. Mont winked ever so quickly, and smiled.

" Are there any remarks? " said Madame President.

Rita looked swiftly about and rose, straight and slender in her brown voile.

" Madame President, if you please — "

" Mrs. Stanhope — "

" I am a new member of Olla Podrida, a new citizen of Detroit, but I should like to say a few words because, in your charming spirit of cordiality, you have made me feel myself to be really one of you, and as one of you, privileged to express myself."

Madame President bowed her pleasure in the new member's happy sense of congeniality and Rita continued:

" From the very first of my membership I saw that Olla Podrida stood for the best and broadest and most liberal interpretation of life. We come here to our discussions free from any restrictions of prejudice. We are untrammeled by creeds or intolerance and, being so, are able to look out upon the world as from a mountain top, with nothing to veil our visions or deflect our judgment. This is a treasure, an attribute of rare enlightenment. It is a possession of the few, the very few, of the highest order of intelligence."

Rita's eyes swept the room and met nods and superior smiles, not flagrantly superior, of course, but delicate recognition of the truth. Finally resting on Mrs. Grieve, whose sweet, grave face was lifted to her, Rita met a look of perplexity. There was in it a little questioning and something of alarm.

" I mean by all this," Rita answered the look, " that it is a pity, a very great pity, to take any step that would tend to destroy this frank, honest discussion of the arts. We cannot set a bigot in our midst and preserve our spirit of tolerance. One who regards her own opinions as final and right, in accord with deity and therefore sacred, cannot be an ornament to this club. There are others here who agree with me. I refer, of course, to Mrs. Angus Stevenson, whose bigoted husband, unfortunately — "

Mrs. Grieve had sprung to her feet. She leaned toward Rita. " Mrs. Stanhope, I beg of you — "

Rita stood silent, her lips parted.

" You cannot know what you are saying. Mrs. Stevenson is much beloved by all of us here. She is present to-day, in this room now; she is to give us a paper on oratorio music, which she will illustrate with her own beautiful voice. Mrs. Stevenson will be an ornament to this club. Will other members express themselves on this matter ? "

A dozen women jumped to their feet. Rita was blind, deaf, sick. She knew only that the room hummed and her face was aflame. She slipped into the hall and ran upstairs, staggering. The hostess followed her.

" How did they dare to have somebody here who was not already a member ? How could I, a new member, know you would do anything so irregular, so unparliamentary ? " She flung these questions at her hostess as she stood with her back to the dresser, gnawing her lips. " It's disappointing to know this club could do such a thing. Preposterous ! "

" I am so sorry. It is too bad. You see, you don't know Detroit very well — "

" I know Mrs. Mont doesn't want Mrs. Stevenson in the club. She as much as told me so."

" She did ? " Silence. " It is not that we all agree with Doctor Stevenson in his religious beliefs, Mrs. Stanhope. We don't. He belongs to the old school and we, mostly, are less positive that we know just what God wants us to think, but we love Mrs. Stevenson. She is to sing 'The Messiah' next week as soprano soloist with the Apollo Club. You must hear her."

Rita left the house, slipping out by the carriage entrance, hot, cold, angry and ashamed — but this last she would not admit.

II

Mary gave her paper, "The Great Oratorios," but not as she had planned to give it. She had written it swiftly that morning. She meant to read it, pausing to sing or play by way of illustration. Instead she stood beside the piano and talked quietly. She was pale. There was a circle of white close about her lips and the gray eyes that looked out at her audience were shadowed by the hurt of the cutting words that tapped ceaselessly through her mind, — "there are others here who agree with me — whose bigoted husband, unfortunately — one who regards her own opinions as final — " and again that "others here who agree with me." Others with less courage than Mrs. Stanhope, evidently, Mary told herself bitterly, for immediately after Mrs. Stanhope's departure Mary had been elected a member of the club by a unanimous rising vote that was followed by quick, warm applause. Whoever had agreed with the aggressive Mrs. Stanhope had lacked the will to stand true to her gossiping. She — they perhaps — were here in this room now, hiding under the cloak of silence.

All this Mary thought as the color ebbed and flowed in her face during the few long minutes before she got herself in hand. Her impulse had been to rise and refuse membership since "there were others there — " but no, she held herself to silence.

Who were her enemies? Who of those smiling,

friendly women with sympathetic or indignant eyes? Certainly not Mrs. Grieve, whose quick, short speech had come from a heart shocked and aching for a friend. Not she. If only she could slip out and go home or hide herself as Mrs. Stanhope had done. But no. She could not — not Mary. She had promised to give the program and she would see it through.

She concentrated on the oratorios and when the moment came for her to begin, something of dignity and pride called out the best that she had to give of this familiar subject. Notes were as unnecessary as if it were the twenty-third psalm she was about to recite. She gave herself to it.

When she came to discussion of the Woman of Samaria, she saw Angus' face and floating, like a color mosaic behind her thought, the clear blue of his dear eyes; the ash of rose silk he loved; the tanned faces of the twins giving her motionless attention and — the pink of Francie's cheeks wet with tears. It was thus they gave audience to her at home in the shabby living room. She saw, the picture shifting, the wide black pit of the Opera House auditorium with its dimly discerned rows of seats; near the front, Frances, a little bunched figure with white face lifted to her — the instruments of the players reflecting the stage lights in polished wood and metal, and herself, in coat and hat, rehearsing her solos with the orchestra.

She had sung looking down at Frances who, alone, was audience that afternoon for she had hoped to impress upon the child in that strange setting the words she believed, " God is a spirit and they that worship Him must worship Him in spirit and in truth." Had Francie understood? Mary believed that she had. There were tears on her cheeks when they met and Francie cried, " I saw you standing there! I saw you." The only words she could find. Mary understood the emotion that had overwhelmed the child when she, alone, in that empty house, had seen her own mother, aloof, on high, divided from her by a group of strange men with strange instruments, and the moving beauty of the music.

Mary sang to her club members that Monday afternoon as she had sung to Frances a few days before. Her sweet voice rose and ceased in the long, impressive pauses of the soprano part, the piano gave its echo, the clearly enunciated words filled the hushed room.

"God is a spir-it — God is a spir-it — and they — that worship Him, — and they" (the long, upward sweep of voice) "that worship Him — must worship Him, must worship Him in spirit and in truth."

It was an answer to Rita Stanhope. It was a recitation to those "others here who agree with me" of Mary's creed.

CHAPTER VII

I

SIR WALTER SCOTT sat on the front porch of the Stevenson house and watched, with every sense alert, for the home-coming of the family.

By a very narrow squeak he had just missed all the fun and privilege of getting inside the kitchen when the twins arrived. They had come running cross-lots in their baseball suits, padding through the soft grass, and Sir Walter had not known they were at hand until he heard voices at the back door. Bounding six feet at a leap he had made the distance from front to back in three wags of his tail, and had arrived at the very moment the door slammed shut, forcing a burst of pleasant dinner odors into the nippy air. He stood looking at the door, his head gracefully turned on one side, then the other, as he listened for the return of feet. It was warm inside. He could smell the warmth. Maggie was muttering as she rushed the last preparations for dinner. The surpassingly delicious odor of meat, meat pie or hash or stew, since it was Monday, the day after the Sunday roast, made him wag in an ecstasy of desire.

Inside now he could hear faint thumpings and the staccato of voices. The twins changing their clothes, their shouts, their affectionate names for each other.

A soft, wistful wail of loneliness began low down in Sir Walter's vitals and rose to a sharp, short bark. So plainly it said, " John — Jim — let me in. It's Sir Walter wanting to be with you." He waited. No response, no feet hurrying to the door. He could expect nothing of Maggie. Long ago he had learned that she was utterly lacking in sympathy for his dependence. She muttered over his mud and complained of his appetite.

He barked again and was rewarded by the sound of a window being pushed up. Jimmie's head appeared in the opening.

"Hello there, old Scott. Hello there! Want to come in? Come on!" He whistled invitingly, with that note of cordiality that drops a little as it seems to add, "Well, really, old man, if you don't care to — of course — " Sir Walter went mad with despair, barking, wagging, jumping, telling his young master as best he could that the window was too far away, he couldn't make it on the jump.

John's head appeared in the window beside his brother's.

"What's matter, Walt? Come on up. Gee, old man, we'd like to have you join us," and so on until poor Sir Walter sat upon the ground and, lifting up his voice, wailed his anguish.

The sound of running water, a certain thundering, vibrating down the very walls, told Sir Walter the twins were about to perform in their splashing manner in the bathroom. No hope for him if they were at that, and what was more, thought of the water and their method of sharing it dampened his desire to join them. He listened a moment longer before trotting around to the front porch again to await the others.

II

Mary arrived home first. She came walking down Second Avenue, swaying easily as was her way, not hurried or flurried by all the clamoring for attention she

knew she would encounter at home.   She was tired, spent
with the surge of emotion that had caught her in the
afternoon.   It had "taken the tuck out of her" as she
would have said herself had she felt less hurt and more
humor in the incident.   But she saw no humor this afternoon and she walked slowly, breathing deeply the refresh-
ing ozone of the bright cool air.   She had this little time
for re-creation before she let herself into the problems
that awaited her.   She would be met by Sir Walter —
she was sure of that — and she could not fail to give him
the greeting he would deserve when he came bounding
toward her, tongue out, face grinning with delight.   He
would trot beside her very proudly, holding the edge of
her coat between his teeth, his forefeet lifting with the
importance and pleasure of this service.   She would have
to talk to him and put her hand on his head as she walked.

And then, having arrived at home, there would be dinner to supervise and help with; old Maggie muttering and
rushing about; the silver laid crooked on the table and
half the things forgotten.

The twins would follow about, telling her their affairs
and demanding that she nod and laugh and say " Really "
and " Good for you! " in sympathy or triumph or reproof or grief, as the case might be, and then, whether
late or early she could not guess, there would be Francie
to bend over and listen to — the tooth, the doll carriage.
Angus would want to tell her everything the child had
said.   He so seldom took her with him on either his
errands or hers.

III

Dinner was a lively occasion.   After the plates were
served and the first edge of hunger dulled, the talk and
laughter broke out.   Everybody had so much to tell.
Frances' experiences were of tremendous importance;

the boys had won the ball game for their side, according
to the accounts they gave; Angus told about his call from
Jack Mason and the twins hung on his words. They
laughed a great deal as they ate and talked, and everybody told some adventure of the day. All but Mary.
She was quiet, listening, and made no bids for the floor in
recital of her afternoon. That, she thought, could come
later when Maggie was not present.

Sir Walter lay under the table at Frances' feet. He
told himself that his nose had guessed the truth. The
dinner did include meat pie from yesterday's roast. Sir
Walter sighed heavily, his nostrils quivering. He was
content because he knew no other way than to wait his
turn for dinner, and the pie was well worth the price of
patience. It was large and round and deep. Onion
atoms lurked in the gravy that made a rich brown lake
for the meat under the biscuit crust which was held just
above the gravy line by an inverted jelly glass, in the
middle of the pan.

The children had watched Angus cut the crust in
eight, wedge-shaped pieces and neatly extract the glass
that Maggie received on a saucer and carried away to the
kitchen. For that moment of pleasant observation the
family were quiet enough to hear Maggie's mutterings
as she waited for the jelly glass, mutterings that told
about the crust and the lard, and the onions " sprouting
so's they're that soft." Nobody listened to her consciously. Her voice hardly articulated but mumbled
rapidly. It was her chronic state. She asked no audience and expected no answers. It was simply that the
machinery of her poor, halting mind creaked as it
worked. Nobody minded.

Maggie was faithful. She was kind, a burden bearer,
and the worst of her disapproval was worked off in the
mutterings. It was a miracle that she cooked so well.

What her mind lacked her hands somehow made good in the humble service that was her happiness. To get all the dishes and silver and accessories on the table for a meal without assistance was an impossibility, but to achieve a great, crusty, swimming meat pie was simplicity itself.

IV

Maggie was not beautiful. Her straight dark hair was slicked back into a hard little knot at the wrong angle upon the crown of her head. Her too long upper lip and too tip-tilted nose above a pointed and slightly receding chin were uncharmingly Irish, but — (it was Mary who insisted that the family make note of this rather than the other features) her eyes were darkly blue and large, soft with gentleness and lit with her affection for the only family who had ever been kind to her.

"Let's always mention Maggie's lovely eyes instead of her funny nose," Mary said. "And her kind heart instead of her fluttering ways. She is so good to us."

In her youth Maggie had trundled babies about while she played or worked; big babies and tiny babies, there were always several of the former and one of the latter in her home. The history of her childhood labor was written on the sagging back and rounded shoulders. She walked with long, running strides, eager, hurried, her big apron rolling up roundly in front, her skirt trailing sadly in back. And because of her speed, her wide apron sashes, stiff with starch, floated out in back with the startled and fleeing look of one pursued.

The twins made a song about Maggie. They sang some of it rapidly, and drawled some of it lugubriously, to an accompanying duet upon the piano that shook the chandelier.

Maggie, Rose of Erin, see me at your feet,
Bend you now, in pity, Mag. Give me food to eat.
I will chant a poem while you razz the dough,
Put the mutt in mutton chop, muttering as you go.

Artist of the juicy pie, slinger of the hash,
Flapping flap-jacks as you flap your gingham apron sash,
Maggie! Oh, Macushla, with your Tipperary nose
Blooming out between your cheeks, the color o' the rose.

Maggie, Rose of Erin, muttering as you go;
Tell me, Fair One, where you got your figure, high and low.
High it is across the front, sagging low in back;
I am moved to tearlets, Mag. 'Tis bustle that you lack.

Artist of the juicy pie, slinger of the hash,
Flapping flap-jacks as you flap your gingham apron sash,
Maggie! Oh, Macushla, with your Tipperary nose
Blooming out between your cheeks, the color o' the rose.

Perhaps it was the happy introduction of minor chords
in the accompaniment that made Ireland's Rose an especially appealing composition. The twins had unusual
voices, full and sweet and somehow so directly connected
with their big, pulsing hearts as to be the very channel
of outlet for their sympathy and tenderness and stupendous, fun-making propensity. When they sat at the
piano, their strong, young hands spread on the keys,
their mouths wide with song, they compelled attention.
It was not possible to remain indifferent. They sang
Ireland's Rose always on Thursdays to celebrate Maggie's day out, sang it with splendid expression and loud,
close harmony that served to drown for a few minutes
Mary's calls from the kitchen for assistance.

One Thursday just as they were about to give full
voice to their composition, Maggie walked in the back
door. It was after dinner but earlier than usual for her

return. She had come home to nurse a poor bunioned foot.

From the back stairs she heard all the verses as they were strung out with tenor echoes of bass recitative, fortissimo, pianissimo, harmony, chords, wailing duet and then at the end Jimmie — persuasively — imitating a famous evangelist, " Now all together, friends! Let us repeat the chorus softly."

Jimmie: Artist of the juicy pie
John: — the juicy pie.
Jimmie: Slinger of the hash — hasheash,
Both: Flapping flap-jacks as you flap your gingham apron sash.
Jimmie: Maggie (passionate, pleading voice)! Oh, Macushla (wailing tenderness),
John: With your Tip — a — rare — ey nose
Jimmie: Blooming — out — between — your — cheeks,
Both: The color of the rose, of the rose, oh, of — the — rose (Falsetto high G).

Confused Maggie might be when her work called for her full powers of concentration, but she understood the song and sitting on the back stairs she heard the chorus repeated with a soft sibilance that stung her ears and flooded her eyes with tears. She wept for some time before she felt anger along with an impulse to descend on Mary and resign her job.

It had taken Mary a full minute to understand what she was talking about; the flow of words was like a stream from a fireman's hose to one who is used to the gentle drip of a leaking faucet.

Her voice was shrill. She hardly punctuated her remarks:

" All this time I'm workin' gladly cleanin' up after their mud an' all. Cookin' an' ironin' their clo's an' them that mean makin' fun of the likes of them that's old enough to be their mothers. Maybe they think I ain't got sense understandin' all that, but I know well enough who they're hollerin' about. After all this time livin' with you up early and to bed late nights an' then just comin' home a little early so as to fix me bunions up, and that's what happens — "

She packed, muttering, her hat with its single upstanding, red rose awry, her coat straining across the shoulders. She did not pause long enough to unfasten the poor, black fur that sagged round her neck.

Mary tried to soothe her and apologize for the boys who were sitting in awed silence downstairs. They could hear their mother's gentle voice.

"They wouldn't hurt your feelings for the world, Maggie. They are truly fond of you; we all are, and we do appreciate what you do for us. The boys are just young and foolish and enjoy their silly jokes. They joke about everything, you know. You mustn't take it so hard, Maggie."

The only answer was the muttering that had not ceased during Mary's talk. It flowed on even as the poor limping soul left the house an hour later. Mary saw her out, still trying to soothe. "Take a few days' vacation and get your foot well, Maggie, before you come back. We'll be glad to see you."

A week had passed and Mary was beginning to look about for another "girl" when one morning she stepped out upon the back porch to get the milk and saw Maggie sitting on the lowest step, huddled over her bundle, the red rose, the black fur, the straining coat all exactly as if they had not been off her since she packed.

Mary's welcome was a mixture of surprise, relief and amusement. She was cordial, and at her, "Come right in and get warm and have some coffee," Maggie muttered that she guessed she'd go to her room " if some other girl ain't in it " and put on her old dress.

She looked at Mary and there was gentle contrition in the bovine eyes. Mary patted her arm as she shuffled past and said the room was waiting for her. They never referred to the song or the unhappiness of that time, but ever after, Maggie dated all events from " before my vacation " or " after my vacation."

V

Now Maggie was in the last month of the second year of her reign with the Stevensons. She seemed never to change. She adhered religiously to a program for her work. Each day was sacred to its particular line of achievement and to add a detail further was to bring confusion upon the poor, slavish mind. Mary could ask no help of her for the lighter and more numerous tasks of the homemaking that crowded upon her along with the children, the church work and her music. And yet she was content with Maggie. Coming as she had after Ella, she was peace and comfort.

The affair of Ella was a sordid thing. It was a dark spot in the Stevenson family life and yet not profitless.

Mary reviewed it again there at the table while Angus and the children talked and Maggie muttered. She was probing her heart with exacting honesty in search of flaws that might justify the criticism she had met in the afternoon, wondering, puzzled, if their altruism, Angus' and hers, might have been misconstrued. There had been so many cases like Ella's when they had had to choose between the world's way and Christ's. With the simplest of motives they had striven always to be consistent with their high calling.

Ella had come to them in answer to an advertisement

for a helper at housework. She had almost pleaded to be taken, though Mary had seen from the first that she was not the usual sort and had sensed a mystery. But the very nature of the girl's appeal made it impossible, in mercy, to turn her away and Mary had watched her the first few days about her work with a deepening of her distrust. " She is hiding," she had concluded. " Perhaps she is a thief," but the thought — " We have nothing worth stealing. She would hardly waste her time on us " — disposed of that.

It was less than six weeks after Ella came that Mary, returning home one afternoon earlier than she was expected, found Ella at the piano. Without notes she was sweeping a Chopin scherzo from the keyboard. Her passion, her control, her brilliant interpretation held Mary silent with admiration in the hall.

" Housework! Indeed. That means years in a conservatory! She's an artist. It must be *the* tragedy, the old, old tragedy."

Mary stepped into the room. Ella was huddled on the piano stool, sobbing into her crossed arms.

" Ella — " Mary had been very gentle. " There is something you want to tell me. I've known since the first that there was a mystery."

It was, as Mary had thought, the great tragedy of girlhood. " I'm not married. I couldn't tell my parents. They think I'm teaching music here."

" And your music. Where did you study? You play so beautifully."

" The New England conservatory and last year I was in Vienna and Berlin. It was when I came home — a man I knew. I don't love him. I hate him. He hates me."

In so few words the mystery was dispelled. There arose no question in Angus' and Mary's minds as to their own responsibility. " We must keep her here and help her. She must be saved from all sorts of danger, bitterness, hate — " The list lengthened. They thought of the boys. " We can turn it to use as a means of teaching them the truth about this phase of life — justice, tenderness, but chiefly the cruel injustice of it all."

Angus had felt not so much sympathy for Ella as championship of the helpless unborn and wrath that Ella's partner in guilt had no share in the price of it. He was gentle with Ella and persuasive; his way with her sent her to her knees in humility and gratitude, and he succeeded, after a long struggle with her reserves, in learning the name of the " miserable scoundrel who deserved a sound beating."

The wretched business of it all dragged through months of that winter. Angus finally forced Alfred Meyerheim to come to Detroit. He took Ella with him for the triangular interview and by skillful work as mediator, led them to discuss their mutual problem from the angle of the helpless product of their wrong-doing rather than their own selfish preferences.

It had been characteristic that Angus, when they had reached a deadlock and Meyerheim, stolid and sullen, insulting to both Ella and Angus in his refusal to accept responsibility, had sent Ella home to rest and had turned to Meyerheim, willing to continue the battle alone.

" Meyerheim," he had said, looking straight and terribly into his hot eyes, " you've beaten Ella with your insolence. Your insults have driven her away. But you can't get rid of me. I shall force you to decency if I have to go to the law to do it."

Meyerheim had shrugged. " Don't fool yourself on Ella. You can't insult a girl like that."

" That's enough. You skunk! You can't talk that way about her to me."

At last they had moved on from argument and persuasion to open hostility. Angus almost struck the man. He wanted to. His hands jerked with repressed desire to beat the sneering, bored face before him. Instead he talked. He let his tongue fight for Ella and he managed not to be abusive.

"Ella is an artist;" he began, snapping out the words. "She is temperamental, emotional. She is carried away by a force that I would be satisfied to call the passion of genius. I believe she will yet be called great by a critical world. I have never heard anybody make a piano speak so convincingly. I do not idealize her nor exonerate her from blame. She has done wrong. She has soiled herself unspeakably, but the test is not so much in what we do as in the way we react to our wrong-doing. Ella has gone to the bottom of the fiery furnace. She is being burned white. She will rise from the ashes of her dead self a splendid, repentant, wise, brilliant woman. She will be worthy of motherhood and of the love of a big-souled man. But it won't be you, Meyerheim. Your hide is too tough to feel the flames. You are used to the scorching of sin. You've baked your conscience in it till it's like a piece of asbestos." Angus' lips shut with a snap on his short rapid sentences. The slouch of Meyerheim's figure was fuel for his wrath. "Now, sir," Angus paused, but glimpsed no response from the young man before him, "I haven't many weapons to use against you, but such as I have I will use. For the sake of your own child you — are — going — to — marry — her. And how much money are you going to send her?"

"That's my business."

"It is my business. She will live in my house and under my protection. She shall have every comfort and you will pay for it — not her board. We will continue

to pay her wages and give her board, but other things —
doctors, the best hospital — it is expensive."

Angus glared. Meyerheim deliberately felt in his
pocket for his cigarette case, opened it and went with the
utmost calm through the business of making a selection
and closing the case. He searched for matches and as
deliberately lighted the cigarette that hung waiting
between his lips. When he had tossed the match over his
shoulder, he took a great draught of smoke and blew it
toward the ceiling. Then he looked at Angus, sidewise,
his face slightly awry.

"Have you finished with me, Doctor Stevenson? If
so —" he moved backward.

Angus' expressive face had passed through several
changes during this silence, but Meyerheim had not
looked directly at him for some moments. He saw him
now distinctly, and his own face changed as if by shock.
Angus' eyes were gentle, shining with a dawning look of
understanding. He smiled slightly and his lips had
parted. His whole aspect was one of eager kindliness.

"Meyerheim, it has just come to me — the reason for
all this cruelty in you." Meyerheim blinked rapidly and
stared. "At some time in your youth somebody has
sinned against you. Somebody has failed you, as you
are now failing your wife — and child. You're *ignorant.*
Your sense of justice is not developed. Sit over here by
me and tell me about yourself." He turned persuasively
and indicated a seat on the settee.

Meyerheim moved forward a step and grunted inquiringly. But Angus, his hand extended, kept the
steady magnetic gaze on his face and smiled ever so little,
waiting. The hard eyes turned from Angus, after a
moment of sneering scrutiny, and he sat down.

They talked for two hours. Angus told Mary and the
boys all about it. "God gave me vision," he said, his

eyes shining. "I was led to say the right things. The fellow melted utterly and told me his whole, bitter, childhood story. Before he finished he was sobbing and not ashamed of it. He wanted to hear anything I would say. His stubbornness broke completely." Angus' voice sank to a whisper. "I — prayed with him!"

"And then?" said Mary, to whom repentant sinners were not a novelty.

"Then he asked me to make Ella understand that he felt differently; that he would marry her and care for her. I think the man honestly wants to do right. The seal of the fountain is broken. He'll come to-night for her answer. They'll be married here and you and the boys will be witnesses. I believe they'll manage to come out decently yet, maybe stronger and better, but oh, boys . . . boys . . ." Angus had turned to his sons.

"No." Mary concluded there at the table, when she had remembered it all again. "It isn't for that sort of thing that we are called bigots. It is for that that we are loved in spite of our old-fashioned orthodoxy."

VI

"Well," said Angus, lingering over his dessert, "this is the first evening I have been able to call my own in about three weeks. I can stay right here with you all."

There was a chorus of cheers.

"No old committees? No prayer meetings? No speeches to be made?"

"Not one. I belong to myself this night. How much studying have you, boys?"

"Latin."

"Math. and history."

"Let's have music till Frances goes to bed; then I'll help you with your Latin."

Angus enjoyed helping with the Latin, though he was chary about giving aid since the chief benefit of the study was discipline for the boys, but he had a natural aptitude for languages and delighted in pitting his memory from some forty years back against their fresh-from-the-classroom knowledge. Invariably he translated more rapidly than they, had his vocabulary at his tongue's end and took a tone of impatience with the boys' groping hesitation that, they knew, was assumed more to conceal his own delight in beating them than disgust with their limitations as Latinists. He liked to lean back in his chair and tell them the stories of word building, using the Latin root to raise a structure of many stories. Words were individuals to him, with histories, personalities and character, like people.

" There's that word Cæsar uses — *impedimenta*. It's one of my friends. *Impedimentum*—neuter gender, but a humorous chap nevertheless. Baggage; encumbrance; something that hinders progress. Whenever I see a dandy going about in street cars and cabs with a walking stick I say to myself, " There's my friend *Impedimentum* laughing up his sleeve."

The twins liked this sort of thing. It helped them to remember.

An evening of music in the Stevenson living room could not, consistently, be classified as Chamber Music. Unless Mary performed it was not apt to be in the least restrained, although the twins' repertory included many of the best things along with the rag and rabble of the lesser lights.

- The program was a thing of mood, impromptu and as variable as the tastes of the performers.

They began that Monday night with the only two comic operas they had ever been permitted to see, Robin Hood and Foxy Quiller. They knew the score of the former from beginning to end and acted the parts and sang the choruses and laughed at each other immoderately. Jimmie as the Sheriff of Nottingham, John as Friar Tuck, Jimmie as Foxy Quiller, John as Tutso, made Angus roll in his chair and beg for mercy.

If the stage had lost a light when it lost Angus — as was often said, it should have mourned triply for Angus and Jimmie and John, born comedians all three of them.

Even Frances was pressed into the chorus and she shadowed the Sheriff of Nottingham when he roared, "I am the Sheriff of Nottingham. My eye is like the eagle — ", acted the chorus and made the response with Mary, who sat in the lamplight with a piece of sewing and trilled, "Bow low! Bow low!" in the right places.

John, in his brief white track pants, a sleeveless shirt and tennis shoes, entered at the right moment, his hair erect, his eyes crossed and staring, his knees flexed, and did Friar Tuck straight through. The boys managed to change off as orchestra. For Jimmie's solos John played, and for John's solos Jimmie played, though Mary often did the whole score for them.

Jimmie, who was a little livelier than John, was an accomplished clogger and in perfecting the art had clogged his way through three coats of varnish and half an inch of boarding. One spot was allotted him for his performances and when not thus used it was covered by an old Turkish prayer rug.

It was after Frances had gone to bed that Mary gathered her three boys about her and told them of her afternoon's experience, Mrs. Stanhope's speech, her election to the club membership, her paper.

Angus asked her a few questions but made no comment. He rose though, and walked up and down before the fireplace, head bowed, his hands thrust deep in his pockets.

John leaned toward his mother and kissed her. " We know, mom," he said. " We get it at school. Worse. A lot worse than that. You and dad don't know."

CHAPTER VIII

I

RITA STANHOPE refused to admit to Felix that anything had gone wrong at the meeting of Olla Podrida.
She was a little reproachful in her replies when he questioned her and asked if a severe headache were not
sufficient reason for leaving early and refusing dinner.
He put no pressure upon her but he thought he knew
much that she would not tell.

He was very busy at the factory and it was Thursday
before he had further light on the affair that already had
grown dim in his mind.

The playground committee was to meet again at
luncheon Thursday noon. Felix, entirely ignorant of
Rita's offense against the Stevensons, arrived a little late
and, pressing his way through the thronged lobby of the
Russell House, offered his hand to Angus. He liked
Angus and remembered his first meeting with him so
pleasantly that he had decided to invite him to call on
them some evening. Back of his intention he entertained
a hope that Angus might be generous-minded enough to
discuss Nietzsche and Ingersoll with him dispassionately.
He rather longed for such a pleasure with its attendant
clash of convictions and intellect.

His proffered hand was accepted after a moment of
hesitation, while Angus regarded him inquiringly. Felix,
puzzled, glanced about him at the familiar faces of the
committeemen. " You expected me? " he asked quickly,
made doubtful by Angus' long unsmiling look.

Angus released his hand. "Yes, yes." He seemed to have roused himself. "Certainly. Shall we go in? The mayor is to join us later. He asked us not to wait."

Felix was on guard. Doctor Stevenson's unsmiling greeting and the look of surprise, with something of quickly masked resentment, were significant. For some reason he had not been expected to-day.

In the shifting about for places at the table it fell to Felix' lot to sit on Angus' left. He was content that it should be so. It would give him opportunity to watch for an explanation of his behavior. There was something, certainly, to be learned.

They began almost at once upon the business of the day. Angus was happy to report that through the estate of the late beloved Colonel Herrick the committee was to have a piece of ground in the most congested residence section below Jefferson Avenue for a playground, three acres flanked by warehouses and surrounded by dilapidated mansions of past glory and present squalor, land — plenty of land where they needed it most.

As Angus made the report the glow came into his eyes and lit his whole expression with a radiance that Felix watched intently through his heavy lenses. What a look, shining, joyous. Felix' glance swept the circle of faces. The difference. To the others this was a business meeting, a matter of getting land grants for a good purpose, philanthropy, but good business for the city's future; nothing to shine about, only one of the day's jobs, luncheon, a little talk and back to business. To Felix' mind there came a quotation. It flitted across his thought, the inspired look on Angus' face accounting for it. "Suffer little children to come unto Me and forbid them not, for of such — etc." This playground committee meant *that* to him.

What was it Ingersoll had said? "More crimes have

been committed against little children in the name of the Scripture's ' Spare the rod and spoil the child' than for any other one sentiment ever written." Something like that. Oh, well, of course there were Christians and Christians. Judging by most of them, it was to be hoped there were others of a different stripe.

Before the committee disbanded Felix said, watching Angus' face keenly, " Doctor Stevenson, I'd be delighted to have you drop in on us some evening. I am usually at home. We are in your immediate neighborhood, I understand."

Angus turned on him with a glance like a searchlight. " You would like me to call? I had intended doing so. Last Monday afternoon I passed your house and made a note of the address. Later I felt I could not be acceptable to you. You are agnostic, I believe."

" We are nothing much. I wanted to know you personally, as a neighbor rather than professionally, but perhaps — "

Their eyes met, the blue and the black, and after a moment of scrutiny Angus said, " I will call. I shall be glad to — some evening soon."

Felix carried the memory of these two brief encounters back to his office and sat before his desk, pondering them. " I felt I could not be acceptable to you," sounded like the touchy Christianity stuff that says, " You insult my Master with your doubts." Yet that wasn't Stevenson's sort. He didn't seem the chip-on-my-shoulder sort of clergyman. That shining look, the different look when his eyes met Felix', a man proud, on guard, resenting something. By George, there had been resentment in it!

Henry Grieve threw open the door and hurried in with some papers.

" Look over these. I want to have a talk with you. I

wanted you to lunch with me but you got away. Where do you lunch, Stanhope? We must put you up at the Detroit Club."

"I'm on a committee that met this noon at the Russell House. By the way, what do you know about this man, Angus Stevenson?"

Into Henry Grieve's eyes came something of the look that Felix had met in Angus.

"I know he's a remarkable man, an unusual sort, the kind the world needs worse than it needs any other thing under God's sky," he said pugnaciously. "That answers your question. May I ask what you have against him? That little affair Monday rather upset us. Mrs. Grieve and I hardly knew what to do. She felt that it was up to her to smooth things. How did Mrs. Stanhope feel about the suggestion that she call there personally and make amends? Or write — I believe a note was decided upon as less embarrassing."

"That little affair Monday" — "Mrs. Grieve, Mrs. Stanhope" — "make amends" — Angus' scrutinizing eyes.

Felix dropped down in his chair. He had the story, most of it, from Henry Grieve in a few minutes; learned of Rita's speech; Mrs. Stevenson's election to membership unanimously; of the call Mr. and Mrs. Grieve made upon the Stevensons late that Monday evening and the fine, generous spirit they found. "Wonderful people. Best sort in the world, I tell you, standing strong on their beliefs. Tell you what, Stanhope, this young country's got to come back to a lot of hard and fast, right and wrong, hell and damnation religion or go on the rocks. The man's right. Human nature can't go easy and stay well-balanced."

"Or go religious and stay well-balanced, either."

"Maybe not, but that's the safe side to have the scales

sag on. By golly, I don't know what my boy's riding for, but it isn't the thing his grandfather lived by, and his grandfather is the real man, the real American of us all." He moved toward the door and Felix, rising, brought him back to the case of Rita. His voice was husky. The blood was pounding in his eyes. Henry Grieve was sorry for him.

"And then, of course, Mrs. Grieve told my wife she must call or write and apologize?"

"She saw your wife the next morning and asked her to do that. Of course a club like that has to have harmony or — or resignations. It's hardly possible to — a —"

"Of course," said Felix. "Mrs. Stanhope wrote, I haven't a doubt." There was interrogation in his voice.

"Not yet, I take it, but I don't know. She may have. It was hard to do, of course. They don't meet again for another ten days. There's time."

Mr. Grieve was glad to get away. Disagreeable business, but he had gotten into it unawares. No use floundering in a thing like that. Damn shame Mrs. Stanhope hadn't 'fessed up the whole business to her husband. What kind of a rotter was she, anyway? And so on, his thought, while he crossed the hall and seated himself at his own desk.

Felix was left cold and still in his swivel chair. He swung slowly toward a window and sat looking out toward a patch of vivid blue sky that was framed by a wing of the factory and a warehouse to the north. Through the open window, the rattle of traffic in the yards below made inharmonious accompaniment to the song of a robin that balanced on a wire strung across the street. The wind came in and fluttered the papers on Felix' desk.

It was not very long that he sat there, but afterward it

seemed to him to have been most of the afternoon. And remembering, he knew that in that brief space had come to him the realization that the bonds of love, of children, of home were beginning to fray under the knife of Rita's flagrant selfishness.

II

During the twenty-four hours that followed Felix gave Rita every opportunity to tell him the story of her humiliation. He was gentle with her but he hinted and invited confidence until he knew she understood that he had come into knowledge of the affair through Henry Grieve.

Still her stubborn silence held. She took on a manner of self-pity that angered Felix, and at last, in acute distaste, on the second evening of their silent struggle, he moved his belongings to the back of the house, to the room Rita had labeled the little guest chamber. This change that required but a brief half-hour for accomplishment was, nevertheless, a domestic earthquake that opened a gulf which, for Felix, never could be bridged. He tried to be casual about it, but his heart was torn and he was grateful for the refuge Dick offered the next morning when he said, with shining eagerness, " Are you going to stay in that room always, dad? Near me, like two fellows together? "

" Always," said Felix, smiling into his adoring eyes and conscious of Rita's listening ears. " Like two of the very best of fellows and I think we'll know how to keep bachelor hall at that end of the house, won't we, old man? "

Dick expanded in pride and pleasure. He said no more just then, but he pondered his good fortune on the way to school. His father had chosen to be near him, men together! Their tastes and ways would be alike.

" It's time I began to act more like a man," he concluded, adding to himself, " When your father prefers you to the rest of the family, it's time you showed what's in you."

III

The Irving School is on Willis Avenue. It stands behind a row of maples that lock arms, so closely are they set, and form, with other maples across the street, an arched tunnel above the pavement. The grass plot about the building is a weakling thing that makes no attempt at verdure in the play yards and holds its own, as a front decoration, only through constant and careful nursing. There are signs upon the lawn from early spring till late fall that read, " Please keep off the grass." But there are, besides the usual lawless lot, those daily attendants of Room One, first floor to the left as you enter, who cannot read and because of their benighted ignorance there are spots of one-time fertile soil now pounded into arid sterility by the pressure of little feet.

It was after recess Friday afternoon when the din of squealing and shouting, tramping and laughing had been suddenly and completely silenced, that teacher, who was the beloved Miss Brinton, made an announcement to the second grade.

There were forty-three of the second grade, the B class numbering twenty-four and the A class nineteen. They sat in their little seats facing the blackboard, their hands primly folded, their feet, for the most part, flat upon the floor, and gave wide-eyed attention to teacher.

She was smiling. Her dimples had deepened so far that Frances thought the bottoms of them must surely touch her teeth, and one slender finger was held out straight, pointed nail shining, while surprise, a secret, twinkled in her eyes.

"Children, be very still. I have something nice to tell you. Don't anybody move till I have finished and then perhaps you will want to clap. Before I tell you, I want to ask you what day this is. Hands."

She had said "hands" too late. From forty-three throats was shouted loudly, "Friday."

"How do we know it's Friday?"

"Dancing school," shrilled a half-dozen voices, and, from one, "The girls are all dressed up."

"Don't all talk at once, please, children. Charlotte Stanhope, you tell us how we know it's Friday."

Charlotte's dimples reflected teacher's dimples. Her eyes danced. "It's the last day of school this week, and dancing-school day when we wear our second-best dresses."

"I don't wear my second-best dresses," came Francie's deep voice deliberately. "Because I don't go to dancing school."

"No. You don't go to dancing school," said teacher, moving her head negatively and making no mention of the awful fact that Frances had spoken without permission. Truth was that teacher loved Francie especially, and found it very easy to overlook her naïve superiority to rules. The child spoke when she had something to say and blinked with a puzzled look of wonder when she was reproved — a little guileless manner that Miss Brinton found appealing. It worried Miss Brinton that Frances alone, of all the little B class, never wore a second-best dress on Fridays. She was conspicuous in her ordinary little school dress among the sashes and ruffles of gala apparel. Miss Brinton did not know the Stevensons personally, but she rather fancied they had principles of some sort against finery. It was too bad, for the children, cruel little things in their ignorance, teased Frances, and more than once Miss Brinton had seen tears in

Francie's eyes.   She had decided to do something about it and she unfolded her plan to the children.

" Now we all agree that this is Friday, but who can tell me what month it is? "

" May! "

" May, teacher."

" Yes, that's enough.   One answer will do.   It's May and next month school will close for the summer.   It is just four weeks now before that time when we will all say good-by and carry our books and pencils home and put them in the attic for the long ten weeks' vacation. And so — "

" I'm going to the seashore for my vacation."

" We aren't; we're going to Grosse Isle."

" Children.   Quiet!   I want to tell you our surprise. We're going to have last-day exercises the day school closes for the summer.   Pieces and songs and maybe — refreshments."

" Ice cream, ice cream! "

" Hush.   Quiet again.   Tell me how many of you want to speak pieces or sing songs."

" I — I — I — I — I."

" Not everybody? " cried teacher incredulously.

Yes, nearly everybody, apparently.   The response was overwhelming.   Volunteers shouted their repertories. while Miss Brinton rapped for order.

" We aren't going to talk about it any more to-day. Those of you who know pieces and want to give them on the last day stay in at recess Monday morning.   In a few days I will make out the program and let you each know your part.   Now listen to this: each Friday afternoon after this we will have rehearsal.   We'll go through our pieces and songs and have a lovely afternoon.   And it might be a good idea, if you want to, for us all to be especially clean that afternoon in second-best dresses and blouses. Not only the dancing school class *but everybody!*"

Miss Brinton was very expressive, very emphatic in her speech. As she said, "but everybody," she clasped her hands together in a gesture of ecstasy and looked down, dimpling, to see Frances raise her pudgy hands in an imitative gesture of ecstasy and echo, delightedly, "Everybody!"

Miss Brinton was content. The right one had gotten the suggestion. Perhaps this would end the teasing.

When school was out and the children formed in line, Francie stood hugging her sweater, which was rolled into an irregular bundle, one sleeve trailing, and gazed up at Miss Brinton. Miss Brinton smiled and won the response of a smile, put the tips of her pointed fingers on Francie's brown curls and directed the children to move forward slowly. She kept close to Frances as they advanced, and when her fingers slipped from the curls and hung at her side she felt with a thrill the warm, cuddling nestle of Francie's hand against her palm. She gave it a quick squeeze and held it fast, and Frances was content to have it so. The line moved more rapidly and the first little ones to pass through the door burst into shouts and running as they reached the walk below.

Miss Brinton impulsively drew Frances out of line. The others passed on. A moment and they were alone in the hall. They could hear the heavy tramp of the big children on the floor above forming for dismissal; the piano in the eighth grade room was sending forth a lively march.

Miss Brinton stooped beside the little girl and put an arm about her. Frances' small body gave softly, and pressed with warm coziness against the teacher whom she loved.

"You tell mother, Frances, that everybody is going to

wear best dresses on Friday, every Friday until school closes, and you have somebody teach you a little piece."

" I know a little piece! " Frances was all eagerness. The veins in her neck swelled and the pink of her cheeks deepened warmly. " It's about Honora Malally and I say it loud."

" Daddy and mother don't want you to go to dancing school, but they don't mind having you speak pieces or wear your pretty dresses on Fridays, do they? "

" Oh, no! " Frances assured her as to that. " Dancing school is foolish and silly and leads to no good end, but speaking pieces isn't silly. We speak pieces in our Sunday school and wear best dresses."

" That's so, you do. Of course! "

" I have a best dress that my mother made. It used to be her own. It has little flowers all over it and a pink sash and sleeves so short I show way up to here."

" Oh, lovely! I know it's beautiful. I want to see it so much I can hardly wait till next Friday." She gave Frances a final squeeze and the child skipped delightedly into the sunshine.

IV

It was warm and beautiful, a smelly day. Frances walked backward toward Cass Avenue, looking up into the trees that moved gently in the breeze. A magnolia, in the front yard of the house next to the school, was in full flower and some of the great, waxen petals lay scattered on the grass. They looked very beautiful to Frances, lying palely pink against the green. She passed the house slowly and again turned to walk backward, counting her steps.

She was very happy. She felt warm and glowing inside around her heart. She caught her breath with a little squeaking sound. Fridays, after this, she would wear her pink sash and the short sleeves and say her piece! Love of teacher, love of life, love of summer and pink sashes and short sleeves flooded her soul with wordless ecstasy. She hopped up and down for sheer joy in it all.

In just the minute that she had given to jumping, all but a few little children had disappeared, she noticed, and the big boys and girls were marching down the school steps. She had the sidewalk almost to herself for walking backward. She did it with intent interest, her short legs striding waveringly over the stones.

Behind her at the corner she heard Charlotte's voice calling something to somebody. That Charlotte thought she was smart because she was an A Second and went to dancing school! Francie paid no attention. She was walking away from the school but facing toward it and she saw big Richard Stanhope leaping in great bounds as he advanced upon her. He would look at her shoes. She had better hurry.

She turned around and hopped along, trailing her sweater, her curls bouncing up and down upon her shoulders. Such lots of fun to hop and feel the cool air on her face!

Richard overtook her at the corner. They met there, the three, and he reached down, lifted her sweater and tossed it over her head as he went leaping past.

"What you hanging around here for, Charlotte?" he demanded, stopping suddenly before his sister. She sat on the smooth, iron pipe fence that ran diagonally across the lawn of the corner house to keep the children from tramping down the grass. A vain endeavor, for the fence was to them an invitation to gymnastics and not a day passed that some hundred or more did not jump over it, swing upon it, crawl under it or use it as a saddle bar. There was no grass at all for it to protect by the time school closed in June, but it stood there year after year and told the neighbors thereabout that at least an effort was being made to keep young hoodlums off.

Charlotte, sitting on this iron pipe, balanced airily, her short skirts puffed out about her. She made an impish face at Richard and informed him loftily that it was none of his business. His reply was given with a quick jerk of his arm and Charlotte was off the fence, squealing and kicking. "You let me alone," she shrieked. "I'm waiting for Zoe to get her slippers, Smarty."

Frances stared in alarm. Richard would muss Charlotte's dress if he pulled her like that! She longed to go to Charlotte's assistance, but the futility of small girls against large boys was one of the few things she knew well. She stood back, watching.

The big children flowed around and past, and Frances joined the last straggling few, walking slowly backward again, her eyes on Charlotte, who was on the fence once more. Richard was engaged in sudden and deep confidences with another boy who had joined him. They were swopping. Frances saw a sling shot change hands and something else — something wrapped in paper. Candy! Frances' mouth watered.

Charlotte saw her staring. "Francie's teacher's pet. Francie's teacher's pet," she sang, making a face at Francie.

Francie stared harder, forgetting to walk backward.

"Francie is a big-gut, Francie is a big-gut. Her father won't let her go to dancing school, and that's a big-gut, big-gut, big-gut."

Another face, and from Francie the worst face of all, a dreadful thing with tongue sticking out and nose quite wrinkled and hideous.

"Bla, bla, bla," said Frances furiously. "I am not big-gut."

"You are too, and you haven't any best dresses. Francie's poo-er. Francie, Francie's poo-er!" Charlotte slid down off the fence and advanced upon Francie. "Big-gut."

Not the very least idea did Frances have as to the nature of a big-gut, but she guessed fast enough, though what it had to do with not going to dancing school she couldn't think. Big was an easy word and the other one the boys said sometimes. She had heard.

She stood glaring as Charlotte approached, her little face red and serious. Charlotte sparkled with joy in mischief. Her dimples flashed, she minced her walk, looking Francie over with a supercilious stare. "Francie's poo-er," she sang again and again. "Francie hasn't any best dresses," and suddenly changing, "Francie has funny shoes", and thrust her tongue way out in a red point that maddened Frances. Big-gut and poor and taunts on dancing school she could bear, but her shoes were a sore point. She howled with rage and flew at Charlotte, her face puckered into wrinkles of wrath, her hands — the very hand that had clung confidently like a warm little bird in Miss Brinton's clasp not ten minutes before — lifted in dreadful claws that attacked Charlotte's face with bloody intent.

They fought like small wildcats. Frances scratched and Charlotte, grasping at Francie's curls, pulled with all her might. Not a sound came from them at first. They clutched in terrible combat and their strength was well matched.

Richard pulled them apart and as they felt his strong grasp on their shoulders they broke into tears. Charlotte's face was streaked with blood from Frances' nails and Frances, panting with rage and exhaustion, looked wildly out from a disarray of curls that was, for all the world, like a kitten with fur on end.

"My — my *shoes,*" sobbed Francie. "I hate her. I hate her," and she lunged forward.

Richard held them apart until Zoe, with her mother at her heels, took Charlotte from him and folded her in her arms.

"You take Charlotte to dancing school," Richard ordered, disposing of his sister, "and wash her face, and I'll take this little cat home. What did you scratch Charlotte like that for, Frances? What's the matter with you kids?"

He could not have expected an answer to his questions. Frances was sobbing. Her whole body was jarred and shaken with the force of great, terrible sobs. She couldn't walk and she stood bent forward, gasping, raining tears upon the sidewalk.

Over his shoulder Richard saw Zoe's mother taking Charlotte into the house. He knelt, giving one knicker-bockered knee to it, before Frances and fished for his handkerchief. Luck was with him. He had one — such as it was.

"Gee whiz, Frances, don't cry so hard. Gosh, you sure can go it!" He applied the handkerchief as only a big brother can, firmly and effectively — but firmly. Frances, lifting her face for his ministrations, leaned wearily, her rioting hair brushing his face. She burst into sobbing review of the encounter.

"Char-Char-Charlotte called me big-gut. She — she said I have no best dr-dr-dresses. I am n-not big-gut." Woe bore her down and she collapsed weeping in Richard's arms.

He glanced around quickly. A friendly clump of lilacs was most conveniently placed to screen them and he dared to pat her rather tenderly, saying comforting things about teaching Charlotte not to pick on little girls, and she mustn't mind teasing, anyway. Feeling very

much a man, he tried to behave as he knew his father
would under the same circumstances.

Francie was used to boys. Their rough sympathy was
perfectly acceptable to her and she clung and wept, rubbing her wet nose on Richard's coat.

He took her home, walking slowly, carrying her
sweater over his shoulder, holding the hand that had
scratched so viciously, and feeling several sorts of mild
emotion. Nice, cute little kid, this Francie, and friendly
as the dickens. Gee, the way she hung on to him as if he
was her mother.

He looked down at the shoes pat, patting on the walk,
short steps, short feet, one tassel bobbing, the other sadly
missing, lost in battle. Poor little kid!

She had nothing more to say, no need for words. The
tired droop of her head, the last shaking sobs that caught
at her throat, the clinging hand were sufficient speech.

Richard took her to her own back gate. In its shadow
he knelt before her again. "Alrighty now?" he asked
pleasantly. "Here, wipe your nose again. There now,
go on in to your mother." He gave her a little shove,
but leaned forward and kissed her cheek and she stood
looking up at him, wet eyes, rosy cheeks and mouth all
round with wonder.

A very pleasant feeling tingled down his spine. He
called a hasty "so long" and, leaping, cleared the fence.

BOOK TWO

IN WHICH THE SONS AND DAUGHTERS OF THE STANHOPES
AND THE STEVENSONS GROW UP AND CREATE
COMPLICATIONS THAT BECOME ACUTE
IN THE SPRING OF 1917

BOOK TWO

CHAPTER I

I

LOOKING back along the twenty-eight years of his
service in Detroit as a minister of the gospel — for it was
as such Angus classified himself — he perceived that the
spring of 1905 was the time when the tide of his affairs
had begun to ebb. In perspective, events which once
seemed small often take on looming proportions, while
events that at the time seemed large may have dwindled
to surprising smallness.

It was so with Angus. He began to search for the
reason when he realized that his memory of May, 1905,
held a portent of trouble inexplicably interwoven in his
thought of it, with the change in the Sunday baseball
laws and the clash between the Stanhope family and his
own.

At the time it had not seemed of as much moment as
other affairs not recorded here. There was always
strife for Sabbath observance on Angus' program, there
were always new people of various sorts crossing his
path. His family, like every other family, had its social
inharmonies. Committees were the rule of his busy days
and yet, in looking back, he saw, distinct among the
shadowy memories of that time, Felix Stanhope's face,
the playground committee, Mary's still whiteness and the
story of her afternoon at club, followed within the week
by Frances, gory with battle, and the baseball incident.

Angus had taken defeat in the matter of the Sunday ball war characteristically. He had fought hard and with the best of himself. On the occasion of his dinner with the players as Jack Mason's guest, he had perceived that he was combating the sinned against as well as the sinning, and he had returned home that night to say soberly to Mary, " We'll have Sunday ball. The players themselves want it. They were cordial to me, very courteous, did me all the honors, but they want Sunday ball. It's coming. Somehow they made me feel a fool for standing champion of their rights. They don't want their rights. They'd rather shine in the limelight than anything else under heaven. They don't want a day kept sacred to God."

He stood by the mantel in the living room and gazed, with farseeing eyes, at the opposite wall where, like a panorama, he saw the valley of life with its struggling swarms of souls, little souls and big, jostling each other in the mêlée; rampant bands of marauders riding the plentiful valleys for privilege; raising a din in the name of Personal Liberty; waving the banners of pseudo progress. He saw the small and earnest bands of the righteous making their fight of resistance, mounting guard on the bulwarks of conservatism, pointing agonized and unobserved to the cross that was all but obscured by the smoke of materialism. So few they seemed, a giant here and there among them, but for the most part (and this, to Angus, was the pain of it) a straggling band of ineffectuals pressed upon by the shifting millions of the indifferent. The Indifferent! Going their pleasant way unruffled by the conflict so long as their troughs were not upset in the struggle.

It was unjust and strange that his mind viewed it so — the influence of Saint Paul, no doubt, with his exhortation against sins of omission — but Angus saw, in his vision, that the indifferent and the ineffectuals were greater enemies of right than the rampant marauders for wrong. A strong man feels kinship with a strong man. It had ever been so with Angus. He felt an understanding of the aggressive sinner; whatever he was he was fighting for the thing he wanted. Whatever his sins, he wanted something enough to fight for it. But the indifferent, the ineffectuals, jellyfishing their way through life — for them contempt and their just deserts — oblivion.

Sunday ball was provided for through law that year, and when Angus received his season pass, with the usual note from the club secretary, who was genial and Irish and both an admirer and enemy of Angus, Angus read it with a clouded face.

Dr. Angus Stevenson,
Detroit.

Dear Father:

Enclosed is your season's pass and I want to say again what so often I have said before, — that it does me good to send it to you. I like to see you at the games with your twins, rooting for the Tigers.

I hear often the story of your dinner with the boys recently, and of the fine speech you made. The fellows liked you fine and what you said did them good.

Hoping to see you often in the grand stand this summer,

I am, yours respectfully,

Terrence O'Keefe.

Angus dropped the letter on his blotter and read the pass. For how many years had he been receiving them and counting them one of his greatest delights? The Tigers were heroes to Angus, slim young creatures of brain and brawn; plenty of brain, the game wasn't merely a brute affair. That was the beauty of it and the thing that would keep it alive as the national sport. More and more it would become a matter of mind and the type would be correspondingly finer. He loved the game. Of all life's pleasures it was one of the few that remained for him. He thrilled to the drama and in his college days he had had a place in the dramatic club where he had shone as a comedian. He had played Macbeth once with strength and poise, but, since Princeton days, the theater had been closed to him. "Immorality is their one theme. They keep the sex problem uppermost and they never solve it. They exploit it. I won't support, in any way whatever, the crew of loose-lived, half-baked egoists who call themselves actors in these days. They debase a great art. They merely amuse and that not creditably."

In the house of mirth Angus found open doors, but investigation ended ever in his voluntarily closing them. He shut himself out through choice, feeling only distaste for the things that might have been recreative pleasure but for the degrading extremes to which they were carried.

"What's wrong in a quiet game of cards?" he was asked.

And for answer he said, "The thing that's wrong is the thing that makes gamblers and tricksters and idlers of the people who begin by playing a quiet game."

All but baseball! Baseball, until now, had been a sport apart.

Angus reread Terrence O'Keefe's note and smiled. "'Dear Father!'" he quoted. "Very respectful is Terrence, who doesn't know we don't call 'em 'Father.' Well, this is the end for me." He reached for a sheet of paper and wrote rapidly:

My dear O'Keefe:

I thank you for the pass. For many years it has been received with the very keenest delight and used with both pleasure and profit. My sons are great fans for the Tigers and they, with me, regret exceedingly that the games are closed to us from now on.

I have made a hard fight against your invasion of the day that I believe to be sacred to God. You, too, have fought, not harder than I, but on the winning side, and from now on you are to have your Sunday game with its yelling and din, and the big gate receipts.

I shall continue to combat you, and some day a miracle may happen to turn the tables God's way.

Enclosed is the pass which I return. Thank you for sending it.

I am, as ever, sincerely yours,

ANGUS STEVENSON.

With the mailing of that note Angus closed and locked the last door in the house of mirth that had stood wide for him. If he were an extremist, if he were unreasonable, he was at least consistent. He stood upon his principle, a figure of bronze on a base of granite, and the sea of pleasure-loving, gain-greedy Detroit washed like a tide of ooze about his feet.

He never again went to a league game. He asked the twins not to go, but he suspected — and rightly — that they did as they pleased upon occasion.

In looking back it is not strange that he remembered that incident of the baseball pass in 1905.

II

As to the Stanhopes. Why did he remember them especially? Felix' peering black eyes looked out at him

across the years, puzzled, questioning, hurt — yes, hurt.
The man carried wounds that, later, he had hidden under
an impermeable and aloof exterior. He had wanted
Angus to call, but Angus had not done so at once, and,
almost immediately, that club affair had made it impossible. But the playground committee had continued
to function that year, and Felix had not missed a meeting. They met with outward show of amity. Angus
had promised himself that he would be quick to make
more friendly advances should Mrs. Stanhope fulfill the
requirements Mrs. Grieve had laid upon her in the matter
of apology. Since she had failed to do that he could
only accept her silence as settling the matter of their
personal relationship.

Mary reported that Mrs. Stanhope had appeared at the
first of the fall meetings and had made herself very
charming indeed, but she had never been present after
that, and Mary learned that she had been asked to resign.
Mrs. Grieve had pressed the matter to a conclusion in her
loyalty to the Stevensons.

So little had been said about the affair that Angus
remembered only Felix' face and the gradual change that
had taken place there, mirroring, he thought, the man's
soul. And yet — if to understand all things is to forgive
all things — how great the pity that understanding is
not made simpler.

Angus sighed. He was sorry he had not swallowed
his pride and gone to offer friendliness where once it
had been requested. Well, there was excuse enough.
Charlotte's attack upon Frances, the epithet "biggut"
as pronounced by Francie, added its weight to Rita's
speech. The Stanhopes had talked at home unkindly
enough to impress an eight-year-old with their enmity.
Perhaps, in doing the natural thing, he had been right,
after all.

The two families met here and there about the city, but they avoided each other when possible. Charlotte and Francie were frankly enemies, but Frances could not speak of the family or see young Richard without coloring. Mary had called his attention to the fact. Such, probably, was the nature of a feud, even so intelligent a feud, Angus mused. Fiction seemed to think so, at least. Through antagonism a shaft of sympathy, the tightening of some subtle bond denied, for to be able to hate, one must be capable of love. To feel continued animosity one must know the pain of contumely. Mere indifference would have sounded the death note to feeling long since. After all, the affair centered in Frances. Looking deep, that was the point to seize upon. Not Mary, not Angus — save for a disturbing sense of regret — but Frances who became firm-chinned when Charlotte was mentioned and flamed with color at word of that handsome, black-haired Dick.

III

Frances at seventeen, in 1916, was that idealistic type of girl whose vogue was to suffer eclipse during the next four years. She was, judged by post-war standards of her own generation, too naïvely simple. She wore no rouge. Her soft, dark hair was unlit by henna and her eyebrows arched naturally above eyes that looked out with the wonder of innocence upon ways denied her. To-day's mode calls for the artificial, but yesterday's did not, and Frances, even though she was held back by Angus' strong prejudices from the sophistications of her compeers, was, nevertheless, considered pretty and popular. Her ingenuous manner was partly the result of the rigorous training of her brothers, who had agreed that their sister was to be the " rightest sort of a girl."

Winking a wise eye at her, Jimmie had advised, " Keep your skirt down half-way between your ankle and your knee, Frances. Don't show anything. And never be sentimental. 'No tears under any circumstances. Be a thorough sport, but don't be fresh. Some girls get away with it for a while, but the fellows get tired of them. They like girl-girls, and I won't have my sister talked about. Leave it to us. John and I will introduce you to real men when you're old enough.".

These instructions were given when Frances was just glimpsing the dawn of her teens. It was the wink of understanding fellowship that sent the advice to a place of remembrance, for she never forgot it. Jimmie had a way with him, and he had succeeded in making his guileless young sister feel that, quite free of legitimate charge, she had been given advice that was priceless. When Frances was an impressionable small woman in the making Jimmie and John were men who disappeared collegeward and returned periodically with an air indescribable, a fund of foolishness and a vocabulary convincingly careless. They thrilled Frances, who shadowed them on their vacations at home and gave them the shining glory of her adoring gaze.

When she was seventeen the twins were long out of college and gone from home into the world of their professions, — Jimmie to admiralty law with an old established firm in New York, and John as special writer for the *New York Herald*. They had a small suite in an old building on West Forty-sixth Street, up two flights, over a milliner's shop, where their college paraphernalia and a few comfortable willow chairs were magically made to create an atmosphere of artistic bachelordom that charmed Frances when she visited them.

She had lived, in her days of obedience, on that promise made by Jimmie when he had winked The Wink, —

" I will introduce you to real men when you're old enough," but he had not felt, evidently, that she ever would be old enough.

She was lonely at home with Angus and Mary, and strange outside her home, and it was that strangeness that made the knot in the problem of her youth.

CHAPTER II

I

Until Frances visited her brothers in New York and realized, through them, her mother's concern for her, she had not known her youth was in any way a problem. That she offered interesting material for a study in psychology she did not dream for a moment. Like her father, she considered herself transparently simple, the very thing her mirror showed her to be, a young girl at once both wistful and rebellious.

It was Mary who understood, and though Frances was never to know, it was Mary who wrote to the boys two months before Frances' birthday with a suggestion.

Sitting at her old, oak desk with its sagging writing board, she began a letter one April morning, but paused after she had written the salutation, " My dearest boys ", to pull out the top drawer and thus give the slanting writing board a prop. She looked through the scrim curtains that hung between her and the outer world and saw in memory the twins playing shinny in the street, while Frances, cuddling herself into a heap too small to menace the progress of the game, watched her brothers knock a stone over the asphalt. It seemed such a little time ago, to Mary, that they had all been there with her, content in the happy family life, with no yearnings beyond the fun of their own making.

Mary sighed and wrote, making an effort not to reveal her heart hunger for her sons.

My dearest Boys:

Your fine letters, which I wanted to answer immediately, came the day I had to leave for Mt. Clemens to preside over the synodical meeting — annual, you know, and very important. This is the first year I have not been president and · I was feeling like a colt turned out to pasture with the rope of that responsibility taken off my neck, when word came that the president was suddenly ill and I, who thought the vice-presidency was to be a sinecure, had to assume her responsibilities at a moment's notice. That is why I did not write to you sooner.

I am glad you remembered to answer my question as to what you think of New York as a city, for I really wanted your impressions, and I was much interested in your reactions to its tremendous effect. I agree with you; it offers everything, and its inhabitants have but to choose what they will take. I remember a Sunday there that was more peaceful than Detroit. The library in our hotel was as quiet as the country. Fifth Avenue was leisurely and almost deserted. I remember a night that was lurid with lights and drunkenness and wretched women. It all revolted me, until I was physically ill, yet I was on the outside looking in. I have had a sun bath on a bench in the Battery in the middle of a working day as peacefully as any ruben snoozing on the edge of his half-plowed field. All things to all people might be the city's slogan.

You say you have learned much there in the new life, chiefly to despise woolen union suits and flannelette pajamas. From that I should judge that you are living the steam-heated life, night and day. If you were not, the Atlantic winds would nip your skins and remind you of woolly comforts. I think the human animal will soon be growing fur again in self-protection, for the young moderns are all, it seems, reducing their amount of clothing. Frances wears a scrap or two of nothing under her dresses, but when I remonstrate and urge something warm she assures me, with pain in her voice, that she is " so hot " she couldn't stand more!

You want to know about her. You asked especially, and I suppose you realize that at her age she changes rapidly, so that even we, who see her daily, are constantly aware of her growing charm. She is a young person of temperament. She has character and a something I can't name, but it has to do with her exquisite whiteness. It is as if the lovely pallor of her face were an inner light, not so much a characteristic of her skin as of her quality. There is nothing madcap or flyaway about Frances. Her animation is from within. When she is hurt or angry (and I assure you she is not without her tempers) her face whitens, and the dark of her eyes deepens. The heat of her temperament is like father's. It is dangerous and beautiful and I have sincere respect for its blazing.

This ought to make you want to see her. She will have a birthday, you know, in a little less than two months. Of course you won't forget it, but you will wait until the last moment before you ask me — by telegraph probably — what to send her. Anticipating that, I am going to suggest that you make a visit to you your gift to her. She would love it, and she would make you happy if cozy suppers and things are possible in your rooms.

You have often accused me of playing too much the diplomat with you, twisting you all around my finger and never letting any of you know what my real purposes are. This time I am not concealing anything. I won't pretend that I want Frances to visit you for your sakes. It is for her that I want it. She needs it. I am troubled about her, and I want her to get away from home for a time. If we could afford to send her to boarding school, we would, but — that is another story. The church.

It happened just before I went to Mt. Clemens. It was at the annual meeting and the treasurer's reports showed an alarming deficit. There had been extra expense and pledges had fallen off. I can't go into the reasons, but your father, in his high idealism suggested that the church solve the financial problem by reducing his salary, and . . . they did it. In place of the munificent sum of $4,000 a year

they now pay him $3,000. Mr. MacLaren made a speech
to the effect, that, since " our beloved pastor does not now
have to support his sons, this reduction in his salary can
hardly be called an injustice." My emotions seethed. I
wanted father to rise and resign, and I sat there, making a
speech that would have raised the roof. Mrs. MacLaren
was behind me. She slipped into the chair beside me and I
thought she looked ashamed — as she should be — of her
small, small husband! She whispered, " I am so amazed
at Thomas these days. I tell him he talks ' rainy day ' at
home so much that his mind dwells continuously ' in
wet weather.' " She is sweet, of course. Too sweet.
A little pepper in her dealings with Thomas might
have made a bigger man of him. The church accepted father's proposition. They voted to reduce his salary. I can't
express to you my feelings. I don't know whether you remember it or not, but this is the second time they have done
that same thing. Back in 1898 when you were little and
Frances coming, father made that same offer and it was
accepted. Then later the church was more prosperous and
his salary was raised to $4,000, but now, on $250.00 a month
we must keep up our home, educate our daughter and live a
full life in the service of church and city. Of course Francie
can't go to boarding school.

I told your father so. He had not let down a peg below
his high mood of sacrifice. He lingered after the meeting,
attending to details, but I slipped out as soon as possible
and came home. I couldn't talk to anybody, or smile. To
think that after nearly thirty years they would let him
take that cut just when Frances is most expensive and we
ought to be saving for our old age. Of course I can't tell
you all I felt. I don't need to, but I was hot with indignation.
I walked the living-room floor feeling that we were in a
trap, and trying, with all my intensity, to discover a way
out. I want father to leave this church, and yet I know I
might as well want to transplant a hundred-year-old oak
and have it live in alien soil. His heart roots are so deep in
Detroit they couldn't be dug out alive.

I wondered how he would feel when he found that the people had blandly, and as if it were the usual procedure, accepted his offer. Before he came I had control of myself and had lighted the lamps and brought in apples. I was ready to comfort him, but I saw at once that he had no more need of my solace than if he had just inherited a million dollars. He came in shining, his eyes like stars, his face white with that transparency he seems to have when he has been long in prayer. He said, " A burden has been lifted from us all! The church expense was too heavy. Constant need for money cripples our spiritual life. I am glad that difficulty is settled so."

He seemed not to see me. He was looking into other worlds, as oblivious of himself and his own finances as ever Christ was, and I — looking at him and remembering Thomas MacLaren's face — I failed him. I pulled him down from his exaltation by saying — " I am glad you feel relief, Angus. As I see it, Francie pays the church deficit. There can be no college for her on this salary."

He wilted, recoiled as if I had struck him, and I seemed to see his spirit descend from the heights to the enclosure of our four walls. He looked about and said, " Francie — not — go — to — college." I pitied him then. He loves us all, but he loves the church best and first, always.

In writing this I want your sympathy for him who deserves your adoration and needs the warmth of your understanding love. Give it to him while he lives, and in spite of your exasperation on Francie's account, try to appreciate him anyway.

There came back from Jimmie, by special delivery, a letter rapidly written, judging by the trailing scrawl, that dealt vigorously with affairs in the church after a paragraph of preamble —

John has gone awooing. You may as well know it. He is in love and I am left a little too often to suit my taste, to ruminate upon life and matrimony as they touch my brother. As to Frances, I will write her, inviting her to come, and send a check. Maybe it would be as well to let her think we boys thought of it without a nudge from you. We should have done that, but we're careless. Only don't tell her. She's the only girl who really appreciates me.

As to the church affair, I am red hot. You want us to appreciate father. You say he is rare. We do, and he is, but we're the only people who do appreciate him. He is as wasted on that bunch of earthworms he serves as a pearl is wasted in a swine's trough. I know, mother, you and dad have always refused to let us blow off steam about the church. You're right and I do admit that the church is the best institution the world has, and as such we must stand by it and each do our best to hold its standards high. I know the church can never be better than the people that run it, and that the thing to do is not criticize, but pitch in and make it better. You see I have recited my little piece so that you won't think I have failed to get the spirit of your life's teaching, but on this occasion of father's reduced salary I shall permit myself a few remarks, and I beg of you to read them for your soul's good. You know, mother, you can't say damn, but you can have a good, comfortable time letting me write it for you. Well, damn, then. That's the way I feel about Thomas MacLaren. He's as small a potato as the Creator ever condescended to make, and as long as pigmies of his caliber run the church the big minds can't and won't mess up in it all. There are exceptions, like Henry Grieve, but the MacLarens so outweigh them that the whole business is an unbalanced hodgepodge. Young Walter MacLaren will follow in his father's footsteps. Fussing up the works in the church is just about his speed, and he'll throw a monkey wrench in some time that will break a crank-shaft. He'll dominate the others, and you want to keep your eye on him and Jack Small. That's the pair that will bring father's gray head in sorrow to the grave.

Ideals are great, mother — greatest thing there is. Without them the world would long ago have drowned in a wallow of its own rottenness, but ideals that animate a man to high thinking and clean living mustn't expect to reach too far or they'll overreach themselves. When father not only lets his ideals as a follower of Jesus Christ animate his life, but tries to apply it to a Thos. MacLaren, he's simply offering himself for crucifixion. I don't like to hurt you, dear, but I am going shy on the church just now. John and I walk Sunday mornings way out along the Hudson, do some good reading when we get home and call it a day. What do you think of that? Haven't we done enough church in our young lives to last a few years? I think we have. This would hurt father to the soul, so don't tell him, but you — it won't hurt you. You knew it would be just this way with us. A light attack of religious indigestion. We'll get over it and be better for the rest we're taking.

As to Francie. I know why you are worried about her. It is the church versus the world and little Francie squeezed between the two. I know what she's up against. Cards, dancing, matinées, the only diversions of the girls she likes, and father's finality about such things. Of course, I suppose you knew John and I sneaked to things when we could get the money. We saw plenty of shows from the gallery and, rather often, when you thought we were at the Y gym we were dancing, innocently enough, but dancing just the same and enjoying it without much pricking of conscience. Francie can't do that sort of thing the way we boys could. For goodness' sake, don't tell us we are to keep her from dancing here in New York. She needs to forget her father's profession for a while and be free, as other girls are free. We don't know young chaps, not many, but we know men who will enjoy her and give her a good time. Francie is old for her years. We can make her happy.

You don't mention the war, mother. I wonder if you have any idea what a terrific thing it is —

II

Since Jimmie thought he knew the cause of the worry over Frances, Mary did not further enlighten him. She meant, for a few days after receiving his letter, to tell him and John the whole story, but later she felt that the less they knew the easier it would be for them to do for Frances the very things her hungry youth desired.

They understood perfectly the case in general, Frances caught in the jam between two worlds; further details were, after all, Francie's own secret. It was not fair that they should know from Mary. If Frances chose to tell them it would be because the old bond of sympathy had endured through separation and growth, and was worthy of confidences.

At their first glimpse of her the boys were a little subdued by her very evident maturity. Since they had last seen her the great potter had had her on his wheel for shaping and tinting. The little jug-like proportions of her childhood, chubby and round, had been drawn upward, elongated, molded into the curved, vascular slenderness and swelling fullness of young womanhood. As their mother had said, she was less pink. Less infantile in every way they found her. Her beautiful youth was enhanced by the thoughtfulness of her demeanor. Her eyes, once so wide and guileless, had contracted as a result of the thinking she had begun to do for herself; they were bright and steady, but their baby blue had deepened until they seemed the very color of her densely dark hair, softly dull in tone yet shining with vitality and contrasting with the whiteness of her skin as moonlight contrasts with shadow.

On the first evening of her visit she sat in the lamplit living room of their suite, at ease in a deep wicker chair that was set against an open window where a light June breeze stirred pleasantly. She was dressed entirely in white, her background the white of swaying curtains, and in the picture that she made the only line of color was the warmth of her lips.

It seemed to her brothers, watching her as she talked of home, their parents and the church, that she was a bit aloof from them with something in her face that had been caught and held from Angus' shining moments.

That the "something in her face" which held her aloof from them had not been there two months before they could not know. She told them nothing, on·that first evening, of her own experiences, except that she described the prolonged visit of one Antony Remington, the Egyptologist, friend of their father's, who had come to Detroit to give a course of lectures. He had stayed at their house as a guest, she said.

The boys gathered that Francie's young-old ways, and her intelligent comprehension of his profession, had captivated him. He had enjoyed talking with her of his work. As Francie told it, her brothers lounged, smiling, content to listen to the treble cadences of her voice and laugh. They smoked and drowsed lightly, their eyes at rest upon her whiteness.

"He couldn't understand at first that I was really interested in his Egyptology." She smiled. "He thought because I was not quite eighteen that I must be vacuous, and his face was radiant when I caught his ideas and became excited over the excavations and the way they worked out a key to the writing on the tombs. It's much more fascinating than Latin. I loved it. He and I are great friends and I have a standing offer, when I've finished school, to be his secretary. He has outlined a course of reading for me in Egyptology and he says I'll be well prepared if I add shorthand and typewriting to

my course. Would you think it a good idea for me to
be secretary to an Egyptologist and go over there?"

"Sounds as right as possible! Must have pleased
father."

"It didn't please him half as much as Doctor Remington's amazement annoyed him. He said, 'Do you
think we specialize in cocoons, Antony, here at our house?
We discourage the frivolities in our children!' Doctor
Remington thought that quite a pity, too. He told father
he thought his high devotions were being misused if they
denied me my butterfly days." Frances dropped her eyes
and, lifting the handkerchief in her lap, ran its hems
slowly through her fingers. "He said every girl ought,
perfectly legitimately, to be utterly frivolous at some time
in her teens."

"How did father take that?"

"Flamingly. You know how. He used the words
vapid and inane rather recklessly. It made me feel so
hopeless. I can't tell you how hopeless."

She gave her attention to the handkerchief. John and
Jimmie exchanged a quick glance.

"Did Remington make love to you, Francie?" John
asked.

"Oh, not at all. He's really wonderful. Not the
least like that — soppy, you know, and looking things.
He's eager about his work and so alive. He's an interesting contrast to his subject. Egypt seems to me to
be one vast tomb and he a living searchlight in the midst
of it all. I have decided, definitely, to be his secretary.
His wife travels with him, you know," she added.
"Father is willing."

She had "decided definitely." She moved, turning
her face from her brothers to the window and, looping
back the curtain, sat gazing up at the stars in a sky made
pale by the city's lights. Her thought carried back to a

brief two months before, on a night when the sky had been black like a canopy of deep pile velvet, star-spangled and lightly brushed by a spring wind. The memory of it was as close as the beating of her heart. She had been driven recklessly in an open car. She felt the moist breeze from the river on her face as she rode, felt the backward straining of her uncovered hair, smelt the sweetness of the April fields — youth and speed and spring in her heart, tears and the shine of eyes above her own.

Love had come to Frances on that night.

III

She relived it all, in that time of silence, as she sat there with the boys. It had happened during the spring vacation, when Francie's college friends were at home for a holiday. There had been a few hiking parties which she had been permitted to join, and a few informal gatherings when they had danced to victrola music, but Frances was barred from the formal dances — three very especially inviting ones.

This wall, which Frances called " the-thou-shalt-not," was working a change in her because, as she rapidly grew eligible for social life, she more and more felt shut away from others of her kind. It was not that she wanted to be frivolous, she explained to Angus patiently, " but I do want to do what the others do."

" Do, do, do," Angus echoed fondly. " I think it is delightful to have you different."

" But I don't want to be different, daddy dearest. I want to be like other people. It makes me queer."

" More queer girls like you, Francie, would result in a better world. I can't give my consent to anything that would make you common."

This conversation came before the spring holiday, just after Doctor Remington's visit and weeks of Egyptology.

Frances closed her lips. A flame of temper burned her. She remembered Doctor Remington's words, "Every girl ought perfectly legitimately to be utterly frivolous at some time in her teens."

She had gone to her room and closed the door and she stood, one hand still on the knob, thinking new and rebellious thoughts.

On an impulse she turned and went back to Angus.

"Father," she said, a challenge in her voice, "you admire Doctor Remington, don't you? You think him unusual and well-bred and clean-minded."

"Certainly I do."

"He would let me dance. He would want me to be foolish sometimes if I were his daughter. He thinks it is legitimate."

"Just remember, Frances, that he has no daughter. He has never seen a dear young thing he loves asking to be allowed to go into the tents of mammon. You might as well ask me to let you go about the world half naked because the Zulus do, as ask me to let you press your body against some young chap's and go moving about to music with him. I can't endure it."

"I don't press — It isn't that. You ought not to say such things."

"You don't see it that way. No! But the young men do. Don't talk of it. Don't. That question was settled before you were born. Birds don't languish because they can't be lizards crawling in slime. My daughter mustn't find sorrow in the fact that she can't play in the ooze of iniquity."

It had such a horrid sound, coming thus, from Angus. Frances turned away again but was called back.

"Francie —" Angus rose and went toward her as she moved slowly nearer, her rebellious face lifted to him — "I love you more than you can possibly imagine. Not until you have a little flower daughter of your own can you know. I wouldn't hurt you for the world. It is only that I know, and you must trust me." He put a hand under her chin and lifted it gently. He kissed her forehead but she made no response.

To herself she said again and again, "The worst of it is he thinks he knows and he doesn't. It's I who know. Dancing is all right. I know, I know, for I have done it, and he hasn't. Doctor Remington knows it's all right. He has danced. He's been to balls and balls. — He loves me like a daughter. He would let me."

Mary knew what had happened. She said to herself, "It has come. Francie's rebellion. They are alike. She's not the sort that accepts dictation."

That night she went to Frances' room when she was ready for bed. She brought with her two tall glasses of iced chocolate.

Frances sat up cross-legged and stared. She thought, "I know what's coming. Mother's suspicious of me. Well, what if she is! I can't help it."

Mary said, trying to look as if iced chocolate were the one thing above all else her soul craved, "What does this remind you of?" and joined Frances in her quick ripple of laughter as she remembered.

"The time I wanted you to be like the Little Colonel's mother and sip iced chocolate at night and exchange confidences. I called it being an idle mother and the boys teased me terribly for saying idle for ideal. How old was I then?"

"About ten," said Mary, "and you thought anything I decreed was absolutely right."

Frances ruffled her white forehead becomingly. "I do

now," she said sweetly, raising her glass to her lips. Her eyes were half closed in deliberate anticipation of the syrupy drink. After the first long sip she continued, " When you advise me on the things you *know*, I take it. But you and daddy don't know about dancing as it is done now. Of course you have come to talk over the things he and I said to-day. He thinks the subject is closed, but it isn't."

" That's what I thought. There is something I must say to you because I do understand your desire to do the usual things. It's a phase, a part of your growth. You don't yet appreciate the distinctiveness of being different. We call it the herd age."

" And I suppose ' it too will pass away.' "

Mary heard the scorn in Francie's voice. She made an effort to smile and looked up above the little dresser where the quotation hung framed in dull gold. For a moment she re-lived the time when they had planned a room for Frances on the occasion of her graduation from a crib, and Mary had especially wanted that quotation where she would be reminded of the ephemeral phases of childhood. For fourteen years it had hung above the little white dresser in the blue and white bower that had been prepared for innocence. There were pictures selected from an old art album by Angus, copies in color of famous masterpieces—Hoffman's Boy Christ, the Stewart Baby, the Della Robbia Bambino and Mary's quotation — black lettering on maize: This Too Will Pass Away.

Recently Frances had been adding photographs and banners, souvenirs and copies of modern art to the more chaste collection, but this was the first time Mary had known the quotation above the dresser was a thing despised. She felt a dart of regret, but remembered the quotation in time to think, " Her superiority will pass away too. Some time she will want to hang this same one in her own nursery."

"When I spoke of the herd age I meant to go on right then and say that you will soon begin to appreciate indi-viduality. To be different, to have a distinct personality that sets you in relief against the mob, is very desirable. As your father has said of you, ' When I see Frances with other young things her quality is enchantingly dis-tinctive. We think you an orchid — among gera-niums.' "

"Lovely, if you like orchids. A good, healthy red geranium is happier than any old lonely orchid. I feel like a pumpkin among roses when I'm out with people, I'm so different."

Mary shook her head, smiling. A pumpkin! That vivid, beautiful vessel of youth opposite her in the lamp's warm glow, eyes like starlit pools, velvet skin and rounded modeling of shoulders and breasts glimpsed through sheer muslin. Her mind wandered away from the old war of the church and the world to the miracle of life. It was almost a daily marveling that the love of Angus for her, and her for Angus had flowered — in Frances. The flesh of two made one. Living, sentient! Love incarnate. Oh — nothing in all the realm of crea-tion was so supremely beautiful.

"The trouble is," Frances went straight to the point, "Father thinks he knows, but he doesn't. He thinks it's rather nasty — dancing. But he doesn't know."

"He knows as much as any one person can know. We none of us know more than our own experience plus what we are told by others. You see, your father at your age was very worldly."

"Ooo, he was?" Frances sat up straighter and low-ered her glass of chocolate. "Really? Tell me."

"Oh, nothing to tell," said Mary, wishing she hadn't

gone into the past. "He was not converted until he was nearly eighteen."

"Then he ought to know that a Stevenson can be frivolous for a few years and still be saved."

This was pert. Mary knew no answer save the obvious one. She sipped her chocolate a moment before she said:

"I didn't come here to combat you, Frances. I know how you feel. I see how unreasonable father seems to you. But after all, his child can hardly expect to be as free as other girls. I thought I could make renunciation easier for you maybe. You see, I have had to give up things too, things I would have enjoyed so much; some of the good plays and operas, because a really successful minister must stand very strong if he would hold his people true to an ideal. I might know that Peter Pan and the Maude Adams company are very different from the Milk White Flag, for instance, but if I went to see Peter Pan the people who look to us for leadership would see only what they consider our weakness. We have dedicated our lives to helping them in their limitations of judgment. I have had to work out my own vision of life. I try to see it all as an adventure, a thrilling adventure in goodness. I try to play up to my belief that this life is but a test of us, an overture to an eternity of spiritual adventure. I should be ashamed to fail when I was tested and, besides, it's as easy to thrill to good as to a good time, so called. It's all in the way you look at it. Somehow I doubt, if you were given your chance, if you would enjoy the things you crave. It might be like the time you longed for charlotte russe and helped yourself to five."

"I can't endure them now, but I had the satisfaction of getting enough for once. Perhaps father did too, back in those old days before he was eighteen — got chuck full of fun, heaps and heaps of jolly fun." With an air of reckless finality she tipped up her glass and let the last, heavy drops of syrup roll slowly down into the red of her waiting mouth. She set the glass on her bedside table.

"You're welcome to your adventures in goodness, Molly dearest. I'll try that — some time — but not this spring."

She pursed her lips and blinked solemnly at Mary through darting lights of mischief. " In the meantime I want you to know that I think you and father have done your — full — duty — by me. I know the ten commandments by heart, and the twenty-third psalm, and the Lord's prayer, and the thirteenth chapter of First Corinthians, and I can lead a prayer meeting, and play all the hymn book. I know all about our ideals and I anticipate every word of father's prayer in the morning and — "

Mary had risen. She bent now above her sparkling daughter. " Stop, you bad child! Francie — " They looked long in each other's eyes, Mary troubled and searching, Frances restraining the mirth that, in spite of her efforts, brimmed over into laughter. She kissed Mary impulsively and hugged her with a violence that relaxed only to tighten childishly. Clinging, she made a little whimpering sound. " Don't leave me," she whispered pleadingly and, a moment later, suddenly released her mother, crying, " Aren't we too silly? "

Mary put her hand on Francie's forehead, thinking rapidly, " She's going to disobey, she's giving warning, she's already in revolt. Combating her will only make things worse. If our teaching hasn't done its work by this time we have failed." She bent above her daughter and looked straight into her eyes. " Frances, when you are of age, twenty-one, you may choose for yourself.

You will belong to yourself then and we will either have failed or succeeded in molding you to a high ideal. Until then you are our child. Don't do anything you will regret. Remember that. Don't do anything you will regret."

" I'm not a child in my feeling. At twenty-one I will be so old and serious that my dancing zest will be dead. You know yourself you always say if we don't develop our gifts when they make themselves felt, we deny them life. Well? Well? You see? "

When the door closed and Frances was alone in the dark, she lay very still, thinking. Rebellion and love, hunger for life and loyalty to her parents stormed her heart. " Maybe I'll hate it. Maybe I have no capacity for enjoying such things. Maybe it will be like the charlotte russe, but — nevertheless — I will test it out and know. Father never will give his consent. I will have to take matters in my own hands."

She turned, bouncing about to settle herself for the night, but sat up and saw before her, like a light in the darkness, Mary's face, and heard her voice — " I try to see it all as a thrilling adventure in goodness. I try to play up to my belief that this life is but a test of us, an overture to an eternity of spiritual adventure. It's as easy to thrill to good as to a good time, so called." Oh, botheration.

Francie turned abruptly from the vision and the voice. She had made up her mind. She would not be headed off, but she was not at all surprised when she found that she was crying.

CHAPTER III

I

WHEN Frances waked the next morning her resolution to go to the Boat Club dance, whether or not, and a fig for the consequences, held firm. It was to be such a wonderful dance and Tubby — young Theodore Buschnell — had asked her to " see if her governor wouldn't grant her a reprieve just this once."

She had known when Tubby put it that way that he had no sympathy at all with her father's discriminations against dancing. " He'll think father is just an old Has Been if I tell him he refuses. He won't admire father at all. I sha'n't tell, but I'll go."

Other than the ever pressing agony of clothes the only complication that bothered Frances in making her plans was that the dance came on prayer-meeting night. She would have to make a good excuse to be let off from accompanying her mother and, once excused, she would have to dress and be ready rather early for Tubby.

She decided against taking Tubby into her confidence. One must closet one's family skeleton. But later, warmed by his delight at her acceptance, she felt him to be worthy of her trust and told him all about her difficulty, warning him not to let the secret out. She put it in a note which she wrote on lavender paper and sealed with a large blob of silver wax into which she pressed the single initial S.

My dear Tubby:

Maybe it would be best for you to know that in going to the dance with you I have had to act upon my own authority. Father steadfastly refuses to say *yes*. I feel that the time has come for me to decide for myself. I cannot too long remain in the nest or my wings will not be strong enough to fly — later. Anyway, of course I can't tell either my mother or my father. They were born free to do as they pleased, and they had a lovely time before they became converted. I, on the other hand, was born to conversion and have never, therefore, experienced it. That creates a situation. I intend from now on to have as much good time as I can, but please don't tell or let the cat out of the bag when you are at our house.

Wednesday is prayer-meeting night, so please wait till after it begins before you call for me. If by any chance mother does not go, I would be in an awful situation and might have to get out a window. My bedroom window opens on the roof of the porch, but, then, I forgot — there is always the back door.

I will have to manage the best way I can, but so you'll surely know, you had better telephone at a quarter to eight. If mother answers you will know she isn't going to prayer-meeting and that I am, to say the least, *embarrassed.* If mother says anything about my not coming to the telephone because I am not well, or very tired, and have gone to bed, you can know that you'll have to collect me at the back fence or somewhere like that. I am sorry my parents are so different from other people, but their ideals are very, very high and that is a beautiful thing, of course, in this world with the war and everything as awful as it is. I have a good many ideals, too, but they don't affect dancing.

Hoping all goes well and that it stays sub rosa,

I am, your friend,

FRANCES.

II

Tubby called around the next evening to suggest that Frances plan to spend Wednesday night with one of the girls and thus be free to dress and go out as she pleased. Frances thought about it. The evening was warm and they sat on the top step of the Stevenson porch to discuss ways and means.

Soberly, weighing her words and with an air of wisdom, Frances said, " It doesn't seem fair to the other girls' mothers. If anybody found out, they would think me horrid to use their houses as a place of — of, well, disobedience; and besides, Tubby, I don't know any of the girls who are going so awfully well. All that crowd are perfect highflyers and I'm not. They often ask me to go with them but I never can, and you know you stay on rather formal terms when things are that way."

Tubby knew. Tubby knew a very great deal. He was one of the men — age nineteen — the girls all liked, especially younger girls, for he had gone to college at sixteen and now at nineteen was a very knowing Junior at the University of Michigan. His friendship was so valuable to one still lingering in her seventeenth year that to seek his advice was the part of wisdom.

" Knowing all that, don't you think I ought not to spend the night any other place? What do you think, Tubby? "

" I wish," said Tubby, beating his palm with his golf cap, " that I had a sister you could spend the night with. We wouldn't tell mother at all, and what she didn't know she wouldn't be to blame for. It's a rotten shame. I tell you what, Francie, your folks force you to do things on your own hook. If you get caught you don't need to be ashamed at all, not a bit."

" Oh, no. Of course I won't." Frances looked him squarely in the eyes. " I wouldn't do anything I would be ashamed of. I am proud to have the courage of my convictions. They force me to sneak out. If I said, ' Father, mother, I have decided to do as I please. I think dancing is all right and I cannot do as you wish about it,' they would lock me up, maybe. It isn't a question of shame, Tubby. It is just a matter of — of *convictions.*"

Tubby understood that perfectly. He was entirely in sympathy. He liked Frances better than any girl he knew. She had a brain in her head. She could talk about real things, the college sports and the different professions a fellow might want to go into. She knew about all kinds of law, corporation, trial, criminal, admiralty. She had heard her brothers discuss it, and she told Tubby, wisely, that studying law couldn't be a mistake because it was a foundation for any profession or business he might later have a chance at and like better. She was so well informed you liked to listen to her. You liked to look at her, too, and you thought it a rotten shame her folks made things so tough for her.

Before he left her Tubby suggested a code of signals. As he came along Second Avenue Wednesday night he would look at the window that let on to the porch roof. If it were open halfway it meant that Frances was in the room, that the coast was clear and she was listening for his whistle to tell her he approached. If the window were up just a few inches he would know there was a blockade and he would have to wait around at the end of the yard, in the shadow of the fence, till Francie joined him.

" I am sorry to make you do such a back alley thing, but I don't believe it will happen that way. Mother surely will go to prayer meeting and I can then walk

down and out the front door just as if I had her blessing
and father's too."

III

How to get out wasn't half the worry just then that
clothes were. Frances just had no clothes fit for a
dance. She had a beautiful new spring dress — brown
crêpe de chine. She had worn it to dinner at Grieve's
and she had felt very correct in it with amber beads, real
amber that her mother had worn years before. Mrs.
Grieve had spoken of her looks and called her dress a
"lovely little gown." But lovely though it might be, she
couldn't wear it to a dance — and the Boat Club of all
places, where one wanted to look especially correct.

There were, of course, her last summer dresses. There
had been a white crêpe that Frances had thought very
chic, clingy and narrow, with short sleeves. She had
white pumps too, and yet, how she did wish — She
dawdled over her breakfast, evoking visions of billowy
tulle, sequins, net over lace, floating sash ends and French-
heeled slippers. She could see herself whirling, stepping, turning, backing through the new dances with
Tubby and — perhaps, but no, probably not — Dick
Stanhope. Dick Stanhope was older than Tubby's set,
twenty-three about, in Harvard Law School and oh,
wonderful, with that air — that calm, aloof superiority
that distinguished him. His smile, slow in coming, the
downturned corners of his lips, the copper lights in his
skin. Frances wriggled her toes in her morning slippers.

IV

She had to hurry with her breakfast at the last. Her
father was waiting morning prayers for her. He
seemed to be very impatient of delay. "Frances, what

are you dreaming about in there? You've been long
enough to have eaten more than two small girls could
need. Hurry, dear!"

Over her shoulder Frances saw her father sitting tense
and frowning, an open Bible in his hand, his keen blue
eyes on her. Her mother was bending above a Boston
fern, picking off dead leaves. Even Maggie was ready,
Maggie who usually shuffled in at the last minute and
slid into a dining chair over the threshold from the living
room.

Frances gulped down the last of her doughnut, drank
half a glass of water hastily and wished she hadn't eaten
anything at all. Her stomach felt suddenly unhappy.
That was the fault of her early training, she thought, as
she sat on the piano stool while her father read one of the
psalms. She had always been made to eat what was on
her plate, eat it all up and not fuss, and now when food
wasn't so important as it once was, she mechanically
waded through things she didn't want at all. She had not
wanted the doughnut, but she had eaten it, obedient to
habit, while she thought about party dresses and Dick.
She had seen Dick Stanhope just a minute on the street
downtown recently. He had crossed over to her with
that smile — and held out his hand. He had held her
hand ever so nicely for a long minute as he stood in the
April wind, bareheaded, talking to her. She had noticed
the crisp curliness of his hair and the black that was so
dense, even the spring sun had not been reflected in its
lights. He had been nice — oh — She had left him
feeling a glow of something and wondering why she
hadn't invited him to call. But no. She was glad now
she hadn't asked him. A Stevenson couldn't ask a Stanhope. They could be friends when they met that way.
No more. Besides, he couldn't like her so very well, he a
second year student in law school and *twenty-three!* He

cared for racier girls, like Tot Bradley and Kathryn Jaster, Charlotte's set. No, it was better not to have invited him than to have invited him and had him — Charlotte's brother — make excuses. If he wanted to come he would anyway. Their only bond was that memory of long ago when he had brought her home after the fight and had kissed her. That had colored all their brief meetings ever after with kindliness. He remembered her as a dependent, small girl whom his sharp little sister had hurt. She remembered him as a hero to the rescue, a knight — Oh —

Angus was saying, "And so endeth the reading of the twenty-second psalm." He looked at Frances. "Frances, tell me in your own words what I have read."

Frances gasped but caught her lip between her teeth, lifting reflective eyes to the ceiling. Finding no reminder there, she dropped them to Sir Walter Scott who lay at her feet, gently thumping the floor with his tail.

"Well," she said slowly, "it was very lovely and musical, all about praise to the Lord and glory to His name. The Lord is my comforter, my refuge and strength. David wrote them. He was a very wonderful king and the father of Solomon."

Frances rubbed Sir Walter with her foot. From the corner of her eye she saw her mother raise a handkerchief to her lips. Mary was laughing at her.

Angus said, after a silence that was painful to Frances, "I thought you were not listening. I think for a few mornings we'll have you do the reading and see if you get the meaning better that way. Let us pray."

As they knelt Angus crossed over to Frances and dropped on one knee beside her, bowing above her, his arm about her shoulders, his hand softly patting her as he prayed, prayed earnestly for many things, grace and purity, forgiveness and mercy; asked that "the words of our mouths and the meditations of our hearts be acceptable in thy sight, O Lord, our strength and our redeemer"; prayed for " All of us here, strength to resist the temptations of the day, courage for difficult tasks, bravery in the face of discouragement." He gave thanks for the unnumbered mercies of the night and, gently, with a deepening note of tenderness — " Oh, God, bless our dear Frances. Help her to live nobly and beautifully in thy service. Make her worthy to be called — thy child." He did it exquisitely. The impatience was gone from his voice. It was deep, tender, thrilling with love and anxiety for his beloved little daughter.

Oh, dear! Frances would *not* sniff. She felt a tear inside her nose, tickling at her nostril. If Angus had to be stern about worldly pleasures why couldn't he be stern all the time and not make her heart all icy, only to melt it again? Well. She would have to kiss him after prayers and say she would be more attentive hereafter. He would hug her tight and say, " Little wanton." A dreadful word, but said so affectionately it meant nothing.

V

All this made it very hard to go about the business of secretly preparing raiment for the dance. She almost weakened, hated everything in the world, loved her father with a sudden warmth of passion and reacted as quickly with a rush of resentment.

She had to watch her chance to slip up to the attic unobserved, but it came before nine o'clock and she tip-toed to the storeroom, taking long steps over the bare floor. There were three packing trunks and she searched all the way to the lower part of the third before she came to the white crêpe. Bending over the trunks the unhappiness returned to her stomach, her hands trembled and a terrible feeling of guilt shook her with chill. But she would not admit a sense of guilt, not for a minute. She would not even go so far as to deny it.

"It's cold up here," she thought. "I'm all goose-fleshy. I wish I hadn't eaten that doughnut. It makes me feel so funny and horrid."

The white crêpe was folded flat and buried under pounds of summer things. She shook it till it snapped, so vigorously did she attack its crushed and wrinkled limpness. It looked soiled. She examined it, frowning, and decided that it would have to be washed. Trained in practicality, Frances examined the seams. They were, as she supposed, generous, and a wide hem had allowed for shrinkage and growth. Closing the trunk very gently she danced on her toes to the stairs and ran down. At the foot she listened and heard Mary's voice at the telephone. She darted to her room and tossed the dress beneath the bed to wait till such time as the coast would be clear for laundering and altering it to the new mode.

Her opportunity came that afternoon. Maggie in the kitchen, muttering as she ironed, and Frances upstairs in her room, were alone in the house. Frances locked her door and tried on the dress.

It looked a hopeless mess. For a moment, standing before the mirror, Frances' heart sank. She had grown like a child since last summer. Of all things! At her age! The dress was short-waisted and tight across the bust, all twisted and funny. She used her hand mirror, turning slowly, studying herself from all angles. At last she stood gazing dejectedly at the strained folds of the crêpe where they crossed her small breast. Her face was a study in defiance and shame. "Why do I have to grow straight out in the front like that, poking out so conspicuously? I think it's horrid. Those points! They embarrass me." She tried to turn the neck in and by lowering the opening ease the strain, but that brought no relief. She pulled and shook herself down into shape, stood on a chair to see the bottom of the skirt, and finally, her buoyant spirits rising, decided to let out all the seams she could, wash it and press it and see if it would look better. But no matter what, even if it came out lovely and smooth and stretched, she would have to have a new sash. A sash could be so put on as to lengthen the waist for one thing, and it would give color and style and the necessary finish. But in the matter of the sash she would have to do a sneaky thing. She would have to charge it to her mother and, when the bill came in, face the awful consequences. There was no use anticipating trouble, however. There was always the chance for a miracle — that the saleswoman would forget to charge it, or her mother would not notice the item or — something. Between the day of buying and the first of May there might be ever so many chances for Francie to earn the price of it and pay for it herself.

Washing the dress was easy after the tiresome hour of ripping the underarm seams and sewing them up close to the edge. Fortunately it was made in the kimono style and when she discovered an extra inch in the waist length she was as happy as if she had come upon a Cinderella outfit.

As she sewed she listened. The throbbing of guilt in her heart was almost a pain. Every creak set her pulse to racing. It was not that her convictions lacked strength. She was as strong as Angus, but she hated the locked door and the secret consciousness of her disobedience. She made a poem that began:

A prisoner of righteousness I am,
Forced 'gainst my will into a life of sham,
Strong my convictions as my keeper's are,
Strongly I will arise and break my prison bar . . .

She sang it softly, improvising a moving, minor air that sent the quick tears of self-pity to her eyes, so perfectly did it express martyrdom, anguish, imperishable hope, unbroken will. " It's very like Henley's 'Out of the night that covers me ' . . . Invictus ! " She lifted her arm and held the scissors high aloft as if they were a torch to light a prison fastness.

" I will *not* be conquered! I will arise and stand strong for my convictions, for the things I — have — be — lieve — ed ! "

VI

Late that afternoon, when the dress was carefully ironed and hanging in the basement to dry, things looked happier for Frances. She evolved the very excellent idea of reading late that night in bed with her door locked. This dissipation would cause her to sleep late in the morning, she could plead feeling " perfectly awful " with truth, and act languid all day so that her request to be excused from prayer meeting would not be a surprise to her parents. Also, she would be released from having to read at prayers. She felt that her father, knowing her spirit of rebellion, was trying to touch her conscience. He would choose a very tender psalm and pray a very touching prayer, disturbing treatment for a young rebel.

She was enjoying her happy inspiration when Tubby telephoned to ask " how's every little thing ? " and she had trilled that all was well and for him not to forget their code of signals. They talked of nothing long and feelingly before Tubby said, " Oh, say. I saw Dick Stanhope to-day. He's a Sigma Tau and he's going to be there to-morrow night. He said to have you save some dances for him. He said ' Tell Frances to keep half a dozen for me.' I didn't know you knew him so well."

" Oh-o-o, I don't, not well, but a long time. I hate
his sister. She's snobby, but he isn't. He tries to make
up for Charlotte."

Frances went dancing from the telephone. This would
make the matter of getting out easier. She'd have more
courage now, since there was so much to make it worth
the dreadful fuss and worry.

Half a dozen dances with Dick, half a dozen! She
sobered. That would mean that she'd save four but tell
him to take three, and then, later, she'd arrange the fourth
if he seemed really to want it. She breathed deeply and
clasped her hands tightly together. Oh, joy, oh, joy, oh,
joy! To-morrow night!

VII

Wednesday night brought its complications. The day
had gone slowly, dragging, but with no particular discouragements. She had slept late but not late enough.
Her father had heard her open her door just as they
were beginning prayers and he had called her to come
down in her bathrobe. They would wait.

Making her voice very sleepy and childish she had
replied, " Oh, no, daddy, I can't this morning. I feel so
awful — " and she had gone back into her room and
crept into bed. They let her alone. She heard her
mother say, outside her door, " This is her vacation. I
want her to get well rested for the last weeks of the
school year."

Darling mother! Always understanding that nice way.
Frances buried her face between two pillows.

Later, when she rose, Mary thought she looked very
limp and wan. She ate no breakfast but said she must
drag herself downtown to the library and get some books
of history — school reading that must be done. She

dressed languidly and strolled forth into the bright noontime, watched by Mary, who thought, "She's not at all herself this morning. I wonder what's up."

Downtown she went at once to a ribbon counter and, walking slowly along the case, reviewed the colors set out in pyramids, all the shades in satin and taffeta and moiré. There was American beauty, so lovely with white; blues, pinks; yellows that would match her beads; green — She paused before the greens. They looked springlike and cool, jade and emerald and a soft light green like lettuce in crisp taffeta and very wide. It was a dollar a yard and the clerk thought she would want four yards. Needing all the courage of her much bolstered convictions, Frances decided for the lettuce-green taffeta at a dollar a yard. She hesitated — surely four yards would be too much. The clerk was very kind. They measured. Yes, to go around the waist and be drawn down, to make two loops and two long ends would take four yards.

"Well," said Frances hesitatingly and swallowing several lumps, "I'll take it then. Four yards."

While the clerk measured again she looked in the show case. There was a small ribbon bag trimmed with flowers. "It's to carry to a party for your vanity case and handkerchief," the clerk explained. "We haven't a green one, but you could make one yourself in a few minutes. It takes half a yard and some narrow ribbon."

Frances took an extra half yard and the narrow ribbon but refused the flowers. "There are some in our attic, I'm sure," she explained simply.

She went to the library for the books, but made quick work of it and hurried home to make the bag. Again fortune smiled for her mother was out. She rummaged for the flowers and found forget-me-nots. They looked very French, she thought, on the green with small, dark foliage. She saturated a handkerchief with cologne and tucked it into the bag, which she put with her white shoes and stockings and all the clean things she would wear that were laid ready in her drawer.

At dinner she was pale and silent. It was not feigned; she suffered to think of the ribbon, almost five dollars' worth, charged to her mother "by daughter Frances." She hated the secret, the guilt, the lie of it all. Oh, why need her parents be so queer, so different?

Leaving the table before the dessert she said, swaying, one hand on her chair, " I want to go to bed, daddy. If I don't feel better by half-past seven I think I'll have to be excused from prayer meeting." Angus gave her the long look she expected with its suggestion of hurt, its patient " Certainly," as if he were the sufferer, and Mary said, " Go to bed, dear, and I'll come up and see you later."

VIII

At half-past seven Mary was ready to go to church. She paused in Francie's doorway, looking with expectant eyes toward the crumpled figure on the bed. Francie heard her, waited for her to pass, and when she did not, turned to look at her.

" Oh! " Frances saw at once that Mary was wearing a different hat and waiting for her to notice it.

" Your best new spring hat? "

" What do you think? "

Frances sat erect, suddenly alive and interested. " You aren't going to keep it? It isn't yours? "

Mary only smiled, waiting.

" Why, mother, that's your old last year's hat with that perfectly ancient feather sticking up in front. It isn't any of it new! "

" No." Mary walked into the room and stood before

the mirror. "Isn't it too elegant?" She sighed happily. "All style! I love the effect of that standuppish rooster tail. I knew you would too."

They began to laugh. Frances, watching her mother's reflection in the mirror, rocked with merriment. Mary was not pretty, not even a little chic. She was sweet, wholesome, radiant at times with buoyant personality and often extremely amusing. "Oh, you're going to be funny!" Francie cried. "Tell me where you got that hat. It's a pill of a thing."

"This, Francie dear, is not my best new Easter bonnet. It's to save my best new one. It's our old friend, the lid of last year; and our older friend, the rooster tail of the year before; and our oldest friend, the velvet ribbon of ancient history. I am going to call it my Prayer Meeting Hat."

"Oh! and make prayer meeting more gloomy than ever! The rooster looks so *fagged,* like a fighting cock the day after. The velvet ribbon has the mange. Whatever did that creation cost you?"

Mary used the hand mirror, surveying the hat doubtfully. "You see, the back's rather chic and, as I always sit way forward in prayer meeting, only the back will show and daddy won't mind the front of it."

"It will upset him when he ought to pray. He'll snort in the middle as sure as pop!"

Frances fell back on her pillow and laughed irrepressibly. "Drape a veil over it, mother, and get a Madonna expression, or you'll break up the spiritual benediction of the meeting." Frances sobered and sat up straight and still. The clock in the lower hall had struck the half hour. Her eyes widened and darkened. "Why," she said, "it's half-past seven already. You'll be late."

Mary saw the look. "You're so white, Francie. Do you feel really ill? Maybe I ought not to leave you. I

could be persuaded to stay here if you said you needed
me."

" Oh, no. Why, *no*. I really am not sick. I am lazy.
Mother, to save you worry, I'll tell you a secret." Frances
was panicky. If Mary stayed at home — that would be
a complication that no cleverness could overcome. The
truth right now would save her. " The reason I am so
worn out is that I sat up all night in bed reading. It was
vacation and I thought it didn't matter if I had a book
spree. I just need sleep."

Mary was looking at her, noticing the veil that cur-
tained her eyes. There was secrecy there, self-consciousness and distress. She said nothing, waiting. Her
eyes traveled about the room. There was no evidence of
anything unusual.

" You're sure you were reading."

" Oh, mother ! " Reproach from Francie.

Mary stooped and kissed her. " All right. There, the
telephone is ringing; I must hurry."

Frances knew it was Tubby. As soon as Mary had
disappeared on the staircase she ran softly to the banister.
She heard her mother say, " Frances is here but she isn't
well. Who is it, please? Oh, Tubby — "

Frances flew downstairs. " Mother dear, let me speak
to him, please." She took the receiver and gave her
mother a quick kiss on the cheek. " Good-by," she said.
" I'll only talk a minute."

When she called " Hullo ", Tubby began, " Your
mother is still there. Are you having troubles? If you
are having trouble and can't talk, begin now to tell me
something about a book you're reading. Something like
that."

Frances was grateful for his understanding. She
began by telling him about the novel she had read the
night before.

The conversation sounded innocent enough. Mary
stepped out upon the porch and shut the door. Francie
heard it click.

"Oh, Tubby," she began in a different voice. "Mother
has just gone. I haven't begun to dress but I can start
now. It won't take me more than half an hour, I'm
sure."

Tubby laughed. "Take your time dressing. We can
get over there in half an hour. Well — so long. As I
come up Second, I'll look for the signal. Don't forget.
Gee, Frances, this is awfully tough luck on a girl like
you! Your folks ought to be a little more human."

IX

At a quarter past eight Frances was ready but Tubby
had not arrived. She set the "all well" signal and
climbed upon a chair for the third time to look at herself.
The crêpe dress didn't hang exactly right. It still strained
over the bust, but it was smooth and creamy white and
the green sash turned the trick for style. Frances was
willing to believe the best. She thought she looked parti-
fied and clean even if she wasn't gorgeous. "I'll try to
be very dear and lovely. I'll be as entertaining as possible and the boys won't notice my clothes — so much."

She turned out her light and peeked under the shade.
Automobiles were passing. It was quite dark. The
headlights of the speeding cars lit the street. Frances
thought of Dick Stanhope and his beautiful car, a long
low roadster painted French blue and gray. She had seen
him in it with Charlotte. When he was with Charlotte
she always looked away. Charlotte and she spoke when
their eyes met accidentally, Frances quietly, Charlotte
breezily, the roguish dimples of her childhood still giving
her face an elfin look. Charlotte delighted in mischief-

making, and she enjoyed Francie's white embarrassment. If Charlotte were at the party to-night Francie would — would not be self-conscious, but very cool and well poised.

Oh, Tubby! At last his car was stopping at the curb. She turned from the window but spun around again. From the corner of her eye she had seen — Mary! Mary getting out of the car at the curb and being helped by some woman. They were coming in. She stood paralyzed, watching. They were walking slowly; Mary was ill evidently, for she limped badly. They would come in and Frances would be called. Oh, what should she do? She ran to her door and locked it. Ran back to the window and fixed the signal "blockade" for Tubby; stood breathless, her eyes staring wide into the darkness. She heard Tubby's whistle, peeked out and saw his car slowly turning the corner. He slid along the curb and stopped at the back in the shadow. Frances tiptoed to the door and listened. There was no sound for a moment, then she heard steps on the stairs, some woman's voice saying encouragingly, with sick-room cheerfulness, "There you are, another step. You're doing fine. It doesn't hurt so much now, does it? There."

Mary was hurt, her foot or something. Cold perspiration stood on Francie's forehead. She tried not to breathe and her breath, disobedient as never before, boomed through her nostrils. She heard Maggie shuffling down the hall and Mary's voice, weak and strained, "Maggie, see if Frances is awake. If she is asleep, let her alone. We can manage." Then the woman — who was it? Mrs. Small? "I can stay right here till Doctor Stevenson comes. No need to wake Frances."

With the informality of expediency, Maggie turned the knob of Francie's door, pushed against it and called loudly enough to have wakened Francie, "She's asleep."

Frances relaxed against the door frame and leaned her head upon her arm. "Mother is hurt. Mother needs me. Oh, Oh! What shall I do?"

She heard Tubby's whistle under her back window. Tiptoeing very softly, she crossed the room and gently raised the sash. Tubby was below. She saw his white face and the white of his shirt front.

"Tubby, listen. Can you hear me?" She whispered very softly.

"Yes. I saw your mother come home. What are you going to do?"

"Oh, Tubby, I'll **have to** stay. I can't leave her." Her voice trembled with emotion.

Tubby made a wild gesture. "Oh, sure you can. Don't cave in, Francie, there's a woman with her. Say, haven't you got a ladder?"

"Yes."

"Where is it?"

Francie's white arm was on the sill. She pointed toward the back. "Little door by the back porch. Under the house."

Tubby disappeared and almost immediately Francie heard Sir Walter's alarmed barking. He was shut in the kitchen. Fortunately Tubby knew his kind old heart. He wouldn't be afraid. A moment more and Tubby returned, dragging the ladder up the lawn. He put it against the porch roof. It made a dull thump. Frances knelt on the floor and pressed her hand against her lips. Her heart was beating so violently it jarred her whole body. She loathed herself for a sneak and an ingrate. Why, why had she thought she would enjoy this sort of thing?

She heard Tubby's whistle again, softly impatient. She raised the window and stepped out upon the roof. "Tubby, I feel terrible. I can't go through with it."

Tubby ran up the ladder. Frances stooped low and he stopped, when his face was opposite hers just above the railing. " You mustn't get cold feet and leave me in the lurch like this! Come on now. Your mother and the maid are all right together. If you were at boarding school they'd get along. Your father will be back in an hour. Come on. Don't get nerves."

A man's scorn of nerves. It was the clinching taunt. Frances reached into the room for her coat, dragged it over the sill and silently wrapped herself in its dark folds. She fastened it close about her neck and, giving her hand to Tubby, stepped over the railing. It was easy enough to reach the ground. Tubby seized the ladder. " Run for the car," he whispered and Frances obeyed. She wanted to help Tubby with the ladder. He was having a hard time. Frances felt that she would have to be very nice indeed to make up to him for all the bother, but just now — she couldn't talk.

CHAPTER IV

I

THEY drove down Cass Avenue, angling through mean, little cross streets toward Jefferson Avenue, where the stream of traffic was decreasing as the theater hour closed. Tubby kept his foot on the accelerator and gave his entire attention to the driving. Frances, victim of acute nostalgia, oppressed by her sin, cuddled into her coat and let the wind have its way in her hair.

As they left the bridge and turned toward the lights of the Boat Club Frances began to talk. " Thank you, Tubby, for being so nice to me — and understanding. I never did anything like this before. I feel better now, though."

" You're all right. The first time is always the hardest. When you're in college you'll remember this and ha-ha about it. This is nothing to the stunts you'll pull then. You must forget all about it, and have a dandy time now. Your folks think you're getting your beauty sleep while a white-winged angel aeroplanes around the head of your bed."

" Oh, no. They don't think that," Frances protested, murmuring. " They aren't like that, Tubby. As they see things, they're exactly right. They are very, very courageous. Very strong — "

She stopped short. The defense of her own was forgotten at sight of Dick Stanhope's car. It was parked near the entrance to the club. A near-by arc light threw shadows of lacy branches over the long radiator. Over

Frances they trembled too, and like the web of the sorcerer, drew her into the land of romance.

They passed close by the car and Frances shyly stretched forth a hand and touched a fender. Oh, beautiful night, beautiful light, beautiful world!

Tubby's hand was on her elbow. They ran up the long flight of steps to the club. In the hall they parted with a gay little gesture of au revoir and Frances tripped into the dressing room. All the strain of her stricken conscience was magically wiped off her face. She heard the squeak and scrape of orchestral tunings, saw gaily dressed girls and lounging young men grouped about the dancing floor. Her feet flew, but halfway down the room she stopped and turned, busying her hands with the fastenings of her coat. Charlotte Stanhope sat before a dressing table arranging her hair.

From the cloakroom came voices, and Charlotte made bantering reply. Frances had seen her whole costume in the one quick glance she had given her. She was perfectly dressed in turquoise blue. She sparkled with crystals. Her bare arms and shoulders were softly pink. There were dazzling stones in her hair.

Like the hand of the harpist on the golden strings of his instrument, the hand of emotion swept Frances' nerves. A chill of depression ran down her spine, a hot wave of self-consciousness flamed in her face. She wanted to run away. She wanted to stay and not care. A maid approached her quietly and took her cloak from her shoulders. Frances' back straightened as she faced her enemy, and her head went up. The desire to scratch Charlotte's saucy, mocking face tingled in her finger tips. Instead she smiled with only her lips and said, " Good evening " — very casually.

Charlotte swept Francie's length with a cool eye. " Oh, Francie," she said. " You here? "

Frances did not reply. Charlotte had called her Francie. Francie, her special pet name from her worst enemy! She walked to the dressing table and, holding her hands steady, tried to remedy the havoc the wind had made in her hair. The maid helped her and she welcomed the woman's kindliness. She left the work to her and saw her hairpins all removed and returned, each to a different place, with the result that a soft and very charming effect had been achieved. "How skillful you are; how nice you make me! Thank you so much!"

Frances rose and turned to find Charlotte surveying her from a short distance. The look and smile on Charlotte's lips told her more plainly than words that she had overdone her thanks to the maid. Charlotte would have said a careless word, patronizing but appreciative. She turned her back and strolled toward the hall. Charlotte had followed. They stood, side by side, between the velvet curtains a moment before Tubby rushed forward to Frances and Charlotte, coolly nodding, advanced to meet Dick, who was coming down the hall.

"We have programs to-night, Frances," Tubby was saying excitedly. "I have taken these dances with the crosses. See? That name is Bim Burnes and that's Jack Ranney and this is Kendall Stearns — thought maybe you couldn't read the writing." Frances heard, but the eyes that appeared to be regarding the program were noting Dick's swift advance and the slow, conscious smile that twitched at the corners of his lips. She saw too, in a flashing glance, the superiority of the girls about her — their toilets. They were decolletté, they moved with easy assurance, they were at home in the ballroom, they belonged. Dick would see the difference at once; he must be seeing it now! He wouldn't want to dance six times with a recluse. As she agonized she glanced up at Tubby and her trembling lips formed a smile.

Dick was beside her at last, his hand outstretched, the
warm color rising under his dark skin. He had gone
past Charlotte without seeing her, and she had turned and
was watching him resentfully.

"Frances!" Their hands met and parted and Dick
reached for the program Tubby still held for her inspection. "I'm mighty glad you're here to-night. I've never
seen you at a dance before. Did Tubby tell you I had
asked him to save me six?" He held up as many fingers
and looked questioningly into her shy eyes. "I hoped
we could have a chance to talk to-night. You've grown
up so fast lately I'll have to get acquainted with you from
the beginning. I'm going to take this dance"—he
glanced over his shoulder at Tubby, who was melting
away—"and these three here together, when we can be
comfortable and talk. And then two more together.
May I? What say?"

II

What Frances said was, "Well, but—" and paused,
smiling at him from under her lashes. Her heart was
racing, she hardly knew what to say but heard her own
voice. "What if we disagree in our talk during the three
and loathe the thought of the two?"

"We won't. Let's plan not to disagree till we are
having the second one of the last two."

He had taken her program from Tubby. He had
eliminated Tubby altogether, he was so easy and unem-
barrassed. Frances wondered if her excitement showed
in her eyes. She wanted it not to. She could be high-
handed with other young men she knew, cooler than
they, even patronizing. She must make an effort to be
as pleasantly impersonal with Dick. She would banter.
She was quick enough at that. Dick handed her the

program and she crinkled her brow as she studied it.
" R. S. is you," she said, smiling. " What a pity it isn't
R. L. S. I love him so."

He gave her a quick response. " You do? So do I.
I grew up on him. That's a fine idea for me. I'll be
R. L. S. too. L stands for love, love of his books, you
know." He took the program from her and drew a
heavy line through his initials and wrote, six times,
R. L. S. " That was a very good suggestion of yours,
that L stands for love." He laughed teasingly at the
round-eyed, round-mouthed face Francie made at him.
" Are you related to Stevenson, Robert Louis? Your
names are spelt the same. I never thought of it before."

" Oh, yes, indeed." Frances nodded soberly. " His
father and my grandfather were brothers," she said
proudly. " I — I think that's quite nice, don't you? "

" Very." Dick regarded her gravely. Her lips had
begun to quiver into a smile she could not repress. " On
my life," he said very slowly in a sad voice, shaking his
head, " I believe you're eligible right this minute for the
Ananias Club. You look innocent enough, but I believe
you're fibbing."

" Well, perhaps I am. But why not have him my
cousin, since we don't know he isn't? " She shrugged.
" I had never thought to find out that he is. I'm willing
to accept him without investigation. There are a thousand chances that he might be."

Her tongue ran glibly. All embarrassment was gone
in the atmosphere of Dick's sympathetic kindliness. He
understood and made her comfortable. She was herself.
He joked and pretended mournfulness that luck so
favored " some chaps that they were accepted without
investigation — quick — like that," and shook his head
over the injustice of it while his look ran over her face,
weaving back and forth from the smiling curve of her

lips to the dancing light in her eyes. He seemed not to notice her clothes nor the clothes of the other girls, and Frances, chattering, thought how much easier it was to talk to him than to boys of her own age with their slang; thought how nicely he stood, one hand in his pocket, one shoulder dropped a little, in a confidential attitude, as if he desired to be nearer her level. Certainly he seemed to have no thought for any other person present, for his eyes did not once wander from her.

Frances asked, glancing toward Charlotte, who was practicing a new step at one end of the ballroom, " You brought your sister to-night?"

"Her crowd was coming. I tagged along." His eyes swept the room and found Charlotte. " Perhaps I did bring her. I hadn't thought. I must go back and see about her program. You'll excuse me? And don't you cut any dances with R. L. S."

He left her and she watched him as he walked toward his sister; saw the smile Charlotte gave him; saw her say something rapidly, glancing toward Frances. Dick's answer was a clenched fist shaken under Charlotte's nose. It was all play, but Frances felt the heat in her cheeks. She could guess what Charlotte had said. For a moment Frances was alone in a crowd of young people she did not know. Again she noticed that not one girl within sight was dressed as she was, in a summer frock and white pumps. All were in evening dress and dancing slippers. " I mustn't think of myself. I mustn't let it spoil things. I wanted to come and here I am, but oh, what if I hadn't bought the sash! That old sash, added to this dress, would have been too awful." The music began with a burst, a one-step, and Tubby arrived, breathless and eager.

" Here, give me your program. I want to put down these names. By heck, the same guy has taken the eighth, ninth and tenth. Who's R. L. S.? I promised two of those to other fellows. Well, what do we care; come on. Who is R. L. S., anyway?"

They were dancing. The music filled the place with throbbing sound. Frances felt her depression drop from her. She breathed freely at last, taking draughts of delight as they moved and stepped, walked and ran, turned and dipped. Oh, what dandy fun! How much nicer than dancing to a victrola on a thick rug. "Tubby, this is wonderful," she breathed. "I'm glad now I came."

"Sure thing you are. You're some dancer. Say, why don't we go to the Saturday night dance at the Athletic Club? You probably wouldn't have as bad luck again as you had to-night getting out. We could say we were going for a ride and then just drop in at the club. You can wear regular dresses there, and hats, you know."

"I'd love it. Oh, Tubby, I love this so; let's not talk."

They finished the dance in silence.

III

It seemed to Frances that all her courage, all her delight in Dick and her firm resolution to forget herself were not enough to make her immune to the look in Charlotte's eyes. Charlotte was not dancing much. She looked bored, and sat on a cushioned window seat tapping time to the music with her silver slipper while she watched the dancers. Frances saw her eyebrows mount whenever she danced past, saw her eyes run over her dress and shoes, her sash and the little green bag that dangled from her arm. Charlotte made no effort to conceal the fact that she was entertaining her partners with her sharp sallies about the dancers. Over her shoulder she threw remarks that kept the young men who sprawled beside her grinning with amusement.

When Frances danced with Dick, Charlotte made a face at him and, rising, strolled out of the room. Frances sighed. "I'm glad your sister has gone. She never forgets to hate me."

Dick did not smile as he said, "Oh, you mustn't mind Charlotte. She's a ragger. Really, you know, she s witty. She ought to write the stuff she says. It's very keen."

"Wit at the expense of others is — is — " Frances was going to say "bad taste," but she would spare Dick. Instead she said "not kind."

"No, but Charlotte doesn't specialize in kindness. She leaves that to me." He sighed. Frances thought he looked tired.

She did not answer at once. Dancing this way, to this music, on this floor with Dick was too perfect to spoil by thinking of Charlotte, but, unable to resist, Frances said at last, "You are joking, of course, but just the same I fancy that is true. But for you — your niceness — we would not be friends at all. I have a vicious disposition and unless you were very polite I should ignore you — because of your sister."

Dick held her off and looked at her with raised brows. "I recognize the little wildcat of the fight long ago in that speech. Do you remember your scrap with Charlotte?"

"I do. I remember it so well I can still feel Charlotte's fingers twisting in my hair. I haven't forgiven her, Richard."

"Why, Francie, you of the Christian virtues? Why don't you turn the other cheek?"

"Oh, please unsay that. Because my father is — is my father, you needn't be sarcastic about the Bible."

He made no answer and they danced on with swimming grace and rhythm, in silence, until Richard said soberly, "You love to dance, Frances. You were made to. I am wondering where you learned."

Frances was a little ashamed of her tempery speech. She was glad of a new subject. She made her voice very sweet. "I can't remember learning. My brothers knew how and they just took me in hand so early I don't know when it began. I think, as you say, I was made to and yet — do you know how I came here to-night?"

"With Tubby? He drove over, didn't he?"

The dance was ended. There was no chance to answer while Dick clapped as noisily as possible. During the encore they were silent except when Frances breathed, "Oh, I do love this. I can imagine I am a puff of summer wind blowing over the grass. Summer wind is never tired. Nor am I."

"I can easily imagine that you are summer wind. I love it too — with you."

IV

When the music started for the next dance they were still discussing plans for the three.

"I hoped we'd wrap up in our coats and walk on the veranda. Have you noticed what a night this is?"

"Oh, yes, and to walk there above the river — " wistfully. "But the dancing is so delicious and I have so few chances."

"You do?" Dick regarded her curiously. "I am beginning to suspect there's a sorrow in your young life. Let's compromise. We'll dance the first and half of the second, and walk the rest of the time that's left."

"You are generous. I want to be generous too. Let's walk and talk the first half, and dance the last. If the talk is terribly interesting, I won't want to dance."

They left it that way and when the time came for their walk Dick, who was ready in his top coat with collar turned up, found Frances on her way to the dressing room.

"Wrap up warmly," he advised. "It's cold out there."

She had only her spring coat, but she buttoned it tight around her neck and they stepped out upon the porch that overhung the river. As Dick closed the door behind them he shut out the pleasant swing of the music with its invitation to dance. They had passed from sound to silence, from light into darkness. The night received them and a soft wind blew them up the veranda, walking north.

Dick took firm possession of Francie's arm and tucked it under his own. "It isn't as cold as I thought it would be here over the water. I know a sheltered corner where we can talk. Do you care for water, black like that and mysterious, or does it make you afraid?"

"Water?" Frances moved more slowly, softly, listening. "I hear it gurgling about the boat landing," she said, whispering. "I'm not afraid of it. I love it, and yet I feel about it as I do lots of things. It's best to love it from a distance."

They leaned on the railing and looked down. The water was black, restless, lapping. Reflected lights moved and shifted in its surface. Across the channel the city blazed and was mirrored brilliantly. Few boats were moving. The season was early. Even yet great chunks of ice found their way down from the waters of Superior. Dick moved around to Francie's left to shield her from the wind and as she turned her face to him in the dim light, her hair was lifted and held back from her forehead.

" Duck lower," said Dick. " I'll play wind shield."

Frances sat on the railing, cuddled down snugly, her hands in her coat pockets.

" What shall we talk about? " she asked. " The time has arrived."

She looked at Dick's profile. How interesting it was with its drooping lines and the lift of his cheek bones; clean and lean and fine. He stared out at the river a moment before he turned his eyes full on her.

" I want to talk about you. You do remember that scrap with Charlotte. I have often wondered."

" How could I have forgotten? "

" You were very little. You cried on me."

Frances laughed and Dick watched her. He did not smile. " Do you remember that I wiped your nose and told you to blow it? And mopped up your tears? And walked home with you, holding your hand? "

" I do." Frances bit her lips, nodding. " Of course I do."

" You hung on to my hand as if — as if I were your mother."

" I did? "

" You had forgotten that? "

" I didn't know."

" You wore funny, stubby shoes."

" I remember that you always looked at them, and I hated so to meet you. I wish now I had sat down on the sidewalk when I saw you coming."

Dick laughed. " I wasn't exactly polished in those days. I'm sorry. What else do you remember, Frances? "

" I remember the names Charlotte called me well enough." Francie's eyes snapped, but Richard did not see. He heard the new note in her voice. " She called me bigot. I didn't know what it meant then. But I do now. Dick, I don't forgive Charlotte for that nor any of the things she has done to me all my life. Why does Charlotte dislike me so? Why does it give her pleasure to make sport of me? "

After a pause Dick said, " Do you want me to answer that honestly? Are you ready to talk about it? "

" Yes. I want to know."

" I want to tell you. I want to have this talk with you, Frances. I have a reason — if you can stand it."

Something clutched at Frances' heart, squeezed, and let go. " I can stand it."

" It began with our parents, that old trouble. I suppose you know."

" I know. But Charlotte — Charlotte makes fun of me. Of my clothes, Dick. Always she has."

" Yes. Clothes are life to Charlotte, and ragging. She's that way. Some people are; but she needn't bother us. But about our parents — our mothers? Do you know what has happened to me? "

" No. You must tell me."

" My mother and father have separated, Frances. I wanted to tell you myself. My mother has gone back to her father in Chicago. Charlotte's going to her soon — to stay — and my father's going to live here in Detroit at a club alone, except when I am in town." He had spoken in a voice so low and deliberate that Frances bent to hear him. With his words came the wet gurgle of the water caressing the spiles. Far off the staccato of a launch engine tapped the silence.

A great lump filled Francie's throat. " Oh," she said, and waited.

" I had to choose," he went on quietly. " Between my mother — and my father. Not the courts; they didn't care because I'm of age, but my mother forced it. She made me choose." There was a long silence before he continued. " Charlotte chose mother and they thought I would too. The money's there, but I didn't." Again a pause. " I couldn't turn away from my father. I chose to stay with him."

" Oh, Richard."

" I knew you'd feel it, Francie, I knew you would. — Do you realize what it means to have to say, to choose which parent you — care most for? "

He put both hands on the railing and leaned forward. His head dropped until his chin touched his coat. Frances put a timid hand on his arm. " I suppose," she began, trying to imagine herself choosing between Mary and Angus and failing, though all her heart cried out to her mother, " I suppose some big, big reason made you turn from your mother."

" A big, big reason," he repeated deliberately. " Yet — since it's done I seem always to be carrying a living fiend in me, here. It tears at my heart all the time. I can't change my mind. I can't go back on my father. If only mother hadn't made me choose I could have spent some time with her, but now — She thinks I am against her and — it's hell, Frances."

" Oh, it must be! It must be! Why did your mother force you to decision? "

" That's it. That's the heart of the whole trouble. Things like that mother does — to anybody, everybody. It's her way. To your mother too, that time. That nearly lost my father his happiness in the Northern Motors. The Grieves are strong for your family." A long silence. " Well, Frances, these are my troubles. Do you know why I wanted to tell you myself? "

" You knew I would sympathize. You knew I was your friend even — even though we almost never meet."

"Yes, and because of that day. It is a strange thing. When this awful decision was forced on me — only last Saturday it was — when I came home from Cambridge and I was feeling — this way, you understand, I met you downtown. Right then I found out that of all the people I have known in my life I remembered best that day when you hung on to my hand, the way you did it, and when you cried on me — and I kissed you. You remember that?"

"Yes."

" Old Hugo Munsterberg explains all those things. I had him in psychology. You know who he is? "

Frances nodded, staring straight before her down the river.

"And yet, isn't it a queer thing that hardly ever seeing you and knowing lots of girls, it should be like that? You said when we were dancing you could still feel Charlotte's fingers twisting in your hair. Well, I still feel your fingers clinging to my hand." He reached down and drew Frances' hand from her pocket. "I want it now, that same way. Frances."

Francie's hand, drawn from the depth of her pocket, was warm and soft. She could not speak. Her throat ached with unshed tears. Emotion, deep, hurting, stabbing with exquisite cruelty, shook her. She gave her hand and let her fingers curl around Richard's as he caressed and pressed it.

At last she found words in her struggle to be practical, grasping for solid facts in a sea of swirling sensations. "I suppose," she cleared her throat to free it of the pressure of tears, "that is because you were with me in my trouble and we had been sober together, and I had cried. You naturally thought of me when you were in trouble — and — and tears."

"At times like that the real things in our lives make

themselves known. The false things drop away. You thought I joked about your Christian virtues when we were dancing, but I do want you to be generous with Charlotte. There is a strain like that in our family, and Charlotte had it handed to her. She didn't choose to have her disposition. When she knows you she will be dear to you. She doesn't know you, and my mother — my mother and my father too are prejudiced against your family. But we are friends — you and I — always."

"You hate religion and churches. You are — infidel."

"Agnostic."

"You too, Dick? Not you?"

Frances drew her hand from his clasp and thrust it deep into her pocket.

"You are cold," said Dick, avoiding her question. "Let's move on to a sheltered place." And later, when he led her around the corner of the porch, "This bench. See? It's almost warm here out of the wind. Tell me about yourself, Frances. What do you do?"

Francie's imagination was stirred as it had never been stirred before. No dream of her maiden romancing had ever pictured Dick more truly the ideal than the reality was proving him to be. He was a man, gentle, tender, wise. Like Jimmie; *dear*, like Jimmie. All the boys she had known had been like Tubby, young — oh, so young they seemed now — slangy, self-conscious, awkward in their moments of love-making. With Dick she soared. He made all things simple and natural. There had been no self-consciousness in the eyes that had held her gaze while he caressed her hand.

Every thought, every sensation that swept through her was poetry. Words came to her, ideas in pictures that were colorful and vivid. Her eyes had darkened and

Dick thought as he watched her leaning slightly forward when she talked, that they were like the river, deep, living, starlit.

"What do I do, you asked me. Dick, I am Eve alone in the garden. All the world is a beautiful garden about me and wherever I go, wherever I look I see always, always, until I am weary with the sight of it, "Thou shalt not" and "Thou shalt not." God told Adam and Eve not to eat of just one tree, but in my garden there are a dozen trees I may not touch. My brothers used to play with me and we had so much fun at home we didn't mind, but they are gone now and I am alone. And my father is old and my mother has to stand by him and I too — must stand by him and not make his work harder, because it is very hard to be a minister in a gay and foolish city; but oh, Dick, it's so lonely in the garden with just mother and father — and the thou-shalt nots!"

Dick had straightened. He bent toward her, his eyes alight. He was about to speak, but she continued, sure of his sympathy. "You don't understand father's ideals, I know. The worldly pleasures are all denied me. Father can't see why I mind giving them up. He says my wanting them is like preferring unclean food to clean, foul air to fresh. You see, his whole effort is toward the spiritual. It's the only real thing in life to him. He wants me to get up a quartet of musical instruments for fun, a dramatic club where we write our own plays and act them the way the colleges do. Things like that, that I would enjoy well enough but none of the girls and — and men, will do it." (Frances was going to say "boys" but that word she felt, to Dick, would be confession of her own immaturity. She said "men" instead, biting her lip as she did so over her memory of some of the "men" she had tried to interest.) "Such things bore them, of course," she went on, "because everybody's crazy over the worldly things I am not allowed to do." She sighed heavily. " I have to go to prayer meeting every Wednesday night and to five services every Sunday. Just think, Dick, we have a blessing at breakfast, of course, but that isn't supposed to count; then we have family prayers after breakfast. Church, Sunday school, young people's meeting at six-thirty and church again at seven-forty-five. The junior children have a service in the afternoon and I am often asked to help with that. I am getting so I want to scream, I'm so tired of it. Sometimes after church at night I run home, run and run as fast as I can, and cry. It's like eating and eating charlotte russe hours after you've had enough and being starved for other things you want. Richard," the words poured from her. She had taken her hands from her pockets to gesticulate and she clasped them now tightly in her lap. " I climbed out a window to-night and down a ladder — to come here."

" Frances! You nervy little sport. By George, I'm glad you did."

" No. No, you aren't. You hate me for doing it because — what else do you think I did? I left my mother sick, needing me. She — she went to prayer meeting alone, so sweet and patient, standing it all these years, and then she must have sprained her ankle or something. I don't know. No sooner had they got her home and upstairs than I climbed out the window and came here." She had risen. There were tears in her voice. " Don't sympathize with me, Dick. Scold me. You told me about your mother and it tore my heart. But I've deserted my mother. Oh, I wish I hadn't."

Richard, too, rose and stood close before her, bending over her. " No!" he said. " Listen." He took her clasped hands and pressed them, emphasizing his words. " There was somebody with your mother, wasn't there?"

" Yes, two women."

" Then forget that. Drop it out of your mind. I suppose they thought you were asleep. You have a right to your own life. That's just the sort of thing I expect of a Puritan like your father, shutting you up in the orchard of thou-shalt-nots. His mind is evil or he wouldn't see evil in so many things. You have to think for yourself, Frances. You can't let bigotry rule your life. You were not born to your father's beliefs — nor was he. He acquired them. You must acquire your own. You're living back in the eighteenth century. Child! Don't you know? Don't you, a young modern, realize that the Bible is just a collection of vague writings by the Jews about themselves? Think of Revelation and the description of heaven. A Hebrew paradise. Golden streets and pearly gates, diamonds all over the landscape, and emeralds. What a place? Fancy trading the green grass we have for gold pavements, yellow and hard; fancy emerald seas when we have water. Would you trade the stars for diamonds stuck up in the sky? That's a Jew's paradise. You worship a Jew, you live by the teachings of a Jew, you obey Jewish laws, but do you mingle with Jews here in Detroit? No. You don't. Then why with your Bible? "

" Oh, but Dick — " Frances was shocked almost beyond her power of expression. She had never heard such talk. It was blasphemy, dreadful, wicked blasphemy. She looked about her in her distress, hunting for words with which to impress on Dick the enormity of his offense. The only utterance she could make was the, to her, final fact. " The Bible is different, divinely inspired by God himself. It's the *Bible*, Dick. God's word, the only word of His we have to guide us."

" No, it isn't," Dick cut in. " That's your first great basic error. It isn't all that. It's a very faulty compilation of ancient writings to which much has been added by those who thought God wanted to speak through them. It's great literature. It is unusual, beautiful English, worth studying, inspiring in places, but immoral, indecent in spots, cruel often." Dick was enjoying himself. He was astride a hobby.

"Richard! No. Not immoral, not cruel. It's sacred. You mustn't say such things. It's blasphemy. I can't listen."

Her voice had dropped a tone lower. He noticed its quality and thrilled to it, saying, "Have you never heard these facts before?"

"These aren't facts. They're the words of the devil." Tears had rushed to her eyes. She was quarreling with Dick, she was shocked, repulsed. Dick, her dream, to talk this way after their quick, wonderful recognition of an old bond. It had all been so beautiful till now. Through tears she strained to see his face, but the darkness covered him. His voice was eager as if he had brought her here to convert her to his way, as if he were clutching to get a hold on her mind. She didn't notice what he was saying now, her emotion was so woven with the pain of disappointment. A minute ago she had felt happier with Dick, arm in arm against him, than she could remember ever having been in her life. They belonged; and now he was thrusting her away from him. She acted on impulse, animated by a sense of disloyalty to her father and a consciousness of guilt toward her mother that, mingled with Dick's frank, terrible talk, wrenched her spirit from him and made his presence an atmosphere impossible to endure. She began to back away from him and his voice ceased. She turned and looked about her, at the void of darkness above the river, at the door to the hall and on to a distant window where the shadows of dancers were thrown on the curtains.

He said, stepping forward, "What is wrong; where are you going?" He had just perceived the change that had come to her. "What is wrong?" he repeated.

"Oh, Dick, you are an infidel. It is true." He heard her labored breathing and the passion of her voice. "I shouldn't have come here. I disobeyed. I criticized my wonderful parents — to an — infidel. Charlotte — Charlotte would spoil anything for me and I — Oh, don't follow me like that. Stay there, where you are." She was still moving backward, her eyes on Dick, now, as if she were being pulled away from him against her longing by a stronger force. "I have to go home." She turned and ran to the door they had come out, and slammed it after her.

Dick stood petrified. He had been so wrapped in his own logic that he had not even sensed the rising storm of protest. Of course she had defended her old stand but why so feelingly? His astonishment grew. Not ten minutes ago she had complained of her religion and its restrictions; why should she not want to discuss it further? Why the nerves and passion when, by the very nature of their discussion, they were proving the bond that had always held them together in spirit? It was as true with her as with himself; he knew, for he had seen it in her eyes and heard it in her voice, that to her he was different as that to him she was different; that and the beautiful sympathy of their contact they had both recognized and accepted, yet now, in the midst of their talk, to have it suddenly end like this — with a show of temper — it was all wrong, inexplicable.

He made a move forward. He must follow her and bring her back and make peace. He must soothe her emotion and make her see that these things were a matter of mind, not nerves. He could do it and he would do it. He had come to this dance to find her and test her attraction for him, and it had been proven to be so real that he could not have it marred by her resentment of a thing misunderstood. He smiled, seeing, in the spirited personality of young womanhood, the little fury he had first known way back long years ago.

The memory of her baby rage released him from astonishment and doubt, and he jumped forward to the door in pursuit of her.

CHAPTER V

I

AT home, in the old house that the Stevensons had been renting since before Francie's birth, there was consternation of a different stripe.

Angus had discovered that Frances was not in her bed, not in her room, not even in the house, and so far as he could tell none of her clothes were missing.

It was half-past eleven. Mary sat in her bed pale with pain. Angus stood in the middle of the room, his white hair upstanding, his face wrinkled with distress.

They had gone to sleep after the doctor had bandaged Mary's ankle and quieted her with bromide, but she had waked with a chill and Angus had suggested a hot-water bottle.

He rose sleepily and went to the bathroom, but returned at once to say that the bottle did not hang in its accustomed place, and looking as helpless as an infant among the trappings of civilization, he stood in the middle of the room, gazed around at the walls and floor and said he didn't see it anywhere.

"No," said Mary, "neither do I, and I don't believe it would come if you whistled. It probably is in Francie's room."

"Her door is locked. I tried it when I first came home. She ought not to do that, lock herself in. Young things sleep so profoundly it is not safe."

Mary shook with chill again and gazed at him helplessly. "If I could only get up — " she complained.

"I'll wake Francie." He left the room quickly and Mary heard him knocking, calling. He waited, then rattled the door knob and called again. Returning to Mary, he got his old bathrobe, lapped it about him so that from the rear he looked like a long brown cornucopia, and opened the window to the porch roof.

"Her window is up. I'll crawl out on the roof and into her room and get the bottle. Her door ought to be unlocked, anyway. Why in the world she should lock the door at all —" he fussed, talking to himself as he went.

Mary forgot to listen after that. The shock of her accident had been slow in reacting, but now as she shivered with cold, her breath came in sharp, labored puffs. She had no idea how she had happened to slip. She was mounting the church steps and, raising her foot to the porch, she seemed to miss it, failed to reach far enough, whirled, clutching for the banister which eluded her, and fell forward and sideways, twisting her ankle.

Prayer meeting had begun. The people were singing "Abide with Me" — beautiful thing but dragging it — and she had to lie there until the hymn ended and she could call Ham Heath.

What was keeping Angus? He was fussing at Francie's door inside. There was silence until she heard him again on the roof. He thrust a white face in at the window. The hot-water bottle was in his hand. He groaned as he crawled into the room.

"Mary! Frances is not in her room. The door is locked and the key gone. Her bed is made up but turned down ready for her. Where is she?"

"Where? Frances not in her room?"

"She is not in this house."

They went over the evidence step by step. Frances had been there, in her nightgown, at half-past seven, at the telephone talking to Tubby about books. At a quarter past eight, when Mary had returned, Frances' room was dark and quiet.

Angus filled the hot-water bottle and tucked Mary in with it for comfort. He hunted up odd keys and tried to open the locked door. None would quite do it.

Returning to Mary, he said, " I think you guess where she is."

" I think I do," said Mary, " and if I guess right she will return before very long. Angus, this is a critical moment in her development. I believe she has gone to a — a party, something we would have denied her had she asked."

" She did ask and was denied."

Angus sat on the bed. His face was drawn and old. The sight of it hurt Mary. She clenched her hands under the covers.

" What shall we do? "

" Come to bed. Lie here and rest and wait. When we hear her come in, let's make no sound. We can wait till morning and give her a chance to confess. Oh, don't let's be hasty now! We must not do anything we would regret."

Angus sat there, his elbows on his knees, his head in his hands. Between his fingers tufts of silky white hair stood erect. He was saying her name, " Francie, Francie, Francie."

He would not come to bed. Mary pleaded but he stood irresolute a moment and then said, " I'll wait downstairs for her. I couldn't rest. I'll walk about and wait."

" And make a scene when she comes. Angus! Don't."

II

By the time Richard had followed Frances into the club she had passed through it and gone. The orchestra was swinging through a waltz with soft, sinuous delight and from the look of the deserted hall everybody was dancing. He blinked in the bright light and glanced about. Frances was not there, but of course she wouldn't be. He made the round of the club rooms looking for her.

It was less than three minutes after their parting that Richard, remembering her cry, " I have to go home," hastened out the same door he had come in. He hurried around the veranda and ran, three steps at a time, down the long flight to his car.

He turned on the switch and stepped on the starter. A roar from the motor disturbed the quiet night; he shot forward a few feet, reversed, swooped around a conclave of parked cars and dashed out into the boulevard.

The Detroit Boat Club is but a short quarter-mile from the old Belle Isle bridge, and Richard had hardly gotten under way when he saw Frances cross the road just ahead and run up the approach to the bridge. There was an arc light there and he saw distinctly her white face between the dark of her hair and the coat collar she had turned high about her neck.

Immediately he throttled his engine and crept slowly in muffled silence along the road, following her. He drove up the approach and stopped, waiting till Frances, half running, passed into shadow. He could see her small white shoes wink-winking through the darkness and he smiled, shaking his head as he remembered her passionate outburst.

Slipping his gear into high he moved forward and ran ahead of her a few yards before he jumped over the side of the car.

She had seen him and when he turned back toward her she was standing perfectly still in the middle of the walk.

As he neared her, moving deliberately, Richard extended a hand after the approved manner of approach to a runaway colt. Through the darkness their eyes strained, each dimly perceiving, as they drew closer together, the gravity of the white face opposite. To Frances came, with relief, the knowledge that Richard was not laughing at her. His face was sober.

" Frances. Where were you going? "

" Home."

" How? Have you any money?" His voice was very quiet.

" No."

" I thought not. You must come with me. I will take you home."

He drove slowly across the bridge. Neither spoke. The river lay to the right and to the left, midnight black between its shores, far strung with lights. On the Detroit side a fleet of tiny sailing yachts rocked at anchor. Frances watched the tip of a mast sway sleepily with the movement of the water. It soothed her. She was very tired. She closed her eyes, but the swaying mast became an illumined baton that moved back and forth, back and forth in time to a measure of dance music that was beating in her ears. Her emotions rose and fell, with the rhythm of the mast, regret for her impulsiveness, pain for her faithlessness to her parents, gratitude to Dick for his thought of her, and, over and under all, like the soprano ecstasy of the violin in the song that sang through her senses, the fact that Dick had cared enough to follow. That was the great fact, that he had not only forgiven her heated repulse but he had cared enough to follow! She loved him as she had always loved him, but to-night the dazzling glory that until now had been but the flushing rose of sunrise became visible to her in all its radiance. In its light the religious differences that had loomed like a barrier of mountains between them appeared to be cleft by a shining road for them to travel together. If Dick would take back the things he had said, if he would forgive her passionate outburst, she surely could forgive him enough of his differences to be patient until he learned.

She opened her eyes and looked at Dick. In the illumination of an electric sign she saw his firm profile and almost immediately the flash of his eyes as he turned and glanced at her. But neither spoke until they had crossed Jefferson Avenue and were headed north on the boulevard. When the lights of the denser quarter were behind Dick slowed the car and turned a little toward Frances. He wanted to see her face and read what he could of her changed mood. He had no way of guessing what she was feeling. She had seemed to care, he had felt her sympathy at the club, until suddenly she had turned from him and fled and, perhaps, had permitted his approach later, only because she had had no money with which to get home alone. Whether he were suffered now merely as a vehicle or — for a better reason — he had no idea, he told himself. What to think was puzzle enough; much less could he know what to say, especially as everything was yet to be said and crowding forward in his mind for release. He felt no swimming music of delight. He was conscious, with the physical pain of tense longing, that this hour would bring one of the great moments of his life. Before its sixty minutes passed into history he would know whether Frances was to be his by natural attraction or his by conquest. He felt, without defining it, that of all the girls he had known, Frances was the most genuine. She was sincere, and she would know whether or not her heart spoke to his without the triflings and twaddle of courtship. For himself he knew, and if Frances did not — could not answer from her heart honestly and surely to-night — he would suffer his first great disappointment in her. He wanted her to speak first. He wanted the key to her mood and he let his silence put a burden upon her. At last she stirred and said slowly, " Dick? " doubtfully, as if she were beginning to question the motive for his care of her. " You were — very kind to follow me."

Dick smiled quickly and sighed his relief. The voice had brimmed with contrition and besought understanding. She was evidently as uncertain of his state of mind as he had been of hers. He said, " It wasn't kind. I couldn't do anything else."

" You mean you felt — felt responsible? "

" That and — more. I wanted to follow you. I couldn't let you go. Surely, Frances, you didn't want our evening to end so. You didn't wish it? "

" No. No. I didn't, but I couldn't bear what you said. I couldn't hear such things about my father without — without losing my — control."

" I am sorry I shocked you so. I couldn't know you had never even heard such things before. I felt very much in sympathy with you. I had told you my trouble and you had been — everything I had hoped you would be and then, when you told me your loneliness, I understood and wanted to help you. I am sorry."

" Oh," Frances clasped her hands tightly in the intensity of her relief. " It's all right. It's all right if you said the things just to comfort me. I thought at the time you meant them, but I didn't see how you could! You see, Dick, anybody who believed as you talked couldn't be a friend of mine. It wouldn't be possible. I did wrong to complain of my father. He is next to God with me, he is so brave and self-sacrificing and that was one of the chief hurts,— that I had said and done things against him until I had made you think I would listen to such talk."

"But, Frances — " Dick's courage was almost unequal to the confession. "I did mean what I said. I am not taking it back. That is what I believe. But why should it make any difference to us? I don't mind what you believe."

"Oh." It was a sigh and a moan and it stabbed Dick to the heart. Impulsively he reached for Frances' hand and the touch of her fingers against his own drove the fire of an electric shock through his body. With his free hand he swung the car to the curb and stopped.

"Frances, don't take it like that. Don't *care*. It doesn't matter. You and I can never be held apart by differences. They aren't vital to life, but we are vital to each other. I am not going to live without you. Look at me, Frances, and see how little I care what you believe!"

He leaned toward her, the arm he had flung along the back of the seat drew her closer, but she held away from him and he did not break her resistance. Through the dimness he saw that her eyes were on his face, searching, searching — and in the long silence they gazed — she in an abandonment of passionate questioning, he endeavoring with all the strength of his will to reassure her. Slowly he moved nearer her, and dropping his head suddenly, he lifted her hands and kissed them.

"Dick — Dick — " a broken whispering, her head bent low near his.

"Frances — I love you. You knew it. I seem to have been shouting it all evening. Look at me again. Tell me you see it." He kissed her lips and felt her draw back from him and turn away.

Her voice was choked with tears. "No — No. You shouldn't — I can't. I mustn't want your love — I have no right." She stopped and beat her clenched hands together softly as if speech, her voice — life itself — had failed her. But immediately she cried, "Take me home. Please go on. Why did you follow me if it was only to make things worse?"

Dick sat motionless gazing at her in despair and amazement. He had stalled his motor and the silence was broken only by their quick hard breathing. He made no slightest move to do as she had asked. Instead he kept his steady, narrowed eyes on her profile. At last Frances pleaded, "Are you going to take me home?"

"No. Not yet."

"Why? It's no use, Dick. Even if I wanted to, I couldn't turn against my father for you. Something in me couldn't."

"Nothing in you need turn against him. Frances," he waited till she lifted her eyes to him. "I want you to believe me when I say that I love you for your loyalty to him. I want you to be loyal, but I want you to be intelligent too. If when you know what I believe you still agree with your father, I shall never question it, but that has nothing to do with us. We always have, we always will love each other in spite of everything. Be honest with me. Can you look at me and say you do not love me?"

"Dick — I can't love you."

"Say it again — and look at me."

"I can't — I don't — Dick, I won't." She was not looking at him. She was pulling at something in her lap, something she could not see for tears, but knew suddenly to be the little green bag with its forget-me-nots and ribbons. Her lips were moving. " I can't — I can't."

Dick moved nearer her and took her, protesting, into his arms. " But you do. And nothing else matters. Nothing — nothing — but this — " He kissed her and held her. She heard his urgent voice close to her ear. " Say you knew that you did, Frances. Tell me that you knew."

She was powerless to move. Dick's arms, his cheek against hers, the warmth of his breath on her neck had conquered her efforts at resistance. She had dreamed of loving him, but never of this delight in contact. She felt the beat of her pulse and with every throb a syllable, as if her heart were echoing his words, " Nothing matters but this. Nothing, nothing matters but this." But she could not speak.

She knew Dick was waiting. The silence pressed upon her and suddenly, as she hesitated, Dick's clasp loosened and he turned from her, one arm thrown upward before his face. The movement was like a cry of reproach.

Frances caught at his right hand in a panic of regret. " Dick — Dick — forgive me." The tide of her love rose like a wave and swept over her; it drowned the little voices of prophecy and washed Angus completely out of her consciousness. She lifted Dick's hand and put her quivering lips into the cup of his palm. " Oh, I love you, I do love you," Dick heard her cry.

Again the silence and to Dick, at last, the orchestra of the heart. Familiar sounds came to him with a thrill of ecstasy, and crashed and chorused like the wind sweetness from the pipes of a great organ built around the world of the night. He heard a distant train whistle, a quick minor wail like the cry of a flute; he heard the whirring accompaniment of a passing car and the tapping triangle of gravel on its fenders.

Frances' yielding lips had finished the answer he had wanted and he held the moment breathlessly, motionless in his rapture.

It was later that the wind began to rise and briskly scuttling among the clouds, tossed them up and away, ragging them, tearing them till only wisps of tattered gray floated below the stars. The frosted silver of the Milky Way brightened and shone upon the long, low car as it crept through the shadows of the boulevard. Houses lay dark and still in the midnight quiet. From the river the deep, hoarse boom of a freighter shook the very earth, and set the lacy branches of the trees to trembling. Frances and Dick talked in low tones and sensed the tingling moment of their delight. The breath of young clover and freshly made gardens was blown into their faces caressingly. They drew it in with the deep sighing thrill of their happiness and the perfume of it was woven into the tapestry of memory.

III

Angus, waiting for Francie's return, paced the living-room rug and watched the clock. The house was cold, his bare ankles were like ice between the hem of the old brown robe and the felt slippers that clothed his feet. He had turned on a lamp when he first went down but he soon switched it off that he might the better discern the light of a motor stopping at his door.

He walked nervously back and forth, back and forth, pausing each time he reached the front windows to look out into the street. He moved like a shadow among shadows, silent, bowed, his head hanging forward, his hands working tensely in the pockets of his bathrobe.

One of Angus' favorite admonitions to others — especially his children — was, " Distinguish between feeling and thinking. You are expressing your emotion, not your thought." He said this to himself now. " This is feeling. This is my feeling, my emotion, my hurt. I must try to think. In justice to Francie, I must try to think. I must remember her youth. I must remember that she is not yet eighteen." But instead of remembering Francie's youth, he remembered the boys at seventeen and contrasted her with them. They had been reasonable, amenable to discipline, jolly — not passionate, making the best of things as they were, not striving for forbidden fruit.

Life had dealt kindly with Angus as it does with those who give themselves over into divine guidance. Whatever the psychology of the thing, whether explained by religionist or scientist, he whose unceasing prayer is for guidance, and wisdom — whose waiting ear is tuned for a voice from the infinite — will receive guidance, will find wisdom. The hardest lesson Angus had had to learn after his conversion was — to use his own phrase — " to await the Lord's leisure."

To a less spiritual man than Angus, the state of mind and soul he sought was best described by the psychologist's " relaxing into the subjective state," or the prepsychologic, " waiting for something to tell you."

But to-night Angus was far from prayer. For the first time in his twenty-eight years of parenthood he was experiencing the poignancy of shaken trust in his children, faith abused.

They had all, always, seemed to him high-minded, fine-spirited. They had seemed of another breed than the careless, young moderns he saw all about him, pursuing the fleshpots or bowed in worship before the golden calf. He had found, in thought of them, solace from

a world gone mad with materialism.   They, crowned by
the stars of self-denial, were confirmation of his belief
that youth, as well as age, may live and live fully and
joyously, animated by the high fires of the spirit's
desires.

To have gone on so, through the boys' difficult years
with hardly a ripple on the deep-flowing surface of his
fatherhood and then, through his little daughter, his idol,
his white rose of love, to have this flagrant insubordina-
tion!   No, there was no distinguishing between feeling
and thinking for him to-night.   He only felt, and that
with a pain that was sharpened because it was new.

Angus would have said he loved music had he been
asked.   That he was entirely indifferent to it in all but
two very limited senses he would not have admitted.
But it was true.   He enjoyed the hymn singing in church
and thrilled to the boom of the organ and the voices of
massed worshipers raised in praise.   That, because it
was part of his work, while in his home he loved song
and piano because it had ever been the heart of the family
life.   Where another household would have gathered
oftenest about the hearth, the Stevensons gathered about
the piano.   Such music was expressive of happiness, of
merriment.   The voices under his own roof were the
voices that he loved.   But rhythm, the rhythm of a waltz,
the invitation of the tango, the exhilaration of the march
passed him by.   He was an odd combination of sentimen-
tality, practicality and spirituality.   Poetry, the æsthetic,
the wild, free colorful imagination of the artist was not
his.   He had danced in his youth in Virginia but he retained little memory of it beyond the temptation to which
it had stirred him.   He remembered moments of intoxication when every sense had been roused — every sense
except his sense of rhythm.   A smiling girl in his arms,
soft lights, perfume, the brushing of hair across his face,

the trill of a voice at his ear, — these were the remembered joys, not the orchestra in the hall.

His mind was just. He prayed for vision, but he had never even dimly perceived that the love of dancing might be simply a form of musical expression. As he thought of Frances giving her young beauty into the embrace of the average American youth as Angus saw him — undisciplined, reckless — yielding to the pressure of strange arms, he shook with disgust and fear, fear for Frances and her unawakened passions. That they were 'there, sleeping within her virgin breast, unrecognized by herself, he knew, for she was his child, his temperament, his blood come through Mary miraculously, without taking with it the tempering chill of Mary's cool sweetness.

As his darting thought stabbed into the past he saw Francie illumined in perspective; saw her whiteness and the soft darkness of her hair and eyes above the warm red of her curling lips. He saw her as she had leaned toward Antony Remington, kindling to his detailed story of the deciphering of the hieroglyphics on Egyptian tombs. "We found that meant king," he had said, himself animated, scintillating with the remembered joy of discovery, "so when we came to a tomb bearing the same word twice, we knew it meant — "

"King of Kings," Francie had cried, cutting in excitedly.

"Exactly! Exactly! You see it — " And so on through hours he taught and Francie followed, or anticipated, breathless at times with acquisitive delight.

And now to-night she — that same Francie — had climbed out her window to sneak away — and dance —

Incalculable creature!

Ah, she was so worth while, so beautifully alive, a treasure to give for the world's betterment. She would be a strong force for good if she chose. If she failed to choose for God, chose mammon, how needless a loss for God, and for Angus what pain of failure. How not fail with her? How keep her close? It lay with him. He must learn, be willing to listen and learn.

The clock struck the half-hour after twelve. Angus started. Past midnight. Was it right for him to wait thus, assuming that she would return? Might she not have been kidnapped, or lost, wandering alone, sick perhaps and helpless somewhere out in the darkness? He went into the back hall off the dining room and turned on the small telephone light. The police headquarters number stared up at him from the back cover of the directory. He had never noticed it before. There it was, brief, easily pronounced by a tongue agued with fear. Should he call and give his name, thus to adver- tise his daughter's delinquency? No. Delinquency! Vile word to use of Francie. He thought of its Latin root. Where had she gone, what ball? He tried to remember the society columns of the newspapers. Where were balls given? He would telephone. Why hadn't he thought of this before, Strasburg's, the Woman's Club, the Statler, any hotel. Possible places came flocking to his mind, the Athletic Club . . . all the clubs and hotels and dancing schools and auditoriums in town. Dozens, hundreds, if he counted the rough as well as the polite. There had been a time when the church had been the gathering place of the nation; now the dance halls, the theaters were the choice of the people. Oh, the little handful, the pitiful little handful, that stood true. Even the churches, some of them, were having theatricals and dances in their parish houses, baiting God with the flesh of mammon.

He made a sweeping gesture with his arms as if to push the whole mass of humanity away from him. Its stench was in his nostrils, and yet, like a voice within him, the word why, why, why, beat on his mind. He sat down in the dining room, his knees apart, his arms hanging between. Why? Is it the fault of the church? What can the church do? To himself in the depths he said, " The church is no more, no less than the people in it. As much of God as they permit within their organization, that much will God be present. God forces no issues. He is there, eternally and unchangingly there, infinite love, to be taken or denied. If he is not wanted, he is not to be had. When the people will to make the church the temple of God, it will be the temple of God, not before. One man is no more than one man. He can give of himself, dedicate himself to God's service. Beyond that he cannot go. The fault is not with the church but with the time. Money hunger, war hate, pleasure madness, flesh love, — these are the pipers who play for the people to dance. It is true that the majority should rule. I believe that politically, but can I learn to believe it ecclesiastically? Is the majority right? Is life a meaningless opportunity for sensuousness? Can it be that Omar and his appealing philosophy are true and Christ wrong? So easy! So pleasant and easy to let go and drown care in a goblet of wine. Life — great, moving, throbbing creation of mystery; man, of all living things the soul, the heart, intelligence. Can it be that for him there is nothing more than that

Man wakens from his sleep within the womb,
Cries, laughs and yawns; then sleeps within the tomb?

Laughs and yawns! Laughs at simplicity, yawns at virtue — even Francie — Francie deploring her simplicity.

Deep water this, for Angus; discouragement, bitterness, imponderable problems of the spirit. He began to

pray in broken phrases, his eyelids pressed close upon
smarting balls of fire. His tongue stumbled, words
eluded him, but his groping consciousness pressed forward.

"God, show me the way. Show me the way. Am I
serving a lost cause? Am I the blind and foolish one?
God, thou art the creator. The Mind that could create
the heavens and the earth, stars and the mountains, a
field flower and the drop of dew within its cup; the Mind
that made man with a soul to suffer and a heart to be
glad, had a purpose. God, show me that purpose. Lead
me. I am a worshiper, a soldier for righteousness.
Wherein lies righteousness? Where? Where? — Reveal it to me. — I follow the only light I see. Does it
lead me in false paths? Francie. God, bring Francie
safely back to me. If through her I may learn, give me
generosity of mind. Open my eyes, give me an understanding heart." His breath labored, his lips moved on
soundlessly. He called upon God again and again, waiting for an answer. In deep silence he sat silent, his face
lifted a little, in an attitude of listening. For a moment
his thought was suspended, hanging, it seemed to him in
a shifting vapor of great stillness. His eyes were closed
but light pierced the nebulous darkness, color bloomed
and faded and bloomed again. Thought began to form.
Slowly, distinctly he began to repeat the words he saw
in relief against the trailing dimness. Sentences from
the Bible, scraps from his reading, strong, quiet mes-
sengers of peace. He said them aloud, haltingly, waiting for revelation.

"I am the light of the world — he that followeth me
shall not walk in darkness but shall have the light of
life. Be strong — fear not for I am with thee alway,
even unto the end of the world. He maketh the judges
of the earth as vanity. — He shall blow upon them and

they shall wither. They that wait upon the Lord shall renew their strength, they shall mount up with wings as eagles; they shall run and not be weary; they shall walk and not faint." Angus' lips quivered into a smile. "They shall mount up as eagles; they shall run and not be weary." He breathed more easily. "God is truth and God is love. The gift of truth is freedom; the gift of love is purity. Truth and love. Give me love sufficient for my child's need. Help me to make her see. Help her to make me see. Hand in hand, O God, let us walk in light, seeing Thee in all things, seeing the beauty of complete oneness with Thee. God, help Francie to turn away from self, to find renunciation of fleshly things robbed of the pain of sacrifice in love of Thee who art love, and joy and life eternal." He felt, stealing through his halting thought, the returning tide of courage. God's response, the gift of courage, the victory over doubt. Vagrantly, lines from some poem read and remembered thrust themselves forward for attention. "Have you heard that it was good to gain the day? I also say it is good to fall; battles are lost in the same spirit in which they are won."

Battles lost in a spirit of victory. This resistance from Francie, defiance, falsehood. — Francie! A battle lost in the spirit of victory. Yes, the victory, for Angus, of humility. "My child's sin is my sin. I am hers and she is mine — my Francie."

IV

While Angus sat deep in sorrow, Richard's car slid up to the curb and stopped. He jumped out and went around to the other side, where he gave his hand to Frances. She looked fearfully up at the house. It seemed to her she had been gone a lifetime. She had sneaked out, a foolish child; she returned a young woman, betrothed.

Dick took her arm and they quietly mounted the steps. She fumbled in a little green bag and found her key. Dick took it from her.

"I will come to-morrow afternoon," he whispered. "We'll drive somewhere. Frances —" He held her face between his hands and looked deep into her eyes. "This — is destiny."

"It must be, Dick. Only God could bring us together from our separate worlds."

"Yes." Their gaze held, beautiful, clear, breathless.

"I should love to think —" Frances began, whispering, but stopped, her lips parted.

"Tell me."

"I should love to think that after you were born — a little boy, in Pennsylvania — God planned me to be part of you, to finish you and make you — whole."

Dick's breath caught. He drew Frances to him and held her close against his heart. "Think it; believe it; and help me never to forget it!" Frances' face was hidden, he pressed his lips to her soft hair and they remained so in the silence and the shadow until Dick whispered, "This has been the saddest week of my life — and the happiest. I lost my mother, but I found you."

While they lingered, oblivious to time in the beautiful exaltation of their love, Angus, renewed by his revery, walked back into the living room and saw the lights of a motor at the curb. He turned to the hall, hurried, trembling with eagerness, and threw the door open.

"Oh!" The cry came from Angus. Frances! Frances in the arms of — He stared and found himself gazing into the startled eyes of a stranger.

"Frances!"

"Father?"

Angus stepped back against the wide swung door and pointed inward to the hall.

"Doctor Stevenson, one moment — "

"No." It was Frances. She stretched an arm to bar Dick's advance. "Please go. Please. Not to-night. I want you to go."

Dick hesitated but Frances went forward, past Angus, through the doorway and was shut away from him.

He took one step down, paused, looking back at the blank panels of the door and beat one fist upon his palm. "It would be just his stripe, just his damned righteous sort, to whip her for running away, the stiff old Puritan!"

Angus was conscious only of towering wrath when he saw his daughter move from the embrace of a stranger and walk into the house she had left in disobedience. He forgot his prayer for light and guidance. The tender mood of his own responsibility in Frances' defection was swept from him by the maddening knowledge that she had lied, had sneaked, had given herself to a stranger — her lips — her body.

Looking at him in the suddenly flooding light, Frances saw his horrified face and felt, with a great sinking of her spirit, that nothing she could say or do now would right her in his eyes.

"Frances!" Angus towered above her. "Who was that?"

"Richard Stanhope." Frances realized that she was spent by emotion. She dropped into a chair and sat sidewise, her arm across the back, her head supported by her hand.

"Richard Stanhope, the son of Felix Stanhope? That family?"

"Yes, father. Richard and I have always been friends. You remember that."

"Friends — and I found you in his arms! Friends — the son of his mother. Where have you been?"

"At the Boat Club."

"Dancing?"

"Yes — a little. I came away early."

"You call this early? It is after twelve, well after twelve. Frances — " So comminatory was the voice that Frances raised her eyes to her father in alarm. "I believe you left after your mother came home. I believe you knew she was hurt. Answer me. Is that so?"

"I didn't know — I heard her come home. Yes, I knew — Daddy, don't you want to hear — "

Angus cut in. "How long has this been going on? This evening at the table you said you were tired; you went to bed, then you dressed and sneaked out with that Stanhope! How long have you been living a lie?"

"I don't live a lie. Oh! This has never happened before." Tears started from Frances' eyes. "Won't you hear my story?"

"You've never done this before? Am I to believe you when already to-night you have deceived me? What story can you tell that will explain what I have just seen?"

"I am engaged to Dick, father. I — "

Angus had lost control of himself. He laughed. He wanted to shake Frances, to shake and shake her till she rattled. He took a step nearer and thrust his hands hard into the pockets of his robe. "You are engaged! You — a child. You mean you are allowing yourself license in — indecency." He looked with burning eyes into the startled whiteness of his daughter's face and met eyes not less burning than his own and deep with passionate anger. Frances rose slowly. Tears dried on her cheeks. She moved forward, holding his gaze, and Angus knew he was witnessing his own white hot

temper of indignation. " You — take — that — back,"
Frances said, panting.

Angus' whole body sank inches in a long sigh. He
lifted his face and his eyelids dropped until the lashes
pressed on his quivering cheeks. " Thank God, thank
God, it isn't true."

She was in his arms, trembling, sobbing, clutching his
gown to hold him closer. " Unsay it, daddy. Unsay
it," she cried.

" Darling. My Frances. My child, it isn't true. I
know. It was my fear for you, my terrible fear. My
beautiful child — " He could say no more. They grew
quiet there together in the silence, clinging close until
Frances, gently removing herself, went slowly toward
the stairs and up.

When she knelt beside her mother's bed with Mary's
arms about her and Mary's soothing voice in her ears,
she lay inert, weighted by her heavy heart, her guilt,
her hopeless love. She felt herself a prisoner thrust
back into the garden of thou-shalt-nots. Richard could
never be hers. They were worlds apart, worlds and
worlds apart. She had had her flight. She had defied
lightning and been struck. She had tasted the world
and found the flesh and the devil. It was not for her,
not for her. Wings had Richard, and a cloven hoof.
He loved her, and he tempted her. He loved her, and
he tried to turn her from her father. It was thus the
serpent had talked to Eve. He had tempted Eve — and
now Frances, in her garden of thou-shalt-nots.

CHAPTER VI

I

Richard Stanhope was as perfectly the product of his environment as Frances was of hers. Less pressure had been put behind his home training in agnosticism than had been expended on Frances' intensive religious culture. It had come easily, no faster than his developing young mind could accept, and with no exactions of service. Combined with his father's amiability of temperament, he had much of his mother's tense seriousness and not a little of her intellectual snobbery. He had always considered himself a peg more acute mentally than his associates, and by natural selection he had chosen activity in the literary and debating clubs of high school rather than in athletics. Before he was fifteen, he was pronounced one born to the law, so logically, so keenly, did his mind operate under opposition. He had a natural gift for seeing around his subject and, whatever his convictions might be, he easily switched to the other side when he met his own logical arguments. To provoke discussion was breath of life to him. He delighted in arguing against himself that he might have the pleasure of winning debate on purely logical and intellectual grounds unaided by the fire of conviction.

The night after Dick's impetuous love-making, he could not sleep. He was thrilled into tingling wakefulness by Francie's qualities. He was in love, tremendously and blindly, and though the physical intoxication was a continuously recurring pain of delight, his thought was engaged with the spirit of Frances, her mind, her temper and her responsiveness. To overcome her resistance to his teaching would be the first need, then to see her accepting pure logic in place of emotionalism would be perfect accompaniment to his love for her; and to have her beautiful, intelligent, his — to hold, to teach — ah, ecstasy. He clutched a pillow close in his arms and pressed his burning face against its coolness.

He loved her for her loyalty. He loved her passionate defense of her father. Just as passionately would he defend his mother against doubt and ridicule, always, and just as devotedly. Some day, Frances would fight for him — Dick — and his logic, as she had fought for her father and his superstitions.

He thought back over the years of their acquaintance. He had been twelve. For eleven years she had been deep in his heart and he had hardly guessed it until that Saturday when, with his mother's demand that he choose breaking his heart, he had met her and felt her hand in his again, and seen the deep blue of her grave eyes lifted to him. There had been girls. Lord! He flopped over in bed. Dozens. Dancing girls, serious girls, jolly girls and sweethearts. All, like a bouquet of yesterday's roses, wafted into the past, with Frances filling the dawn of the present. He went back over their talk, everything, the ride, the misunderstanding, the moment when, desperate, in love, he had taken her and won her. Her yielding body and pulsing lips — so sweet — so fragrant.

He marveled at her youth, smiling. Eighteen. Hardly that! A child, infancy viewed from the height of twenty-three. But a wise child, a wise little tempest of a child, old beyond her years, thoughtful, wistful. He felt again the pressure of her lips in his palm; he felt her fingers in his hand, clinging. She was like her own hand, alive, thrilling straight through to the heart of him.

He longed for morning and activity. How should he stay away until afternoon? He feared for her in her father's hands. There was something about the Disciples of Christ that made them brutal. He tried to think his way through that. The spare-the-rod-and-spoil-the-child admonition that gave every beastly hypocrite a right to beat a dependent creature. Wife-beating was denied the Christian, but not child-beating. If Angus tried — Dick saw red. If he had done any of his Puritan hellishness on Frances, he would be made to regret it. He'd meet a fist. Dick clenched both fists and punched the mattress.

Morning brought activity that precluded Frances. Felix needed Dick to help him plan. They were shut in the library until lunch time and his heart, that had thrilled to the dream of union with Frances, dulled into sickening pain for the wreck of his parents' marriage.

II

It was two o'clock when he rang the Stevenson bell. He was eager and fearful. He hardly noticed the worn porch or the old oak door with the marks of Sir Walter's scratching. But he entered the living room when Maggie showed him in with something of a shock. It was shabby. Coming as he had from the luxurious home of his mother's making, it startled him for a moment. The rug was almost threadbare in one place; the whole room was lean with simplicity. He looked about. He was alone. The house was very quiet. He noticed the loud ticking of the mantel clock. On closer inspection the room showed itself intelligent. He admitted charm and a something that might be called personality. There was a blue bowl full of apple blossoms on the bookcase, some hammered brass of great age, cushions of dull amber on a window seat, and music on the open piano. It was a room lived in. He strolled to the table where a row of books a yard long stretched between bronze elephants. Novels. Of all things, novels in a Puritan's house! George Eliot, Trollope, side by side with Arnold Bennett and Edith Wharton. Poetry, modern stuff, Masefield and Amy Lowell. A book on music, Kipling; Journeys to Bagdad, Roosevelt. An *Atlantic Monthly* lay beside a pile of papers, the *Herald* and *Presbyter*. Somebody was reading a history of France. Its place was marked by a pencil on which the book was closed.

Dick heard a step. He wheeled about to face Maggie, who stood shyly before him, extending a letter at arm's length.

"Mrs. Stevenson she says tell you please wait after you read this." Maggie reached for an apron string and held to it during this embarrassing interview. That she was dressed especially for the occasion Dick did not know. She looked a very ordinary maid to him in her shapeless black with clean white apron. She seemed to have more to say but difficulty in getting it out. "And — you're to have a chair." She gave a large chair a tentative shove. "Have a chair."

"Thank you." Richard waited, expecting from her attitude further instructions, but none came. "Is that all?"

"Yes, sir. That's all. You're to have a chair." She backed out, muttering.

Richard walked to the window-seat and sat down among the amber cushions. The letter was from Frances. His fingers were cold as he tore the envelope.

Dick dearest, it began. How could we have hoped to belong to each other? Romeo and Juliet were never farther apart than we, because it is religion that divides us. I didn't realize last night how wrong I had been nor how foolish. I left my mother knowing she was hurt. I was worse than you know. We have had a long talk this morning, mother and father and I, and they say we can't be engaged. Not yet, anyway. Father says we would have to wait years, and if our love is real it will last until I am old enough. My father is going to see you this afternoon when you call. He is willing to listen to anything you have to say about our being engaged or about religion, and not only to please me but because, after last night, he wants to understand our generation and everything. I hope you will talk to him. He scares boys who come here sometimes, but I don't think he'll affect you that way. You aren't a boy.

Dick, I have had to promise not to try to see you before you go back to Cambridge, but oh, I want to so much that if you try I will help you. If we don't write too often we can have the comfort of each other's letters, — and, anyway, whether I see you again or not, whether you write to me or not, I want you to know that I love you more than all the world and I shall wear the memory of your love like a flower upon my heart. I can't get over the marvelousness of our loving each other this way. To think that all these years when I have dreamed of you, you, too, have dreamed of me, and that at last we came together. I shall live on the happiness of that memory until I see you again.

God bless you, dearest. And Dick — think kindly of God. He is the only way there is across the gulf that divides us, and I want you to bridge that gulf and come over here to me.

Always and forever yours,

FRANCES.

There were tears in Dick's eyes when he finished reading. He coughed to clear his throat of the choking pressure of emotion that caught him. Frances was sad. She had been beaten into submission and convinced of wickedness! She was upstairs now, locked in her room probably, alone with a wrathful God. Her father would soon be down. Well, damn him, let him come and if he wanted to know how the present generation believed he'd get an earful from one who had never felt lack of words with which to express himself.

He waited, listening, glowering through the curtain at the sunny street.

Some boys were playing ball in a yard. opposite, he could hear their shrill voices in continuous wrangle. A dog barked somewhere. A door closed upstairs. Dick rose. A sense of cold anger straightened his drooping lips into a hard line. He folded his arms and stood with his back against the mantel, waiting.

When Richard heard Angus' heavy step on the stair he turned toward the door prepared to meet his adversary. He enjoyed, for the moment, the sensation of perfect calm with which he faced the interview. It was pleasant to feel emotion held in check by the steel grip of his nerves. He had trained himself for such moments as this. To remain unperturbed in the face of fire was one of the strongest links in the chain of qualifications he was forging for the law. His chin was stern under the youthful freshness of his mouth; his black eyes were hard, cold-lit with animosity. He visualized Angus as he had been the night before, a shocked ascetic, wrapped in the robe of a monk, the very voice of denunciation — such he had seemed — coming suddenly upon them out of the darkness. Whether he came to-day as ascetic or Pharisee, priest or prophet, he doubtless would appear austere in clerical habiliment; somber, implacable with righteous wrath that should have its answer of unrighteous wrath. They would face each other, divided, as Frances had written, by a gulf of differences. Hardly, it seemed to Dick, would their voices carry across the vastness of that chasm, yet, bound as they were by their mutual love for Frances, they must strive for understanding.

It was with a start of surprise that the man of steel-gripped nerves faced Angus when he appeared between the portières and stood poised a moment before advancing. He showed no more trace of the night's agitation than did Richard. He was clear-eyed, clean-shaven, alert. The upstanding hair of the night before was brushed flatly across his head from a side parting and the shapeless monk's robe had been changed for a close-fitting suit of dark gray serge. His effect upon the quiet sunny room was as of a rush of spring wind through a wide-flung door. He stepped forward quickly and offered a large hand.

"Mr. Stanhope, how are you, sir? I am sorry to have kept you waiting so long. Please be seated." He had given Richard's hand a warm, strong pressure. He waved him to a chair and himself sat opposite on the window seat, fixing his grave attention on the young man who for a moment — Dick hoped it was but for a moment — had lost his perfect calm.

"You have Frances' letter," Angus began, thinking Richard's self-consciousness might be surprise at his appearance in place of Frances. "She is feeling very badly to-day. Quite used up. I want to thank you for bringing her home. Had you not followed her when you did, we might have realized our worst fears. We are grateful to you — for that."

He waited for Richard to speak and Richard, thus given opportunity, found himself tongue-tied. It was not so easy to address this clear-eyed man as he had planned. He felt himself in the presence of a force rather than a personality. Every line and quiver of Angus' expressive face was animated by a life behind a life, a literal *vis a tergo*. He said, for lack of anything better, "I believe you have met my father."

"Very pleasantly," said Angus. He reached behind him and pulled a cushion away from his back as if its softness annoyed him. "I met him years ago. I thought at that time we might be friends. I meant to call upon your parents but unfortunately — later it seemed inadvisable. You are very like your father, Mr. Stanhope. I think I should have known you were his son."

"Thank you." Again there was a pause before Richard said, "My father liked you too, I remember, Doctor Stevenson. He regretted — that things were — as they were. My mother —" Dick paused. He could not go on with the sentence he had begun, but he was impelled to expression by a magnetic quality in Angus that seemed to be drawing him closer. He continued and heard the words he uttered with amazed disapproval, "I suppose you know that my parents are in great trouble. They are both very unhappy and — for me it is trouble too."

Five minutes before Richard would not have believed it possible that he could, freely, against his every inclination, yet with keen desire for understanding, have told Angus Stevenson — the bigot, the Puritan — the deepest, most intimate trouble of his life. Sitting opposite him, the coldness of his eyes replaced by a troubled frown, he told the story and heard Angus answer kindly, with sympathetic understanding. When he said, "It is probably best under the circumstances that this break has come since things were so unhappy for you all," Dick exclaimed, "Do you mean that you believe in divorce?"

"Not at all. No. But I believe in peace. You said your parents had separated. That is not divorce."

"It is the first step. It means that."

"Not necessarily. Not by any means, not if you do

your part, Richard." The blue eyes were boring into the
black.

" My part? "

" Certainly your part. You and Charlotte will have
to be the magnets that will draw your parents together
again. You, more than Charlotte, for your mother and
father both share Charlotte but you are estranged from
your mother. That can't be. It is for you to make her
feel the tug of your deep affection. Don't let her lose
you. She doesn't want to, and she can't if you play
your part. I said the separation was probably for the
best because absence is salutary. In the silence and solitude of this new arrangement they may see things differently and in time be reconciled and happier than before
because they will be wiser after this — or ought to be."

" I have never fancied myself in the rôle of little
peacemaker — a dove is hardly my style."

Angus smiled. " You are going into the law, I believe?
You will have opportunity for just such service there.
This is something of a test of your quality in that line.
All the odds are yours in this case, however, Dick. You
have elastic youth, courage, hope and all the love of
your parents for their only son. You can do it if you
try."

" I am captain of my soul? You believe that? "

" I do."

Dick's smile was edged with weariness. " I'm afraid
I have not succeeded in convincing you of the reality of
this trouble. It is not new. It is very old. You give
me hope, however. I will try." He paused. " And to-
day — I came here to — to see Frances. Her note said
you would see me instead. Am I not to see Frances at
all? Is it forbidden? "

Richard had recovered his poise. He had adjusted
himself to Angus, the reality, but it had been a wrench to

meet, in place of the man his imagination had created, a personality so compellingly sympathetic, so strongly kind. His very strength had driven to Richard's weakest point and upset him on the eve of his great victory of logic over emotion.

Angus had not answered the question about Frances at once. He crossed an ankle over his knee and fixed his penetrating look on Richard for a moment. Richard sustained the scrutiny with the cool frown he had cultivated.

" It is forbidden for to-day," Angus said at last, " and perhaps for always. My instinct leads me to say for always, unconditionally, but I am going to let you settle that question."

" It is a large question — for me. I can hardly conceive the possibility of refusal."

" Why not? "

" This is the twentieth century, a democracy."

" Politically, yes. And I believe in democracy for both men and women — since that is the direction your thought is taking — when they are of age, but Frances is still in her nonage."

" Must she be twenty-one before she chooses her friends for herself? "

" No." Angus smiled and sobered quickly. " But it was not in an attitude usual in friendship that I saw you last night at the door. Explaining that, Frances has told me that you have very rapidly, it seems to me, advanced into something a great deal closer."

" Yes, that is true." Dick felt the blood creeping into his cheeks. Angus saw it rise, copper red under the dark skin. " It was as surprising to us as to you, Doctor Stevenson. It seems to me to have been one of those things that are to be. It was not premeditated — in a way."

" It is no less serious because it was done impulsively. I can see that you are both convinced that you are experiencing the great passion."

" I know I am. I could not plead my case with you if it were not so. There is a tradition in my family — my father's family, that the Stanhope men love but once — and that forever."

" Ah ! " Angus' exclamation was little more than a quick-drawn breath. " That is as it should be. That is beautiful. An ideal for you, and yet, it might lead you into a mistake. There will be an exception some time, of course."

" Not necessarily."

" Your father? It is true with him, you think? "

" It is. That is his great hurt."

" And you, Richard, am I to understand that you have never been in love before? "

Their eyes met. The twinkle in Angus' called out Dick's reluctant smile. The corners of his lips took their downward dip. " I have to confess that I have been *in* love before, but I have never — loved before. I think you know the difference."

" I do and I respect it. If this really is your great love, Dick, it is most unfortunate; for you and Frances belong to different races, you speak a different language. Frances is as remote from you as a South Sea Islander from an Esquimau. I want you to make no mistake in my meaning. You are agnostic. I am Christian. You are about as welcome as a lover for Frances as an anarchist would be to the court of a monarch. You deny every tenet of our faith, you resist every principle for which we live. I would die to preserve the institutions you would destroy."

Dick had risen. This was the sort of thing he had expected at first. He folded his arms and narrowed his eyes, " I am to understand, then, that it is your faith that separates Frances and me? "

" Rather your agnosticism; that and her youth." Angus too had risen. He leaned one arm on the mantel-shelf. As Dick put his question he turned his scrutiny more directly upon the cold young face before him. " It is enough, I think."

" Such a stand hardly seems compatible with the ideals of Christianity. Not to me, anyway."

" You are not an authority on the ideals of Christianity, are you? "

" I am a student of all religions."

" And a convert to none."

" I find all religions rational. The greatest intelligence for me is in knowing that I do not know."

" You are content with that? "

" There is nothing more. A creator explains creation; the rest is mystery, an unsolvable problem."

" Unless faith solves it. Faith is the key."

" The sort of faith of which you speak I find extremely limited. It leads men into making exact statements as to the nature of God and that nature is not known. Creeds are ignorance. My intelligence refuses to subscribe to any creed."

Angus smiled and moved a little impatiently. " I have heard that so often. First of all creed — credo — means ' I believe,' doesn't it? Everybody believes something. Whatever for you that something is, is your creed. But I suppose you mean that you do not believe the — shorter catechism, for instance." Angus' smile took on a twist of twinkling humor but Dick did not see the look. He frowned tensely and Angus, sobering, continued: " But in the matter of knowing you do not know, I want to call your attention to one phase of your condition of mind. You have finished your Harvard course. It is more than four years since you went there a freshman. When you entered, isn't it true that you gave an open mind to every line of thought except the religious? When you think of the sun, you think of it as ninety-three million miles from the earth; you accept that fact from your professor of astronomy. You believe him when he tells you Mercury is the planet nearest the sun and the swiftest traveling. You respect his method of computing these figures and you accept them.

"You have taken Hugo Munsterberg's word for the facts of psychology (if there are any established facts). In short, you went to Harvard with a mind open and receptive; but not to religion. There you had a closed door. In no branch of knowledge, whether it be an exact science or of a philosophical nature, are you proud to say, ' I do not know ' — except in religion. There was pride in your voice and face when you told me a while ago that you found the greatest intelligence in admitting that you do not know. We could say that about any branch of learning. Nothing is stable. Neither life nor knowledge stand still. There was a time when men would have died rather than say there was a unit smaller than the atom. We know now that there is one smaller. We have had to admit recently a fourth dimension. Shades of our grandfathers! You don't appreciate that as I do. Your lack of faith is, to me, a confession of limitation so sad as to be appalling. You are alive but lacking life.

"Richard, as I go about the city in my work, I feel that I am among people who sleep. They live in the flesh — content not to know; yet not content with that, they ridicule those who try to know, who have glimpsed the beyond and heard a whisper of God's purpose. I am such an one. God is close to me. I reach Him through unceasing prayer. He is my life, my reason for being, my aim, my end. Everything! What takes His place in your life? Where are you going? What is your aim?"

"I am content to make the most of this life as I see it. I want success. I want above all things to think, to work thoughtfully and always toward provision for those I love. Essentially I am a materialist, but what I achieve materially shall be actuated by the highest motives of idealism."

"Pagan Idealism."

Both men stood gazing through the window, seeing nothing of the afternoon glory — white piled clouds shadowed on the fresh green of the opposite lawns, gilded roofs and sun-drenched light quivering above the pavement. They heard no sound save the ticking of the clock, no rustle or stealthy footstep, though Frances, who had crept downstairs and was waiting to dart into the shelter of the dining-room portières, felt that they must hear her hurried breathing. The murmur of their voices had reached her mother's room where she watched in silence as her patient slept, and she had dared to tiptoe within earshot.

She was rapidly recovering her balance after the emotional storm of the night. Her sin seemed less scarlet than it had been when it was fresh. She yearned toward Dick and the gray roadster standing motionless in the sunshine. Certainly it could do no harm to listen to a conversation of such great importance to her. "This day," she thought, "this very hour may be the turning point of my life."

Angus moved and spoke. She saw him turn toward Dick and under cover of the sound Frances made her dash to security. She reached the curtains and softly dropping to her knees, leaned her forehead against the door frame. She risked peeping with one eye and found a vista through the living-room table legs to the two figures standing before the fireplace.

Angus had said, remembering his promise to himself in the night, that he would try and see the younger generation's point of view. " I suppose there is no form of argument more futile than the religious. I can hardly hope to make any headway with you nor could you possibly change me, but I want to make you think, to see my point of view if I can and — in justice to Frances, I want to see your mind. When you outlined your aim in life, you spoke of the highest motives of idealism as if ideals were set by a gage. That which may seem to you a very lofty ideal may, to me, seem pitifully small."

" Certainly, but when a man wants to do right he can pretty safely follow his instincts ! "

" No, that is dangerous doctrine. That is the door to moral anarchy. The instincts of the heart are not superior to the statute book. The statute book founded on the principles of Christianity is the epitome of justice."

" Do you think Christianity is a safe guide ? I have known professing Christians who were rotters and I know you have too. "

" I have indeed. Professing Christianity is as easy for a lying rascal as a saint. But the man who has the love of God in his heart and has given his vows to the church will conform to the statute book, whether it is in harmony with the instincts of his heart or not. To give my daughter's happiness to a man who meant to follow *only his own* instincts would be impossible. If two women loved your sort of man, the instinct of your heart might as honestly choose for the new love as for the wife. Men who live by the statute book rarely go so far in their relationships with other women as to have to choose. They put the brakes upon their first desires. Any other way is unsafe."

When Angus had spoken of Frances as his wife, Dick had wheeled about to stroll toward the upper windows. His nerves were jumping under the repression of words he could not utter. He heard Angus distinctly and felt his eyes upon him. He could not stand so longer, away from his adversary. He must face about. His hands were deep in his pockets, jingling keys and coins. He said, turning and glancing sidewise at Angus, "I could be trusted to be true. The point I want to make is that I should do naturally, without the statute books, as you call them, without being leashed by fear, the right thing by — Frances."

"You think so. You are in love now, but love such as you feel at this moment does not last through marriage. Given a chance, helped, nursed, fought for, it shifts and wanes, all but dies, changes and revives. In the end, if it lives it is because husband and wife have willed that it should live. But this — this is beyond your experience. It does not interest you."

The silence hung. The two men stared at the hearth tile, calmed by the April sun that pulsed hotly from the window panes. Dick resisted the insidious quiet that had descended upon him. He roused himself, sighing.

"I suppose, Doctor Stevenson, if I had come here professing Christianity instead of bringing my honest doubt, you would have received me differently. I should think you would want — of all qualities in any man — honesty first and last, and that given honesty you would know the other qualities were pretty sure to be sound." Dick's voice was impatient. He shoved his hands into his pockets and walked up and down before Angus. "There is no use in our arguing. As you say, we make no headway. As I see the church, it is an obstacle to growth instead of a help."

Anger flamed in Angus' face. He turned on Dick

with outstretched hands that trembled with agitation. But Dick did not see him. He had walked beyond Angus. His head was bowed. He chewed his lips. To himself he raged, " Why do I stay? Why do I care? " and he answered himself, " I won't give up till I score a point he can't answer. I won't give up."

The silence tightened until Angus, clearing his throat and clenching his hands, said quietly, " You would clear out the churches, shut them up? "

" I would."

" And you would doubtless be glad to do away with the good the churches have built up? Make a clean sweep? " This aloud. To himself Angus was saying, " The young ass! The preposterous, rude young ass. If I can keep my patience, give him rope — I'll see him hang himself yet."

Frances, kneeling behind the portières, covered her face with her cold hands. Her cheeks were on fire. " How did Dick dare? How did he ever dare to say such things? "

" I wouldn't shut them up, no," Dick said, " I would turn the churches into libraries and lecture rooms. I would have men speak who knew what they were talking about, men who had enough respect for the idealism of Jesus Christ to be honest with themselves and all Pharisees. I would have these talks cultural. I would raise the intelligence of the people in a war on superstition, and in the end I believe the true spirit of religion — of all religions, for all are rational — would prevail and be reëstablished with worthy leaders. The world is over-fed religiously. A little healthy starvation would be tremendously effective. But for now — *now,* I would sweep it out, the whole church as it stands to-day."

Frances — knowing her father — could feel the passion of Angus' silence. He leaned against the mantel, his narrowing eyes fixed on Richard's face. " He wants to beat him. He can hardly keep from striking him. Oh, this is my fault! This is what I've done! "

When Angus spoke, his voice was quiet. Dick, walk- ing back and forth, back and forth, his head bowed, his eyes on the rug, was insensitive to the menace behind his words.

" And these worthy leaders who would arise? What of them? "

" To accomplish anything, the leaders would have, lit- erally, to be leaders." Dick looked up. He took his right hand from his pocket and gesticulated dramatically. " That's the greatest trouble with your church to-day. It lacks men of personality, of brain, of leadership. With sheep in the pulpit the people have lost interest. If Henry Ward Beecher and Campbell Morgan and Billy Sunday — men with tremendous personalities — came to Detroit, you'd have no cause to wonder what is wrong with the church. People are hungry for religion, Doctor Stevenson. I suppose the fact that I think about it so much shows that there is a hunger in me somewhere. The average person has to worship something. They only lack leadership. The standards of intelligence are so high these days compared to the old times when reli- gion flourished that people are bored by the preachers they hear. They can stay at home and read, in any one of half a dozen magazines on their table, better and more thoughtful stuff than the pulpit can give them. And ministers — ! I know a chap who'll graduate from theo- logical seminary this June. He's a finished product, ready for the pulpit, and his voice, his personality, his manner as a speaker are the poorest thing about him. He'll stand up before people as intelligent as he is, and try to put his zeal, his sincerity, his faith across in a sing- song voice, with an apologetic manner. He'll fail; he'd fail as a trial lawyer, as an actor; he'd fail anywhere that personality is needed."

Dick stopped, stared straight into Angus' tense face and said quietly, " I suppose you resent that — but it's the truth."

" I do resent it. I resent it with all my soul and body. It's merely another way of blaming the church for the sins of the world. In all the talk as to what's wrong with the war-mad world, everybody is blamed except the sinners." Angus shut the clamp of repression on his tongue. Arguments, sharp retorts crowded to his lips. He seethed with passionate denial, but he could not speak. There was truth in the boy's statement, but it was not for Angus to admit it. Watching Angus' white face, Dick knew he had come as near scoring as he ever would. Angus had seen the truth but could not admit it. To admit that the church lacked leaders of personality and magnetism would be to let down a degree more of his resistance than was possible for his nature. He said, " Mr. Stanhope, you are not merely careless of religion, indifferent as youth often is indifferent to the profounder aspects of life; you are not ignorantly prejudiced, you are thoughtfully, intelligently agnostic; antagonistic to both Christianity and the church and probably also — I say this deliberately because I have found it to be the third leg of the triangle usually — extremely easy in your moral life. I find you utterly unworthy of even Frances' friendship and I feel, after this talk, no hesitation whatever in asking you not to try to see Frances again. I shall forbid her to have any communication with you and I shall enforce obedience."

" You accuse me of immorality! Do you think I can let that stand with Frances' father? "

" Convince me that I am wrong and I will make my apology. I have no desire to think ill of you."

" I don't know how to convince you. You would not honor my word and I have nothing else but my word."

" I will take your word. If you can look me in the eyes and tell me — you are immaculate — I will believe you."

Angus' steadfast eyes had softened but they continued, relentlessly, the gaze that ripped through the veils of deceit. Dick's eyes wavered and fell.

" There is a vast gulf between the word morality, used ethically, and the fact of being immaculate. I am moral. I have a moral conscience. There is not a man of my age anywhere that is cleaner."

A pitying smile crept into Angus' face. He sighed heavily and passed his hand across his eyes. " Ah," he said, shaking his head, " moral, but not immaculate! How we juggle words. And if Frances were moral, but not immaculate, it would be perfectly acceptable to you? " Angus' voice was very low. He spoke with deliberation. " Richard, I came to this talk to-day willing to learn from you if I could. Willing to listen to the voice of your generation if it should speak through you to me and — I have learned. For one thing, I have learned why Ingersoll and his kind are dear to you. You have lived according to the senses. You have believed that there is nothing more than the senses. You have indulged yourself. It has been an offense to your splendid intelligence — but deliberately walking on the lower planes of virtue, it has been pleasant, a solace to your protesting soul, to read convincing arguments to the effect that no man knows whether there be a higher. I see in you a great opportunity gone astray." Angus stepped nearer Dick, put a hand on his shoulder and compelled his eyes to turn from their tense gazing through the window to meet his own. " With your gifts, your personality, your intelligence, you could be a leader in God's service.

God wants you to be one of his captains, one of his generals. Can't you get the vision? If you can't glimpse it now, won't you try? Isn't its bigness, its very difficulty a challenge to you? You're a fighter. I want you — for God." A shining mist like silver light shone in Angus' face and eyes. His voice vibrated with feeling. The hand on Dick's shoulder seemed to lift as it gripped. " The thing I have learned from you to-day, Dick, is the desperate need of your generation for Jesus Christ. You need Him as the pagan philosophers needed Him. When He came with His gospel of unselfishness, their world died — and His was born. He is the greatest fact in recorded history." Angus' voice ceased but the shining look held, and the smile, and the hand on Richard's shoulder.

Dick moved and the hand slipped off and dropped to Angus' side. He turned toward the door, looked for his hat and found it, hesitated on the threshold and glanced back. Angus was standing where he had left him, motionless. Dick took a quick step forward and Angus offered his hand. It was accepted and in silence they gripped a moment before Dick returned to the door and passed out.

CHAPTER VII

I

WHEN Angus told Frances the story of his talk with Richard he did not know of her eavesdropping. He had remained in the living room a few minutes after the door closed on his young antagonist and had not heard Frances when she rose from her knees and crept upstairs to her room. He found her door locked and wondered that, true to her frank young curiosity, she was not waiting on tiptoe for a report of their interview.

Her eyes were darker than he had ever seen them when she admitted him, and she sat on the side of her bed looking at a handkerchief she twisted nervously as he told her their conversation. He went over it carefully for her, slowly, making an effort to be fair, and when he repeated Dick's analysis of the church situation he said, " He classifies me with the others, of course, one of a type who fail because we have not large enough qualifications for our job. It is not the people's fault that the church suffers by their indifference but the clergy's. He would do away with the whole institution, sweep it out. Frances, there could be no other answer to such a stand on his part than the one I made. I have forbidden him ever to come here or to communicate with you in any way. Over him, however, I have no authority. It is to you I look for obedience. He is not a fit friend for you." Angus leaned toward her. He had spoken the last words deliberately, hoping to draw her look upward, to meet his own. But she did not lift her eyes. She pressed the handkerchief against her lips. He saw the quivering of her chin. "This is hard for you, but it is all part of the disobedience of last night. You will forget him. You can do it. I still have faith in your loyalty and purity of motive. You will not try to do what you know would bring so much sorrow on us who love you."

He waited, his keen, clear blue gaze on her face. All the love of his heart for this headstrong child was in his look. And while he waited, Frances waited. Surely he would go on and tell her that most vital part of the story, which he had not yet mentioned; that last terrible revelation.

She lifted her eyes. "Then it is our faith — and his unbelief — *only that,*" she asked, "that is to keep us apart?"

"Isn't that enough?"

"If you liked him — you might admire him enough as a man to want to help me change him." She would make Angus tell if she could.

"I think I wouldn't hold to that hope if I were you. A man — of his type — Francie, is more apt to hurt your beautiful faith than to accept it for himself. He is clever, convincing. I feel that he would do you more harm than you could do him good."

He wouldn't tell! He wouldn't hurt her so. He loved her enough to keep Dick's image clean in her thought. He staked everything on her loyalty to her own blood. He had faith enough in her — yet — for that. If now she disobeyed he would still hold the secret he guarded for later use against Dick. Impulsively she promised herself never to make that a necessity. Rising quickly, she went to him and he received her into his arms.

"I would have spared you this. I would have saved you from the world's cruelty. It is life that is hurting you, Francie, not I. You believe that?"

"Yes." She did believe it. Dick himself had hurt her, not Angus. Angus, guardian of Dick's honor in her sight, had put a new twist in her relationship to the two men. She pondered it. In her own heart she classified them the Christian gentleman and the pagan. "When Christ was born there were pagan gentlemen — plenty. Dick's sort of fineness, his culture, is as old as civilization. Father's is the new sort Christ gave us."

II

Between the interval of her great experience and her trip to New York, she was very busy with the closing of the school term and preparation for her journey, but not so busy that there was not always room for Richard in her thought. She carried him there consciously with heartache and longing that made their marks in her face and checked the gay impulsiveness of her manner. She matured rapidly and on her eighteenth birthday she sat long in revery upon the imponderable mystery of life, the whence and wherefore of her course. Egypt she clung to for its promise of heart's ease in adventure, new scenes, new life, new faces. She planned to give the summer to special study in preparation for her work.

Richard wrote her long argumentative letters of love and pleading.

"You have been too sheltered. You don't know life, Frances. When you meet men and women of the great world, you will be wiser, less keen to judge — " and, " I am engaged to you just as truly as if you were not estranged from me. You are free, but I am not nor desire to be." And again he pleaded with her to suspend judgment until years brought the knowledge that would make her fit to judge. " You have been shocked by the interpretation your father has put on my honesty. I love you for it too, strange to say, and my faith in your love gives me hope that you will change, understand, and tell me that you understand."

To this Frances made answer. "You have shocked me in two ways so terribly that I feel my father was right. We are of different races. We see things differently. I can never forget what you confessed — my great wonder is that a man of your sort should want a girl of my sort."

Reading this, Richard knew Frances to be but a precocious child. " She will change. She will understand and change. Strange that she should comprehend archæology and not the great facts in the daily lives of men ! "

III

Frances had not been long in New York until she realized that her brothers were watching her with silent questioning. They gave her opportunity to unburden herself, which she ignored. She would not tell Richard's secret. To her it was shame that she shared with him remotely through the bondage of her love, for it never occurred to her to deny her love. It had always been there. It would always be there. She found it hard to resist the appeal of Jimmie's eyes and smile. He understood that there was trouble. He wanted to share it. It was he who in the end won a measure of her confidence.

They started out one evening dressed in their most fashionable light apparel to drift with the current of summer pleasure-seekers; John and his fiancée, Edith Hetherington; Jimmie and Frances. From the boys' apartment they strolled down Fifth Avenue, lingering before the perennially fascinating shop windows, to Enrico's, where the smell of broiling chicken, cigarettes and garlic were accepted smilingly as appetizing forerunners to the ceremony of dining. They laughed and chatted through five courses as they played a game of spotting the sightseers and, in the hunt, discovered a famous actor who was observing them.

" He's watching the people too," Edith said. " I wonder what he is thinking about us. He's been staring. I noticed him before I recognized him. Wouldn't you like to ask him what he thinks of us? "

Said Jimmie, " I know without asking. I can tell by his face. He thinks you and John are a charming American couple from the Middle West, showing your two high-school children the sights of New York."

Edith made a small face at him and rose. " That's enough to break up the party. Let's leave before he sees the truth. I wouldn't want to disillusion him. Come, children."

She suggested the Battery for the twilight hour. They would watch the strollers and the boats.

The breeze from the river bound them to the spot till long after dark. They heard the orchestra of the city dimly and forgot it in the nearer interest of lighted ships and strolling lovers who waited impatiently for the deepening of the long June twilight.

Leaving John and Edith alone on their bench, Jimmie drew Frances' arm through his and led her away for a walk close to the water's edge.

" I'm glad you're here, Francie," he began, when they were beyond chance of being heard. " I can't get used to sharing John. Old nut to desert like this! "

" Oh, now," Francie protested. " He's in love. What else could he do? You'll have to find a girl for yourself, Jimmie."

" I have you, little one, to love; and a new mistress

for my devotion. Shall I tell you about that? I want you to know. I can't tell John."

Frances' heart set up a tumult of rapid beating. She had misunderstood. She thought at once, " Dick. Now Jimmie! It can't be. Not Jimmie. Dick couldn't be right in believing that other men, nice men — like Jimmie — "

" Tell me," she whispered. Jimmie heard the small voice and thought it the effect of the magical evening. He spoke lower with long pauses. His arm pressed hers.

" See the lighted ships out there gliding through the harbor gates? See the Goddess of Liberty with her torch? How still it is here, how safe and peaceful and good to live in. Beyond the sea lies Europe, Francie, reeking with gunpowder, dying, I think, her long, slow death and not so slow either, if we don't go to her aid. I'm going over. I'm going soon. I wish I hadn't had to wait so long."

" Jimmie — and that — war — Europe is your new — "

" My new devotion, yes. I'm ashamed of my country's stupidity. We have eyes but we see not, ears and we hear not. I have long hoped America would go in, but we haven't, and I can't wait. I'm going over. I'll enlist in Canada — after this little visit with you."

He paused and they stood silent against a group of spiles. Frances' quick, firm clasp on his arm was her only answer. As yet war meant so little to her, a great, vague, terrible fact, but it caught her emotionally in response to the thrill in Jimmie's voice. Her thought had gone on another line, pursuing the first mistaken impression she had gotten from his words. She had linked Jimmie with Dick for a moment, wondering. Almost she had hoped to find Jimmie, her idol, no higher than Dick, her love.

"I haven't told mother yet, or father," Jimmie was saying. "No use till it's all settled. My firm know and approve. America will be in soon, Francie. We can't stay out long. That chap you're dreaming about these days when your eyes are dark and misty will be over there before long — if he's old enough." He paused.

"He is."

"Oh, well. War — hell and damnation. I didn't realize it till last summer."

"Tell me. Why haven't I realized it, Jimmie?"

"Don't know. Few Americans have. Last summer John and I went up into the Hudson Bay country, you know. We were just out for vacation fun and adventure. We canoed all day, making long portages, worked like sledge dogs, breathed the keen, piny air; ate enormously; lay around our camp fires at night and watched the stars. It was great and wonderful. Every step we went North was a step nearer life and away from artificiality. The life of the winds of heaven. I loved it. I could have stayed forever; the right woman, work and health up there where nothing counts but ability and character. It would be a life worth living, no flimflam stuff to waste time. Just the essentials and heaps of the poetry. One night we took a traveling Englishmen into camp, a rugged old fellow buying up lumber for his government. He talked war; about us and our stupendous ignorance of it all. He said we were nursing our ignorance under a dollar mark. He wasn't a sorehead. He seemed to understand pretty well. He said, 'If you few individuals see things as they are, in their proper values, why don't you prove it by coming over? How can you go laughing on through the weeks and months and years of that hell over there without offering help?' Words like that he said and it got me. I had resisted him at first, explained, defended. I changed fronts and told him I'd come over."

Francie interrupted, squeezing Jimmie's arm. "Oh, good for you! Oh, Jimmie, I'm glad. I want you to. And I want to go. Take me too, Jimmie. I could work. I could learn nursing, anything. I can do anything I try to do."

"I know you can. I know that, but you aren't cut out to be a nurse. Why not stay right here and influence the chaps you know to go over? That one who's old enough to go — the dream god."

"Oh — the dream god — Dick —" And that was the way it came about — the telling of the story of Dick and the great and terrible gulf between them.

IV

Jimmie found an unoccupied bench and they sat very close together as she talked. Jimmie had stirred all the romantic hunger in her heart. She felt again somewhat as she had felt on that night in April on the clubhouse porch with the river at her feet, lapping the spiling, gurgling like a living thing with rapture for her happiness. She felt again the pressure of Dick's hands and heard his voice as he said, "I can still feel your fingers clinging to mine — I want them again that way — Frances." Lights were mirrored in the river, soft wind blew, the dome of the sky shimmered above their heads; she was dizzy for a while with the beauty and thrill of life, nameless, illusive beauty like the blue-gray mistiness of the night. Out there, beyond the sea, over near the dawn, was the great magnet war attracting the steel of youth. All the metal in her character felt the pull of it and longed to be drawn closer.

Through the stir of emotion that ran in her veins,

Frances talked quietly of Dick. She sketched his handsome face and compelling personality, trying not to be superlative and schoolgirlishly rapturous. But Jimmie heard the tremor of her voice. He remembered Dick well, admitted the charm of his sort, smiled at his memory of the Stanhope-Stevenson feud. Toward the end he turned more directly to his sister and fixed his eyes on her face. Lovely she was, simple and clear-eyed. How fearless she looked as she told him of facing their father's wrath at midnight. Her voice went on; he could see the old home as it must have looked when Dick called, the battered piano and its heaped-up music. Memories stirred and hurt. She was telling him of her eavesdropping, the discussion she had heard and, at the end, after giving Dick's analysis of the church situation, she made a sudden finish. "That's about all. You see, it's hopeless."

Jimmie frowned into the dimness. "Hopeless! Tommyrot. It's just begun. Get busy and make him think your way. You're on the right side; he's overboard. You can make him come part way over. Dear child, you don't have to agree absolutely on religion to be happy. He's Protestant, at least. He admits a God. You can do the rest if you try."

Frances was silent.

"Are you leaving it there?" By his voice Frances knew he thought her love a small and childish thing, not worth considering.

"No, *he* didn't leave it there," she cried, challenged. "Father accused him of — easy morals as part of his stand against the church and religion. He denied it and I was convinced. I believed him — but father — father pressed and he couldn't deny it — the way father put it. He admitted — by his silence, things I can never forget."

"I suppose he claimed to be moral but couldn't look

dad in the eyes! Well, I get the distinction." How matter-of-fact was Jimmie!

Frances had expected a different answer. She had supposed Jimmie would turn against Dick immediately when he knew. His words suggested tolerance. She stared at him and heard herself say merely, " Oh."

" You don't? " Jimmie asked.

" How is there a distinction? I try to see but I can't." She put a hand to her face and closed her eyes. " It's like saying ' I'm white but I have colored blood in my veins.' The white skin means nothing if the colored blood is there. And yet all the time I seem to be waiting for something to make me understand. You see — " she spoke slowly, " when a girl has had you — you, Jimmie, and John and father, and has been brought up on Sir Galahad, any degree less is — hardly thinkable." Jimmie made an impatient gesture. She touched his hand. " Of course, I know Sir Galahad is a long way back in the past, but you aren't. If one man can be what you are, nothing less than that will meet — my dream."

Jimmie twisted around on the bench and leaned forward, his elbows on his knees. He held his stick between his hands and tapped the pavement with it restlessly. What to say. What advice. He was too long silent.

" Jimmie, say something. You're thinking so hard I can hear it tick."

" There is so much to say. I see all around this problem. I don't know how to advise you. Life is so complex. Your love might be so tremendous it would ride over every restriction you yourself had placed upon it. It's a grave thing to lay hands on another's heart affairs. For you," Jimmie twisted about again and looked down into her luminous eyes, " I want the cleanest and best, the bravest and truest, but your love may not choose that way. Women are inexplicable. I don't understand them.

They find it so easy to forgive. How they do it! I have seen it so often; women I would have called high-minded, proud, forgiving things no man would stand for. I can't understand even you, of course, because you're one of 'em." He smiled and touched her chin. " You are not in the least unreasonable in demanding the utmost cleanliness in the man you love. It can be done. Men can keep immaculate if they want to. It's a fight, a constant battle, but it can be done. It is done more than the worldly world believes, I think. Many a manly chap is fastidious, innately shy. There are a few monogamists in the world and a good many fellows whose ideals reach as far as personal cleanliness. But it isn't usual. I have known chaps who 'fessed up to me as if it were a guilty secret, that they were immaculate. They'd never tell another fellow whom they knew was not. The sort who don't put up the fight say it can't be done, is impossible, absurd, or a proof of being — effeminate. They believe it and it isn't entirely their fault. They don't know it can be done."

" Whose fault is it? " Frances asked, still gazing at him.

" Pretty much everybody's. Their parents most of all. Their fathers have told their mothers it's a losing fight. Their mothers, like the sheep women often are with the men they love, believe it. Great heavens, Francie, you women do sometimes swallow bait, hook, sinker and all. Fatuous credulity! You see, the boy starts out without any strong, clean teaching from his parents. Mother is sweet and sad; son hates to do anything she wouldn't like, but, being only sweet, she hasn't given him any sort of moral foundation to stand on. Fathers — even the best of them — talk with embarrassment to their sons, say a few things they only half believe and give advice they didn't take themselves when they were young, and don't expect their sons to take. And there you are. What can you expect? The boy goes out into life and meets temptation. He finds the nice girls extremely indifferent to his moral character. They thrill over a dark past and make fun of a chap who has modesty enough to blush on occasion. That sort isn't popular. Girls in their abysmal ignorance help the bad work along."

"I know that's so," Francie agreed. On this point she was wise. She knew.

"I think—" Jimmie gave his attention to the stick again, scowling at its tip. "I don't like to say this, but I think the sweet" (he said the word with exaggerated unction) "kind of mother does about as much harm as good in this world. The truest aphorism I know is that every strong man has had a strong mother. The branches of a tree can't grow wider than its roots. If the roots are weak the branches are weak. I dislike sweet girls. I want them like our mother, strong, fine, gentle. A gentlewoman is the biggest power in the world. A sweet woman — bah, I hate 'em. They shouldn't have sons. Think how gentle mother is, gentlest woman in the world and strong as braided silk. John and I don't deserve credit for our winning fight in the sort of thing we're talking about. We had father's kind of teaching, an intimate personal God — and we needed Him — home discipline that was discipline, not soppy advice — and mother. Do you remember that maid we had — Ella? Mother used her case to teach us the greatest lesson of our lives. I'll never forget her face when she showed us the clothes Ella had for her baby — little bits of things, so little you'd hardly think a human being could get into them — and mother's talk on injustice. You see, Francie, if John and I couldn't look dad in the eyes on that question we'd deserve what we'd get."

They were silent several moments. The stick swung

like a pendulum from Jimmie's hands. Francie could not see his face he leaned so far forward, his elbows on his knees. She watched the stick. At last she said shyly, " I suppose by all that you mean that there might be some excuse for Dick."

" Yes. I'm sure there is. I'm the last fellow to blame another chap for being different. Mrs. Stanhope is the sort of tree that could hardly have very wide branches. The old man's all right and Dick may have sensed his mother's weakness and taken his father for an example. If he did, he found nothing that would keep him off the primrose path probably. I don't know though. That's just my guess. Dick may have a fine moral conscience. He may be fastidious, and yet there might be that in his memory that would make it impossible to look dad in the eyes. But really, you know, he had courage. He might even have been excused for lying at that moment. Credit him with that. One thing certain, people of our sort have got to be big enough, generous enough to be tolerant. That's one of the several jokers in Christianity. Christ wants us to be gentle in our judgments, but gentle judgment makes the sinner bolder and worse. I think about it so much and wish I could be the fellow to work out the new philosophy — interpreting the teachings of Christ that would answer the present need of the world."

" It wouldn't be Presbyterian? " Francie asked, mildly surprised.

Jimmie laughed. " Not entirely," he said dryly.

" What would it be? "

" It would be as strong as Presbyterianism. That's what keeps the old religions alive. They are strong, hard to believe, hard to understand, the deuce to live up to. People want strength in religion and medicine, something that tastes so bad they don't forget it once that they've had

it." He laughed. " It would be more literally according
to Christ's teaching than the hardest of the old faiths
though. It would teach literally that the power of Christ
was a healing power for soul and body both. It would
put the soft pedal on the physical. We're all beginning
to understand that we eat too much, for instance. You
know the old joke about the alimentary canal being so
named because most of the human ailments come from
the overstuffed stomach? And the saying that we dig our
graves with our teeth? In my new philosophy we would
make less of food, we would eat less and more simply.
Christ walking through the fields took some grains of
wheat and ate them just as they were. Bread and fish
was another meal, bread and wine — you remember. If
religion could solve the great eating problem, simplify it,
the sickness problem and healing, the over-population
problem and sustenance problems would take care of
themselves. Then — and of greatest importance —
would be the stress on the spiritual side of life, not
spiritual as expressed in prayer meetings Wednesday
nights, but daily, hourly spirituality to such a degree that
all life was tuned up to the spiritual instead of down to
the physical. To-day our world is physical ninety per
cent and spiritual ten per cent. Christ tried to make us
see that we must be spiritual ninety per cent and physical
ten per cent. It can be done. That's what people want,
Francie. They are tired of a church that tells them it is
more blessed to give than to receive. They won't go on
sitting in the pews giving their attention, their time, their
support, their interest, when they get so little in return.
They want the power of Christ to heal their diseases,
physical as well as mental and moral. They want death
really robbed of its sting through the triumph of the
spiritual over the grave. Christ said all these things
would come to pass if we followed Him. People to-day

want to follow Him that far — or not at all. And it *can be done*. It's all in the way we think and believe."

"Father wouldn't agree with you. Does he know you think these things?"

"No. What's the use? His way suits him. I wouldn't offend him by offering my thought. Any system that succeeds as dad's has succeeded with him should be let alone where he is concerned. Unfortunately his followers aren't so successful. If I am ever as fine as dad, I can do some talking. I'd like to, for as I see things now, civilization will certainly be lost, unless men, women, races, nations apply the eleventh and greatest commandment. The Golden Rule is the only solution to the disease we call life at present."

He leaned back and laid his stick across his lap. Frances looked up into his face, expecting to see it illumined. It was not. It was just Jimmie, scowling into the twilight, his square chin and straight mouth tensely earnest. Frances wondered suddenly if Christ himself hadn't had just such a thoughtful, strong face, if he hadn't scowled too over the very problems that Jimmie pondered. She said, "And yet, believing that, you are willing to go to Europe and kill a few Germans."

"Yep," said Jimmie unheroically. "I am, I want to. There is no other way now."

They had gotten far from Dick in their talk. Frances' thought came back to him but Jimmie's did not. Her lips moved. To herself she was saying, "He thinks there may be excuse for Dick. He advises tolerance. He doesn't blame him entirely but he thinks women are sheep for forgiving as much as they do. He wants me to be gentle and strong, not sweet." There was no one thing in it all to tie to. Jimmie had solved nothing. "You have no advice for me then — about Dick?" she said aloud at last.

"Yes." Jimmie sighed, rousing from his reverie. "Yes, I have. Judge not. Be charitable, but don't cheapen yourself. Hold yourself just as high as you always have. Either your love will prove itself big enough to forgive, or your ideals will be big enough to cure your love. Time will show you. But remember this, if you decide you can't give him up; if you love him enough to forgive him, then be sure your forgiveness is big enough to include forgetting. Don't marry him unless you can forget that you have forgiven — and never throw it up to him."

CHAPTER VIII

I

BEFORE the year was out, Jimmie was in France and John in Plattsburg. After that idle month in New York, life had caught the Stevenson family in a vortex of change.

Antony Remington returned to Detroit to help Frances arrange for a special course of study in preparation for her work with him. He wanted her sooner than he had at first thought, for war had changed his plans. He would not return to Egypt at once but would lecture in the universities. He needed a secretary.

She was eager to begin the new life. The action of the Second Church in reducing Angus' salary had made college impossible for her, though Jimmie and John insisted there was no need for her to give it up. But she could accept nothing from men called to war, she said, and the very nature of her life and work with Doctor Remington would be an education.

But in all the change the only real trouble came through the church. Murmurs of unrest and dissatisfaction had begun to press upon Angus. He was quick to feel it. Small criticism reached his ears, his plans for work were disregarded and others substituted in a way he had never before been obliged to endure.

The history of any church is a history of disagreement, compromise and small wars. There had been less of this in Angus' parish than is usual because his leadership had never been challenged. Many of those who, until

now, had accepted his edicts, were moving away. The
far north side called; the Indian village offered much to
the prosperous. The old Piety Hill district had become
congested. The change came about rapidly. The war in
Europe had brought prosperity to America. Detroit business boomed. The manufacture of motors was a twenty-
four-hour round of achievement. Trucks, speed boats,
army transports, Fords were ordered by the thousand.
The supply was not equal to the demand. Small clerks in
the offices of the factories, quiet members of Angus'
church, leaped into salaries that fulfilled their dreams.
In a single fall thirty families moved from the Second
Church district and Angus, surveying his congregation
from the old pulpit, knew that the flower of his flock had
gone. Few but the thorns were left. He found himself
only nominal leader of a handful of small-souled members whose church was their social playground, their
political arena, their intellectual center. The life of the
institution shrank to their measure and it was very small
indeed.

Returning from a session meeting one night, Angus
walked the floor of the living room. "My hour has
struck," he was saying to himself. "My day has ended.
I irritate them with my leadership. They want a young
man, new ideas, new methods. They want play, not
spirituality. Church suppers and bazaars, games and pic-
nics. A social center — I shall resign."

During Jimmie's visit he made no mention of his
decline. It was enough for the boy and his mother that
war was to separate them. His sorrow could wait.

It was on his seventieth birthday that he wrote his
letter of resignation. It was very simply worded and
unemotional. He reviewed the happy years of his service and asked that only the good that he had done
might be remembered.

It caused a small tempest in a small teapot. Angus had expected nothing less. It was, he knew, but part of the ceremony of the severed connection. Very soon, to his ears, by ways round about, came news of a search for his successor. He was to be young, modern and "not so expensive." Through the strong influence of a group of old members who could not endure that less should be done for Angus, whom they dearly loved, he was named pastor emeritus at a salary of one thousand dollars a year, the new status to begin in ninety days.

During those ninety days only the ever-strengthening nearness of his God kept Angus up. His pride was in rags. His heart all but broke. To the world there was no evidence of this. It seemed a natural enough arrangement. Doctor Stevenson at seventy had retired "after some thirty years of splendid service. He would live in Detroit and, as pastor emeritus of the church he had built and guided through the vicissitudes of more than a quarter-century, he would continue to bless and minister to his people. But a younger man would carry the burden in his stead." The newspapers were very complimentary. They dubbed Angus the bishop of Detroit, the city's father confessor and congratulated him, Detroit, the Second Church and everybody generally on everything generally. Angus took it all standing, straight-backed, high-headed, a smile in his keen blue eyes. To himself he thought the word failure. He was old, no good any more. A burden. He had wanted to die in harness but at seventy he was young — and not wanted.

To Mary and Frances, the pinch of the reduced income was of first concern. The thousand dollars a year would not be their entire income, for Angus would still preach and lecture and write. Old Maggie, twisting an apron sash, vowed eternal fealty and said she would rather stay

for less wages than leave. From France, when he heard
it, Jimmie wrote that his firm would send his parents a
check each month, " just a small one to remind you I am
to be counted in until I get back to my work and provide
a wallow of luxury for your old age."

Frances gave her days and part of her nights to study
in a feverish desire to be ready to join Doctor Remington.

II

When April brought the great event of America's entry
in the war, Frances was nearing the end of her intensive
training.

She heard through Tubby that Dick had said he would
be the first man to enlist upon the declaration of war.
He, too, like John, had been at Plattsburg and expected
to be made an officer at once. Frances tried to write to
him on the night of the anniversary of their meeting at
the Boat Club. She was alone in her room, studying,
fighting her desire to put into writing all her longing and
heartache. It was her daily struggle and on that night,
when memory was sharpened by the fact of the anniversary, the desire was too strong for her resistance. But,
with her pen on the paper, she could not find the words
she wanted to tell him all she would have said. Her love,
her dreams, her hope were all for him; there could be no
other and she could not relinquish the belief that somewhere, if she waited, all would be made right. As she
wrote, seeing his handsome, drooping profile, the idealized
Amerindian type of his features, high cheek bones,
bronzed skin, the flash of his eyes and teeth, tears and a
sense of futility stayed her hand. Why should she hope
on for a bridge across the gulf that separated them?
Why should she wait and what for? Even if, as Jimmie
had thought possible, they should overcome the religious

difficulties, there was that other thing, that unspeakable other thing she could not forgive. How could it be that she still loved Dick? Were women like that in life as well as in books? She had always thought sin was death to love — that kind of sin — that kind of love. But here was she living the mystery, proving the truth of the fictionists.

Dick's face was not always distinct in her memory. Often it was blurred and refused to be recalled. But to-night his presence was vividly with her. She paused in her writing and glanced over her shoulder. The little familiar room looked strange, for he was there, very near, very clear. She seemed to look directly into his troubled eyes. She saw the droop of his lips in a tremulous smile. For a long moment she held the vision, breathless lest it vanish. "Are you near me?" her heart asked. "Are you here in Detroit — near me?" Unkind quirk of her stubborn mind: around Dick's face she saw other faces, lewd, leering, tawdry. Women, vaguely comprehended, but vividly imagined. They surrounded him, passed between him and her and blotted him out of the picture. Ignorance is the father of cruelty; Frances' own imagination was the instrument of her torture. Tears blinded her. She snatched up her letter and tore it into tiny bits, tossing it from her. It showered, like enormous snowflakes, on the floor about her. She hurried from the room and down. She would go out into the night and try, through the velvety darkness with the help of the stars and the April winds, to recapture the mood of a year ago, — to remember only the beauty and none of the hurt; to dwell upon the good and the future and forget the past.

She took a coat from the hall closet and ran out on the porch. It was very dark. There was no moon. The sky was black. Only the street lights shone in that hour.

Walking rapidly up Second Avenue she felt crowded upon, watched. The street was filled with motors; a continuous procession whirled by. There was no solitude any more. Everywhere the pleasure car carried its idlers. She stood irresolute on the corner, trying to remember a quiet spot where she might be alone with the night. She longed for the whisper of leaves or water, for the stillness of the stars — clouds traveling across vast spaces of the heavens would carry her spirit with them into the far reaches of beautiful to-morrows.

As she hesitated, rain fell on her face, a few drops at first, then more until she turned and made her way back down the street toward home. By the time she had reached Hancock Avenue the rain had settled to a fine mist. It shone like dew on her hair when she passed under a street light. She lifted her face to receive it and welcomed the cool moisture on her lowered eyelids. She wondered, " Why do I run from rain when I have a need for the elements, wind and clouds and the light of the stars? Why isn't rain a solace as well?" Answering her own question, she turned about impulsively and walked east. The menace of dampness had driven many motors from the streets. The wet asphalt reflected the lights; the moisture carried sounds to Frances that stabbed her with loneliness; a piano near an open door sent out strange, wistful music to which presently a voice was added.

Frances paused, head on one side, listening. A baritone — illusively familiar. She thought of Jimmie; he had sung that same music and with the association she placed it. The " Persian Garden "! The words came to her. Unconsciously she had memorized them.

The bass ceased and a contralto voice continued and was succeeded by a soprano, then a tenor. There was an abrupt end of the music and a burst of laughter. Frances heard a woman say, " Begin there again, Bob, and make your recitative more impressive."

The bass began and Frances heard every word as clearly as if she were in the room with the singers.

Myself when young did eagerly frequent
Doctor and Saint and heard great argument —
.   .   .   .   .   but evermore
Came out by that same door wherein I went.
With them the Seed of Wisdom did I sow,
And with my own Hand labored it to grow,
And this was all the Harvest that I reap'd, —
I came like Water, and like Wind I go.
Why all the Saints and Sages who discuss'd
Of the two Worlds so learnedly, are thrust
Like foolish Prophets forth; their words to scorn
Are scatter'd, and their Mouths are stopt with Dust.

Then came the recitative that Bob had been told to make impressive. Frances thought he obeyed with the greatest possible success.   The words thrilled her.

Ah, make the most of what we yet may spend,
Before we, too, into the Dust descend.

And as if that were not sufficient warning for the thoughtless waster, the contralto took up the advice:

When You and I behind the Veil are past,
Oh, but the long, long while the World shall last.

Frances stood thinking while the piano wove strange minor ecstasies about her. " When You and I behind the Veil are past, Oh, but the long, long while the World shall last," she repeated slowly, sensing each word. She caught her breath, Dick, her love and the fleeting moment of life, so brief, slipping from her while she yearned in bondage.

The tenor sang:

Alas that Spring should vanish with the Rose,
That Youth's sweet-scented Manuscript should close,
The Nightingale that in the branches sang,
Ah, whence, and whither flown again — who knows?

His sweet voice died and the dripping of rain echoed
its sadness. Frances walked slowly on, but the piano
followed her, and the poet's summing up of life:

The Worldly Hope men set their Hearts upon
Turns Ashes, or it prospers; and anon,
Like Snow upon the desert's dusty Face,
Lighting a little hour or two — is gone.

There was more that she did not hear and then, as if
flung after her through the night, a prod to her dalliance,
came the last clear notes, "Waste — not — your hour."
Ah! Her rapid steps ceased and she turned to look
back in the direction of the voice. "Waste — not —
your hour." It seemed to echo through the wet whispering of rain as words cried out through tears. A voice
from the infinite surely, an answer to her bewildered questioning, this admonition of the great philosopher. All
her emotion surged toward Dick. It mattered not how
great his fault in the past; she loved him, he was hers and
this, their hour, was passing. She leaned in the direction
of the music but there was no further sound. She was
alone in the street with the stillness and soft odors of
wet earth. Turning, she walked on again, making an
effort to recall the Rubaiyat as Jimmie had read it to her.
She had not understood it then as she did now on this
night, when it had spoken to her troubled heart, though
she had thought she did. She reflected that before the
hour when Dick had taken her and loved her into con-

sciousness of life she had understood nothing at all —
nothing worth while, though she had been living with
those who were perceiving and weighing. Jimmie, jolly
and affectionate, had been wading through just such deep
streams of thought as these that eddied about her. Jimmie had wondered and doubted and questioned and —
decided. At some time he had quietly cut loose from his
father's theology, as she was cutting loose now.
She caught her breath over the admission. She had
dared to recognize her doubt and its right to recognition. The cage door swung a little outward, invitingly, and Frances heard again, "Waste not —
your hour." Her hour and Dick's! Perhaps it had
come — and gone. Again the thought of Jimmie on the
Battery bench steadied her racing emotions. How calm
he was, and fair when he had assumed quite simply that
there might be another way of looking at things than the
Presbyterian way. Wonderful Jimmie, whose balance
was rarely disturbed. He had told her she must not
judge. Would he advise her to seize her hour? If he
loved as she loved, would he " make the most of what he
yet might spend? "

She turned a corner and was on Woodward Avenue.
Three doors up the street was Dick's old home. Her
feet, unconsciously, had brought her to his door. She
went on. The house was lighted. Her heart leaped and
pounded. Perhaps — he might be there. She had felt
his presence, he was near her.

In the shadow of grouped shrubbery she stopped, looking up at the great stone front. A long flight of wide
steps led from the walk to the entrance. The first-floor
windows were high above her head. She could see nothing but lights. As she waited, a car drew up at the curb
and Charlotte, wrapped in a dark coat, stepped out. She
called something over her shoulder to the driver and

ran up the walk.   Frances moved forward, " Charlotte."

Charlotte wheeled and peered into the darkness.

" It's Frances Stevenson.   Charlotte — I want to speak to you."   Frances had walked rapidly until she stood close to Charlotte and offered her hand.   Still peering doubtfully, Charlotte accepted it, but stiffly.

" You're getting wet.   It's raining."

" I know.   I like it."

" Really.   Well? "

Frances pressed the gloved fingers in her hand and lifted her face.   " Charlotte — tell me.   Dick is going to France? "

" Yes."

" He is in town now.   When does he leave? "

" He will arrive in the morning.   We have no idea when he'll go over."

" My brother, Jimmie, is over there now — C. E. F. — and John is going.   Are you? "

Charlotte's unresponsive fingers had relaxed.   She bent toward Frances and gave her hand a little squeeze.

" I want to terribly.   My mother won't consent.   Are you going? "

" No, I'm not old enough, and I couldn't finance myself.   Go, Charlotte, if you can.   I'm going to be secretary to Doctor Remington, Egyptologist.   You know him."

" Yes — are you?   That's wonderful!   I didn't know. If I don't go over, I'll concentrate on the Red Cross here, I think.   I have an opportunity."

" Oh, that's something.   Lots, I think.   Only when the boys — your brothers are over there, you want to be there too."

" Did you come up to see Dick to-night? "   Frances heard the mocking note that, until now, had been absent, miraculously, from Charlotte's voice.

"No. I had no idea your house was open. It's been so dark and still all winter. I hoped when I saw it lighted that you — you were all united again."

"Not that. We're here to close the sale of the house and see Dick. Frances" — Charlotte gave Frances' hand a pat and dropped it quickly. "If you want me to give Dick a message, I will."

Frances' moment of hesitation was not long. "Tell him we met — and talked — this way. He would be glad. He said I would love you if I knew you — well."

"Dick did? Dick said that? Well, and do you?" Charlotte laughed.

"I'd like to. Honestly, Charlotte, I would like to. That's why I spoke."

Charlotte laughed again. "Well, Frances! You're always the most surprising little thing! I never know." She put a finger under Frances' chin and lifted it. Their eyes strained through the darkness and met laughing. "Dick said the very same thing to me about you!" Charlotte put a hand on each of Frances' arms and squeezed. "I'm sure I don't know why we shouldn't be friends. I'd like you to love me — if you can."

"I can. I do; really I do."

Again Charlotte's laugh, amused this time, interested. Frances took a step backward.

"I am terribly sorry I scratched your face."

"Well, good work! I'm glad to hear it. I'm sorry I pulled your hair." They were both laughing. Charlotte drew Frances closer. "Really, you know, I'm glad you spoke to me. Detroit seems too desolate when we drop in like this. We lose all the threads while we're gone. Wait for me in the car. I have to go in, but when I come out I can drive you home and we can talk."

Frances was suddenly shy. "No, I want exercise. I must run home. More rain won't hurt me now." As she talked she walked backward. Charlotte stood still watching her. " Good-by."

" Good-by, and say, Frances, I'll telephone you soon and we'll make an engagement. Shall we ? "

" Please do. Any time." She waved her hand and, turning, ran down the deserted street toward home.

III

On the following morning it was necessary for Frances to go to the public library for reference work. She desired above all things to stay at home near the telephone. Surely there would be some message from Dick. He would try to see her. Even her father would not forbid them a moment together on the eve of parting, he for war and she perhaps for Egypt before they two should meet again. This day might be their last opportunity to be together in life — at best, the last for many months.

It was eleven o'clock when she left the library and walked out toward Woodward Avenue for a car.

The air was dense with moisture. Heavy curtains of gray mist trailed over the high buildings and dimmed the light. A sharp ripple of thunder mingled with the din of traffic.

On Woodward Avenue a thin line of dully garbed people stood along the curbing, waiting for something, it seemed, yet there was no evidence of anything unusual. Frances made her way across the street and stood in a safety zone, waiting for her car. Before it came, two mounted policemen emerged from the traffic at the Campus Martius, and as they approached, waving pedestrians back with their riding crops, a band, walking behind them, burst into the new English war song, " Keep the Home Fires Burning."

Frances went back to the curb and found a place in the crowd. The band swung past playing energetically. It was not much of a band, a few cornets, a drum and some pipes. Followed a police guard, a company of soldiers from the fort, regular army men in khaki who marched as if they were physically constructed to do nothing but march. Behind them in carriages and on foot were the city's few remaining G. A. R. veterans, feeble and bent but military to the last, and consciously proud in remembered glory.

There was a little perfunctory cheering, but the dampness and thunder checked any demonstration of enthusiasm the band had aroused as it passed. A girl near Frances talked excitedly to her mother. "Here they come now! This is them!"

Some young men walking by fours came next. They had no banner or badges that Frances could see. They walked along in step, their eyes downcast. Frances was about to ask who they were when a man near her began to harangue.

"Three cheers now!" he shouted. "Three cheers for the first enlisted men. That's right, yell *loud,* you Americans, yell good and loud."

Not a sound had come from the crowd. It stood in solemn silence, gazing at the equally solemn young men walking past.

"This is the way to send them off to war, with cheers and tears and a rain of flowers. You're the sort!" Frances looked up at him. His face was distorted with the bitterness of his sarcasm. "My God, ain't you appreciative though! Wish I was going over to France to fight for you folks."

The excited girl near Frances was leaning out into the street, scanning the lines. "He's drunk, I bet. Only a drunk would talk like that."

From the distance, the last notes of " Keep the Home Fires Burning" were lost in thunder. Thrills, chills, played on Francie's spine. She wished she wanted to cheer. She longed to express her inexpressible appreciation, but she could make no sound. She glanced to right and left at the faces near her. Solemn, almost stupid they looked, feeling emotion too deep for noisy cheers and yelling. The city seemed very still to Frances. She heard nothing but the shiff, shiff, shiff of the marchers' feet on the asphalt. Their faces were terrible to her. The pallor of winter was still on them, heightened by the pallor of emotion. She saw one young man whose lips looked stiff and waxen. His face was like chalk, his eyes staring. "He's walking to his death; that's what they are feeling. They're walking to their death." These men had enlisted immediately upon declaration of war. Like Dick, like John — they would soon be in the hell of it.

Passing her were three boys she had known in school, marching together. Oh, they looked so different now, like slaves, creatures of fate, cannon fodder; maybe to end as cannon fodder. Horrible words. Tears rushed to her eyes. The sarcastic man had moved farther up the street; he was still talking. Suddenly the excited girl saw the man she had been waiting for. "Jerry!" she cried, "Jerry," and ran directly into the lines to a grinning chap who hooked his arm in hers and walked her along with him. In all that company he was the only one who had smiled. Frances shrank with shame for the girl's incentiveness. How could she be so conspicuous with her love and her emotions? Her eyes followed them and saw the pressure of their arms together. These were the common people, the people of frank expression. Perhaps their feeling was less terrible because it had more outlet; perhaps it helped them to do hard things more cheerfully. She would never have been able to run out publicly to Dick! She thought with satisfaction of the difference between her brother and her lover and these men before her. John and Dick would go out in uniform, mounted probably on graceful charges, with gloves and swords and clinking spurs; for them picture-book war, glory and music and conspicuous honor. Her thought rose from no fundamental instinct of snobbery. It was that her pride threw up defense for itself in childish visions of a fate less cruel for her men, who would go as they had enlisted, with patrician scorn of demonstrativeness.

She had watched until the girl with her Jerry had been lost in the distance. When she turned to the men still coming in fours she found herself looking straight into Dick's eyes. She started and her lips parted over silence. Her surprise was overwhelming. All the blood in her arteries froze in shocked stillness. He was there, beside her, close enough to touch! He had seen her first, his gaze held her startled eyes; he was smiling faintly but the smile was only of the lips. He made no sound, no move toward her, and the only sign of recognition, other than his look, was the lifting of his gloved hand in salute. It was over in a moment; he had passed and the shiff, shiff, shiff of his feet was in Frances' ears. He must have seen her amazement and horror; he must have seen the color drop from her face; he knew she had made no sound, no gesture toward him. He had gone beyond her voice; she couldn't call; he had gone, shiff, shiff, shiff through the street, walking tragically, simply, with these men marching like herded cattle to the slaughter. These men, these poor men, the Jerrys and Dick together; the ordinary and the brilliant, the mob — with a Dick in its midst!

Tears filled her eyes and hung on her lashes, but she

could see Dick's shoulders twenty feet beyond her now.
Oh, what was he thinking? What did he feel? Would
he have had her run out as the girl had run to Jerry?
Had Jerry had the worthier friend? Jerry had laughed,
but Dick had worn the indescribable pallor; the smile on
his set lips had been worse than no smile. It was his
bravery and loneliness that hurt her so terribly. She felt
that she had failed him. She wanted him to know.
Her heart was at his feet in humility and love. He had
voluntarily marched here with these men, feeling no class
distinction but conscious, as she belatedly was conscious
now,.that all were Americans — ah, *of course,* and she
had thought — had thought — but unworthiness was a
conviction. Shame and remorse filled the chalice of her
soul and she wept there alone on the curb. And now she
felt no scorn of emotion. Let it show, let it express itself, let it stream from her eyes and clutch her throat;
she had no care save to make Dick know the great ache
and tenderness of her heart.

From way up the street she heard the first thrilling
measures of "The Star Spangled Banner." A long,
solemn roll of thunder contrasted with the swift, stirring movement of the song. Distance lent enchantment
to the band and the shiff, shiff, shiff of feet changed to
the staccato padding of marchers. One of the boys
turned to his fellows and smiled, saying something that
he accompanied with a waggish movement of his shoulders. They answered him with a laugh and, for Frances,
the tension relaxed in a thrill of patriotism. The crowd
felt it too and cheered when the flag, carried by a staggering giant, passed.

Frances looked up at the stars and stripes against the
gray mist of noon and loved it, loved it and Dick together with a devotion that welled from her heart like
prayer.

"What would I do for you, you stars and stripes?"
she asked herself.   Pictures of war, bursting shells and
a hailstorm of bullets; wounds and a crippled body filled
her vision, but she said, "That! Anything! Anything
in the world I could, I would do for you."

IV

When Frances left for the library immediately after
morning prayers, Angus took his *Free Press* to a favorite
window and settled himself for an hour of news review.
He had read all the first-page headlines during breakfast.
He knew that General Haig's men had smashed their
way nearer Cambrai and had shattered the very flower of
the German army in the doing.   He knew that the House
of Representatives were debating the selective draft
versus the volunteer system; that local breweries might
have to close to conserve grain; that onion sets were forty
cents a quart and scarce, whereas a year before they had
been ten cents the quart and plentiful.   He knew the
Free Press seeds for war gardens had arrived at last,
and he had assimilated the important fact that circus
fees were to rise along with the price of onions; but he
went over it all again in detail, his habit and the never-
flagging interest in his world.   "Life is sweet," he was
wont to mutter.   "With all its tribulations, life is
sweet."

He turned a page, carefully creasing the long fold,
and read the lesser headlines of the state news aloud:
"'PROMINENT MICHIGAN EDUCATORS MADE
MAN AND WIFE.'   Makes me tired the way newspapers everlastingly talk about 'man and wife'!"

Mary came into the room with water for the ferns.
"What makes you everlastingly tired?"

"I wish people who write for publication would give

more thought to the trite phrases. Constantly talking
about man and wife instead of husband and wife. They
never say husband and woman, why say man and wife? "

" Custom."

" Ignorance. Thoughtlessness. Ah! Here's our
young enemy's name. Young Stanhope."

Mary's hand hung poised above the ferns. " Not in
town? "

" Yes. Arrives this morning to march with the first
enlisted men of the county. A parade. Starts at ten
o'clock. Propaganda stuff to stir enthusiasm, I suppose.
Gatley's band — G. A. R. — regulars from the fort.
Well, we ought to see it. Too bad it's such a dark day.
Young Stanhope's come on from Cambridge for it.
Well — too bad! " He shook his head sadly. " Too
bad." The paper slipped down and Angus, staring out
into the street, sat absorbed in thought. " War, war,
war. I say it to myself and think I must be dreaming.
Sometimes I wonder why I'm not a pacifist. Christ
taught nonresistance and lived it — all but once. ' Love
your enemies,' He said, ' bless those that curse you. Be
merciful to those who despitefully use you and perse-
cute you.' Tremendous! Would we gain our goal more
effectually by nonresistance than by war? I know we
would if, as a nation, we could stand *united*. If we could
return good for evil, if we could do for the other fellow
what we would have him do for us, we'd win him and
our own victories enduringly. War is futile. Carnage.
Waste. Oh, terrible waste. Nonresistance would mean
slavery and death for us. But death to a follower of
Christ is but a translation — not to be feared. I try
to follow Christ literally, taking no thought for the mor-
row, what I shall eat nor what I shall drink. God will
provide for me if I serve Him with my whole heart even
as He provides for the sparrow. And if I lose my life

for Him, it is but to go to the Father. Yet in war the gospel of nonresistance is impossible. I could not preach it. It is beyond us yet. Next to my God is my brotherhood with men. As brothers, we resist the injustice of Germany, her invasion, her cruelty. It is desecration. Christ flogged the money-changers from the temple. Their desecration of a sacred place stirred Him to anger. I'm glad it did. Germany stirs me to anger. I wish I could fight. I wish to God I could!"

Said Mary, "Frances may see the parade. I wonder if she knew Dick was to be here."

"How should she know? She didn't see the paper this morning." Angus was alert again.

Mary turned to look at him in astonishment.

"How should she know? Have you supposed there is no communication between them?"

"I have. She gave me her word. I am trusting her. Until I see with my own eyes her disobedience, I will not believe that she could continue to care for an agnostic —a man of his sort. Frances has character enough to understand values. I believe she has already stamped beneath her feet as dust the memory of that boy." Angus' eyes shone and his nostrils dilated with pride.

"You do. Well, faith is a beautiful thing but sometimes faith misplaced is a loss. Agnosticism to most people isn't one of the seven sins. There are those who can forgive that. When Frances gave you her word, she was shocked. She has had time to think. The church as an institution isn't necessarily as sacred to her as it is to you."

"She is a minor. She has given me her word."

"She is in love."

"She was." Angus had risen. He stood looking at Mary with his boring eyes. "There are times when I suspect that the church is not so sacred to you as it might be."

Mary looked up smiling, met his look and laughed. "Oh, tra la la! Why annihilate me with your lightning glance? I will tell you the truth; no need to probe my guilty heart. Since our experience — recently — I find the church as small as the smallest of its members as well as great like its founders. I think I am growing more and more to believe that though we poor human worshipers try mightily to build our highest aspirations and conceptions into a temple, we *fail* mightily to secure a place of peace and joy. We think it our duty to organize multitudes — to love grand and imposing, visible cathedrals to God, though Christ was trying to teach us that the body, this fleshly tabernacle, is the real temple of the holy spirit."

"You, too, would do away with the church!"

"Oh, no, I didn't say that. That doesn't follow logically on what I said. We were talking about Frances. The church, religious beliefs weighed in the scales against her love, won't count a fraction of an ounce if her love is real."

"Mary, you can't mean that. This chap — who, in this very room, in my own house, said he'd sweep the whole institution of the church out of existence? You know all he said. Frances knows. She couldn't love him after that."

"She could."

Angus turned on his heel and walked away, talking half to himself. "God help us! How little He weighs against the flesh! How can you believe — as you say you believe — the gospel of Jesus Christ and yet lend countenance to this affair? John says, 'He that believeth on Him is not condemned: but he that believeth not is condemned already because he hath not believed in

the name of the only begotten Son of God.' John said
that — John, his dearly beloved disciple, who was closer
to Him during His life and teaching than any other man.
John knew what Christ believed if anybody did. That
verse holds the touchstone of our faith. You apply it
to young Richard and it comes back negative. He
doesn't believe Christ Himself said, 'If ye believe not
that I am He, ye shall die in your sins.' And Richard is
an unbeliever, yet you would give Frances freedom to
bind herself to him! I would take her off down the
river to-day, anywhere, on any excuse to keep her from
him. I can't bear it. I can't compromise with my religion. Until my last breath I shall fight against this
engagement. Frances doesn't know him. It can't hurt
her to be denied this childish love." Angus threw out
his hands in a vehement gesture, opened his lips to continue, but closed them over clenched teeth and turned his
back on Mary.

Mary sat silent, watching him. He stood a moment,
but faced her again and lowered his voice as he said
persuasively, "You were talking about the temple of the
body, Mary, were you not? Don't you see that in just
that little thought on a great subject you defeat yourself? You feel sympathy for this boy, yet he has dese-
crated the temple of his body and you know it. You
have guarded Frances' body as the most precious possession of your heart; you know it to be beautiful and clean'
as rose petals, yet — yet — " Angus groaned.

Mary put a gentle hand on his arm. "My dear, you
feel that way because this case is personal to you. Your
daughter! Even unmoral men feel so about their
daughters. You are judging young Dick on that score
severely. King David was just such a sinner and yet
your sermons, nearly half, I dare say, are built around
texts from his writings."

"David repented of his sin. He was redeemed."

"This boy may repent too. He's young. If Frances loves him, he's sacred to me. If Francie can forgive him, I can hope and pray and believe that he will grow worthy of her. I'll give him every chance. Why can't you? Christ would. God does."

"So do I, but he sha'n't have the reward of Frances till he earns it through repentance and redemption. She shall not be dragged down to his level in order that he may be pulled up to hers."

"No? Well, dear, I am sorry, but deciding that isn't your prerogative, sad to say. Frances will decide for herself. You have had your chance, nineteen years of it, to mold her to the pattern you chose for her. If she is not what you wanted her to be, at least you have tried to make her so. That must be your solace. There is no other for you. But I want you to know that if you restrict her now, to-day, against seeing Richard when he is off on his country's business, with death the price, maybe, I shall think less of you than I do now."

"Mary."

"I mean it. I want you to take yourself off downtown. Stay away where the need for decision will not be put upon you. See not, hear not, ask not. Keep away. Pray. Surround Frances with the spirit of your love and wisdom and understanding and leave the rest to God and the beauty that dwells in her soul. Don't *talk* about trusting her, but trust her. If she fails to do what you would have her do, don't think she has betrayed your trust, but go right on trusting her. That's love."

Poor Angus. The staff of his life had taken to itself legs and had walked off. He stood gazing, wrinkles of distress about his eyes. This from Mary, whom secretly the Adam in him held responsible for the fact of his marriage and fatherhood! She had urged him to it when he had foreseen these very trials for his possible children.

Mary saw the look of helpless dependence, so rare in his face, vanishing before the returning of his compelling convictions.

She said quickly, anticipating his refusal to be influenced. " Think only for a moment of their psychology. These children have known each other for twelve years now. For a year they have been consciously in love. They have spent only one evening together. They know the delight of contact; they are wrapped in the veils of romance. Their love is as blind as love ever is, and as unreasoning and as unreasonable. They think they understand each other, but they don't. We know that. To Dick, Francie is faultless. She is his dream, his ideal, his little nun-like sweetheart. To her, Dick is love's tragedy. She knows enough of his faults to feel great virtue in still loving him. All the maternal in her, all the passion for reform — which she gets from you — is on fire for him." Mary clasped her hands in a gesture of earnest pleading. " If you keep them apart, Angus, you will but feed this passion, give it fuel. Absence won't cure them when war and misunderstanding parents and all the appurtenances of romance are theirs. Let's try the other way. Let's trust Francie's good sense. Let's give her a chance to see his faults. War will separate them after to-day more effectually than you can. This is life, inexorable, dictating, absolute monarch. You can't usurp his throne."

Mary ceased speaking and stood before him, her shining eyes lifted, her face eloquent with thought that went on and on, piling up arguments she felt no need to voice. She saw Angus' lips quiver and the furrows deepen between his eyes. He blinked at her and looked away.

She knew she had almost won. She smiled and lifted herself on tiptoe before him, her hands on his shoulders. "Dearest!" she whispered. "This is the day for you to go to Grosse Pointe to see Grandpa Grieve. You know the last time you saw Henry, he urged you to go out and see the orchids and have lunch and cheer his father. That would be a real service. You'd be doing good."

A long silence. Angus was staring over her head. "Well —" He touched Mary's cheek and looked into her eyes. "My darling . . . I believe you love your child more than you love your husband — or your God."

"No. No, Angus. All together, a concatenation of loves. God's in the soul of me, you're in the heart of me. Frances — is me." She, laughed through tears. "It can't be analyzed, even with all the rules of grammar thrown to the dogs. Come on now. Wear your new tie to-day and get yourself off. You may see the parade as you ride through the city."

V

When Frances returned home, that noon, she flew to her room to make a toilet that would do honor to a call from Dick. She had no idea what to expect from him. He might telephone, but she supposed he would drive up to the door with a rush, jump over the side of the car and run up the steps — all in a second. Whatever he did, she wanted to be ready.

On her little white dresser she found a characteristic note from Mary, rapidly scribbled with a crossed-out line or two:

"Frances, dear, when you come home you'll find your family flown. Your father's gone to Grosse Pointe Farms, your mother's out alone. We won't be home till dinner-time. In fact, it may be dark. It seemed a most inviting day to go off on a lark. You'll have the house quite to yourself, all clean and still for study, or for a caller, should you chance to welcome anybody. There's everything for sandwiches and tea with lemon in it, or marmalade and buttered toast made ready in a minute. Just do whatever you think best, but to yourself be true. No matter what may happen then, you'll know that I love you."

Before she finished the jingle, Frances realized the purpose Mary had had in writing it. At the end she looked up at her reflection in the mirror. "They know Dick's in town," she said slowly. "They've gone out to leave me free to do my own deciding." She reread the note carefully, understanding and lingering on the last lines. "They've put it up to me — alone — at last." Frances was peeling off her coat, but her tempo had been moderated considerably. She said over and over, as she tossed fresh clothing on the bed, "They've done this deliberately to leave me free. It isn't in the least an inviting day for a lark."

Before Frances was dressed, she heard the telephone. She ran downstairs breathless with suspense. Her voice was so low when she spoke that she had to repeat before Dick heard her. He had never talked with her over the telephone. He was not certain it was she.

They rushed over the formalities and then — " I want to see you. When can we meet, Frances? Are you free to talk now?"

"Yes, I'm free. I'm alone. Won't 'you come right out now, Dick? I can't wait."

"Francie! I knew you would. I was afraid you wouldn't." They laughed. "I can't come till after luncheon with father and Charlotte at the Athletic Club, but I can be on my way by two o'clock. Then I must return to see my mother — if she will — before train time. I have a plan for us, Francie. Are you game to go with me?"

"Where?"

"Do you have to know? Can't you trust me?"

"Yes, I can. I'll go anywhere. What kind of clothes shall I wear?"

Dick laughed. "Oh, any old thing that's comfortable and a coat. We'll drive."

"I'll be ready at two."

"If I'm delayed a very little you'll know it's my family. We have a great deal to say, but I want to get to you more than — This is a public telephone. I'll tell you about that later."

When the connection was cut, Frances stood with her hands over her face, trembling.

"I wouldn't have said no if I had wanted to. He's going to war. He's going to war. This is being true to my best self."

She dressed carefully in a new dark-blue taffeta dress Mary had made for her and put the amber beads around her neck. They hung almost to her waist and made a long loop of palely shimmering gold against the dark silk.

When the last little finger-nail was polished, she was quivering with excitement. She walked about her room, striving for calm, and decided finally to go down to the piano and throw all her emotional energy into song. She would play resolutely, make herself play. She laid out the music she wanted to go over and admonished herself not to look at the clock until she had finished it.

She had chosen the cooling freshness of "The Magic Casement" to temper her emotion. It demanded her best effort at expression and, as she played the first rippling accompaniment of the cycle, she knew that she would be able to call from the piano the groan of the billows, the moan of the tempest, "like ghosts of sailors dead." She sang with wistful longing in her voice and a throb of joy in her heart:

> I saw two ships sail by to-day,
>   In the bright April weather.
> Over the sea all blue and gray,
>   Slowly they sailed together.
>
> My breaking heart, it bled to see
>   The blowing sails together;
> For I am lonely, woe is me,
>   In the bright April weather!

Happiness had stimulated her. Love ran riot in her veins and loosed the best of her musical talent. When the last chiming chords of "The Love Ship" were finished and her fingers still held the keys, she turned slowly toward the clock and saw — standing in the doorway, his arms folded across his chest, his head lowered — Dick. His searching eyes looked steadily into hers and he waited motionless for her to speak.

She whispered his name, rose, radiant, blazing with happiness and went swiftly to him.

CHAPTER IX

I

"FRANCES!" Dick circled her face with his hands and looked down into her lifted eyes. "We've been together a whole hour of our time. Can you believe that clock? There's still so much to say, and I can't remember what it is." He smiled tremulously, but Frances, released from the tension of her rapture, laughed at him. He went on, "About your father. Ever since that night a year ago, I have thought around and around our problem and the things he said to me. He was fair to me apparently, but sometimes I feel that his show of fairness was a trick to turn the case against me at the last. He meant right along to get me. He made it seem as if I had defeated myself."

Frances put her hand on his and he took it between his palms, pressing it. "To your father, people are either white with goodness or black with sin. There is no gray or lavender. To me, the great qualities are highmindedness, honesty and courage."

"But, he doesn't think that, Dick. Those qualities are just the beginning for him. The kind of highmindedness is what matters to him. I think he wants to be fair. See," Frances reclaimed her hand and sent it down into the front of her dress for Mary's note which she brought into the light. "Mother wrote this in her funny little way." Dick read it, smiling. "She knew you were in town. She has sent father off to Grosse Pointe and she herself has gone out — to leave me free.

That's fair, isn't it, Dick? It wasn't easy for them to do that."

Dick folded the note and Frances watched his face. It wore still the expression she had seen as he passed her in the morning, set yet tremulous, as if he were making a conscious effort to conceal a grief. She seemed to understand suddenly that Angus was responsible for that look, Angus and herself more than war and the trouble with his mother. He had not looked so when he spoke of them. War he had accepted philosophically, Frances thought. It was inevitable for him. He must go and put it over. He might get "stuck by a Bosch," but he'd survive. "All the allies need is our help to finish up. It won't take long." He had dismissed the tragedy of it as briefly as that. His mother's obdurateness was painful, but he felt conscience-clear, evidently. He had done his utmost for reconciliation. But Frances — the hurt in his eyes, the repression of his lips — these visible marks of a wounded and aching heart were for her. The desire to throw herself on her knees before him and beg his forgiveness rushed upon her. Who was she that she should judge him? She caught her breath and clasped her hands tightly in her lap.

They were sitting on the low rosewood settee that had held several generations of Stevenson lovers in the old Virginia days. Dick still kept Mary's rhymed note; he leaned forward, his elbows on his knees, turning it over and over between his fingers. He had not seen the sweep of emotion over Frances' face. He said, "This note is fair. It leaves it all up to you. I know you're loyal to them. You're a minor but you won't let them decide for you; you couldn't and be you, Frances. I think we all want to be fair. I try. I went away from Detroit angry, after my talk with your father. I wanted to forget you. I tried to shut you out of my thought."

But I might as well have tried to shut the sun out of my days. It's there. It pervades the day — and you, Frances, pervade my life. You always will. You wrote, you know, with that little twist of humor you get from your mother, I suppose — 'Think kindly of God, Dick. He's the only bridge there is across the gulf to me.' Remember? Well — " he turned quickly and smiled at her, his eyes twinkling. " I do think kindly of God. I think about it a great deal, and I'm trying to approach Him in a different way — to see your side. I'd be a Christian if I knew how, but there is no way. It just doesn't appeal to my reason. There's the Malthusian theory, for instance. I believe in it. It solves one of life's most acute problems, but it does not harmonize with Christianity. At least, I can't make it harmonize. But I am trying, Frances, to think in sympathy with you and perhaps I'm making a little headway. I had a — a vision — a revelation. We might call it that — night before last on the train." He drew a deep breath. " I want to tell you. I wish I could make it sound as it appeared to me, but that is seldom possible with — visions."

He rose and took a turn on the hearthrug before he continued. His face was crinkled with thought. He was trying to recapture the vision that he might give it to her with something of the vividness that had startled him.

"You see, I didn't come to Detroit direct from Boston. I went to New York first for something I'll tell you about later, and from there I went to Cleveland. I was a messenger from the class to poor old Ted Candler, who is down with T. B. He has to 'go West.' Of course, he can't enlist and they think he won't live. He's in such a terrible blue funk we wanted to do something to cheer him up. That's why I went to Cleveland.

Well — " he smoothed his thick hair, passing a hand down the back of his head again and again. He was unconscious of the gesture, Frances thought. " He does that when he studies," she said to herself, smiling, and loved every line of his figure as he stood there before her.

" Going from New York to Cleveland on the Pennsylvania, we went through Pittsburgh. It was late night. I don't know what time, but I think I had been asleep." He left the hearthrug and leaned above her, one hand on the back of the old settee. " I was thinking of you. I always think of you with part of my mind. Even when the rest is busy, I am conscious of you. I dream of you, Francie. Sometimes I can't bear the reproach in your eyes. It wakes me often and makes me — miserable. That night I waked and you were there in my thought. I knew we were pulling into a depot and I raised the shade. It was Pittsburgh, black night. The sky above the city was red with reflected fire and draped with smoke. It was startling. Against the flame color, objects, black in the darkness, were sharply silhouetted. I thought, ' This is the altar of materialism. This is the passionate devotion of men that keeps the fires bright to the gods of gain. Their zeal never sleeps. Money, materialism, prosperity, war — they work together to make the hell of it.' " He laughed apologetically. " Those were poetic thoughts for me. I was feeling a good deal of a philosopher. The train was moving slowly all the time into the yards and suddenly my window was opposite a canyon of buildings that made an avenue to the fiery furnace, and right against the reddest part of the sky was the spire of a church with a cross on top against the glare. Perhaps I don't make it sound as dramatic as I felt, but that cross stood out, high above the furnaces, such a simple little thing —

just two straight lines — but a tremendous symbol. I thought it rather triumphed over the materialism below. It's more enduring. It's been a compelling fact for twenty centuries. Of course, you were in the vision, Francie. I remembered, ' Think kindly of God, Dick,' and wanted — I wanted you to know — I was trying."

"Dick." Frances had his hand in hers, against her lips. He felt her tears. "I know, I know. Oh, Dick, you are good. Don't think of me as reproachful. I love you. I love you so much that I can't stop though I've tried. Nothing stops it. I didn't know love was like that. I thought certain things killed love. But they don't. If you can be tolerant of my religion — if you won't say things against it — if you can give me time — I love you for what you are. The past we'll have to forget — as fast — as we can."

"You don't forget easily, Francie. I can see. I wouldn't either, I suppose. Would knowing all the truth help you any? I'll tell you. It's your right to know if you want to know."

Frances sprang to her feet and he rose with her. "Please don't." The words were a whispered cry. She turned her face from him and he walked away down the room. When he returned to her, she was smiling palely. He kissed her hands. There was long silence until he said, constrained, "We can have several hours together. I want to take you away off somewhere. I know a place. Shall we start?"

"And I'm not to know where we are going? That's rather fun!" Her face brightened with happiness. "I'll get ready — a coat."

He detained her, looking deep into her eyes. "Are you willing to go anywhere I take you?"

She nodded and repeated, "Anywhere."

"Suppose I should take you — across the river, to Windsor? We could get a marriage license and — "

"You wouldn't!"

"I would."

"Dick — you are joking."

"I'm not. Do you realize that I am going to France? This may be our last day — our last chance — in this life and — I love you."

She had lowered her eyes. Dick saw the throbbing of her pulse in her throat. The amber beads trembled with her rapid breathing. They caught the light and blazed pale gold in the dimness of the quiet room.

"Don't you care enough to want to have — at least my name?"

"Yes."

"Then you will?"

"No." All the light had gone from Frances' face. She looked pale and tired. The darkness of her eyes was deepened by shadowy distress. "A secret, like that, all the time you were gone. Oh, I couldn't — couldn't bear it — alone."

She glanced up and caught Dick's look. "I suppose I knew you would feel so, Francie, but I hoped you'd want to as much as I." He passed his hand across his face, sighing. "Of course, I can't urge you. We'd both have to desire it irresistibly. You don't want me to urge it? You — are — sure?"

Frances was silent. If she told him how much she wanted him to urge it, the thing would come to pass. She dared not permit herself to speak. She shook her head and bit her lip to hide its trembling. This was her moment — her hour. She heard the slow music of the night before and the words, "Waste — not — your hour." But her eyes beheld her father's face. The music had been the revelation of an emotional moment.

Her father stood for a lifetime of repression. Fear paralyzed desire. The blood pounded in her ears but she heard Dick's deep, urgent voice. He was saying with long pauses between the short sentences, " I've thought about it all so much. I want you so. You can't know. Every way I can, I want to bind you to me. I went to New York for this. I thought girls liked things from Tiffany's. Look, Frances." He was putting a box into her hands.

Tears dropped to her hot cheeks and dried there as she fumbled with the wrappings. Through tears, she saw a ring, all crystal white, a great diamond in a band of diamonds and coiled about it, a little chain.

" You'll wear it for me to-day? Here on your left hand and later, if you can't leave it there, on that little chain around your neck? " He was kissing her eyes. He whispered, " I want to know that something of mine is with you always, close and warm where maybe it will feel the beating of your heart."

Before they left, Frances tried to write an answering rhyme to Mary. She sat on the window seat among the amber cushions and leaned against Dick, who looked over her shoulder as she wrote, and gave advice.

Frances began, " Oh, Molly dear, you are an understander." " You think she is, don't you, Dick? "

" She is. I want to know her."

" You'll love her. What rhymes with understander? "

" Candor. Gander."

Frances laughed. " I can't call the lady a gander, m'lord; 'tis the wrong gender. Candor's all right. I might say, ' Oh, Molly dear, you are an understander. It serves with me as well as brutal candor.' "

" Good! "

" ' Your jolly little joke about the lark, suggested just the thing for us till dark.' "

"Great-o! Some poet, Francie. Go on now, name the villain."

"'Dick Stanhope — came to see me in his car.' It's your father's, but that doesn't matter. 'He promises that he won't take me far — but dinner is the order of the day, and so you'll understand why I'm away.' How's that? Doesn't it just say itself?" Frances waved the pencil.

"Hold! Wait a minute! I have a line. 'We won't stay long for Dick must catch a train, and anyway we know the sky may rain.'"

Frances laughed at him, leaning against his shoulder, her head tipped back. He kissed her smiling lips. They forgot the verse till Frances, rousing gently, suggested, "How's this — 'We won't stay long for Dick must catch a train. I have my winter coat for it may rain.' I don't mean that the coat may rain. You understand?"

"I do. I understand as only the profoundly intelligent, deeply learned, high-browed scholar of the English language can. Proceed."

"I'll have to tell her I'll be true to myself — like Hamlet. I could say, 'I promise to be just as true as you —'" Frances bit the pencil reflectively.

"I have it. Listen. Say, 'I promise to be just as true to you as if your lips had told me what to do.'"

"That's good. That's wonderful, very simple and convincing." Frances wrote, bending above the paper and talked slowly as she erased and punctuated. "This business of being true to oneself is — is difficult because, of necessity, it rules out selfishness. In matters like Windsor, a secret marriage, I suppose the family of the elopers really suffer."

"I suppose so — " grimly.

"I've always felt that it was either a selfish — or a

weak thing to do. We have had eloping couples come
here to be married and I have never liked them. It
seemed to me they were either going against the wishes
of their families or else were not strong enough to be
convincing. For me to do it would be flagrant disloyalty. If, in the end, my parents won't consent to our
marriage, I shall tell them that I am going to do it, and
when. I won't sneak again. I did a sneaky thing once
in my life and that was enough."

Dick smiled, loving her. "What a conscience some
people have! And yet to me — to think that marrying
me — properly — before I go away could be classified
as sneaking — I can't see it so. There comes a time
when we go beyond questions of loyalty or selfishness.
Your relationship to me, mine to you, is the point. It
fills my vision. I can't see anybody else, my eyes are
so full of you. Francie — " He broke off. There
was something more he would have said.

Frances sat staring before her, troubled again by the
urgency in his voice and the hurt. He could think only
of the long separation and his hungry love. Nothing
else was worth considering but this one day — fleeting,
precious — their hour.

He began again. The words were an effort. His
voice halted between phrases. "Frances — can it be
that I have failed to make you feel how much — I love
you! That in my talk of marrying, to-day, you think
I want you just for now, and not — forever."

Frances was startled by his emotion. She lifted her
eyes and met his look and it was as if his thought blazed
there, in letters of fire, for her to read. Her pulse
jumped and fluttered before it raced forward, singing
through her veins. It was a moment of revelation more
vivid, more amazing even than the moment of their recognized love — the revelation to her own consciousness

that in her response to Dick's desire she was one with
him. She — Frances — this —

If he urged her further toward that secret marriage —

She felt the blood drop from her cheeks, from her
heart. The strength poured from her finger tips and left
her spent.

II

Frances was glad to be in the open air. Dick lowered
the windows of the coupe and they sniffed the fragrant
spring. The warm, sweet smell of clover came elusively
with the breath of the moist earth. Birds chirped and
fluttered over the fresh green grass. The gray mist of
the morning had scattered. Ragged clouds hung like
fringe high in the west, still veiling the great eye of day
that sent a golden shaft upward into the arch of the sky.
It bronzed the roofs and streets and tinted the edges of
the clouds with orange.

"It's hard to guess," Frances said, "whether we're
to have more rain or a sudden bursting forth of sunshine. It's warm and smelly and beautiful, anyway."

"I think we'll see a gorgeous sunset."

They were driving down Second Avenue toward the
city. The swift smooth motion of the car, the fragrance
and moist, warm air roused Frances from the strange
throbbing noon of their meeting.

She talked to Dick without restraint, youthfully, telling him the great and small events of her days. He
asked a hundred questions about the men she knew,
where they took her, what she thought of them and —
satisfied — when with lowered voice she told him how
none compared with him, how each had met the test
and failed, he pressed on to Doctor Remington and the
"sort of chap" he might be. On the level? An interesting wife? His looks, his age, his manner.

"Of course," Dick grumbled. "Now that I am go-ing, you'll be coming down to all the universities. I know he's to be at Harvard. I looked it up and I sup-pose Columbia. I could have seen you in any of the eastern college towns. Life's a nasty trickster. How it teases us and plays with our desires. To think we are capable of feeling — what I feel for you to-day — and helpless to force circumstances to my will!"

They did not talk after that. Dick's profile was dark and scowling. Frances felt torn between him and her parents, her love and her loyalty.

There is perhaps no city in the world where there are more motors and less speed limitation than in Detroit. All driving is swift and almost always sure. The traffic restrictions are many and ironclad, but the multitude of drivers, operating within the law, move with a speed that is alarming to the uninitiated. The stream of ve-hicles stops as one, starts as one, moves forward on wings — as one. Dick operated his car automatically, and Frances watched, hardly realizing the course they were taking, so absorbed was she in his movements and the variety of her thought. They had come down Woodward Avenue to Jefferson, but instead of turning eastward, as Frances had vaguely supposed they would, Dick shot across Jefferson Avenue and down the hill toward the river. At the foot of the street, he turned quickly and stopped before the gates of the Windsor ferry. Frances caught her breath.

"Dick!" He was out of the car and away at the ticket booth. When he returned, the gates were swung back for him and he drove through, across the gangplank and on to the ferry. Frances had said nothing more than his name. Her heart was pounding. When he set his brakes and shut off the switch, he turned and looked straight into her eyes.

" This is the Windsor ferry," she said.

" Yes."

" Dick."

" You said you would go anywhere I took you. What kind of a sport are you? "

Frances had not been brought up by two brothers without knowing the ethics of sportsmanship. She smiled at him.

He laughed at her. " That was a very brave little smile. But it didn't get as far as your eyes."

" What was in my eyes? "

" The thumping of your heart. You're afraid of me."

" And you like to tease me."

" No."

The ferry had put out from the landing. Before their eyes, but a little more than a half-mile across the water, the English flag stood out in the breeze. Behind it the sky was palely silver. The clouds had separated and changed from tattered gray to snowy fleece. Frances forced her mind to hold to the commonplace. She wondered why it was easier to be married quickly in Canada than in the United States. She tried to imagine what she would do, if, when they were beneath a different flag, Dick should put all his powers of persuasion into a plea for her relenting. She could hardly breathe as she thought of it. If by some magic she could banish her father and her mother from her thought, if she could feel that she belonged to herself, a free woman, with none to reproach or suffer for her acts, how eagerly would she take the great step of her life.

Dick began to talk. His voice was low. With it Frances felt the throb of the ferry's engines, heard the wash of the water against the hull. The river danced, palely green and silver-edged in the spring light. The flag drooped and hung, rose, waving and stiffened in the breeze.

" This is just the difference in our — philosophies — our religions, I suppose, your stand and mine, Frances, on this thing to-day. To me, heaven is of our own making, around us always for the taking. I live in the present, not a dim, half-promised, wholly uncertain future. Life now is the vital thing, not the hereafter. After this day, alone with you, looms France. War. Years, maybe. If I'm selfish, my love should be the excuse. To leave you unbound to me, so beautiful, so appealing, Francie, for some one nearer to take — jealousy, you see. I'm eaten alive. I want you to *belong* to me. You don't see it so? "

" Yes, I do. I feel as much that way about you as you do about me. I can paint a picture of my fears. You'll go over there where there are women, girls; heavenly, angelic creatures; they'll look to you; appealing, beautiful too. You'll have your great war experience in common. I'll seem a dream to you way back here in America. The dream will dim and vanish, maybe. Do you suppose — I don't want to tie you to me? "

He turned his troubled eyes to her and looked into the face she lifted to him. " I think you do," he said quietly, after a moment.

" If heaven is here — for our own making," Frances went on, trying to find words to define an answering philosophy, " then we must make to-day's heaven in such a way — that it won't spoil to-morrow's. We must make it for all the to-morrows. Disloyalty — " her voice broke. He heard her breath labor and sigh. " I can't express it, Dick. I can't argue about it. I only know I love you and I'm torn to pieces. If you take me — if you make me — I won't be able to resist. I

can't fight it any longer but I beg of you not to take
me — that way — and leave me — secret regrets."

Her hands were locked tightly in her lap. Dick was
watching them, his head lowered. He saw the pressure
of her fingers against the white flesh and the flash of
diamonds, his pledge to her. Her words had stirred
him. She had thrown herself on his mercy. He could
not in honor press further. He would have to go out,
away from her, bound to her only by their promise of
which the blazing white stones were the symbol. Their
word! His pledge to her. It meant all the height and
depth and width of love, fidelity, charity, unselfishness,
understanding — all things, all high qualities of the
heart and soul. And of the body — reverence. The
bigness of it caught him, stirred the very best in him
and made him say, " I give you my word — I will leave
you with nothing to regret. I understand. It's all
right." Their closed car under the low deck was deep
in shadow. He put his hand over hers and tried to make
his voice sound reassuring. "We're going up the river
to dinner, a great old joint that I want to see again,
with you, before I go. Chicken and frogs' legs and a
way of doing things that always interests me." He
smiled, trying to put the tenderness he felt into his look.
She was so white and still. The distress in her eyes
stabbed him with compunction. He talked until he saw
confidence and smiling faith light her face again. " It
is odd, isn't it, how the customs of another country can
hold over here. Canada's as far as the Atlantic is wide
from England and as close as the Detroit River is narrow to the United States, but over there is America and
over here is England. How would you like to drive up
into the shopping district and buy ostrich plumes?
Charlotte did once; got corking, big sporty plumes for
something like nothing. There's a chap here has an

ostrich farm in South Africa, no duty, you know. Shall
we?"

"I'd love to."

"We'll go in and merely say we want to see some
ostrich plumes and in that second they'll know we're
Detroiters, not Canadians. You watch them." He was
watching Frances. Her face was alight again, sweetly
curving lips relaxed in a smile. Mist filled his eyes and
burned there. He turned to the wheel and fumbled at
the switch. The ferry was putting in at the Windsor
dock.

To himself he was saying, "I have to wait. I have
no choice, I've lost. I must go and not have her. Some
day perhaps she'll love me more than she fears her father.
But now it is his inning. The time will come when she
will be independent of him — and that will be the dawn
of my day — if I'm not a dead thing by that time or a
pulpy mass of bloody wounds."

CHAPTER X

I

On his way to Grosse Pointe Angus did see the parade. He sat in the Woodward Avenue car reading the inevitable book that bulged his right-hand pocket. He had chosen the " Journeys to Bagdad " for the long ride and he sat with the slender volume before his eyes, his head tipped back the better to focus through his bifocal lenses, and chuckled appreciatively over the chaste wit of the reincarnated Charles Lamb. Angus' chuckle had taken on a thinner note as age crept upon him. It had once been deep within him, but now it sprang from the very tip of his tongue and was done with a flat A. This change seemed to have grown out of his new habit of sitting with his mouth a little open. He listened, keen, fine eyes alight and emphasized the effect of his concentrated attention by that trick of parted lips that was not vacuous but, rather, expressive of complete self-forgetfulness. Frances was annoyed by the habit. She was wont to tweak his ear when she observed it and remark prophetically, " Some day something is going to walk right in there and sit down on your tongue." The suggestion acted as leverage on the hinges of Angus' jaws and shut them with a click.

Angus was feeling very old these days. Life had slowed down for him and the quickstep of youth, passing him by at its clipping pace, made him both wistful and weary. He had no longing to do youthful things, they tired him, but he dreamed dreams of a youth renewed. To turn back to his eighteenth year, to have Princeton again and the seminary, his work and Mary, to live better and more wisely, if a man might have the chance — He thought of the boys and the mistakes he felt he had made in their training, and he groaned, heavy in spirit. To be more patient, to expect less of the very young, to have more faith in his own strong blood and less in discipline. All that he would do and yet — ah, that brought him up short; here was Francie, still a child, still being disciplined, and he was using the same old method with her. He was forbidding, commanding. He wasn't trusting his own blood in her as Mary thought he should. He often milled over it these days and now, on the street car, he made the usual review and advanced upon the new development.

Wasn't he trusting his own blood in her to-day? He was when he shouldn't be. God only knew where it might lead, this traipsing off to the country that a child might be free with her baby love — little chit of a thing like Frances, enchantingly pretty and slim, handed over to a young, immoral, worldly agnostic like that Stanhope. All right to talk of his blood and Mary's in her veins if she were allowed to follow its instincts, but heady youth like that Richard sometimes gave a girl no chance to decide, decided for her and the mischief was done.

Having reached that climax, which the other fellow in Angus knew was just a bugaboo that bolstered up his resistance to Richard, Angus' thought jumped over to Mary, Mary playing her mother game to get him out of Frances' way! The flat chuckle was lost in the rattle of the car. That Mary was a cute one! She had her way when she wanted it. And she had wanted it this morning; old softy, to give way to Frances in her calf love.

Calf love. He wondered — was it? The child had

had a bad year. She had been brave about it and quite patient, quite prettily patient in a silent way. As Mary said, it was her first sorrow and she bore it well, for there was no doubt but that young Stanhope was the sort a girl would care for. Mary had explained that. A most eligible youth, well educated, handsome, rich, brilliant, popular. " Strange thing that he should have picked out Francie," Mary had said. Well, the young — you couldn't tell a thing about them. They never jumped the way they were headed. Like as not Remington would introduce Francie to some missionary out there in Egypt who would be the real love of her life. It went that way outside of romantic fiction. First loves were wild, incalculable, blind, then there was heartbreak for a while, a very short while, before sanity and the right love came. Look at Mary now and her affairs, dear Mary.

II

The car had reached the shopping district, but Angus, dreaming over his book, mixing Brooks philosophy with rumination, was unobservant of the crowds that lined the street. He was unaware of the approaching parade, which he had hoped to see, until it was upon him blaring out some march or other that mingled with thunder and the rattle of the car. He did not know that Frances and Dick were within a few hundred yards of him, but he thought of them and was sorry, saddened by the spectacle that went swinging past him in the street. He was old and full of memories and he felt, not so much the Great War as he watched the marchers, but the Civil War and the sadness and horror of all wars.

Shiff, shiff, shiff, he heard the feet when the car stopped, and the throaty roll of thunder that startled him, so like the guns of Gettysburg it was. The car, with

unfeeling disregard for the passing tragedy of youth
sacrificed, picked up speed, out of rhythm with the band,
and racketed him along and away down past the marchers so rapidly he could not focus upon them. He had
not heard " The Star Spangled Banner ", but he had seen
the flag and his misty eyes strained back through the
window at its brave colors, its beautiful symbolism, in
relief against the dull buildings that lined the way.

III

The butler at the Grieve country house had sent the
motor to meet Angus' car and he rode in cushioned ease
along the Lake Shore boulevard to the great Italian
house. It was a beautiful ride. Angus was glad
Grandpa Grieve had not come out to meet him; he would
have been obliged to talk, whereas alone he could look
out across the lake to the Canadian shore and watch the
gray clouds trailing low above the water.

The houses and lawns with their beds and borders of
bright spring flowers held his interest less than the budded shrubbery and trees close to the road. The houses
were to him but pretentious mountains of gold, too
expensive to be interesting, too big to be inviting. Archi-
tectural detail was an unopened book to him. The old
southern colonial that he had known was like the memory
of a beloved face, peculiarly his own, removed by tender
association from other styles. None was so beautiful
or so gracious. He was content to pass the houses
by and see only the work of God's hand in the landscape.

As the car rolled up the long drive Angus saw that
Grandpa Grieve had tottered out to meet him. The
feeble old man came shuffling down the path, his trembling head bowed, his flexed knees hardly moving as he
pushed his feet along the walk. He heard the car and

stopped, waved his stick and watched, mouth ajar, while the car drew up and Angus, feeling suddenly spry and youthful, stepped down beside him.

It was a pleasant enough day for Angus. Old Grandpa's deafness and palsied helplessness contrasted so sharply with his own vigor that he felt himself a youth indeed and was convinced, when Mr. Grieve quavered, " Only seventy, you're only seventy? " that he had been making a monkey of himself with his feelings of old age. A man of the senior Grieve's experience could see. It was time to stop such talk. At seventy-five he might have reason to begin again.

It was hard for Angus to keep his mind on the older man's conversation. He lived in his orchids and gardens; the goldfish pool, the birds and the dogs about the place were the centers of his interest. He talked with gentle insistence, retailing to Angus the virtues, the vices, the pedigrees of each pet, and whether it was fish, fowl or beast Angus was bored. He listened and appeared to be interested, but his thought was in the world outside — with Frances for the most part — and though he enjoyed the beauty of the great place and the peace, the friendliness of his host and the delicate food served him, he was restless.

From the first he perceived that his coming had been made an occasion. The placid ripples on the surface of the old gentleman's life had been whipped into waves. He ate his luncheon with an air of adventure and explained gently, " These things are not permitted me unless the untowardness of events warrants. Mush and milk, I have secretly to admit to you, are my nightly portion, while a little lamb chop, a bit of chicken or a delicate arrangement of some fish is my noon dinner usually. I find I prefer to live long rather than to live heartily. I have had to choose as we all must, sooner or later, Doctor." Angus agreed, enjoying his broiled chicken none the less for the threatened abstemiousness. Sufficient unto the day — he would eat now and be thankful.

"I had Amanda telephone my son Henry that you were coming to-day. I was sure he would make it possible to get here for luncheon with us. He is very fond of you, as I have so often told you, very fond, and would be here, I know, were it not for these motors that are needed for the war. He said as much. He made it quite clear to Amanda. Amanda is the maid, a most gentle and considerate woman, a jewel in my days; so kind to me. But Amanda said Henry, my son, might find it possible to get out a little later and motor you back to town."

Angus hoped so. He saw too little of Henry Grieve. The ride with him would be a delight.

IV

Henry came at four and made short work of his visit with his father. He patted the rounded old back and shouted rapidly, "I have to get back to work, father. This war stuff moves so slowly, no matter how we push it, I can't endure any trifling with it. I'm going to bring Celia out to dinner Sunday and Ned, if we can get him. He's going to enlist — Ned. He's too young for the draft but he can enlist, and I want him to. It's what you'd have done yourself."

Henry's presence was like a small thunder storm. His voice boomed through the vast rooms; he strode about in a great stew and hurry, but was ever affectionate and smiling. He joked in parting and if his father failed to catch the point of his chaffing he felt the spirit of it and was cheered.

On the homeward drive Angus ventured, " I'm trying to figure out why you came out to drive me in, Henry. It's a long journey when you're so busy. You didn't think it necessary, did you? "

" Yes. But for another reason than the one you think. I am a self-appointed ambassador. I came because I wanted very much to see you. When father's house-keeper called up to ask me out, I hoped I could make it. I was sure I couldn't! " Henry laughed. " But this afternoon I decided I would have to make it. I had luncheon on the fly down at the Athletic Club with a friend of mine and his children. His son's about to go over to France, a fine chap, been up to Plattsburg and is ready for his war job. The boy interested me im-mensely. Immensely! I assure you. I like him and I felt — well, you know how we older fellows feel when we see these younger chaps shouldering arms to set right a world we've made a wretched mess of. I felt I'd like to serve that young chap if I could; I didn't think how, but if I could I knew it would do me more good than him. To my surprise, my chance came. I found later he needed help and a sort of help I could give him, at that."

Henry paused and let the silence hang a moment. Angus, feeling the need of recognizing this confidence, said, " I know how you feel. I understand. A young chap going out to give everything for his country ought to have every ounce of support we older men can give him." He was thinking of Jimmie, who had gone, and of John, who was going; those two were enough to fill his vision.

" You feel that way too? " said Henry.

" I do. Certainly I do."

" You feel, do you, that we ought to rise above dif-ferences that have mattered in our civic life and get a bigger outlook? You would do that if you were in my place?"

"I don't know why not! I can't imagine quibbling over anything in the face of war. Perhaps I don't just get the idea, Grieve. Does what I think or would do matter so much?"

"Yes. It's what you would do that I want to know. The case is just this. It's my friend Stanhope's son, Richard. Dick, I'd rather call him."

Henry Grieve heard Angus grunt and to himself he said, "Ah! now the shoe pinches. Well, we'll see." To Angus he said, "We'll just drive around by the boulevard, beautiful afternoon for it, and I can work enough later. I want to tell you this Stanhope story, knowing, as I do, that you know my understanding of that old trouble back in the club the women had—I forget its name but we both remember the affair."

"We do, but I don't hold that against young Stanhope, Henry, not for a moment. That was his mother, and I have no rancor there after these ten years or more."

"No, I hope not. They have trouble, that family, but my friend Stanhope is a prince of a fellow. He's as fine an Englishman as was ever absorbed in America. He comes of a long line of Americans but his type holds true. I've been over there and know his sort and he's sterling clean through. His wife's another story and she's made life as unhappy as she well could, but the boy, this Dick, is his father's son."

"You're wrong there, Henry. Just pardon me," said Angus. "I have had dealings with the young man, and he talked to me in my own living room almost as insultingly as his mother talked in the club that day. That much of his mother is in his blood. I've met it."

"Well—" Henry waived that. "Let's begin back.

Let me tell my story. I'll listen later to all you have to say. I went into the club for lunch to-day and near the door saw Stanhope waving to me. The man's face was a light, a torch. I never saw such a look. I went to him and he asked me to join them; he urged it and I saw it would give him pleasure to show off his boy. They had begun luncheon, but I started in with them, and then sat a bit over the coffee. I want to tell you I'd be as proud as Felix if that Dick were mine. I ask no more of Ned than that, at Dick's age, he'll be as fine. Stanhope hailed every familiar face he saw and introduced Dick. The boy had come on from Cambridge to march in that parade, a propaganda stunt and a rather dismal thing, I take it, from what they said. He's a Plattsburg product and must go back to-night and be ready to be sent out anywhere at any time. Well, Dick had an engagement he was evidently thinking about, for he began to watch the time and he said, 'How about a car, dad?' I could see he was on edge with nerves. I broke up the party then by taking Stanhope with me and letting Dick go off alone in his father's coupe, and no sooner were we alone than Felix broke out. He's rather quiet than otherwise, not a complainer, but his heart was sore for Dick, and I had the shock of my life when I found that you were at the bottom of it, Doctor."

Angus made a vehement gesture, but Henry Grieve was not to be stopped. "I know I have seen but one side, and I want yours, but the thing I realize is that we're *in war* and time is precious and youth is valuable and beautiful and ace high right now. Dick has until midnight, and that means you have until midnight to set things right for him before he goes out to face — God knows what."

Henry stopped and pulled his soft felt hat an inch lower on his forehead. Beneath its brim Angus saw the genial face set and tense. He knew it was turned from him. He had said he would hear what Angus had to say, but nothing Angus could say would change his mind. He was in arms for defense of youth sacrificed. He saw nothing else nor would see else. Angus felt several responses to the look on that familiar face. He was resentful and indignant both. He would not admit a degree of shame, but the quality of his indignation included enough to make him uneasy.

"Well, now that your mind is made up in judgment against me, you probably are willing to hear my story. In the first place, Grieve, I know how you feel about these young chaps. I have felt it longer than you have and more keenly, for I have two sons in it now. Furthermore, we are discussing a case that touches intimately and for all time on my young daughter's life. You know Frances and you know young Stanhope. Is your championship of him greater than your consideration for her?"

Henry brought a broad hand down hard on the wheel. "No. It is not. I am here to make you see that the religious opinions of a young chap Dick's age are just college talk. There's every possibility for him to change; an influence like Frances', your influence, if you'd let him feel it. And then this — if you think you're behaving as a disciple of Christ in this matter, you're just plain off your trolley and it's the first time since I've known you that I have felt anything but profound respect, even reverence, for your stand.

. "Doctor Stevenson, if you had heard Felix this noon, you would know that I am fighting you now as much for Christ's sake as for Dick's. In Felix' eyes and Dick's you're not taking the Christian stand. Christ would put his arm about that young man and love him. He wouldn't hold off from a mind, a soul and heart like

Dick's, and Felix knows it. Why haven't you gone
after Dick to get him?"

"I have, as far as possible. You can't force Christianity on a proud young cub who despises your faith as
he despises ours, yours and mine."

"You can have faith and hope and charity. Patience,
and you can set him a good example."

Angus lost his temper. "Look here, Henry!" His
eyes snapped as he leaned forward, looking at his friend.
"The bone of contention in all this mess is my daughter.
Don't forget that."

"No, I won't. But I can tell you that if you are
considering just your daughter, you couldn't do better
for her than to give her her way. She'll bring Dick
home to the truth. She'll do more with her love than
you ever can — and Dick is worth it." He paused and
shook his head impatiently. "I can't see it any other
way. I can't possibly."

Angus sat silent. He felt misunderstood, and to
have it come from Henry Grieve was almost more than
he could bear. But he couldn't suffer in silence. He
had to defend himself. He began in a gentler voice.
"Henry, you want me to do as Christ would do in such
a case. Very well. Let me tell you what I have done.
My daughter climbed out a window to go to a dance.
She left her mother hurt at home, in the care of a
stranger and a stupid maid. She met Dick Stanhope at the party and their long acquaintance burst into
conflagration as they danced together — just what I'd
expect of the wretched business. Dick talked that night
against her religion, tried to teach her his paganism and
I believe succeeded in getting a hold on her mind that
has already done some damage. He brought her home
and I opened the front door to find her in his arms. I
don't hold that against him, for it was mutual. Frances

was in love with him. I decided that night to be as fair
as possible to him, though the son of his mother was not
acceptable to me, I assure you. He came the next day
and insulted me in my own living room. He did it well;
he had his sophomoric arguments down pat and he did it
thoroughly. In the end, he admitted that he is not
morally immaculate and as a result I forbade him to
have anything to do with Frances, but he has written to
her just the same off and on. I don't know how much.
Now to-day my wife, of a mind with the rest of you, has
persuaded me into getting away from home to give them
a day together. Will you tell me what more I could
have done? Frances is too young to be engaged, much
less married. Tell me now, what in the eyes of a
worldly-wise Christian, I should do."

Henry laughed. "That's the story, is it? Well — "
he laughed again as if something amused him mightily.
"That's very interesting. When Frances got out that
window — and went off to the dance — she did just
exactly what you would have done in the same circumstances." Henry slapped Angus' knee. "Chip off the
old block, Doctor! It stumps me the way parents go
on, generation after generation, forbidding things as if
they didn't know that but feeds the desire. Well, so
she climbed out the window!" Henry's voice was so
infectiously brimming with amusement that Angus was
unable to repress a smile. Henry looked at him and
they grinned together irresistibly.

"Then," said Henry, "you took the young fellow's
theology as seriously as if he'd been a backsliding bishop.
You did some more forbidding and you have chalked
Dick's name up in black on the morality count. On
that I do admit a little sympathy for you, but how many
of us were chalked up white by our wives' fathers?
Celia's father didn't ask me, nor did Celia, but if I had

discussed my religion and my morals with him at the
time I fell in love with Celia, I would have been put
down in the black. Were you questioned about it all by
your wife's family?"

"No, I wasn't. That doesn't affect my daughter's
case."

"No? Well, Doctor, after all, this whole business
comes down for you and for me to the matter of deciding what Christ would do in such a case, were He
here in the Great War. I think He'd put a very gentle
arm about Dick and another about Frances and *love*
them — and make His love so strong He'd win them.
That's what I think He'd do and that's what I believe
you're going to do, for to me you walk as surely in
Christ's footsteps as any man who ever lived. When
you strip this case of its very personal aspect and realize
that your love for your daughter is making you a wee
bit jealous, you'll hear God's voice and it will probably
come in the words of Christ when He said, 'Greater
love hath no man than this — that a man lay down his
life for his friends' — that's Dick, you know. That
fits; and then go on to them and quote, 'This is my
commandment — that ye love one another.' You may
as well advise it, Doctor, for they're going to, anyway,
and who are you to say they have chosen wrongly. I
desire only the best for Frances. If my Ned were in
love with her, I'd kidnap her for him, but Dick is of the
best. What more can you want?"

"I want a young man of Christian ideals, since you
ask me. You've been a little slow getting to my objec-
tions, but that's one. He's an agnostic, a pagan, an
anti-Christ. He told me himself he'd sweep the church
out of existence if he had his way. He's no better than
any young blood that hung around Nero's court."

"Rubbish! He's modern, he has brains, courage,

patriotism, money. He has everything I want for my daughter. He's as cram full of American ideals as the Detroit schools and Harvard can stuff him. He's a Christian and doesn't know it. We're none of us Christians for that matter, but he's as full of it as any of us."

"Is that so!" Angus snorted with scorn. "I believe you think you're telling the truth, Grieve. As Christian as any of us! You don't recognize a man's efforts to be a Christian when you see him at it. You are supposed to believe as I do believe, that 'he that believeth not is condemned already, because he hath not believed in the name of the only begotten Son of God.' That is straight English, Henry. There is no compromise in it, no twaddle that can possibly be interpreted as meaning, 'If you're a nice, polite, social being you won't be condemned for not believing upon Christ Jesus.' There is so much driveling nonsense these days about Christ's love. His *love* that forgives all things, understands all things, *permits* all things! Very good, that, very nice and sweet and comforting, but Christ came with love — *and a sword!* I serve him with love — *and a sword,* and I don't like to hear that you've gone over to all this weak one-sided *love* talk.

"There's a wave of criticism going out against the Puritans these days. We are seeing only their hard side, their bigotry and egotism and mercilessness. What blindness, what stupid blindness that we forget what the England was that they left, what they were striving to prevent in this new country. The easy religion and morals, the tolerance and broadmindnesses of this generation are the rot that will eat out the roots of our civilization. Christ didn't prescribe easy, gracious culture. He preached utter spirituality, complete forgetfulness of the flesh and the material. Henry, I'm a seer. I know it, I feel it, and all that in me is genial and

affectionate and merry has had to be sacrificed to the
vision I have of our civilization in decay because of our
easy, slipshod religion. It has become the thing, the
correct, intelligent thing to stand aside and tolerate.
Watch Rome burn. Do you remember that at the
crucifixion of Christ there were those who stood aside
and looked on? They took no part either in the crucifixion or the befriending of Jesus. They stood by, sorry
that life was dealing cruelly with one of their fellows,
but not sorry enough to fight for Him. It's the easiest
way. I could enjoy life more if I would do so. I'd like
immensely to be a gentleman of culture and large indif-
erence to the mob, but that way lies death. That way
lies destruction and as surely as God speaks He com-
mands me to fight on. Now you — even you — come
along and urge me to permit my daughter to sell her
birthright of righteousness for a little mess of spring-
time love pottage!"

"I do. I want you to permit your daughter to live
her own life."

Henry's answer had come so quickly, in a voice so
firmly insistent, that Angus looked at him in amazement,
but saw only his tense profile under the pulled-down
brim of his hat. He had supposed he would win Henry
by this last strong argument. He had expected him to
sigh his concession of victory. That he did not was
proof of the depth of his feeling in the matter. They
rode on in silence and, while Henry's chin held firm,
Angus felt himself sink and sicken with the discouragement of defeat. His great, affectionate heart yearned
toward Henry, for his smile, his sympathy, his fellowship. He seemed to be facing all his dear ones and
seeing, as his eyes met theirs, the averted look of disapproval; Frances reproachful; Mary troubled and out of
sympathy; Henry hard-faced against him.

He said at last, " Henry, I wonder if you know just how much you mean to me, your friendship, your understanding. I wonder if you know."

" Perhaps not and yet I feel free to talk as I have talked to-day because you have so often taken counsel with me. It has made me a better man to have your faith and confidence. I have been made very happy by your acceptance of my judgment. I recall times when you have let me influence you profoundly and have returned to thank me for bucking my judgment against yours. You have been willing at times to see life through my eyes. To-day I have assumed that you are still willing, and yet I know I don't mean as much to you as you do to me. Your strength has pulled me through many a temptation. You are not only my good friend but my priest. I've hung on to you often — the thought of you — when you didn't know and have gotten courage from you. I go about in the clubs and the social life here and see things that sometimes make me feel Detroit's just an oozing sink of iniquity, with you, in the middle of it all, a sort of rock of Gibraltar. The granite of you is of a piece with the rock of ages, Doctor. That's the way I feel."

Angus took this with great humility of spirit. He said slowly, " I don't deserve that. I don't deserve it."

" You do deserve it. You're the only man I know in this city who's ridden over the money hag that goads us all. You've lived tremendously and made so deep a mark on Detroit that now — in this war, I am jealous for you. I want to help you see as I see, for we're alike in thinking we know, and in fighting for our convictions."

" Yes," Angus said. He was feeling deeply. Henry's praise coming at a time when he was sensing failure rather than achievement was humbling. He felt ashamed to hear such good of himself. "Henry," he began when they stopped at the curb before his own door, "as you say, I have accepted your point of view before now in times when I was perplexed and anxious to do the right thing. I'm going to do it again. You haven't convinced me that I am wrong, not in the least, but you show me that convictions can be pressed to the point of fanaticism. If I seem to you to be tyrannical to my own daughter, an ecclesiastical jailer, then I, or something, is wrong! I have only tried to hold her within the boundaries of an ideal that has never cramped me. If it cramps her, and if you see cause for pitying her, I shall let her out. I haven't dreamed that I was imprisoning her. She is so young, you know, and I have felt that soon, soon — any day now, she herself would see what I have been trying to show her. If she sees when it is too late that, perhaps, I must be willing to call — her problem." Angus had opened the door of the car. Slowly he stepped down to the curbing and stood looking up at Henry. His face had changed, Henry saw, and wore a look he had never seen there before. It was as if he had surrendered his sword to the enemy. There was a stillness, a consciousness of rebuke accepted. That he had come representing the enemy Henry suddenly regretted.

"I hope you don't put it, even to yourself, that you are doing this because it is my judgment. If you don't see it yourself — of course — "

"I see — enough. Mary has been trying to show me the light. Frances has kept a strong pressure on me with her patience and silences and — and her eagerness to be off to her work with Remington. The world has tried to show me that it can't be done — that I am wrong, but for myself I find no possible comfort in compromise. Christ said no more about love than He

said about the difficulty of serving two masters. He
said again and again that to follow Him was to carry a
cross, yet, for me, it has been a burden that I love." He
shut the door of the car. " Well, Henry, thank you for
bringing me in. It's all right — our talk. I'll make
your young warrior happy for you." He had backed
away, smiling, his hat in his hand, the sun glinting
warmly on his white hair and the dear shining face from
which the beaming blue of his eyes carried their message
of deep affection.

Henry waved in return and felt a lump in his throat.
He stepped on the starter and slipped his clutch into
second. " God help me," he was saying. " What have
I done now? What have I done?"

CHAPTER XI

I

WHEN they entered the shop of the plumes Frances' first impression was of its repelling disorder. There was no restraint in the arrangement of the cases or counters. Dry goods and notions and ready-made clothing were heaped in confusion everywhere, and there were no shining surfaces of glass or wood to impress the shopper. Dick led the way to the cave of the plumes, a dark aisle's end where an anæmic young woman pulled a string and thereby caused the flame in an arc lamp to leap into white ghastliness.

"We want to see some plumes," said Dick, looking about him, frowning. "Ostrich, you know, and long."

"Yes, sir," said the young woman in a voice and with a pronunciation so English that Frances thought she must surely be a recent acquisition to the store. She bent over a pile of boxes and pulled one over to a littered table. "These are the first-grade plumes," she said; "had you a choice in color?"

Dick looked quickly at Frances, and Frances, meeting his eyes, opened her lips to speak but smiled instead. "You have a choice, haven't you, Dick? What color is it you like?"

"How did you know? Yes, I have a picture of you in that green that isn't bottle green or olive green but —" he looked about searching for something in the desired shade. A swift glance had shown the box to contain only black and white.

"Jade." Frances supplied him, sure that she understood.

"That's it — jade green! I knew it wasn't bottle green. It's that green that's so awfully dashing with white. Green plume, green parasol, green things here and there on white — and white shoes."

"I know. I love that too."

The young woman was peering into a dozen boxes as they talked. She arrived, finally, at the desired collection and opened it for their eager inspection. Great cloudy masses of jade, of coral and orange and purple mingled in brilliant harmony. Dick's hand went swiftly to the green and he shook one in front of Frances. "Isn't that corking, such long thing-a-majigs hanging from the stick! But you choose the colors you like best. As many as you want. You don't need to wear them all on the same hat, you know."

"Oh, no! I know." Frances drew the green plume across her cheek, closing her eyes. "It's lovely. I do want this one. It's more than two feet long, I believe."

"Twenty-six inches," the anæmic young woman offered and to the Detroiters it sounded like twenty-sax anches. "We have some especially fine black ones. Black is always serviceable and we have some that are many colors, very chic."

Frances said, "I like black." She was thinking of her mother and the old rooster tails on the ancient hat. She told herself that plumes lasted a generation and she and her mother could take turn about wearing the black one.

They chose two long black plumes, then Dick asked for those of many colors. "Are they plaid?" he said.

The saleswoman did not smile, but Frances did and squeezed his hand. "I am content with these, Dick. This is tons and tons more than I can wear out in a life-

time." But Dick liked the many-colored plumes that
shaded softly from cream to pale yellow, to deeper
golden tints until at the very tips they were orange and
amber. He bent toward Frances to whisper, " You'll
need them when — you know — " and Frances nodded
like a conspirator.

The saleswoman gathered the plumes they had chosen
in her hand like a bouquet of flowers and said, looking at Frances' hat, " Do you think we can put them
in the crown of your hat? They crush down pretty
well."

Frances blinked at her, not comprehending, until Dick
laughed. " I told you they'd spot you as from over the
river. If you put them in the crown of your hat the
customs officer won't know you have them. A parcel,
you know, excites their greed for duty." Dick was
taking money from a leather bill fold. " How much are
they? " he asked.

The clerk figured a moment on the lid of a box.
" Twenty-three dollars," she said, " and shall I put them
in wrappings? "

Frances took off her hat, but the soft mass was too
large to be accommodated. " Wrap them," Dick decided and turned to Frances. " We'll pay the duty.
You can't go to dinner all smuggled in plumes."

While they waited for change and the package, they
exclaimed in whispers over the absurd price. " I was
worried," Frances admitted. " I thought we'd have to
pawn this — maybe." She indicated her new ring and
they moved closer together.

" Isn't this dingy and uninspiring — this place? We
don't have to pay for mahogany and plate glass, that's
sure. They have the goods and I'll bet when they say
wool is wool here, that it is wool. They are pretty sure
to put all their emphasis on quality and they don't have

to dike the place all up like Tiffany's to get people to buy sham stuff like our stores."

" Then why don't we Detroit people buy here some-times? " Frances asked.

" Duty. You can't avoid it regularly, you know, and the funny sort of things they have in some lines. Get Charlotte to tell you about the embroidered stuff they showed her when she wanted these shimmy shirts you wear. Legs in them, tight, and ruffles hanging way down. And nightgowns with sleeves down to your knuckles and necks way up to your hair. Charlotte says you'd think Queen Victoria was still ruling the world."

Frances was laughing at Dick's descriptions.

" Of course no Anglo-Saxon would ever have in-vented the immoral, little peek-a-boo things you girls wear. He wouldn't believe nice women would buy them, even if he did invent them; but a Frenchman — " Dick shrugged expressively, " takes a veil and some ribbons for over the shoulders and marks it eighteen dollars and you girls all fall for it. For a fact, Sharley has some that haven't an inch of real goods in them. I don't see how she manages to keep them from wear-ing full of holes in an hour."

Surely Dick's mood had changed. He kept Frances laughing during the long drive up the shore toward Lake St. Claire and dinner. She herself said funny things and Dick's mouth was open and every tooth shining when they drove with a great curving sweep into Sam's cindered " front yard " and stopped at the steps.

" I didn't know you could be so funny! " he said, leaning back in the car. " I've laughed till I ache. You ought to be on the stage."

Frances opened her vanity case and consulted it gravely. " You ought to see our family when we get started cutting up. Father's the finest comedian I ever saw. Dick, he's tremendous. He can mimic anybody."

" Your father? " Dick was incredulous. He stared at her, sobering.

" Why, yes! You don't know him! He's a regular good fellow. Once we gave a party. It was the boys' seventeenth birthday and a masquerade but not dancing. Everybody was to come in costume and we played charades and had music and foolishness. Father wouldn't tell us how he was going to dress and when the first people arrived he came stumbling downstairs dressed like a little farm boy in overalls cut off at the knees, a broken suspender, an old straw hat and rope fringed out to look like hair. He did everything exactly as a self-conscious little kid would, stuttered, wiped his nose on his sleeve, sniffed as if he had a cold and kept sticking his tongue out on his upper lip. Nobody was so funny. Everybody watched him and laughed at him as if there weren't another clever costume present, and yet there were a dozen that had taken more time and effort. He has the personality, the magnetism, and every gesture he makes when he is mimicking is exactly true to the type."

Dick sighed soberly. " Oh, Francie, why didn't the gods juggle things so that I could be in Detroit near you for a while, and get acquainted with you and your family? I'd try like the deuce to see your father as you see him." His eyes had saddened. He gazed at Frances wistfully for a moment before pulling himself up. " Well — " he opened the door. " Stay here and I'll root out Sam."

He went bounding up the steps and in. Frances heard him calling. " Hey, Sam. Oh, Sam — ee " — and then greetings and a great slap on somebody's back. In a moment Dick, slim and elegant beside a keg-shaped, wheezing, red-faced old fellow, stepped on to the porch.

Sam had a great, puffy hand on Dick's shoulder. They were talking and from the first sound of his voice Frances was enthralled by Sam's sibilant and whistling pronunciation of the letter S.

They looked down at Frances and the old innkeeper bowed. "It's early in the see-son and I don't got them vegetables effrybody likes, but I got the frogs and the chickens and all the canned stuff you vant. Some noddles too. Some soup."

Dick interrupted. "That's what we want. Never mind the vegetables. You have all that pickled stuff, same as ever, haven't you?"

"Yaw. I got blenty ever'ting like dot. You hang around. I call you ven dinner's ready."

Dick opened the door of the car for Frances. "This is Miss Stevenson, Sam. She's very, very fond of tartar sauce with the frog legs. She wanted me to tell you about that, sure."

Sam winked at Frances. "Yaw, I know about those sauce appetites you got, plamin' it off on a lady." He waved a long arm like a great rope of bologna towards the water. "My skiff's out a'ready. Got her painted fresh up. You take a leedle row whilst I fix up for you."

He turned back into the bare old house as Dick and Frances started for the lake.

It was evening and the long shadows of spring lay lightly on the young grass. From the moment they tepped into the freshly painted skiff the hush of twilight laid its calming touch upon their happiness. Dick took the oars and turned the bow upstream. The deep copper glow of the setting sun was behind Frances, who had wrapped her arms about her knees in a cuddling attitude that was altogether delightful to behold. Her silhouette suggested the sleepy huddling of a young robin

at twilight. She rubbed her cheek against the fur collar
of her coat and gazed far beyond Dick into the shadows
that were deepening along the fringe of shore. Dick
watched her and wondered what she was seeing that she
could be so unself-consciously abstracted under his gaze.
He frankly observed her ankles and feet and found that
they confirmed his dream of their remembered grace.
Her hands, clasped about her knees, were like no other
hands in the world that he had ever seen or touched,
and the turn of her wrists gave him a distinct emotion
of pleasure.

A little puff of wind moved the hair that touched her
cheek and sent the water gurgling about the prow of the
boat. " That sound," Frances said, looking up. " That
sound of water! It belongs with you. That night at
the Boat Club, you remember? The water whispering
around the spiles? "

Dick nodded, but did not pause in his rowing. He
had pulled his hat down and Frances could not see his
eyes. " That sound of water, the peculiar smell of your
cigarettes, a certain sound a motor makes in just some
cars — those things belong with you, are you. While
you are gone — when those things touch me I shall
regret — dreadfully."

Dick held the oars above the water and the drops ran
like a string of beads from the blades. " Regret? " his
voice told his surprise.

" Yes. Of course. You didn't think — I wouldn't."

" Just what will you regret? I want you to tell me."

" That I couldn't — marry you to-day."

There was a long silence. The boat ceased to move
forward. The current annulled the impetus of Dick's
last stroke. " And yet, it was to escape regrets, that you
— didn't."

" Yes. Either way — I have regrets."

The oars dipped into the river but Dick did not row. After a while he said simply, " I suppose so. I can't see it. I can't appreciate control under these circumstances especially, when it was the most highly respectable arrangement known to civilization. ' In the eyes of God and these witnesses,' " he quoted inaccurately. " But I suppose so — that what you say is the way it would have to be — with you. Regrets either way. I thought — " He began rowing and left the sentence unfinished.

" You thought — " Frances reminded. She was studying him now as he had studied her and his eyes were far away on the copper-tinted sky.

" I thought there was no risk of regret for you. I thought if you chose as your father would have you choose, you would be safe from regret."

" Dick! Did you think that? Did you think I didn't want to do as you wished? "

" I thought — Well, Frances, I thought the fact, which was that you had no choice. You had to obey your father. You aren't free. You are bound to him."

Frances was silent. There was no answer, but she wished Dick had not chosen to say it just that way. He turned the boat about and the current caught them. There was no need for rowing and Dick shipped the oars and sat, elbows on knees, watching Frances. She felt his eyes on her face. The full illumination of the afterglow was upon her now, a soft orange light, smoke veiled. Above the distant city the gray of commerce made its blot upon the evening sky and was metamorphosed by the great alchemist into trailing, floating ribbons of chiffon. To both intent young gazers Sam's call to dinner came as a relief. He helloed from the porch of the old gray house and waved the bologna arm.

The warmth of the dining room, with its delicious

odors of fresh food, cheered Dick visibly. He responded
to Sam's joking with good-natured teasing and between
times talked to Frances in undertones about the place, the
food, Sam's goodness and the fun he had had there in
times past. When he was impersonal thus, and grave,
Frances found the expression of his eyes a constant hurt.
It was not that he reproached her, but he was feeling
the consciousness of a greater love than was given him
in return. To Frances the error of this belief was
torment. She longed to make him understand that she
cared as much as he, but words would not convince him.
She must prove it by agreeing to marriage immediately,
and that she could not do, not if it cost her her life's
happiness.

The soup was the perfection of the German art and
they felt no resentment against it or Sam because his beginnings had been in that despised land. The frogs' legs
and tartar sauce, the chicken and noodles with their
butter-browned crumbs, the half-dozen varieties of
pickles were novel and delicious to Frances. She had
no desire for the dessert Sam served, and watched Dick
eat his with thought only for her delight in him, his
appealing modernity and clean-cut features.

It was black dark when they stepped outdoors again.
The river showed reflected lights that made no illumination in the night. There was no moon and the stars
were dimmed by mist. Frances shivered even in her
warm coat and Dick exclaimed, "You're shaking like a
leaf in the wind! Here, take deep, deep breaths and
hold them. That room was warmer than I realized."
He put both arms about her and felt her eyelashes brush
his chin as she stood close against him. "I thought we
could spend our last hour here, but this isn't very inviting. We can't sit on this chilly landscape."

As he spoke the door opened quickly and Sam's

rotundity was silhouetted against the warmly lit interior.

"Hey, I meant to tell you," he shouted kindly, "Oscar's down in the grove burning bonfires. You go down there where it's warm."

"I thought I smelled wood smoke," Frances cried happily, "but I knew it might be the wish for a fire that made the delusion."

They ran down the steps and around the building hand in hand. When they reached the back the bonfire was visible. It was pretty much smudge, but Oscar was leaning above it with a rake, lifting and poking. Dick found a log and dragged it nearer. "Which way's the smoke?" he asked and Oscar, without looking at them, said, "Straight up. Ain't no wind."

They fixed themselves comfortably and watched the climbing flames. Oscar seemed deaf and blind to their presence and raked and piled steadily, stolidly, while the beautiful light crept up into the branches of the trees and lit the tender young leaves that quivered there in the heat. Soon all the grove was filled with the glow and warmth of it and the last of the collected brush had been piled on the pyre. Dick rolled their log back a few feet and, to even up the comfort of the heat, they sat with their backs to the fire for a while. When they turned about they found that Oscar had departed, rake, wheelbarrow and all, and the magic stillness and glow were theirs alone.

Frances thought of Jimmie, lying by northern camp fires that summer when he had heard the call. She delighted in the smell of burning wood and the soft whispering of the leaves about them.

Dick felt none of the poetry of this last quiet hour. He took Frances' hand and closed his eyes as he leaned, elbow on knee, slightly away from her. He saw, with vision made acute by longing, Frances in jade and white

in Egypt, under low-spread awnings. He saw the
movement of a desert wind in her draperies and the
background of desert color. The Remington chap he
saw graceful, attractive, even though middle-aged, in
close conversation with Frances. They held pieces of
stone or something newly excavated. There was thrill
and eagerness and understanding in their attitude — and
a heavy curtain of distance and silence hung between
them and the north where he — Dick — in mud-spat-
tered khaki lay in a trench. "Bah —" He turned
suddenly to Frances and put his hands on her arms.
She looked up into his scintillating eyes, her lips parted
in astonishment.

"Frances," he began vehemently, "we're going to be
thousands of miles apart, maybe thousands of days.
We don't know. We can't guess, but I hate it. I hate
every vision I see of it. This is the last, this now, here
by the fire, and our drive home. I must see my mother
after I take you home; then — I'm going." He ceased
speaking. The words had come rapidly, but he held the
silence while he struggled to get control of his voice.
"I didn't hate this war — not half enough until now. It
was an excitement until to-day. I don't want to kill or
fight. I don't care a damn about the future of Europe.
I want to stay here and practice law and marry you and
live and love —" He broke off abruptly again. "I
didn't feel myself helpless until now. I have to go, I
have to go, and I can't remember ever having to do anything before that I wanted so damnably *not* to do."
Frances put an arm about his shoulders and his face
dropped to the cover of his hands.

She murmured over him, her eyes suddenly wet with
tears that had pressed upon her through all the long,
beautiful, painful hours of their day. Through tears
she saw the play of muscle in Dick's tense cheek and the

fire's reflection in the shining black of his hair. She put
her face down close to his and felt the quivering pulse
of his passionate rebellion. He was breathing stormily,
as bitterly insurgent against his fate as he had been
amenable to it a few days before. The instinct to soothe
left her before it found expression, and she broke into
quick hot sentences.

"We're both having to do a way we don't want to!
We're both letting something else shove us along as if it
were a pistol at our backs. It doesn't seem right. It
isn't right. I'm sick of it; sick, sick, sick of being
made to do what my own conscience tells me is all right.
Can't we find a way out, Dick? Can't we go off to some
place that will be our own world alone? A little island
somewhere with just — oh, just cocoanuts or something
like that, and you and I alone together. Free." She put
her hands on his wrists and pulled his hands from his
eyes. "Aren't we smart enough for that, Dick? Aren't
we? We ought to be smart enough, if we try — to
plan — "

Dick had raised his head. "No," he said roughly,
"we aren't smart enough. There's no smartness smart
enough for that. We can do what any fool would —
run to the end of our rope, then hang for our folly.
The pistol *is* at our backs. We're caught in the jam."
Frances knew by his voice that he was growing quieter.
Her quick response to his mood had been more soothing
than any amount of resistance. If she felt with him, if
they were insurgent together in spirit, there was, at
least, the solace for them both of perfect understanding.

Dick took Frances' hand and pressed her palm against
his lips. Their outburst ended as suddenly as it had
begun, and they sat gazing in the fire several moments
before Dick said, "I want to talk to you about money.
I want you to know that I have had an understanding

with my father. He knows that I am going to make a will at once. You are to have everything that is mine if I'm killed. There will be a regular income from investments my grandfather gave me. I have it now right along. That will be yours and some time something more from him and my father's estate. Your future as a war widow — or whatever you would be called — doesn't bother me. I am thinking of your needs now. You have to earn your living. I suppose you will — being you — send money to your father. But for God's sake, Francie, don't do without the things girls ought to have. I want you to have them, and there's no reason why you shouldn't. I want part of this money I have to be yours, right along now. Don't say anything." Frances had stirred restlessly and tried to speak. " Don't work up a lot of scruples. I'm married to you as far as I am concerned, in the eyes of my own soul, and I don't care for any further ceremony, but I do care that you should be provided for. You won't give me the absolute right, but you needn't make it harder by fussing up hair-splitting reasons why you can't accept it."

" But I can't."

" You can! "

" Dick! " Frances had drawn away. She looked down on his bowed head. " You know I can't."

" Do I? Well, anyway the Union Trust will send you a check every month from now on till I come back. And when I come back you will marry me instantly. You have promised that. That is settled." That he knew it was not settled he made clear by the note of interrogation in his voice. Frances' dignity crumpled into tenderness. Her arm went about his shoulders again.

" Oh, Dick, you're such a darling to me! I can't tell you — I can't ever tell you what I think of you. I'll take your checks and save them for furniture." She laughed and tears brimmed her eyes, but did not dim her smile.

"If you save that for furniture, I shall do just one thing — buy a stove with one check and burn the others in the stove. You're mine, and I have a right to give you money and you have a right to use it, and if civilization won't recognize the honesty and rightness of that, then I'm eternally dingbusted if I fight to save civilization!"

They began to laugh and made a game of abusing civilization and democracy and all the precious privileges that no amount of imagination could picture their lacking. Dick tired of the foolishness of it suddenly, and said, "I knew some artists in Boston when I was a soph. They really believed that way. There was a girl doing portraits and talking all sorts of revolutionary stuff about women and socialism and religion. She out-anarchied the anarchists and even had all children brought up in government homes while their mothers went out in pursuit of their careers. She didn't believe in marriage as approved by the Victorians at all, and while the stuff was new to me then it isn't now, but she thought the week-end husband was the solution of the divorce problem. She was interesting."

"She must have been." Frances thought Dick was but bravely making conversation. She felt no premonition of startling revelation.

"She was a most beautiful girl, tall as I am, and with hair the color of those ostrich plumes you called burnt orange this afternoon."

"You like them so tall?" Frances murmured.

"She was beautiful, very much so, and striking and poor as the deuce. She and two other girls lived in a vile little hole they called a studio, and on certain

evenings nobody could be admitted because their wet
clothes were hung all over the place to dry.   They each
had a night for washing things and the business of it
filled the whole flat.   The one I knew with the red hair
— orange rather — posed as proud and above assistance, but she knew how to work all sorts of games to
get what she wanted.   I thought I was in love with her.
That's why I'm telling you.   I thought I was, but it
makes me sick now — sick — to remember what an
ignorant youngster I was.   She was original.   She had
brains, and I did have immense respect for her mind.   I
still have.   She wasn't common in her ways.   She didn't
give her friendship easily, but she gave me a great deal
too much more — than her friendship."   He paused just
a moment before he said, " That wasn't terrible to hear,
was it?   That is what I wanted to tell you this afternoon.   I knew the truth wouldn't hurt you as much as
your imagination was hurting you.   I had to tell you —
for your own sake."

Frances was petrified.   She sat perfectly motionless,
wondering where her breath had gone.   It returned to
her and she gasped it quickly.

" I grew up that year," Dick continued.   He bent forward, between his knees, and picked small twigs from
the grass at his feet and tossed them on the fire.   " I
began an egotistical, raw-minded kid and ended — a man
with a conscience.   I knew remorse, and the terrible
injustice in the whole arrangement became abhorrent to
me.   I discovered my moral character and I have one.
That's why I told your father I was moral and then —
under his blue-lightning kind of a gaze — remembered
the time when I had not been.   Some men, Frances,
begin moral as boys, and end a world journey from their
first selves.   You understand the difference and are glad
I told you this; aren't you? "

Frances had herself in hand. She said huskily, " Yes
— I think — I'm glad; since you wanted to tell me."
And to cloak her tumultuous thought — " What became
of the — girl? "

" I don't know. That's the trouble. She never
agreed with my change. She professed to think me a
coward, and she drifted away. She didn't return to
Boston one fall and I've lost her. Of course I'm glad.
But I'm sorry too. I would like to know that things —
are right with her. But I am afraid they aren't."

" How could things be right with her? Her ideas are
cruel to herself."

" You have said it. I tried to make her see that, but
she was more independent than most men. She wanted
to do as she wanted to do, and a fig for the consequences.
She lost interest in me when I backslid from her extremes of modernity."

Frances was numbed by the surge of her aching
thoughts. She kept her gaze on the fire, locked in
silence. Dick waited, tossing twigs. He thought, " She
hated that. It cut deep, but she took it straight and not
a whimper. That's the last time, so help me God, I'll
ever hurt her! "

And Frances, biting her lower lip to stop its quivering, was saying to herself bitterly, " He wouldn't have
forgiven that in me. He couldn't have endured it — but
I have to. I did try to get away — but I couldn't."

At last Dick rose, stretching upward, and turning,
drew Frances to her feet. They walked slowly out of
the fire's glow into the shadows of the grove before he
said, " I suppose this would be called a successful adventure — this day. I have said all the things I had to say
and can go now — anywhere I have to go — with a feeling of relief. That, and the money — Frances, it had
to be said."

BOOK THREE

SEES THE COMPLICATIONS SIMPLIFIED AND ONE GREAT
PROBLEM ON THE WAY TO SOLUTION.

BOOK THREE

CHAPTER I

I

FELIX paced the marble corridors of the Michigan Central depot, waiting for Charlotte's train. It was not that the train was late; Felix was early. He was tremulous with eagerness to see his daughter and, as he strolled nervously, his lips moved in absorbed review of the time since he had last had her with him in Detroit.

After Dick had sailed, Rita had decided to go to California for a prolonged stay. She had an opportunity to rent an artist's bungalow in Carmel-by-the-Sea and she was eager to establish herself among producing intellectuals who would feel her sympathy and seek her inspiration and advice along with her tea. She had utterly failed to comprehend how Charlotte could prefer war work in Detroit to a share in her mother's social glory, but when she realized Charlotte's determination, she parted from her as she had parted from Felix and Dick, with no perception of her own shortcomings, but only a bitter realization of their inability to appreciate her rare qualities.

Felix had not tried to influence Charlotte in her choice, but he was delighted that she decided for the hard work in Detroit as against comparative leisure in Carmel. He was proud of her and happy for the few months she was with him before she was summarily ordered to Carmel by Rita's physician. The telegram said flu, and Charlotte arrived five days later to find her mother a triumphant little invalid, self-important and weakly imperious. She had outwitted death and she was giving herself full credit for her unconquerable fighting qualities.

" Just to show her," Charlotte had written her father, " she had a relapse, and so nearly snuffed out that I all but sent for you." But she pulled up once more, only to descend into a series of ailments that finally ended in old-fashioned pneumonia. All this had kept Charlotte engaged and it was thus that Dick had returned from France in bandages and had been with his father two months before Charlotte was free to join them.

Felix believed he anticipated most the sight of his two children reunited. That Dick was his once more, alive, and free from the army forever, was the deepest well of thankfulness his heart had ever known. The boy had done his part, and that his arm had been all but torn off his body in one of his first weeks in the trenches was certainly not his fault, though to hear him talk one would think he thought so.

II

The train arrived on the exact moment it was due and Felix saw Charlotte walking briskly up the incline toward the gates with a great increase of excitement. Beautiful she was to him, beautiful; straight and tall and as softly blonde as her mother was at her age. " Beautiful women in their way — a way I like." Charlotte's laugh was in his ears. He clasped the bundle of serge and blue fox and scented linen that was his daughter and kissed her before blinking at her through a mist that was happiness made suddenly visible.

" Dad, *dear*, it's so dandy to see you again! Are you alone; isn't Dick here? " She peered around her father.

Felix smiled. "No, I wouldn't let him come; he wanted to badly enough but the riding hurts him, the jarring. I do everything I can to keep him quiet."

"Does he show his long illness? Is he thin?"

"A little. I see more change in his eyes and face than in his figure. His eyes look older, much older and tired, and his cheeks are pretty hollow yet."

"Oh, I do want to see him! Mother's able to sit up now. She has a wonderfully devoted nurse. I know it was all right for me to leave, but she didn't see how I could want to. You know she wouldn't."

"I know."

They arrived at the waiting coupe and Felix went into his pocket for a tip to give the red cap who was stowing Charlotte's bag in the car. When they were on their way again, the subject of Rita was not resumed. Charlotte had made the report that she knew was expected.

"I have a surprise for you about Dick. We're not going to the club but to his office, his new office."

"Dick's!" Charlotte was properly surprised. "I can't imagine it. How? Why?"

"Well, you knew he had been reading law ever since he struck this country. I never saw anything to beat his endurance for it. He took the bar examinations and passed. Surely he wrote you that."

"Yes, but the office. So soon!"

"We had the chance to rent a particularly nice little suite in connection with the firm of Gage, Galloway and Vane, and he'll begin by doing some work for them. It's the right thing to do. He isn't able to work more than a few hours a day now, but it's a beginning, and his name's on the door. He's very happy about it. Very."

"He ought to be and I suppose —" Charlotte minced the word.

Felix understood and laughed. "You are quite right in supposing he wants to be married, but — the lady is still among the dead past of Egypt."

"Dick doesn't get over that? I thought — he might."

"On the contrary it is worse, if that be possible. Her letters, it seems, keep her very close to him. She writes well — just as she talks. I like the child through her letters, such as I have seen. Of course you know I am sincerely fond of her father now. You know that."

Charlotte nodded. "I knew you would be. He did come at you with amazing tact and, and — well, charm, I suppose is the word. I liked him myself, what little I saw of him, but it wasn't that. You wanted to like him for Dick's sake. That was half the battle."

"No." Felix brought the car to a stand. He made no effort to duck through the traffic, but waited until the stream had thinned before he crossed any street, Charlotte noted, wondering if it meant that "dad was getting old." "No," Felix repeated, starting forward. "I liked him from the beginning, way back years ago when we first came to Detroit. I hoped then that we would be friends. I felt that we had more in common than differences — and I was right. We have."

"I should think Dick and Frances were enough to have in common, anyway. Is he making a Presbyterian of you?"

"He doesn't try. After that first talk, when he told me how he stood and his desire to rise above differences for Frances' sake and so on, we have not discussed religion."

"Safest not to, of course. People as red-hot orthodox as he can't."

"Now my dear —" Felix' voice was a reproof. "That is not true. We do not avoid it. We have enough to say without getting into it. He lives his religion. I live mine, and Presbyterian and agnostic, our lives are tangent at so many points they overlap. It's a question of character, you know, anyway. Angus Stevenson, whatever he believed, would be a compelling character, a winning force. Of course he says he would have been a force for evil if he had not been caught, ' a brand from the burning, to be used in God's service.' His words those, and I agree that that, most certainly, is true in many cases. I have respect for the work his church does."

"You didn't once, father." Charlotte's voice had an edge. "I feel his influence on you right now. You never said that much good for the church before." She looked at his profile and laughed. "I didn't mean to remind you too much, but you must see that your saying such things is rather a surprise to me."

Felix was biting his lower lip, and he gazed straight ahead at the street. He said, "I wasn't conscious that I had shifted ground. I don't think I have, but as we grow older we either mellow or sharpen, and I hope what you call the change in me is merely the greater wisdom of my years, that I have sense enough not to be blind to any good."

"In that case — you're one angelic, old, dear thing and I know you're right. I'm getting nicer too, as I grow old. What building is that? It's new?"

"That — I call Dick's building. Its other name isn't worth my remembering. One of those windows on the nineteenth floor is Dick's. Rather two of those windows. He has his own private room and he uses the library, the reception room and stenographers of the firm. He is not of the firm, but with it, a most satisfactory arrangement that we made through Mr. Galloway, who lives at the club and has rooms near ours."

III

Charlotte pronounced Dick's building beautiful. She hurried down the marble hall to the door that bore his name, smiling with pleasure. She had only a moment to admire the black and gold lettering — Richard Stanhope, Attorney-at-law — on the ground glass door before the door was flung open by Dick.

"I was watching for your shadows on the glass," he cried, and put his arm around Charlotte. They kissed gently before Charlotte stood him off for inspection.

"Your right arm lacks nothing of its old skill," she laughed, "but that left." She put inquiring finger tips upon his shoulder. "It's helpless?"

"Just temporarily. It'll limber up in time." Dick closed the door and pushed his nicest chair toward his sister, but she was not ready to sit down.

She said, moving closer to Dick and touching his arm caressingly again, "Please, Dick, don't be modest and say it's 'just temporary' and 'a scratch' and all that hero talk. Tell me honest-to-goodness the truth about it. You wouldn't write it and now you must talk it. I want to know how it happened and everything. I deserve to know. I rolled enough bandages and made enough dressings to cure a thousand such arms." She smiled coaxingly and shrugged. "You see, I'm not one atom modest about what I did for the old war."

Dick tweaked her ear. "All right, neither am I modest, but I got so little, compared to millions of fellows, I can't feel that it is anything to fuss about — now."

"You'll admit it was pretty bad at first?"

Dick smiled ruefully. "Rather. Yes." He drew his brows down in a frown. "I'll tell you about it, Sharley. I wasn't heroically in the trenches at all at the

moment. We had been up and were going in again, but
when I was hit we were playing ball ' out back.' It was
shrapnel and it hit hard and gave me no chance to hit
back. I didn't suffer too awfully just at first. I remember the jolting and the — oh, well, it was plain hell — of
the Ford ambulance that took me away, and the darkness,
but I landed finally with the Detroit Base Hospital in
Dijon and after that it wasn't so bad. You can imagine
that it was some compensation to wake up and find
several of my home-town friends about me. They
didn't send me there because I was a Detroiter. It just
happened. The fellows were fine to me and made it as
easy as possible. If my shoulder hadn't been stiff I
could have been returned for service, but its hinges are
out of order. You see I can operate my elbow though,
and they think I may limber up in the shoulder in time.
That's all there is to tell."

Charlotte considered him gravely, then turned to her
father. " I suppose in the course of the next ten years
we'll get a detail here and there of his suffering. We'll
have to take it when we can, and be thankful. But oh,
Dickey, I'm glad you're back! Even if I have to give
you over to another girl right away, I'm glad."

Dick smiled at her and she said, " When is Frances
due? "

" Soon. She wasn't sure, but it won't be long now.
Sailing dates are as uncertain from Egypt as they are
from every other country these days. I suppose we'll
know when she arrives."

He paused and waited for Charlotte to speak. Her
eyes roamed about the office but her face was very still
and thoughtful. That her vision had not registered impressions, Dick knew by the fact that she passed over a
beautiful piece of carved ivory he had brought home,
without noting it. He waited for her to speak and she

said quietly, " To think, after all, after everything since we were little bits of children, you are going to marry Frances, and there's no bloodshed or heartbreak or feud over it. I wouldn't have believed it. Everything is serene and Doctor Stevenson consents? "

Dick ran the pages of a book through his fingers. " He doesn't dissent. He says nothing about it. I have only seen him twice since I returned. But you know, Sharley, this business of feuds and bloodshed in such a case doesn't happen where people are intelligent. I can see how this might have stirred up a devil of a business, but not with our sort. Frances wouldn't elope. That killed one chance for trouble. The Stevensons wouldn't row about it after they saw we were in earnest, and dad here," Dick smiled at his father, " dad's been for it right along."

" Dad's for anything you want," Charlotte said quickly, and added, " Of course, he ought to be."

" Dick rarely wants to do foolish things," Felix announced. " There would be no sense in opposing him. When Doctor Stevenson made the first overtures toward pleasant relations, I could hardly hold back."

Charlotte and Dick found this statement amusing. They exchanged twinkling glances and Felix said, " Did Dick ever tell you about that first meeting? I mean the first time the Stevensons made him welcome? "

" No," said Charlotte, " that was one of the little things Dick has left for me to guess at or ferret out all aloney. Get right at it and tell me now," she commanded.

Dick laughed. " Ancient history, that. I've lived a whole separate and distinct life since then."

" I haven't, go on. It was before you left, of course, spring of 1917, wasn't it? "

" Yes, last of April. It isn't anything you can tell

exactly except that I took Frances over to Sam's for dinner and got a very decided impression from her that her father was as strong against me as possible. When I took her home, their house was lighted, and Frances said they would expect me to come in. Of course I had to. I went, wondering if her father would shoot on sight or let me have some choice of weapons. Instead he was — wonderful." Dick's voice had dropped a note. He looked down at his desk and pushed some papers about absently. " He was everything generous and kind. Of course," he added quickly, smiling ruefully, " he probably is merely tolerating me in the hope that Frances may yet change. But he was so generous in his way of showing his tolerance that he rather — got me."

Dick stopped but did not raise his eyes and Charlotte thought, " Some day I'll find out from Frances what sort of a scene they had that night. It must have been good — to win Dick so."

CHAPTER II

I

BEFORE Richard had been sitting behind his black-and-gold-lettered name two weeks, he had a client that had come through other channels than the firm of Gage, Galloway and Vane. It began in a conversation at the club and developed from that into a consultation and a lawsuit. Dick was delighted. To have this pleasing interlude in the first lap of his long run toward a practice filled his heart with the glow of hope that the rule might be reversed in his case and that he might not have to sit out too long a term of patience.

The armistice had been signed and, as if it had been the touching of a match to a well-laid bonfire, the mountain of business that had accumulated during the stress of a greater cause broke out and swept flamingly through the world of affairs. Men went wild with the joy of business. Wages, profits, fees rose fabulously and Dick, feeling the heat of it in his firm's offices, chafed that he alone, of all his frenzied world, was at leisure.

To Frances he wrote from his heart, " When I see the problems that are being solved and the money that is changing hands in this office, I vow to myself that before the year is out my brain will be doing some of the solving, and some of the money will be sticking to my fingers."

He was alone in his office early one afternoon in November, having but just concluded a satisfactory interview with his one client, when Charlotte put an inquir-

ing face in at his door and came swiftly toward him.
She was dressed in a style Dick affected to despise and
contemptuously dubbed her " stagey stuff ", an extremely
dashing street costume, high-collared, severely buttoned, fur-edged. There were cavalier gloves and shoes
and a small hat that was little short of rakish in its military smartness.

She tossed a corner of her cape back over her shoulder and seated herself upon Dick's desk, pushing him
down with one hand as she did so. " You are not to
rise when I appear! Until you are absolutely and utterly
well, you are not to put any flourishes on your politeness
to me. I know a secret. I've just heard it and I tore
down here to tell you. It's about the Stevensons."
She paused, her eyes hard on Dick's face. She had seen
his quick, quivering response to the name and the com-
pression of his lips, but he merely nodded interrogatively
and reached for a cigarette.

" Yes," said Charlotte ominously, " the Stevensons!
I have to preamble a little, though. You remember Isabelle Rea, lovely girl, thin, with bad teeth and round
shoulders? She and I became very chummy during a
row in the Red Cross once. We agreed when everybody else was mad, and that made a bond between us.
She loves me! She's rather — " Charlotte shrugged,
" rather angelic, always revolving questions of right and
wrong, wondering about her duty. She talks too much.
She likes me because we're so different, I suppose. Well,
it seems she has a suitor. That pimply Walter Mac-
Laren who used to go to the Irving school. Isabelle is
rich and economical. Walter is nothing if not Scotch,
and I imagine he wants her more on the advantages of
warm feet and a cool million than just — Love — "

Dick put his hands to his head and closed his eyes in
mock agony, but Charlotte, with never a smile or a

quiver of laughter, continued, " You'd better listen.   I'm coming to the Stevensons."

" Thank you for that . . . "

" Well, Isabelle had made up her mind that she would tell Walter she was his'n when he called last night.   It was all settled.   She had searched her heart and weighed her conscience and analyzed her duty and hitched her ideals up a notch, and she was going to say, ' Yes ', but it hasn't been said yet and maybe never will be, and that's where the Stevensons come in.   It seems Walter is a member of Doctor Stevenson's church, his ex-church that he resigned from.   He's one of the big men, a pillar, and Isabelle adores him for his high Christian purpose and his work of self-sacrifice!   She told me so, but last night before Isabelle could say the fateful ' Yes ' he began to tell her how smart he was, what a Machiavellian. Evidently he told it with but the single purpose of convincing her of his great astuteness, but it jarred Isabelle's ideals.   She didn't tell Walter so, but she thinks he is doing something *not quite right* and is so awfully upset she had to consult me as to her duty.

" It seems that there is a faction in Stevenson's church that has been, and is now, awfully against him.   When he was running things, he evidently kept them at bay, but now he's gone, they are in power and cracking a whip his way.   Walter is one of these and Isabelle can't see ' what they have against Doctor Stevenson, but there's something ', and now they have cooked up a scheme to stop his emeritus salary.   Isabelle says it doesn't seem right to her and asked me what I thought, and I said it sounded downright rotten to me, but then I didn't have the church kind of a conscience and might be obtuse."

" What's the scheme?   Tell me about it."   Dick was interested at last.

" Oh, I don't know that I can disentangle all the stuff

Isabelle said and make a clear case the way you would want it, but the jumble of Isabelle's sympathy for Doctor Stevenson and her worry over Walter's scheme made me feel that it was something you ought to know. With the Stevenson boys away, not even Frances at home, I thought you might want to do something."

Dick rose and his swivel chair swung with the quickness of his movement. "Of course," he said, "it's a church affair and Doctor Stevenson's church friends will stand by him, but I might find out. In case they need help — Can't you give me a better idea of the scheme?"

"Yes, it's this way. When Doctor Stevenson resigned, they voted to pay him an emeritus salary. Isabelle said a thousand dollars a year, but she meant a thousand a month, of course. They wouldn't pay him a little dab like that — "

"But they would, they did! A thousand a year is the amount of it."

"Really! Why, that's absurd. That isn't a hundred a month! That wouldn't pay their rent!"

"That's the salary, just the same. Go on."

"Well, they voted to pay it; then after he had gone they found it an 'awful burden' and now they are going to sell the church and go in with another one and just dissolve, so that there being no church there can't be a pastor emeritus and therefore no pastor emeritus salary!"

"They can't do that! They can't put over a dirty deal like that!"

"Isabelle seems to think they can. Walter says it's all settled. They wrote Doctor Stevenson a letter and told him so."

Dick stared at Charlotte. "By George! I wonder if the church allows things like that! I wonder if it's possible. Why, Doctor Stevenson has been there thirty-two years. He built the whole thing from a little mission. He did the work. He made it. He has an equity in the plant. They can't pull a trick like that."

Charlotte threw out her hands. "Have it your way, but Isabelle says they have."

After a thoughtful moment, Dick asked, "Does your Isabelle know about Frances and me? Did she know you have any connection with the Stevensons?"

"No! Nobody does. I wish you'd hurry and announce it. I am tired of being popular because I'm your sister. They all think you're on the market and 'inscrutable' and 'too fascinating', and want me to lead them to you."

"Announcing it isn't up to me or I would. That's Frances' affair and you let her do the telling when she comes. Look here, Sharley — " Dick's eyes were scintillating with energy, "I'm going to find out what I can and see if a deal like that can be put over. I've gathered a good deal of Doctor Stevenson's record with that church from Frances, and I don't think they can possibly work any such schemes. I'm going to find out."

Dick seated himself again and reached for his telephone. He called the office of the Northern Motors and asked for Mr. Grieve but was informed that he was out of the city and would not return until morning.

"That's that," he said shortly, hanging up the receiver. "Well, I'll just stroll over and call on Walter. I often see him around. They have a life insurance business over there in the Ford Building.

Dick reached for his coat and Charlotte sprang toward him. "Let me help you in. I want to help you get your bad shoulder in." She held the coat carefully and tucked and patted with extravagant care. "I'll do some shopping and see you at dinner. I hope you punch Walter's face. I never did like his Chessy cat grin."

II

Dick found Walter MacLaren in his office but engaged, and he was obliged to waste a long five minutes in the waiting room before MacLaren opened his door and breezed forward with a greeting, " Well, Dick, hello, this is fine; come in my room here. Meet Mr. Small, Jack Small. You ought to know one another, you two. Guess we all played on the Irving baseball nine back in the dark ages." He shoved chairs, closed a window, laughed, exclaimed and beamed upon his callers, who had shaken hands and recalled baseball memories briefly. They preserved an unemotional exterior in contrast to MacLaren's buoyant cordiality. " Awfully sorry to keep you waiting, but Jack and I are carrying the burdens of our church these days and we have to get our heads together pretty often over affairs. Nothing in it for us but hard work, but somebody has to do it. Somebody has to keep things going. You're an infidel though, aren't you, Dick? You don't go in for that sort of thing. I remember that. Your father has quite a rep. as an infidel, hasn't he? "

" We aren't infidels. We're agnostic. It's quite different. It's Doctor Stevenson's church you're in, isn't it? " Dick's eyes included both men in the question. They exchanged significant glances and MacLaren sighed prodigiously.

" There it is again! We've been trying to conduct an educational campaign for the last two years against that ' Stevenson's church ' talk. It isn't Stevenson's church any more than it's Small's church or MacLaren's church. It's the Second Presbyterian Church. Stevenson's out and we don't like to have his name everlastingly tacked on to it."

" I see. The church property is for sale, I understand.
I came over to ask you about it. What's the price? "

Dick's voice was as even as if he had asked the market
quotation on Miller preferred, but his words brought a
moment of profound silence before Small broke out
excitedly, " That's Stevenson's doing! Stevenson's let
that out! What'd I tell you, Walter? He doesn't
answer our letter, — oh, no, but he's blabbing around
that the property's for sale. Who told you? " he demanded of Dick.

" I got it round-about, but not from the Stevensons.
What's your property out there worth? " Dick's manner
plainly said that he was not to be sidetracked by their
agitation. The property was the only interest he had in
the subject.

" We haven't set a price, but it won't be less than a
hundred thousand. This is premature though. It isn't
on the market yet. It won't be till after to-night. We
have a meeting to-night and after that we can talk business with you. What do you think? Isn't it worth
every cent of a hundred thousand? "

" At present inflated prices it might be. I've never
been inside the building. What equity has Doctor Stevenson in it? "

" *What equity has Doctor Stevenson?* Say, for Pete's
sake, Dick, did you come over here to kid us? How
should Doctor Stevenson have any equity in that property? He resigned from the church nearly two years
ago. He gets his equity out of the church. He never
put any in. We're the fellows that put in the money.
He gets a salary that he doesn't do a lick of work to
earn. But that's just the kind of talk his friends would
get going. What do you know about that? "

Dick said, " I don't know anything about it except his
reputation here and something of his history. The thing

that surprises me is that you seem to have anything against him. What's he done to you? I thought he was extremely popular."

"He is with a certain kind of people, the kind that do a lot of prattling about the 'intellectual' and the 'spiritual.' They talk about his 'magnetism' and all that stuff, but those kind never buck down and wash any church supper dishes or sweat over any debts. Doctor Stevenson was all right in his day, but his day's over and he doesn't find it out." MacLaren looked across at Small again and added meaningly, "But he knows it now, I guess, or ought to."

Dick rose. "Then the property is not for sale until to-morrow?"

"No, but we can talk business with you. If you've got a client we can certainly hear your proposition. There's no law against that, far's I know."

"But this meeting you have on to-night? As I understand it, the property may never be for sale. It hangs on this meeting, doesn't it?"

"Oh no, no. Nothing like that. The property will be for sale all right. We decide that. We *have* decided it. We tell Doctor Stevenson where he gets off. We just wrote him a letter last week, notifying him that his salary as pastor emeritus — his sinecure — would be stopped because the church is going to be sold and the congregation join up with another church. You see, that's the way we work it; if there's no church there's no obligation; if there's no church there's no emeritus pastor and no emeritus salary. That's our plan. We thought Stevenson would answer before this, but we haven't heard anything. He may not appear, may be ashamed to, but if he does — " Again the two churchmen exchanged glances. "If he does, he'll soon know just where he stands. It won't take long."

" You think Doctor Stevenson won't put up a fight? "

"'He may kick, but he has no ground to fight oh."

" Don't be too sure. I think he has."

" How? What? " Here was legal opinion lying around loose to be had for the grabbing. " What grounds could he fight back on? "

Dick made a gesture of apology. " I didn't come here to discuss the legal aspects of this case," he assured them. " I hope you don't think so. You have your own counsel and doubtless Doctor Stevenson has his. The property interest — "

Small interrupted. " Wait a minute. We're glad to discuss the legal aspect. We haven't any lawyer. Do you suppose Stevenson has? "

" Well — " Dick's slow smile twitched at the corners of his mouth. " I have no idea. Why should you suppose he hasn't? Does a man see his income cut off without bestirring himself about it? "

" In this case, you bet your life! " Small jumped from his chair and pounded the desk. " The Second Presbyterian Church is paying that everlasting emeritus salary out of the goodness of its heart. A thousand good round dollars a year in return for — what? Nothing. Furthermore, every dollar of that salary is just another example of the same extravagance the church has always shown Doctor Stevenson. He's always been overpaid. Twice a certain thing happened that proves Doctor Stevenson himself thought he was overpaid. Way back thirty-two years ago, when Stevenson came here to a little bit of a church with only fifty members, they paid him two hundred a month! That was a lot in those days! Then as the church grew they increased it to as much as four thousand a year and twice — mind you *twice* — "

Small's narrow, flushed face was thrust closer to Dick's, " Doctor Stevenson voluntarily offered to have his salary reduced." He paused with a look of triumph. The room was very still. Dick's steady black gaze bored through to Small's meager little soul, but he made no slightest gesture and Small went on with oratorical calm.

" Do you think a man ever gives up any of his salary if his conscience doesn't tell him he isn't earning it? No. You bet your sweet life he doesn't. The history of that church is a history of generosity. After Stevenson first resigned some of his salary they voted it raised again several years later. Generous, princely, they treated him! And he resigned it again after that! The church was in debt. It was his job to see that it got out of debt."

" Yes, and Dick," Walter took up the tale, " Doctor Stevenson doesn't need that emeritus salary. What does he need it for? He's got two sons and a daughter earning money. Why shouldn't they provide for him? Besides that, he earns enough here and there preaching and writing and marrying people, wedding fees. He's ab-so-lute-ly comfortable. We know that."

. MacLaren's voice ceased and Small instantly put in his further observation, " Yes, and I want to tell you it makes me sore, that salary. I support my wife and kids on two thousand a year and have to chip in on that emeritus salary, but Frances Stevenson, she can wear plumes on her hats a yard long. I saw her with clothes on this summer that stood her father something neat, you can bet."

Dick said slowly, his eyes narrow and glinting, " You — damned — mucker."

If he had fired a pistol in the little room he could not have gotten a more immediate response. Both men rose from their chairs as if they were on springs. They gazed at Dick open-mouthed. He returned their regard with tight-shut jaws.

Small was the first to break the tension. "What's eating you? What'd you mean by that?"

"I mean what I said. I'd like to take you two by the necks and beat your peanut heads together till they crack! If Doctor Stevenson doesn't fight you on this thing, I'll find somebody who will. Do you fellows think you can get by with a rotten deal like this?"

"There's nothing rotten about this deal. It's clear justice and you want to watch your step with the things you say to us. What damned business is it of yours anyway? Who are you to judge — *you* — *agnostic!*"

"Do you think because I'm agnostic that I'm a crook? You pusillanimous little short-change artists. Go out on the street and ask the first man you meet what kind of a frame-up this is you're working!" Dick gesticulated fiercely in his anger, but ceased abruptly and turned on his heel. He heard both men's voices in hot protest, talking, explaining, as he flung the door wide and felt it rush to and close behind him.

III

By the time Dick reached the place where his car was parked he had decided that he could waste no time telephoning. He would have to drive at once to Stevenson's and get his bearings after he arrived. He tried to think, as he raced out John R. Street, what Doctor Stevenson's probable response to the committee's action would be. There was nothing tame about Francie's father — none knew that better than Dick, who smiled as he admitted the fact to himself — and there was nothing small. But what he would consider his duty it was impossible to guess, for a church affair might not be conducted on strictly business standards. That it was not, witness the recent revelation of the methods of Small, MacLaren,

et al. Dick still raged with the anger mention of Frances'
clothes had stirred in him. " Small potatoes! " he said.
" Little stinking souls — "

At the Stevenson house Dick could hardly restrain his
impatience to question Mary. His impulse was to sweep
aside the conversational preliminaries, but he sat on the
rosewood settee, sacred to the thrilling memory of an
April afternoon, and listened to Mary's grave, sweet talk
of Frances and the boys. They would all be at home
soon, she was sure. Frances first, probably.

` She showed him a bowl of nasturtiums from her gar-
den and told him she was certain Frances would come
before they stopped blooming. " It is a race between
them," she said, making an effort to smile, and Dick,
looking into her shadowed eyes, was suddenly aware of
her utter unself-consciousness and charm.

He resolved to send her a box of flowers every day and
wondered why he had not thought of it a year before.
" I might have left a regular order with a florist. I'm
an ass. Fancy nursing those nasturtiums along — this
late! "

Aloud he said abruptly, " I came out especially to ask
you if the news I hear about Doctor Stevenson's old
church being for sale is true."

Mary's face quivered. It was a perceptible moment
before she said, " You have heard that? "

" Yes, and I am pretty much stirred up over an interview I have had with your friends, Jack Small and Walter MacLaren. I decided to come straight out here and
see — offer to do anything I can for you."

" You know what has happened? They told you? "

" Enough, yes. We almost came to blows. I'm still
hot. Will Doctor Stevenson be in soon? I'd like to see
him."

Mary's distressed eyes looked beyond Dick to the window and back to her own hands tightly clasped in her lap. " I'm afraid he isn't able to see you. He is here, upstairs, but — He isn't himself, Richard — I — " She could not finish.

" Those fellows," Dick's contemptuous tone implied adjectives he thought best to omit, " think they have got Doctor Stevenson. They don't see that he has every chance for a come-back, that he can fight them and win. Of course Doctor Stevenson is going to fight, isn't he? His friends won't let him take their decision; they'll *do* something, won't they? "

" Oh, Richard, that's it! We aren't doing *anything!* Our friends don't know. Never, never in all this world has anything like this happened to us. My husband is sick and his one plea is that I do nothing. He couldn't bear to fight them about a thing like this. That is not his sort, you know, to fight over money, to quarrel for something they don't want him to have. He couldn't — "

Mary rose and walked to the window. She stood for a moment with her back to Richard and he stepped toward the piano and leaned an elbow on its top. He drew a nasturtium from the bowl before him, and twirled it between his fingers as he waited.

When Mary turned, her face was devoid of any expression of emotion. She said, " If you have talked with them, you know all the arguments on their side. You know the spirit of the letter they wrote to Mr. Stevenson last week. It came on Friday. Mr. Stevenson was here when the postman brought it. I was out. When I returned near evening, entirely ignorant of its existence, I found the house still and dark. Mr. Stevenson's coat was in the hall but there was no other evidence of his presence. I went through the rooms, calling and turning on lights, and when I reached his study at the back of the house upstairs I found him lying on a couch with the letter in his hand. His eyes were open but he made no sign of recognition to me. I spoke and touched him and he said my name several times. Of course I read the letter."

Mary was still standing beside the window. She had made no move toward Dick. As she paused he pushed a chair toward her with a gesture of invitation. She sat down and he made a place for himself close beside her among the cushions on the window seat. Her lifted face was very near his as she continued in a voice so low it was almost a whisper. "I sat down beside him on the lounge and smoothed his forehead and talked to him as if I were trying to wake him from a bad dream, and he tried to talk to me. He said over and over, 'I want to tell you something in a minute. I can't think now. I can't think just now.' He put his hand to his head and tried to concentrate, but he couldn't find the words. I said, 'Angus, you have read this letter, this letter from the church?' and he said, 'Yes, I read it. Yes, I understand *now*. I didn't know they felt that way. I had no idea—'"

"Did he seem sick?" Dick asked.

"He was like a man in a dream, and he is that same way now."

"He hasn't done anything about it? He hasn't taken any action?"

Mary saw that Dick was incredulous. It was unthinkable to him. "No. For him not to take action is as amazing to me as to you. He is so very aggressive, you know, but of course even in his best health he wouldn't resist this. He would accept the decision; any further money from that source would scorch his fingers! But he's ill. That is the dreadful part—" Her voice sank lower. "They have broken his heart. Literally I believe—they have broken his heart."

Dick shoved his hands into his pockets with a vehement movement. "I don't wonder! Confound them! The scurvy dogs!"

Mary spoke quickly in answer to this. "Of course, Richard, you mustn't blame the church as an institution for this sort of thing. This action came from a group of very small individuals. Small people are everywhere in this world. They hold all good things down to earth; it's a universal curse. You mustn't think these men are representatives of our church."

"I am thinking only of you and Doctor Stevenson, the injustice and — cruelty of such a thing at the end of your — very unselfish lives."

"You see our lives so, Richard? Your sympathy is with us?"

"Oh, certainly!" Richard looked straight into her upraised eyes. "Every ounce of my fighting blood, my most ardent championship, are yours, you know."

Mary thought — "and his loyalty to Frances. Splendid Dick! Frances was right. She did know her man." She said, "What would you think we should have done?"

"I didn't guess that far. I don't wonder it has shocked Doctor Stevenson, but I should think your friends — somebody would have acted for you."

"Yes," Mary said quickly, "that is what you would expect, but because Henry Grieve is away, nobody knows. Angus wanted only to wait, to wait for Henry. You know, Mr. Grieve is his dearest friend. It is peculiar, that pair, but it has been so for years, not utter dependence like this now, but a need to discuss everything important with Henry."

Dick was frowning worriedly, "And you? You yourself have done nothing?"

"No, we both are waiting. I have felt that we were on the verge of something. You see, Richard, we — we pray. We get very close to God and He leads us. Our answers come that way. My husband is waiting and praying. He knows the answer will come."

"But he wouldn't be content to wait so if he were not ill, would he?"

"No, not so long. We expect Frances, of course. We expect Henry Grieve."

"I see. I understand. But, Mrs. Stevenson," Richard twirled the flower and gave it his undivided attention, "I might possibly have the answer for you, mightn't I?"

"I thought of that! Yes, when you first spoke of it, and I knew you knew, I thought — 'This is our answer.' Tell me, Richard, what you would have us do?"

They made their plan bit by bit rapidly, and Mary consented wholly to Dick's suggestion that he call for and take Angus to the meeting at the church that evening. "It is at eight. Before then I may be able to accomplish something."

Angus came down at Mary's urging and sat gazing before him while Richard questioned and Mary verified the facts as Richard had gathered them from Small and MacLaren. When Richard addressed him directly, he made an effort to concentrate but could not seem to get beyond the two thoughts that obsessed him, "Don't fuss about it, don't resist them, Richard," and, "Henry Grieve will know what to say for me."

"But, Doctor," Dick cried, leaning toward the big, still figure, "the meeting is to-night. Somebody must reply and Mr. Grieve isn't here."

"Yes." Angus drew his brows together worriedly and gave his head a little impatient shake. "I remember that. The meeting is to-night, but you see it doesn't matter. I have nothing to say. I didn't know they felt that way. I had no idea. I couldn't want to have what would be grudgingly given." He looked up with a quick movement and smiled tremulously, " I'm like a lover, Dick, a lover repulsed. If I'm not wanted I can't blame the loved one."

Dick left his chair and went nearer. He stooped before Angus and fixed his straight, scintillating gaze on his face. " You're not like a lover as I see it, Doctor. You are a man who, through work and sacrifice, devotion and gifts, immeasurable gifts, has earned far more than the little measly stipend they voted to give you. It's yours by right. They voted to do it. They mustn't be let off from their just obligation."

Angus said, putting his head a little on one side as he looked at Dick, " You see it that way? That is your first judgment ? "

" Of course it is. Any decent sense of justice would see it so."

Angus smiled. " Thank you for that, Richard; thank you."

Mary touched Dick's shoulder and made a sign to him. He followed her into the hall. " Talking with him gets no further than that." They looked back at him in silence and saw him motionless, gazing beyond them into depths their sympathy could not plumb.

Dick said, " I don't see how those men have the nerve to face him to-night. Have they no shame, no decency ? "

Mary made quick response, " No, not shame and decency as you know it, Dick. You mustn't blame them, though. They come from small beginnings. It really isn't their fault and rather than wonder why the church doesn't make better men of them, think how much worse they might be but for the church ! "

Dick gazed at her. She meant it. She felt no personal bitterness. There was no slightest note of vindictiveness in her voice. She understood her enemies,

she understood Angus, she understood him — Richard.
She had said to him once, " Certainly, be frank with me,
Richard. Anything you want to say — to me, you
know." She had meant it literally, not merely with the
social instinct for amiability. What a woman! What a
mother to have had. Loyally Dick checked the tendency
of his thought, but he saw, like a picture flashed on a
screen, Rita and the Sensenbrenner millions weighed in
the balance against this Mary and her wealth of understanding love.

IV

As Dick returned to his office he was so intent upon
review of the Stevenson philosophy and his plan for
further championing of their cause, that he failed to
realize his own extreme weariness. He did notice the
time. His wrist watch gave him a start of surprise and
by speeding up considerably he managed to be in his desk
chair some minutes before three o'clock.

Almost constantly for the next two hours Dick's telephone receiver was in his hand. His first need was to
find Henry Grieve and he pursued him by long distance
from Middletown, Ohio, up the State to Cleveland,
where, finally, he located him at the Northern Motor
Company's branch.

Between calls he wrote on his card carefully, with a
sense of affection ill-expressed, " In case the nasturtiums
fail to-night " and despatched the office boy with it to a
florist with an order for roses to be sent at once to Mrs.
Stevenson.

To Henry Grieve, whose genial voice was soon in his
ear, he gave a rapid sketch of Angus' trouble. " I knew
you'd get here to-night and be at that meeting if it was
humanly possible," he said with confidence. " We need
you. I'm handicapped by my lack of knowledge of

church business and I have no time to cook up a good, hair-raising speech, but I can keep Doctor Stevenson from signing anything till you get here."

"Get there! Man, are you crazy? I can't get from Cleveland to Detroit before eight to-night. It's a five-hour run at best."

"Oh, certainly, if you take the train. But you won't wait for that. What are you president of the Northern Motors for if not to travel by air? Father says Ottinger's over there now with the plane. You can get here if you hustle. You can make it by eight easily and I'll talk till you come."

Henry's hesitation was only momentary. His voice grumbled a bit at first as he said, " You're nothing if not speedy! But I'd do more than ride in that dizzy thing for my old friend. Well, all right. Ottinger's here now with me. If the motor is in condition I'll be with you immediately. But in the meantime you call up some other friends of Stevenson's and have them there to-night. A little group of the faithful!" Henry's infectious laugh. "The brethren," he added. "They'll know what to do but you must make a speech, Dick. You're on the job now — we aren't. You've seen Small and MacLaren. You must do the talking. We'll back you up." He gave Dick a list of names and shouted just before ringing off, "Have a car waiting for me at the landing."

V

In telephoning the men whose names Henry had given him, Dick maintained an atmosphere of mystery. "If I rouse their curiosity, I'll get them there." All but two said they were free for the evening and promised their support of anything Mr. Grieve considered important enough to fly from Cleveland to set right.

When his work for the afternoon was finished, Dick leaned back in his chair, one hand over his eyes, and sensed the depth of his own weariness and excitement. His body hummed with fatigue and the old throb had returned to his shoulder. He fixed his mind intently on his desire for strength to pull him through the evening. His part — well done — would tax him to the utmost. He must be clear of mind and free from pain to do his best. As he sat in the darkness his closed eyes made for him, he was able to conjure a vision of Frances smiling at him with dear, understanding eyes, tender with gratitude for his championship of her father. From the side lines, he felt something of her would cheer him to-night. Far away as she might be, she yet would be with them in thought and perhaps his yearning dream of her would call her spirit nearer.

CHAPTER III

I

AT the very moment that Dick, tense with anger, was hurling epithets of contumely in the faces of Angus' enemies, Frances was gazing through the window of a Pullman car at the squalid purlieus of Buffalo. The day was dark and a half-hearted veil of sleet, dotted with an occasional snowflake, fluttered between her and the bleak scenery.

The train rushed past a long shed and the darkness of it made a mirror of her window wherein she saw herself reflected attractively — so attractively that she wondered if Dick would find her changed. But for the consciousness of her complete sophistication (she never doubted the completeness of it) she could perceive no difference except in her clothes, and that they were a vast improvement over the childish things she had worn in his presence she was profoundly thankful. She wondered if he would perceive her smartness. She believed he would, for he had probably deplored her simplicity before he had bought the plumes.

How suddenly, she mused — after that last evening with Dick — she had been able to afford everything she needed. Her salary with Doctor Remington had seemed overwhelmingly large at first and, as she had emerged from a poverty-inflicted severity of raiment into the clever and colorful things she had so long desired, Mrs. Remington had won her from the habit of wearing what everybody wears, before it was formed, and had helped

her to see that to reflect the mode only in spirit is to
achieve distinction.

II

During the long return trip on the water, Mrs. Remington had teased about Frances' reunion with Dick —
what she would wear, what she would say, how she
would wish she had urged Mrs. Remington to prescribe
her wardrobe for the moment of meeting. And Frances,
in amused exasperation, had finally said, "Then prescribe! But if you start with earrings, as you always
do, it will be no use. They would horrify father, and
Dick would think I had grown vampish."

"Vampish! You! But earrings were made for you.
They heighten your naïveté. They exaggerate your ex-
cessive youth and evident brains. In the desert when
you wore them — " Mrs. Remington laughed, half closing her eyes as if to call up the picture, "they were the
oriental touch that proved your Americanism. It was
like having the Stars and Stripes brought out for the
evening."

"And all the time I thought I was looking like Cleo-
patra! You urged them because they *amused* you!"
Frances was reproachful.

All Mrs. Remington's talk began or ended in chaff.
Frances had grown used to it. They had traveled together over most of the central and eastern United States;
had made the round trip to Port Said and lived in the
desert together for more than half a year. They had
suffered the keen disappointment of an expedition made
unsuccessful by the far-flung obstacles of war, and had
stood together, loyally backing Doctor Remington in
the rage of his rebellion against impregnable circumstances.

They had been undecided for a matter of some five

days as to the method of arrival Frances should elect. Whether to telegraph from New York or merely appear in Detroit unannounced had been teasingly discussed until the day before landing, when Mrs. Remington said, "For the one thousand and ninth time may I ask what you are going to do about arriving?" And Frances, lying warm and dreamy in her deck chair, made instant response.

"I have decided that to telegraph from New York would bring them all to the train and I'd have to divide up my greetings till it would be just a disappointing jumble of meaningless talk. I want to make my cake last; so I shall not telegraph a word, but when I get in town I'll take a taxi home and then, later, I can telephone Dick. You understand that that would be much the better plan, don't you?"

Mrs. Remington's amusement brimmed in her eyes. "I understand that it would give you time to primp before Dick gets to you. Oh, Francie, I wish I could go to Detroit with you and see your Dick. I suppose he's rather ordinary and swarthy, still — I'd like to see him. I approve your plan though. It would be uncomfortable having all three meet you. You couldn't be perfectly natural with any one of them."

"Perfectly natural?" Frances echoed, sobering suddenly. "I wonder. That is what I am trying to decide." She drew a long sighing breath of the tangy air and continued slowly, her eyes straight ahead. "I am wondering not so much about our meeting as our lives after we meet. Just how perfectly natural I am going to be with my father. I am wondering if he'll marry us — and bless us. You see, since I first brought father and Dick together like a head-on collision of comets — " she paused to smile, remembering, "I have traveled from orthodoxy to something — of my own — that isn't as extreme as

Dick, not nearly, but is a long way — from the shorter catechism."

"Of course." Mrs. Remington had hoped to have this confidence and to contribute a thought to Frances' perplexity before they parted.

"I think my brother Jimmie and you — have had the greatest influence on my thinking. Your religions are the sanest, the most satisfactory I have ever heard. And I believe — " she paused again, choosing her words, " that I am going to be able to bring Dick that far toward father. I'm going to try to make him see as Jimmie sees, but what Dick will eventually believe doesn't worry me because I am sure I know exactly what he *is*. He may prove to be stronger than I, and take me his way. If he does it will be a good way. I have ceased to think it matters so terribly, but father — Halfway houses have no place in father's scheme of things. And so I am wondering if I must deceive him by silence."

Mrs. Remington said, " Your experience of him makes you feel that you hardly dare be honest, I suppose. He would not forgive you for deserting his faith? "

"It would never get as far as forgiveness. I would wound him dreadfully, and if I wounded him, nothing in the way of forgiveness would matter either to him or me."

"He is old. You are young. Surely he would make allowances for you."

"No, he would not. He would feel, I believe, that he and Dick had had a tug-of-war over my soul and that Dick had — pulled me down." She paused, her far-seeing eyes dark with the gravity of her thought.

There was silence between them until Mrs. Remington spoke. " Frances, I believe that you are carrying over into your maturity the child conception of your father. You are remembering his discipline and restrictions.

You are not allowing for the fact that he, a wise old man, regards you now as a wise and intelligent young woman. He is too fine and keen not to have perceived that the church of his ideals is in a transition state and must be remade by just such thinking young rebels as you. The church, as it has been, doesn't minister to the present youth any more than the stays of their great-grand-mothers suit their outdoor lives or their bodies. You won't make a better church necessarily, you Dicks and Jimmies and Francies, but it will be different and it will suit you, and that is the need, that it minister to you and yours. Your descendants will have to remodel a century from now to suit themselves — and so it goes. Your father knows history too well to be blind to the fact that you and Dick are merely reactionaries. I believe, my dear, I truly do believe that you are going to find that your father does understand. There will be no need for the deception of silence."

To Frances the words were a prophecy.

III

Hardly had Dick arrived at the Athletic Club to rest his aching shoulder than he received a message from Cleveland to the effect that Mr. Grieve had left at four in the hydroaeroplane, Ottinger at the wheel, and might be at the Detroit River landing by six o'clock.

Felix insisted upon driving down to meet him and assured Dick that, knowing Ottinger, he believed they would have Henry with them at the club in time for dinner. He ordered Dick to rest until they appeared, unless at half-past seven they had not arrived, in which event Charlotte was to act as Dick's chauffeur. Under no circumstances was he to drive himself.

True to his record, Ottinger " made it " and it was not

quite six-thirty o'clock when Henry, red and stiff with cold, followed Felix down the hall to Dick's room.

"The fellow's put in too many hours to-day," Felix complained. "He was on edge with weariness and pain. I've been fussing over him like an old hen. I told him he was to have his dinner in bed. When I left, Charlotte was hunting up Bible references, said he had to be fortified with a Biblical vocabulary for to-night." The two men smiled.

Felix opened the door after giving it a quick tap and revealed Dick before his chiffonier pulling on a shirt. "Couldn't stay horizontal any longer, dad," he explained, after he had received Henry. "I ordered dinner for half-past six. I knew you'd be here any moment and I couldn't talk business lying on pillows."

"No," said Henry, laying an affectionate hand on his good shoulder, "but you made me travel all the way over here in that hideous contraption that doesn't care whether you're head up or heels up. We dropped into air pockets as big as the Grand Canyon and climbed air hills as steep as Pike's Peak. I've roller-coasted all the way over and if I had to decide now whether or not the Northern Motors would continue in the aeroplane line, I would decide *Not!*" He thrust his pleasant face close to Dick's and bit off the word. "I tell you in this world of ours there are fish, beasts, birds and human animals. I've heard of flying fish and flying squirrels and of course all birds fly, but never did I know of one of the human species that did. I don't believe people are going to want it developed far. I don't think the average, cautious, intelligent man wants to travel at high speed if he has to do it by flying. It gives me the creeps to think, as we roar along, "I'm not hanging *from* anything, riding *on* anything, or attached *in* any way *to* anything — and it's uncanny. I'm ag'in it, unless traveling so has brought me here in time to help my old friend. What about it, Dick? Tell me the whole thing."

Henry's vehement indignation was tonic to Dick. He had begun to wonder if the " big men " of the old Second Church were, after all, only doing a customary thing in church business. The assurance that they were not, that the trick was unheard-of and Henry's complete denunciation of the whole crew and their method fortified Dick in the memory of his own vehement outbreak to Small and MacLaren.

" I'm glad you let loose on them," Henry cried. " Glad you blackened their eyes. If you get a chance to-night sail in again and remember that if you can keep Doctor Stevenson from signing we can get presbytery after them and have the thing stopped. Presbytery will never allow it to go through, never in the world, even though Doctor Stevenson will not want to oppose them. Presbytery will force them to do the right thing ! "

IV

Immediately after dinner the three friends left for the Stevenson house. Felix drove and he said, as they neared the corner, " I think it might be as well not to let Doctor Stevenson know I am along. Just don't mention my name and he'll suppose I am the chauffeur." As there was no response to this he added, slowly, " Perhaps in his trouble — this kind of trouble — one Stanhope will be as much as he can endure."

Mary met them at the door. Her mobile face told them at once there had been further developments, but she gave Henry a cordial welcome before she explained her evident agitation. " I called the doctor again this afternoon, thinking he could give Angus something to brace him for to-night, but he wouldn't. He said he

couldn't. It seems that he has known for several years
of Angus' condition, a gradual breaking down, arterio-
sclerosis. He had advised light diet, but neither of us
knew — we didn't guess the gravity of it all and now —
this shock, this heartbreak — has done terrible damage.
He ought to stay in bed. He ought not to go out to this
exciting meeting."

" He's in bed now? The doctor insisted? "

" The doctor insisted and he went to bed, but he is up
now, trying to dress, fumbling at buttons and things. I
am very much alarmed. Anything may happen to him
to-night — but I can't make him stay at home."

" No." Henry shook his head. " Don't try. You
can't force that man to coddle himself at a time like this.
He couldn't stay away. If it kills him, his blood is on
their heads, and even if it kills him, he must go and see it
through."

" I suppose I knew that." Mary smiled faintly.
" When he comes home we will begin treatment in earnest. The doctor has put in a call for a nurse. If we
work we may get him better."

They heard the creak of the stairs under a heavy step,
and Mary sprang up with a little cry of tenderness. She
went to him and they heard her gently talking as they
descended to the living room. Henry caught Dick's eye
and shook his head. " This'll kill him," he whispered.
" It's enough to kill him! "

The two men rose as Angus appeared in the door.
Dick, remembering the spring day he had waited so for
him and his surprise when a clean, modern, human breeze
of a man had confronted him, made the comparison with
this broken figure of two and a half years later. There
was no suggestion of breeze in his presence to-night, no
vivid flash of eye and smile. The Angus who stood in
the doorway gave off a stillness, a deep calm as of a spirit

that has passed beyond the shallows of speech into the eternal mystery. A misty tenderness filmed his eyes as he took Henry's big, warm hand. " I knew you'd come. I knew you would not fail me, Henry."

" This boy brought me." Henry put a hand on Dick. " He ordered me to mercury over. But for him I would not have known until too late."

Dick moved uneasily. He wished Grieve wouldn't pile it on. He strolled down the room toward Mary and escaped Angus' look and murmured word of appreciation only to run into Mary's acknowledgment of the roses. " They came at the very moment we most needed the thought of a friend. It was just as the doctor told us the great gravity of this illness. I put them by Angus' bed and he lay very still enjoying them. You've been our good angel to-day, Dick."

Dick raised his hands in mock surrender. " Shoot if you must my old bald head, but don't give me any more thanks, he said." They laughed together and Dick added, " I wish I had been sending you flowers right along. You appreciate them and ought to have them all the time. I want to send you more. I hope you won't think I have to be thanked."

Mary said, " I couldn't possibly refrain from thanking you, Dick. But I can try not to be cloying about it. I know how you feel, there are ways — and ways of saying thank you."

Dick thought, " She does understand — everything." And his heart was very warm toward her. He straightened from his leaning posture against the wall and moved toward the hall, where the delegation of the faithful were filing in as Henry held the door wide and gave them greeting.

" We all met at Handy's and came together," one explained, eyeing Dick, who had taken up Angus' coat and was helping him into it. "And we have each had three guesses as to the mystery."

To the fact that they were all curious, Dick, smiling within himself, attributed the good fortune of their promptness.

As they were about to leave, Mary, who had gone upstairs for the committee's letter which Angus felt he must have in his pocket, returned bringing Dick's roses, and breaking one from its long stem put it into Angus' buttonhole.

"This is to make you look as festive as you ought to feel, with such kind and loyal friends, Angus dear. Please wear it just as if you'd come from a wedding or a party. It gives you a brave front."

Angus smiled at her resolute face upturned to him in parting, and his hand lingered on her arm. "You're my brave front, Mary. It's you who are brave. The rose will bear witness to that."

CHAPTER IV

I

THE committee, which had assembled according to the information given Angus in their letter, to conclude the business of the church's dissolution and take formal action in the matter of offering the property for sale, were gathered about the fireplace in the church parlor when Angus and his friends arrived.

For some reason not clear to Dick, Henry shoved him forward and held Angus back with such adroitness that the " little group of faithful " were the first to enter the stronghold of the enemy, Dick followed, and Angus with Henry came last.

For Dick the next few moments brimmed with dramatic action. He retained no memory of sound other than the crackling of coal in the fireplace and the stir of feet and chairs. No word was spoken, but gestures, movements, attitudes were a pantomime more expressive than speech.

When the door to the church parlor was opened, he saw a room well lit, rosy with the fire's glow but plainly, meagerly furnished. There were pale-green plastered walls, badly stained around the casement windows that swept in a semicircle behind a bare table and a group of straight-backed chairs. There were stringy green silk curtains, too short by several inches, at the windows, and on the mantel over the fireplace a pile of worn, cheaply bound Bibles that sprawled awkwardly, threatening the safety of a brown Rookwood vase.

In unpleasant contrast to the pale green of the stippled plaster, a long battery of sliding doors — golden oak and varnished — had been spread as a substitute for a wall between the parlor and the outer desolation of musty chill. Dick had wondered, when he had heard that the meeting was to be held in the church parlor, what such a room might be like and he felt, fleetingly, as he crossed the threshold that, but for the open fire, it was a lamentable failure at hospitality, if, as was probable, hospitality was its function.

At the first sound of the opening door, every man in the bare enclosure had turned expectantly and with a startled movement that bore witness to his jumpy nerves. Dick, from the shadow, had seen the grave faces of the faithful quickly scanned, recognized and passed for those beyond as yet but dimly discerned. When he stepped into the light he saw that he was known only to Smart and MacLaren, whose tense faces tightened as they met his steady, slightly smiling eyes. By their look of truculence, they made the fact known that this stranger was the stormy petrel of the early afternoon. It was as if they had cried, " And this is the fellow who damned us! The agnostic! We told you he'd show up," which soundless language centered all eyes on Dick while he moved forward into the room, looked about quickly and glanced back toward the door, where Angus stood framed for inspection.

Save for a few of the faithful, not one of the company assembled to witness the crucifixion of his spirit approached Angus' age by so much as twenty years. All were young as compared to the still figure on the threshold. He stood poised a moment against a curtain of darkness that merged with the black of his frock coat and contrasted strikingly with the color and shining radiance of his head. The firelight touched his silver hair

and strong features with warm kindliness, accented the
pink of his Killarney rose and the white expressive hands
at his sides. But effective as were his dignity and calm,
they were less compelling than the clear, deep blue of his
gaze. Except for the quiet movement of his searching
eyes, as they surveyed the group before him, he was
motionless for a brief space.

Dick observed the scene with thrilling pulse. Angus'
quality was magnetic. He was living his part, not playing
it. He had brought, not defiance, not scorn — but the
pride of an indomitable courage to the meet. If there
were humility in his breast it was the humility of greatness. If, at this moment of his defeat, there was less
of aggressive justice than usually burned in his soul, it
was because that soul was sick beyond all healing.

Dick remembered MacLaren's words, "He may be
ashamed to come," and looked for evidence of shame. It
was there in the room, aplenty, but not in Angus' deep-
lined face, nor in the countenances of Angus' friends.

There was a general shoving about of chairs after that
first moment, and Angus stepped into the room followed
immediately by Henry Grieve, who put a gentle hand on
his arm and led him to a chair near the fire.

In the consciousness of Angus' party, who felt neither
shame, guilt nor fear, the silence in the church parlor
was but natural and decent, but to Walter and his committee it was the final tightening twist on a tension that
must be immediately eased lest it snap. And so it was
Walter who broke the constraint. He pulled himself
together as if he had but roused from abstraction and said
gaily, "Well, here's quite a little party of us!"

He whirled on his heel in the business of computing the
number of chairs and snapped a thumb and forefinger
smartly. "Guess we'll have to have a few more brought
in. We want everybody comfy. Can you get some, Jack,

old man? And you, Mortimer, help him. Atta Boy!"

Mortimer and Jack had jumped to obey. They brought chairs and placed them. They moved the table and fussily opened a window an inch, closed it, opened it; guessed if the cold air wasn't too much for anybody, they'd leave it. Walter continued cheery and alert, Jack Small stony, and Mortimer Beamer honestly uncomfortable and awkward. None of the others spoke or smiled. It was a solemn occasion to them all. Nobody offered Dick a chair and he made no move toward one. He had folded his arms and he stood at one end of the fireplace with lowered head, silently enjoying the play.

Angus had remained passive in the seat first placed for him and he sat with his knees crossed, long slender legs toward the fire on the opposite side of the hearth from Dick.

At last all were settled, Walter MacLaren had taken the chair and Jack Small, with neatly sharpened pencil and secretary's book spread open, was ready to call the roll.

It was on Jack that Dick's eyes came to rest as he waited for the formal opening of the meeting. He enjoyed the evidence of his palpitation. There was a white ring around his mouth and his thin nostrils dilated and quivered with every breath, but he held his head stiffly and permitted no slightest expression of his emotion to touch his eyes. "Poor fish," Dick sympathized silently. "He doesn't know what he's up against. He thought it was going to be easy. Now he knows it isn't, and he wishes he hadn't talked so much this noon. Wait till I get done with him to-night." Dick permitted himself to smile inscrutably and it was then that Angus, glancing up, caught the look and dwelt upon it.

"Handsome boy," he mused. "Living eyes, strong mouth. Francie loves him. Well, I took Henry's advice.

Why did I need his advice to start me in my unbending toward the boy? Not a boy, a man. First great bounding flush of manhood on him. Tremendous power for good, if God would only claim him. I must win him for God. I must do it. It is given me to do — before — it is too late. Before it is too late I must win him for God."

As if drawn by his thought of him, Dick's eyes moved from Jack to Angus and met the tender yearning concern in the shining blue. He stepped forward and bent above Angus. "Did you want to speak to me, sir?" he asked, alert for a possible word.

"No," Angus said wonderingly. "No, my son, I didn't."

A copper red crept up into Dick's face as he moved back. "My son!" and the still unconsciousness of the words he had said. They had come forth simply, inquiringly. Even now, judging by his face, Angus was not aware that he had voiced anything unusual. He was still looking at Dick as if he wondered why Dick had thought he spoke.

II

Walter MacLaren, in the fine balance of his poise, saw fit to put his committee through a deal of trivial prattle before he permitted the real issue of the meeting to come forward for discussion.

When finally, all in his own good time, he arrived at that moment, it was with the jaunty air of bonhomie which so palpably but masquerades a palsying fear.

The fateful letter was mentioned, was read by request, and the floor offered Angus, who had raised his head in answer to the expectant hush that again fell on the room. He moved as if to rise, but was instantly checked by a signal from Henry Grieve, which silenced anything

Angus might have begun to say, and thrust Dick forward
into the arena.

All eyes were turned to Dick and he responded with a
quick gesture of acquiescence and a downward glance
upon Angus' averted face that was at once protective and
affectionate.

" Members of the committee and friends," he began
deliberately, " I am speaking to-night for Doctor Stevenson because he is under orders from his physician to keep
perfectly quiet. I am also speaking for Mr. Grieve and
others of Doctor Stevenson's friends because they have
not known until almost this evening of the letter
which you have just read. But over and above these
two good reasons for acting as spokesman, I am going to
talk because I have something to say." Dick's slow smile
deepened and crept upward to the corners of his eyes
until he looked the very personification of amiability.
He talked quietly, and his glance, as it met Henry Grieve's
intent gaze, and Walter's and Jack's and the sober countenances of the faithful, seemed to suggest to each a little
bond of understanding that was like a friendly wink.

" You have heard this letter read dispassionately by the
secretary of the committee, Mr. Small," he said pleasantly, " but words do not always convey the spirit that is
intended, and it is the spirit which has gone into the
writing of the letter and that now animates all I have to
say in reply that counts most.

" From the committee I think the spirit is one of business. They have met a business situation and have solved
it according to a business principle of their own. Doctor
Stevenson's friends, on the other hand, want to be equally
emotionless in their response. We are therefore most
amiably related and ready to lend — each to the other —
the ear of understanding.

" To get ourselves in a proper mental attitude in this

matter, I feel that we ought to make a brief review of Doctor Stevenson's history as pastor of this church. It is an interesting story and I shall touch only the high points." He said this with a little air of haste as if he feared to bore his listeners. He still held the slightly smiling expression of understanding. It had done its work of conciliation, he could see by the more relaxed attitudes of the committeemen. They were all listening with a look of inquiry as if they were not sure which direction the young stranger was headed, but they were willing to follow and find out.

Jack Small held the widest margin of doubt. He was not to be beguiled by any smooth talking. He had not been the target for Dick's invectives at noon for nothing. He had taken alarm more quickly than Walter, and with the memory of Dick's threat in his ears he had scurried from office to office, trying to find a lawyer to stand for the committee's rights at the meeting. He had been laughed at, damned and scorned enough times to feel sore and angry at everything and everybody. Above all others, he hated Walter to-night. Walter had pooh-poohed Dick's denunciatory threats and refused to fear. He had been loud in declaring that no self-confessed agnostic would fight a *minister's* battles, " No money for him; why should he? " he had wanted to know.

Now they were in it. The man who had hurled lightning bolts a few hours before had the floor, inscrutably smiling as he smoothed and soothed through a review of history they all knew. Confounded impertinence of Doctor Stevenson bringing an outsider and an agnostic in to do the talking! But for the formidable presence of Henry Grieve (a financial colossus in the church and business world) the committee would not stand for it.

Small grouched and lifted his narrowed, mean eyes to Dick with a sneer as ugly as it was deliberate. And

Dick, having anticipated such a response, met the look and held it coolly, still slightly smiling, while his quiet voice went on with the speech he had planned.

"Thirty-two years ago," he was saying, "Doctor Stevenson came here to Detroit to take up the work of the struggling little church that is now known as the strong Second Church. There was a building then — such as it was, a little old frame structure, bare and cheerless. There were a few earnest churchmen to stand behind him, but there was nowhere any evidence of wealth, any promise of great pecuniary emolument. The little Second Church was indeed an eleemosynary institution, with Doctor Stevenson its chief asset rather than its chief beneficiary. I mention this bit of history to make it quite clear to you all that Doctor Stevenson could hardly have come to the work with any greedy dream of future wealth. There was no wealth; there was no generosity save the wealth and generosity of the great and fervid heart that beat in his own breast.

"It was agreed at that time that Doctor Stevenson was to draw a salary of two hundred dollars a month. This was for his services alone, yet almost before he began his work he added a bride to his lonely household, and so increased his return for the two hundred dollars a month that, instead of one great and generous heart, there were two — and, I am told, a rich and beautiful voice as well. At that time the people of the Second Church were satisfied with their bargain. They had paid a goodly sum; it had brought them a goodly return, and the work went forward happily. Years passed. There were both prosperity and depression. There were debts and discouragement that sometimes outweighed the warm fellowship and brotherly love of the church life. In one time of prosperity, Doctor Stevenson's salary had been raised by the people to a sum considered princely in those

days, for a servant of Christ. Later, when the stress of
debt was very heavy, it became necessary to recall part of
the generous increase in salary. I do not mean to suggest
for one moment — " Dick raised a hand as if to take oath
to the sincerity of his statement, " that the people even
hinted that Doctor Stevenson's salary be cut! Not at all.
Nobody hinted it. The offer came *from him.* In a
speech delivered at the annual meeting he briefly announced his willingness to have the church's deficit met
by the extra sum that had been voted him. It is probable
that no member of the church would have dreamed of
solving the problem thus. It is probable that none would
have dared suggest it, even had he thought it, for Doctor
Stevenson was so dearly beloved as to be, in truth, a
spiritual father to his parishioners. No, *he* suggested it!
He offered it and the thought at once was born into the
minds of some of his sharper members that the offer
from Doctor Stevenson was the outcome of a consciousness of remuneration not — quite — earned. But, be that
as it may, the fact remains that Doctor Stevenson voluntarily resigned some of his compensation, either because
he felt he was receiving more than he was worth, or,"
Dick shrugged, " because he loved his church and his
people more than he loved himself. Later, this bit of
history was repeated. A raise of salary in prosperous
times, an offer of reduction in depressing times, for, in
the course of more than thirty years, history may repeat
itself without monotony."

There was a creaking at the door and the new janitor,
feeling very conscious and very humble, creaked into the
room with a scuttle of coal. The squeak, squeak of his
best shoes pierced the quiet room. The clatter of his
tongs and the rattle of coal seemed to jar the very walls.
Dick observed him, half smiling, and paused in his speech
as if all the time in the world, all the calm, were his to

command. But there was a restless stirring among the committeemen which Dick sensed and met quickly with a change of manner. His quiet ease dropped from him, his back stiffened and he raised a straight accusing finger above his audience.

"Such, briefly, are the spirit and history of Doctor Stevenson's financial dealings with his people. In thirty-two years he was paid as much as four thousand dollars a year, as little as twenty-four hundred a year. In his voluntary reduction of salary he personally, by daily sacrifice, and his family with him, paid the debt that his people's indifference piled upon his willing shoulders. In that time he built this church that we are in, a house of worship to the God he loved and served. From a membership of fifty he increased the roll to some six hundred and more. From an equity of perhaps five thousand dollars he increased the property holdings to an estimated valuation of one hundred thousand dollars. An increase of more than three thousand dollars a year. A rate of profit, on the original five thousand, of two thousand percent. over a term of thirty years, or a rate of sixty-three percent. a year. Through his efforts, his leadership, his splendid courage, this property was accumulated until it became a very fortune for the people of the Second Presbyterian Church. True, he expected no more for his work than a living, and for his clerk's salary he gave this enormous return to his people. He did not think of it then, nor does he now look upon it, as a great piece of property in which *he has not an inconsiderable equity*. To him, it is God's work, God's house, and his reward has been the joy of service. In service he found his greatest happiness, in service he found riches, in service he poured his great soul into the world."

Dick was talking rapidly now; his vehemence and swift, telling gestures carried his listeners with him. The open mouth of amazement gaped in the faces of the committeemen and contrasted theatrically with the earnest acquiescence of Angus' friends.

Angus himself sat motionless, one elbow on the arm of his chair, his forehead in his hand. Dick could see only the left side of his face and he was startled by the change from the ruddy evidence of his alarmingly high blood pressure to the gray pallor. But for the quivering of his chin and cheek, he gave no sign of feeling. Nobody was observing him. Even Henry Grieve's eyes were on Dick in a look of twinkling amusement and approval.

" There were times, during these long years of struggle and triumph, anguish in prayer and victory in souls, when concern for his old age, for his wife's possible widowhood haunted his nights. At such times he wrestled with his doubts in prayer and — I have it from one of his own family — ever emerged with shining face and tear-bright eyes. He was not left comfortless; he was made to understand that even though men might one day revile him and despitefully use him, yet God would be the stay and solace of his waning years. On one promise in particular he planted his feet. It was the bread of his spirit, the weapon against his discouragements. No doubt, to you who were given the opportunity of his influence, he preached it, but whether he preached it or not, he lived it. This: 'Trust in the Lord — and do good; so shalt thou dwell in the land and verily — thou shalt be fed.' 'Trust in the Lord!' That injunction he obeyed implicitly. . 'Do good.' That certainly was the sum total of his days, and verily, I, his friend, say unto you, his enemies, as the Lord liveth, *he — shall — be — fed.*

" In this letter," Dick pointed toward Jack Small and glared into his livid face, " this committee has twisted and connived to crawl out of its just obligation. When Doctor Stevenson retired, a stipend of one thousand dollars a year was offered him — and accepted. An insulting sum, I should call it, but in his greatness, in the colossal simplicity of his demands he accepted it, as he thought it was offered — *with gratitude*. Gratitude! for a contemptible little old-age pension! Gratitude for the dribbling payment of a debt long overdue! Gratitude for a so-called living that but barely covered the necessaries of rent and heat. Gratitude in his heart and loving understanding of the reasons for its paltry dimensions!

"The committee has suggested, brightly, that with two grown sons and a daughter Doctor Stevenson need lack for none of the material comforts. Quite right! He need not, nor shall he; but he shall eat of the fruit of his *own* efforts, not his children's. He shall know that the long, hard work of his splendid life has provided for his old age; he shall never taste the bitter crust of charity. His effort, his love, his great spirit have built up an investment here in the Second Church that no man shall rob him of. I represent the law in his behalf, but I make no threats. There will be no need to go so far. The governing body of your own organization will stand behind him and around him and for him, and you shall be forced to do that which you yourselves voted to do for him, during the remainder of his life."

The cohorts of the faithful broke into hysterical applause. There was a sudden movement and clatter of tongues that came to Dick as a roar of confusion. He saw Henry Grieve towering in the midst of it, rubbing his nose, his face, his eyes with a large clean handkerchief. He emerged radiant while the committeemen surged around him with a babel of heated argument and gesticulation.

Just what happened next neither Dick nor Henry nor Angus could have described. Walter MacLaren banged for order, but the two who were most deeply concerned

for Angus had attention only for his needs. He had
raised his head, but he seemed dazed, numbed once more,
as he had been in the early afternoon when Dick first saw
him. He made an effort to rise, only to slip back into his
chair.

Dick bent to offer an arm, Henry put a soothing hand
on his shoulder and patted, but both movements were
arrested by the arrival of a newcomer to the room. There
was a gust of fresh, cold air from the open door; a rush
of color and fluttering garments and, with a little croon-
ing cry of tenderness, Frances dropped on her knees
before her father. Her smiling, tear-wet face was raised
to his, her gloved hands touched his shoulders, his cheeks,
his bowed white head and drew him close against her
breast. "Oh, daddy, my daddy! This is what they've
done to you! This is what they've done!"

Dick stooped above her, his senses spinning with confusion and delight. He heard Mary's voice and Henry's,
Frances murmuring tenderly with little choking moans,
and the rattle and clatter of chairs. One photograph was
printed on his memory unforgettably — Jack Small and
Walter MacLaren, their faces straining with astonishment as they witnessed the little scene.

It seemed an eternity, though it must have been but a
moment, before Frances was in his arms and her half-
laughing, half-sobbing lips against his cheek. "Oh,
Dick! I come home to find you over your ears in *church
work!* Quoting scripture, preaching. Dick, Dick, you
did it for my daddy! You fought this fight for my
daddy."

III

It was a long night of pain and tortured nerves for
Dick. He tossed and moaned, smiled into the darkness
and felt tears of pure joy ooze beneath his eyelids to his

hot cheeks.   Over and over he repeated the amazing
words, " I come home to find you over your ears in
church work," and the perfect promise, " Now we can be
married the first minute daddy is well enough."   That
Angus should marry her and bless her, it seemed, were
heart's desire for Frances.

IV

There came a day within the week when Angus,
propped on his pillows, bent the undimmed blue of his
gaze upon Frances and Richard, kneeling close beside his
bed.   In the background Felix and Charlotte, the two
Grieves and Mary, with Maggie close behind, formed a
semicircle.

There were flowers everywhere and sunlight, the white
of linen and the rustle of wedding garments.   In a clear,
sure voice, Angus began the service that so often had
sent the thrill of mystery and solemn beauty through
Frances' veins, " Dearly Beloved — we are gathered together — in the sight of God and in the presence of these
witnesses — to join this man and this woman — in the
bonds of holy matrimony — "

That — but a few days before Thanksgiving, and the
poignant moment after the ceremony when Dick, having
suffered congratulations and half-tearful inanities, returned to Angus to say quietly, " Doctor Stevenson, I
want to tell you that always, so long as I shall live — I
pledge myself to carry on for you — in my own way — "

The lifting of Angus' tear-wet eyes to his, the meeting
of their hands and then, to those who waited, Angus'
breaking voice, " In your own way, Dick.   In your own
way — and may God bless you and use you — in His
kingdom.   I am satisfied."

They drew the propping pillows from under his shoulders and his strong face, alight with tenderness and peace, lay still and flushed against the smooth whiteness.

V

On Christmas day, Frances and Dick stood hand in hand beside Angus' grave. There had been no snow as yet. The trees held the strongest of their leaf children and the light wind sang and fluttered through the groves of Woodlawn.

Brokenly, Frances said, " He loved this spot. He loved its sunny slopes and the thought that his oldest and dearest friends were here. I am glad the struggle is over for him — but I shall not come here to find him, Dick. His spirit is mine, in me — in my heart like a flaming torch. I never belonged so much to him as now. Somehow — some way — I know I shall go on — in his name to the best he hoped — for me."

Dick moved nearer Frances and put his arm close about her. His voice was husky as he said, bending his head to hers, " I read a little poem yesterday — an epitaph by Louise Driscoll that I memorized. I shall always think of it, with him.

> " Here lies the flesh that tried
> To follow the spirit's leading;
> Fallen at last, it died,
> Broken, bruised and bleeding,
> Burned by the high fires
> Of the spirit's desires."

THE END